'A real treat ... [Meaney] wraps her readers in the company and comfort of ordinary strangers' *Sunday Independent*

'Meaney can excavate the core of our human failings and present it to us, mirror-like, on the page ... Which makes her utterly credible, utterly authentic, utterly irresistible' *Irish Independent*

'Warm and insightful ... Roisin Meaney is a skilful storyteller' Sheila O'Flanagan

'Meaney weaves wonderful feel-good tales of a consistently high standard. And that standard rises with each book she writes' *Irish Examiner*

'This book is like chatting with a friend over a cup of tea – full of gossip and speculation, and all the things that make life interesting' *Irish Mail on Sunday*

'An addictive read with engaging, flawed characters and a unique writing flair that pulls you into the plot from the very beginning and keeps you entranced to the very end' Books of All Kinds

'A delightful read about relationships and the complexities associated with family life ... A cosy read for any time of the year, be it in your beach bag or sitting curled up in front of the fire' Swirl and Thread

'It's easy to see why Roisin Meaney is one of Ireland's best-loved authors ... Should you spot this on a bookshelf, grab a copy' Bleach House Library

Roisin Meaney was born in Listowel, County Kerry. She has lived in the US, Canada, Africa and Europe and is now based in Limerick city. She is the author of numerous bestselling novels, including *The Anniversary*, *The Reunion*, *One Summer* and *The Last Week of May*, and has also written several children's books, three of which have been published so far. On the first Saturday of each month, she tells stories to toddlers and their teddies in her local library.

She is a fan of random acts of kindness, and believes in the power of kindness to change mindsets. With a friend, she manages the Random Acts of Kindness Limerick page on Facebook, where RAKs are shared and celebrated.

www.roisinmeaney.com · @roisinmeaney
www.facebook.com/roisinmeaney

ALSO BY ROISIN MEANEY
It's That Time of Year
The Restaurant
The Birthday Party (a Roone novel)
The Anniversary
The Street Where You Live
The Reunion
I'll Be Home for Christmas (a Roone novel)
Two Fridays in April
After the Wedding (a Roone novel)
Something in Common
One Summer (a Roone novel)
The Things We Do for Love
Love in the Making
Half Seven on a Thursday
The People Next Door
The Last Week of May
Putting Out the Stars
The Daisy Picker

CHILDREN'S BOOKS
Puffin with Paulie (with illustrator Louisa Condon)
Don't Even Think About It
See If I Care

Roisin MEANEY

The Book Club

HACHETTE
BOOKS
IRELAND

First published in Ireland in 2021 by HACHETTE BOOKS IRELAND
First published in paperback in 2022

1

Cataloguing in Publication Data is available from the British Library.

Paperback ISBN 978 152935 567 3

Typeset in Adobe Garamond by Bookends Publishing Services, Dublin
Printed and bound in Great Britain by Clays Ltd, Elcograf, S.p.A.

Hachette Books Ireland policy is to use papers that are natural,
renewable and recyclable products and made from wood grown
in sustainable forests. The logging and manufacturing processes
are expected to conform to the environmental regulations
of the country of origin.

Hachette Books Ireland
8 Castlecourt Centre
Castleknock
Dublin 15, Ireland

A division of Hachette UK Ltd
Carmelite House, 50 Victoria Embankment, EC4Y 0DZ
www.hachettebooksireland.ie

For the Savoy Book Club,
in honour of the books, the chats and the wine

Main Characters

Beth Sullivan, 72, retired domestic science teacher

Lil Noonan, 23, her granddaughter

Mark Purcell, 69, retired deliveryman

Fred Purcell, 45, his son, publican

Olive Purcell, 42, Fred's wife, gift-shop owner

Nancy Purcell, 11, Olive and Fred's adopted daughter

Tom McLysaght, 28, newcomer

FAIRWEATHER, 2019

JANUARY

Tom

After accompanying him for most of his journey, drumming on the car roof, spattering against the windscreen, turning potholes into puddles and gutters into rushing miniature canals, the rain finally stopped as he passed a grey rust-spotted sign that read *Welcome to Fairweather*. Fair weather my foot. He hoped to God he hadn't signed up for six months of rain.

He fished the page with his scribbled directions from the door pocket and propped it on the steering wheel. He drove slowly until he found the church – a weary-looking tinsel-draped Christmas tree still on show outside – and the sharp curve to the right afterwards, and the narrow road off to the left after that, all as promised.

He negotiated the rutted lane cautiously. Wouldn't want to meet another vehicle: one of them would have to reverse, and he was in no mood. His stomach growled. All he'd eaten since breakfast was the sausage roll he'd picked up when he'd stopped for petrol a couple of hours back, having refused Joel's offer of an early lunch before setting off from Kildare.

Fairweather had to have at least one chipper. He'd find it once he'd sorted his digs. The thought of food – a hot slab of battered cod, shiny with oil, a pile of vinegar-drenched chips to accompany it – brought a rush of saliva. The Jeep brushed past a dripping wild hedgerow and lurched into a small hollow on the road, and climbed out again. Bloody hell, where was it? How far down the lane had she said? Half a kilometre? A kilometre?

And then he rounded a bend and there it was, pushed back several metres from the lane, and surrounded on all sides by shoulder-high hedging. He pulled in before the smaller of the two gates, ignoring the larger open one that led into a paved driveway: better wait until he was officially installed before making himself at home.

He switched off the engine and remained where he was, tilting his head this way and that, clenching and releasing his shoulders, rotating wrists and ankles. Undoing the kinks, loosening everything out. Something cracked, softly and not unpleasantly, in his neck.

Past four o'clock, the light draining already from the cloud-filled sky, pulling colours with it. Eleventh of January, still a long way to go to a stretch in the evening. He looked out the passenger window and saw a path beyond the gate that led straight to the front door, from whose glass side panel yellow light spilled. The walls of the house looked white in the dusk – he'd thought pale blue from the website. Not that it made a difference: they could be black for all he cared.

It was a lot bigger than he needed. A window on each side of the front door, three set into the second storey. Altogether too big a house for a man on his own, but he didn't care about that either. What he cared about was rent he could afford, and being left alone. He didn't imagine a lot of folk were looking for a long-term let in a place like Fairweather, not at this time of the year. Glad to get him, maybe. Glad to get anyone.

Was that a curl of smoke from one of the two chimneys? He recalled a working fireplace in the description, so hopefully his new landlady had thought to light a fire in it. Open fires were a rarity in central London, and Joel and Sarah's house had none, but Tom was a fan of the real thing.

He shifted his gaze to what he could see of the property on the far side of the high hedge. Similar in size to his but stone-fronted, with ivy fanning upwards from one corner. A maroon-coloured car was parked outside, turned in his direction. Six years old, the numberplate told him.

We live next door, she'd said in her last email, not

explaining who 'we' were, and his heart had dropped. He'd thought the house to be more isolated, not a sign of the other in any of the photos. Too late to pull out by then, his deposit and first month's rent paid. He'd just have to hope they left him alone.

Beyond the two houses the lane petered out, a line of trees beyond. Just one set of neighbours, at least. He took his phone from the door pocket and selected Joel's number. *Landed*, he texted. *All OK. Will be in touch*. Pre-empting the call that would come otherwise. Just checking, his brother would say, and Tom would be compelled to give an account of the journey and the house, and he had no appetite for that just now.

Safe trip, Joel had said earlier, having taken the morning off work to say goodbye. Standing by the gate as Tom banged closed the boot. All the best, Joel had said, giving a hug to the brother who was putting pretty much the width of the country between them. The brother who was beginning again, or attempting to.

Beginning again. Shifting gear, taking his life in an entirely new direction, and leaving so much behind. Could he? Was it possible? Did he have the energy, the will for it?

He had no idea. He also had no other option,

having leant on Joel and Sarah for more than long enough. Come back if it doesn't work out, Joel had said, but back was the last direction Tom was planning to go. Onwards, not back. Never back.

He stepped from the Jeep, leg muscles stiff, spine putting up a mild protest. The damp air had a clean, sharp tang to it. The sea couldn't be far away. He'd caught glimpses of it as he'd drawn closer to his destination, white slices of it on the horizon when he'd rounded a bend, cut off by a rise in the land a second later.

He'd never lived on the coast before. You couldn't count Dublin, the nearest coastline a half-hour drive from the city centre square where he'd grown up. The house flashed for an instant through his mind's eye – the Georgian elegance of it, the steps climbing from the path to the black front door, the panelled sash windows, the wrought iron balconies – before he shunted it away. Never again.

He wondered how far the sea was from this house, and if there was a beach within walking distance. Not that he was planning a swim at this time of the year – leave that to the local fanatics, bound to be a few – but he liked a walk, and beaches had that wide-open feel he craved these days.

He closed his door, the startling loudness of it

making him realise how utterly quiet the place was. No birdsong, must be gone to bed already. He cocked an ear and heard nothing but the staccato drip, drip of rainwater from leaves – and then he slowly became aware of another more distant sound, a kind of low rhythmic rising and falling.

He tried to identify it. Traffic on a distant motorway, the sound of it travelling far in the silence? Machinery of some kind in a local manufacturing plant? Whatever it was, it didn't intrude. On the contrary he found it soothing, like the bass notes in a soft jazzy tune.

He opened the boot and hauled out the canvas bag that held his clothes. Everything else could wait until tomorrow. He pushed at the small iron gate, which was ajar, and which didn't budge. He crouched to examine it and saw the bent hinge that was responsible for tilting the other end onto the path. A simple fix, if anyone could be bothered.

He scanned the overgrown lawn beyond the gate, the unkempt hedges on either side, the weeds that pushed between the paving stones of the drive. Some kind of briar had climbed halfway up the double doors of the garage to the left of the house.

He wondered if the neglect on the outside was mirrored inside; might account for the low rent. Place could be riddled with damp if it had lain empty for a while, which the condition of the outside suggested. Central heating had been mentioned, along with the fireplace, but central heating had to be switched on to make a difference. Had he signed a six-month lease on a dump?

He hoisted the little gate and swung it open. His boots were loud on the path. He'd never lived in a place so quiet. He sniffed smoke as he approached the front door: at least one room should be warm. He shifted his bag from one hand to the other and reached for the doorbell.

'I'm here.'

The disembodied voice startled him. He turned to see her rounding the side of the house. She wore a silver-grey hat whose shallow brim shadowed her eyes and a coat the colour of raspberries that stopped at her knee, and dark boots beneath. She was shorter than him by a good eighteen inches. Between that and the failing light, he couldn't make out her features with any clarity.

'I saw you coming,' she said. 'I was looking out for you.' She extended a gloved hand. 'I'm Beth Sullivan.' Cool, unsmiling. He wished he could see her eyes properly.

'Tom McLysaght,' he told her. 'Pleased to meet you.'

Her gloves were soft leather. Her grip was firm.

He felt a yawn rising, and stifled it. He'd been awake since before dawn, lying in Joel's spare room while he'd waited for morning to peel away the dark. He hoped she wouldn't hang around. He'd be happy to be let in and left to find things for himself.

She pulled off a glove and took a key from her pocket and pushed it into the front-door lock. 'I have a fire lit.'

'I can smell the smoke.'

She made no response. He followed her into a hallway that felt no warmer than the outside. Behind the door was an old-fashioned wooden hallstand, its various knobs and hooks bare. Walnut, he thought. Stairs climbed up on the left, carpeted in an oatmeal shade. Black and white tiles on the floor, paper on the walls the colour of milky coffee, with a small green leaf print.

'The heating should have come on,' she said, mouth pursing as she touched the radiator with her ungloved hand. 'I'll have to investigate.'

Heating on the blink. Good start. He dropped his bag by the hallstand and left his jacket on.

'Sitting room, dining room, downstairs toilet,' she said, indicating doors as she passed but leaving them unopened, to his relief. Seemed she didn't want the grand tour any more than he did. 'Kitchen,' she said, entering the room at the end of the corridor, flicking on the light. 'There should be plenty of everything you need, saucepans and crockery and the like.'

He saw cream worktops and units, and a white sink, and dark red tiles on the floor. White roller blinds were pulled down on the two windows, one of which faced her house, the other set into the back wall. A red kettle on the hob. A wooden bread bin on the worktop, empty.

'Your keys,' she said, taking them from her pocket and placing them on the table. 'Back and front doors. The garage doesn't have a key – it was lost years ago and never replaced.'

'OK.' Presumably burglary not an issue in Fairweather.

Older, he thought, going by the maturity of the voice, the faint suggestion of jowls, the skin that was slightly pleated around her mouth. The hat covered her hair completely, so no clues there. Still slightly disconcerting that he couldn't tell if she was looking directly at him or not.

'The back door lock sticks a bit; you have to jiggle the key. You'll find some fuel in the shed. I can let you have more turf when you need it, we have plenty to spare, but coal and briquettes you'll have to get yourself at the petrol station you passed on the way into town. We have a man who delivers good dry logs, four euro a bag. Let me know if you want him to call here.'

'Right.' He tried to keep up. Her voice didn't change. Was her accent a Kerry one? She didn't sound remotely like the two brothers in the Dáil, but he suspected a bit of artistic licence there.

'What else? Bin collections. We stopped the service for this house, so feel free to put your waste in our bins. Recycling is blue, organic brown, everything else green. We keep them in the side passage; come in our big front gate and you'll see them. I've written the collection days for you.' Pointing to a folded page lying next to the keys. 'There's a bottle bank in town, at the end of the prom. You can bring your glass and cans there.'

'OK.'

Both gloves off now, a gold ring visible on her left hand, a diamond one next to it. A husband next door then, to explain the 'we'. Wife in charge, by the look of it.

'You've got three bedrooms upstairs. I've made up the bed in the main room. More sheets and pillowcases in the hot press, and towels too. Help yourself to whatever you find.'

'Thank you.' Sarah had given him towels and

bed linen. They're not normally provided in an Irish rental, she'd said, but they were here. He might not have heat, but he had sheets.

His landlady had crossed to the back door. 'I'll show you the boiler,' she said, disappearing. 'Mind the step.'

He followed her out and down a shallow step to a paved patio. The rear garden beyond it was narrow and long – a hundred yards? Two hundred? – and every bit as neglected as the front, with its own overgrown hedging and weed-filled lawn, and shrubs to one side that were lopsided and misshapen for want of a secateurs.

On one side of the patio was a concrete shed, and beyond it a dark green oil tank. She opened the shed door and he saw a large boiler on the wall inside.

She took a slim torch from her coat pocket and aimed it at a dial. 'The clock is wrong – I didn't notice when I set it to come on earlier. At least it's not broken.' She made some adjustment, and seconds later a soft thrum sounded. 'It doesn't take long to heat up. Anyway, like I said, there's a fire in the sitting room.' She fiddled with a dial before turning back to him. 'Are you familiar with this type of boiler?'

'Yes.' He wasn't. He'd figure it out. There wasn't a machine or a device that had defeated him yet.

'Well, it's on now. I suggest you leave it on overnight, and set it as you wish in the morning. There's plenty of oil in the tank for the next few months.'

'And how do I pay you for it?'

She gave a dismissive gesture as she closed the door. 'Don't worry about that.'

'... Thank you.' Free oil, free turf, reasonable rent and sheets on the bed. He wasn't doing too badly so far.

'The solid fuel is in there,' she went on, pointing to a small wooden shed on the far side of the patio.

'Right.'

'This house isn't mine,' she said, back in the kitchen. 'It belongs to my granddaughter, Lil. The electricity account is in her name. Are you alright with that, or would you prefer to put it in yours?'

'I'm fine with that.' He wondered where Lil lived, and why she'd surrendered her house to him, and why her grandmother was here showing him around instead of her. 'So the bill will come here, to this address?'

'It will. Feel free to open it, and we can add it on to your rent. I took a meter reading when I was lighting the fire – it's on that page with the bin days, and I've kept a note of it too, so we can work out how much of the next bill is yours. The meter is located at the side of the house, key is in that drawer. Please feel free to check it.'

'OK.' He wouldn't bother. He doubted that she was trying to pull a fast one.

'Utility room,' she said, and he walked after her into a little space off the kitchen. 'Washing machine, tumble dryer. Manuals are gone, I'm afraid, but they're pretty straightforward. Ask me if you have any questions. There's a clothesline out the back if you'd prefer to hang out your laundry. You'll see it tomorrow in the daylight. Pegs on the shelf.'

'OK.'

They returned to the kitchen. From what he'd seen of it so far, the place appeared to be in good enough nick. No ominous patches on walls or ceilings, no damp whiff, no obvious signs of disrepair. Then again, he hadn't seen a whole lot of it.

'Garage is through there,' she said, pointing to a door that hadn't registered with him, tucked into a small alcove. 'I've put milk in the fridge, and there's tea in that caddy. I forgot sugar, but if you need it tonight come back with me and I'll give you some.'

'I'm OK,' he told her. 'Is there a takeaway nearby?'

'There is, on the way into town. Go back up the

lane and turn right. There's another one at the other end of town – you can walk to it in ten minutes on the cliff path, but not in the dark, when you don't know it.'

'The cliff path?'

'Bottom of the garden, turn left. You'll need a torch around here – do you have one?'

'No.' He'd never thought of a torch.

'I'll leave you this one until you get your own.'

'Thank you.'

She was perfectly civil, but her tone remained impartial, almost curt. She was supplying all the information he needed but she hadn't smiled once, or given him more than a passing glance. It would seem that the sign at the edge of the town was the only welcome to Fairweather he was getting. On the upside, he didn't think she'd be dropping in for tea and a chat.

'You'll get your bearings soon enough,' she said. 'It's not that big a place, and the natives are generally friendly.'

Again, no hint of a smile. He couldn't tell if she was joking.

'What do you do, if I can ask?' Tilting her head to look at him properly for the first time. Her eyes, he saw now, were a definite blue. Her face was striking rather than beautiful. Regular features, good bone structure. She looked after herself.

'I'm between jobs,' he said carefully. 'I'm hoping to pick up work here.'

'What kind of work?'

'Handyman stuff. DIY, repairs, that kind of thing.'

'Plumbing? Electrical?'

'Any of that, as long as it's not too big a job. Painting too. Houses, I mean, not pictures.'

'How about computers, phones, that kind of thing?'

A beat passed. He decided he could admit to it. 'Yeah, I know my way around them too.'

She held his gaze for another few seconds. He began to feel uncomfortable. Was she waiting for more information?

'I can turn my hand to most things. I've always been like that. I used to take stuff apart as a kid, and put it back together. I like knowing how something works, and I catch on quick.'

She nodded. 'You could have dinner with us this evening, if you'd like a home-cooked meal. Beef casserole. We eat at six.'

He was thrown by the sudden shift of topic, and by the offer. A dinner invitation was the last thing he'd expected, and the last thing he wanted. He imagined sitting down with her and her husband, trotting out the lies, or the half-truths, he'd prepared about what had led to his coming to Fairweather. Trying to avoid giving away anything more than he had to. No, couldn't do it, not this evening.

'Thanks, but it's been a long day and I'm wrecked. If you don't mind, I'll just grab a takeaway and crash.'

Something, a sort of grimace, flitted briefly across her face – had he insulted her with his refusal? 'Suit yourself,' she said, in the same cool tone. 'Do you have any questions?'

'Not really.' He'd forgotten about half of everything she'd just told him, but he'd figure things out as he went along.

'If that's it, I'll bid you goodnight. You have my mobile number if you need to use it.'

'I have.' He wondered if he should call her Beth, or stick with Mrs Sullivan. Maybe best to use nothing for the moment. He walked back through the hall with her and waited for her to leave.

She opened the door and turned back to fix him with another direct stare. 'One thing I should mention. You'll hear it eventually, so it may as well come from me.' She paused. She made a small movement with her mouth, a kind of twitch, and a brief pressing together of her lips. 'Lil, my granddaughter Lil, has lived with me for the past two years. In that time, this house has remained empty.' She blinked, twice, without taking her eyes from his face. 'There was an accident, and she moved in with me.'

'I'm sorry,' he put in – but she wasn't listening.

'She doesn't talk, which is why I'm here now instead of her. You're bound to meet her in due course, but she won't talk to you. It's best that you know this, so you're prepared. If you have any problems with the house, or any questions, kindly bring them to me.'

He nodded.

Her eyes remained on his face for a second more than was comfortable. 'Goodnight then,' she said, stepping out. 'I hope you sleep well.' She pulled the door closed, and he heard the faint sound of her retreating steps.

He folded his arms, digesting what he'd just been told. An accident of some kind, a granddaughter who didn't speak. Weird. Lil has lived with me, she'd said. With me, not with us – so that meant, didn't it, that it was just the two of them next door? Husband gone to his heavenly reward, or made his escape via the divorce courts.

He'd imagined Lil an adult when he'd heard that the house belonged to her – but now he thought she might be a child who'd inherited the place after whatever accident had occurred, and was living with her grandmother because she was too young to be on her own. Or maybe she'd been injured in the accident, and couldn't live independently any more. The grandmother's sketchy account told him very little.

He looked up the stairs. They disappeared into a darkness that now seemed slightly sinister. His forehead was clammy: he ran a sleeve over it. He touched the radiator and found it to be hot. At least the heating worked. He let his gaze roam about the space, noting the ceiling spotlight that was out, the not quite accurate meeting of two lengths of wallpaper, the fruit carved into the sides of the hallstand.

It looked bleak with nothing hanging on it. Hallstands should never be empty: they should be full of things. He took off his jacket and propped it on a hook. It didn't make much of an improvement.

He felt gloom descending. What was he doing here? What the hell was he doing here? He should be married now. He should still be living in London, working in the job he'd loved, with no money worries and a full social life. Instead here he was, unemployed and miles from anything and anyone familiar, with the last of his savings to live on.

He opened the door on the right, next to the radiator. The sitting room, he thought – but he was wrong. This room held a mahogany dining table and six chairs, and a sideboard that didn't match, and three shelves set into an alcove with nothing at all on them.

The floor was wooden. The walls were papered in a blue-green shade, with paler rectangles here and there where paintings or photos must have hung. This was a room for family meals, or maybe dinner parties; not for him with his single plate.

He closed the door. He stepped across the hall and found the sitting room, which was altogether cosier. Cream walls, a pair of grey tweed couches and a red armchair, a cream marble fireplace in which sat a nicely reddened coal fire, a large wicker basket nearby full of turf and logs. A rug in patched terracotta and ochre shades covered at least half of the wooden floor. A television hung on the wall above the mantelpiece; an empty bookshelf was set into the alcove on the right of the chimney breast.

He tried out a couch and found it comfortable. He pulled the heavy grey curtains closed. This room he would use in the evenings, to watch television or search YouTube for something diverting.

He thought again of how much quieter his life

had become. He hadn't gone near his usual social media sites since August. He'd closed all his accounts, ignoring the questions that had started to come in as word of what had happened got around. He hadn't had a night out in five months, hadn't set foot inside a pub or a restaurant. He couldn't remember the last gig he'd been to, the last film he'd seen in a cinema.

Back in the hall he looked up the stairs again. What the hell was spooking him? What could there possibly be to fear up there? Nothing but empty rooms, and a bed prepared for him with clean sheets, and fresh towels in the bathroom. With any luck, she'd left him a bar of soap too.

He pulled his jacket on again. He'd hunt down some food, and maybe he'd find an off-licence, and after that he'd have an early night. A soak in a bath if there was one, and if the heating did a proper job with the water. Melt away the nameless unsettlement he'd felt since her mention of an accident, fill the silence with the comforting everyday sound of water running through pipes.

On the point of leaving the house, he remembered the two keys on the kitchen table. He returned and retrieved them, and locked the back door. He threaded the keys onto his Jeep key-ring, which until this morning had also held Joel's spare house key.

Hang on to it, Joel had said, but Tom had taken it off and handed it back.

He opened the front door and stepped outside. The last of the light was draining from the sky, a thin crescent of moon rising. He searched for stars and found none, or nearly none. Too cloudy – but he bet that on a clear night, with no competing street lights, they'd crowd out the sky here. He zipped up his jacket, feeling the bite of a January evening.

He decided to have a quick look around the back again, go to the end of the garden, see what there was to be seen while he still could. In the passage he brushed against wet hedging; plenty of clipping to keep him busy. Maybe he should ask permission – but why would she object to his improving the place?

He rounded the corner and saw the rear garden disappearing into the near darkness. The light from the kitchen window was muted by the pulled-down blind, and the sliver of moon didn't help much. He'd left her torch on the kitchen table, and he couldn't be bothered going back in for it.

He walked to the edge of the patio and squinted down into the high grass. Was there no pathway through it? He prodded about with a boot and discovered a flat stone set into the ground. He stepped on it and searched for another, and one by one he found the rest of them. They made little difference to his progress, the grass having pretty much closed in around them, and the ends of his jeans quickly became damp. He persevered through the gloom and was approaching the end of the garden – he could make out a low wall and a gate ahead – when a movement off to his right, a quick flash of something, a small rustling sound, caught his attention.

He turned and saw a gap in the hedging, roughly the width of a door. Beyond it, in the neighbouring garden, he discerned the looming shape of a biggish building, a shed or cabin of some kind. Must be set right up against the garden wall. He saw the shine of windows, three of them. They emitted no light from within, reflecting only the faint illumination that came from the sky.

'Hello? Is someone there?'

His voice broke through the stillness. No response came. It might have been an animal, a dog or a cat. But wouldn't an animal react in some way to a human voice, either by approaching or darting away? He felt a small crawling in the skin of his scalp, imagining someone, or something, watching him silently. Waiting to pounce.

He shook off the feeling. Cop on, he told himself. It was his imagination, fired up by the empty house, and an accident associated with it that hadn't been explained, and a night that was darker and quieter than he was used to.

He covered the short distance to the end of his own garden, and found the cliff path his landlady had spoken of. It looked to be about four feet in width, and as far as he could tell not paved or finished in any way. Packed earth it looked like, worn smooth by the passage of those who'd trodden it.

He didn't open the small gate. He could hear rather than see what lay beyond the fence that bordered the path on the far side. He understood then that the rumbling sound wasn't caused by a motorway, or by machinery. He stood listening to the low music of the Atlantic, the wash and pull that would be the soundtrack to his life here. He could hardly have chosen a property much closer to it, unless he'd rented out the shed he'd just spotted next door.

He caught a whiff of the catch-in-the-throat tang of seaweed. He'd had a seaweed bath once, and had been surprised by how it had confounded his cynical expectations. He'd loved the sensation of the oily water, the way his skin had smelt, and felt, afterwards. Might pick up a bit on a beach here, try it again.

If the bedroom she'd made up was at the rear of the house he'd leave his window cracked open tonight, see if the sound and scent of the sea helped him to sleep. See if he had any better luck here.

He wondered how high the cliff was. He should have asked her more. Tomorrow he'd take a walk, get his bearings. A growl in his stomach reminded him that he needed food now. He retraced his steps up through the lawn and across the patio. In the dark he lurched against the hedge in the side passage, causing rainwater to shower onto him.

Before getting into the Jeep he shot another glance towards his neighbour's house, and wondered again about the owner of the one he'd taken. She doesn't talk, the grandmother had said. Not can't, but doesn't. She won't talk to you. Strange way to put it, almost as if it was a choice the granddaughter had made.

He sat into the Jeep, rubbing hands together to take the cold away. He looked at the cardboard box on the passenger seat. He lifted it onto his lap and opened it, and took out a house.

He ran a thumb over the smooth warmth of the wood. He brought it to his nose to inhale the smell that always calmed him. He thought of the classes that had been his sanctuary, when he could lose himself in his task, blot out the horror of his reality for a couple of hours twice a week.

He traced with his fingers the skewed chimney on the crooked roof, and the walls that didn't quite meet at the corners, and the front door that was anything but a true rectangle. Twenty houses in total, each the rough size of a half-pound of butter, each different in style and colour from its companions.

Bits of nonsense, that was all they were. Quirky and lopsided and useless. He didn't know why he'd even brought them here, why he hadn't donated them to his little niece and nephew, who might well have got a kick out of them. What was he to do with them here?

He replaced the house and closed the box. He set it back on the passenger seat and looked out once more at the house that was to be his home for the next six months. He thought how absolutely different it was to the last place he'd called home, and how much Vivienne would hate it.

He switched on the radio. He turned the dial until he found music, and raised the volume high. He swung around carelessly, coming too close to the opposite hedge. He heard it scratch and claw its way along the side of the Jeep. He drove off, unaware that he was being watched.

Five Years Earlier

His first sight of her was in the church. From his seat in the top pew next to Joel, waiting for Sarah who was late like all brides, he glanced behind at the small gathering and spotted straight off – how could he miss it? – the little lime green hat with its ludicrously tall feather, and the tumble of blue-black hair beneath it, and the face under that. Full red mouth, eyes outlined starkly in black, an upward feline flick at the outer corners. Amy Winehouse, he thought. Same striking exotic features.

She caught him looking, and winked – or he thought she did. A lightning dip of an eyelid, or not? Hard to be sure, no alteration in her expression – and just then the organist started up, and the ceremony got under way.

He swept the churchyard afterwards and found her chatting with a couple he didn't know. She was considerably taller than Amy Winehouse, nearly as tall as himself. She burst into a loud peal of laughter as he watched, raising a hand to press it to the whiteness of her throat. Red nails. Good teeth.

Her dress, buttercup yellow, clung to her curves, ending just above shapely knees. A wisp of a scarf in a paler green than the hat slithered from a shoulder to rest in the crook of her elbow until she hitched it back up.

She didn't appear to be accompanied: no sign of a hovering man, or woman. Tom had broken up with his last girlfriend a few weeks previously, their six-month relationship, his longest to date, needing to be ended

*when she'd begun hinting about moving in together.
Since then he'd done his share of flirting at bar counters,
and following up with a few one-night stands. He was
twenty-three, and in no hurry to commit.*

*You want to bring someone to the wedding? Joel
had asked, and Tom had said no. I'll hook up with the
bridesmaid, he'd joked. He was glad now he hadn't tied
himself to anyone, glad he was free to investigate this
interesting new person.*

*It took a while. At the hotel he was ambushed during
the champagne reception by an aunt of his father's, a
woman he normally met only at funerals. The woman's
hearing had been on the decline for as long as he'd
known her: he was acutely conscious of his side of their
conversation being audible to everyone in the vicinity.
He escaped when dinner was announced, and took
his place at the top table between his brother and his
father.*

*He located the dark-haired woman at a nearby table,
her hat missing. Her hair, messy in a way he suspected
was quite studied, gleamed in the sunlight that poured
in through the long windows. He looked directly at her
a few times during his speech, and she didn't look away.
As soon as they could move around again, he'd go over
and introduce himself.*

She got there first.

Vivienne Chambers, she said, slipping into the chair vacated by his father between dessert and coffee. First cousin of the bride.

English accent, polished. Up close he could smell her musky scent.

You've been eyeing me up, she went on, so I thought I'd better check you out.

He grinned. He enjoyed a brazen woman. Guilty as charged. Tom McLysaght.

She took the hand he offered, held on to it for longer than she needed. Oh, I know your name. I've done my research.

She'd been asking about him. He was inordinately pleased to hear it. So what else do you know?

She used his fingers to count off. Well, you're Joel's little brother, obviously, and you're currently unattached, and you've just finished college, and you still live at home with Daddy. Oh, and you've been snapped up by Google, because you're a bit of a wunderkind *in the computing world.*

He tried hard to hide his increasing delight. I interned with Google – they went for the devil they knew.

Don't be modest, she said. It doesn't become you.

He held up his hands. OK, it's true – I'm a

wunderkind. *But now I'm at a disadvantage, because I know nothing about you. You live in England?*

I do. I'm English by birth, Irish by blood. She finally relinquished his hand: he had to resist the urge to grab hers, to claim it like she'd claimed his. *Mum is Sarah's aunt, her father's sister. She crossed the sea and was snapped up by Dad in London. They're divorced now, but she never came home.*

You sound posh, he told her. *Like the queen* — and she gave the same loud guffaw he'd heard outside the church, and told him there the similarity ended. *I'm afraid I'm all fur coat and no knickers,* she said, and he experienced a stab of desire, which he suspected was exactly what she'd intended.

Hello.

They both looked up. Tom's father had returned from the Gents. *My dad,* Tom said.

George, his father added, extending his hand.

The lauded cardiologist, she said, rising to her feet with their handshake. *Congratulations, you have two fine-looking sons — and I can see where they get their looks.*

His father smiled. *And you are …?*

Vivienne, Tom said quickly, before she could. He'd wondered afterwards, long afterwards, if he'd wanted *to stake his claim on her, even then. Sarah's cousin, he told his father.*

I shall have to find you both later, she said, for a dance. In her mouth it was dahnse.

After she'd left them, his father reclaimed his seat. Confident young lady, he remarked, and Tom followed her with his eyes, and saw the sway of her hips, and knew she was going to be significant.

Beth

He was troubled. It came off him like a smell. He was running away from something, or someone. She hoped his troubles wouldn't catch up with him: they had enough of their own here.

Still in his twenties, she thought, and on his own by the look of it. Could of course be widowed like herself; that might account for the haunted look.

She'd heard Dublin in his accent. Not the colourful Dublin of Moore Street, less earthy than that, but his roots were definitely in the capital. Coming here had put plenty of distance, almost four hundred kilometres, between him and Dublin.

She was cross with herself for not having noticed that the boiler clock was off: must have gone wrong in a power cut sometime. Good job she'd thought to light the fire, but annoying that he'd walked into a freezing house.

She should have told him more than she had. He probably had a right to know, but she couldn't. An accident was all she could bring herself to say, which told him nothing. He'd hear the rest in town, as soon as people knew where he was staying. He'd wonder why she'd given away so little, and maybe resent her for it. Couldn't be helped.

The eleventh of January today, the date Maria and Killian had flown off on their last holiday, a week before the world had hurtled off its course. She should have asked him to come the day before, or the day after. She could have said she was busy on the eleventh. Then again, what did it matter what date he moved in? What did it change? Nothing at all.

She watched the red taillights of his car until they vanished around the bend. Gone off to get his burger from Caffrey's, having turned down the invitation she'd felt obliged to proffer on his first night, which was a relief. I'll just grab a takeaway somewhere and crash, he'd said, not knowing the effect that word had on her now, the wallop it brought with it, regardless of its context.

Crash. She was allergic to a word.

She hadn't been exactly welcoming. She'd heard the coolness in her tone as she'd taken him through the house. Chitchat and niceties had never come easily to her. She was efficient, she got things done – and she was fair, and always honest, even if the truth wasn't always welcome – but she lacked the warmth of others, didn't gush and flatter like they did, and because of this they judged her to be unfeeling.

How little they knew.

As she turned from the window her eye fell on the two smooth round pebbles of a pale pinkish colour, each roughly the size of a pullet's egg, that she'd come on by the front door earlier and left on the worktop for Lil. Picked up on a beach, most likely. Little paperweights they'd make, or just something pretty for a shelf or a mantel.

She'd been wondering when the next would arrive. A couple of weeks after the accident it had started, little random deposits left every so often on a windowsill, or at one of the doors. Pretty shells, a pair of baby oranges, a jar of honey, clutches of greenery or flowers. A shard of blue sea glass once, its edges rounded by salt water and sand. A small battered box another time that she thought might be silver, badly tarnished and spotted but still capable of being opened and closed. A trinket box, you'd call it. She'd polished it with Silvo and it had come up quite nicely, and now it sat on Lil's dressing table and held her hair slides.

Harmless things, placed there by someone with no malice. A young man with his eye on Lil, she guessed. Too shy to come forward, inhibited possibly by Lil's silence. No harm for someone to show an interest: might be just what she needed to bring her back.

Beth hadn't voiced this opinion, in case she was wrong. Our mystery deliveries, she called them, and Lil didn't seem to place any particular significance on them. But what other explanation could there be? At seventy-two, Beth hardly had a secret admirer.

It was easy for someone to leave things at the house without being spotted. People came through the garden from the lane several times a day when the library was open. Something could be dropped quietly at one of the doors, or on the kitchen sill if Beth was absent.

'I forgot to tell him about the library,' she said. 'He may not be a reader, but I'll mention it next time I see him. His hair is dreadful, badly needs cutting. Why anyone would let himself go like that is beyond me. Still, as long as he pays his rent and looks after the place, his appearance is of no consequence.'

Talking to herself, like she did a lot of the time. Nobody in the kitchen but the cat, and he only heeded her if she was filling his bowl. He didn't stir now from his doze on Lil's chair, didn't even cock an ear at the sound of Beth's voice.

Funny how he always chose that chair, never any of the others. Lil would scoop him up when she came in and place him on another, but he'd hop down to the floor and pad away to the sitting-room couch instead.

'Needed a shave too,' Beth went on, stooping to pick something – what? A papery curve of onion skin – from the floor. 'Nails were bitten, horrible habit. Mannerly, though. Educated, I'd say – so why is he making himself out to be a jack-of-all-trades?'

The fact that this new man had shown up a few months after Jimmy Talbot, the town's handyman for years, had fallen off a ladder and broken his neck didn't strike her as strange in the least. That was simply how things worked. Some would call it coincidence, or serendipity – foolish word, she'd never had time for it – but she knew better. A gap was created, and sooner or later someone came to fill it. Happened all the time, if folk would only sit up and take notice.

The rich aroma of the casserole wafted about the kitchen. 'I wonder what brings him to Fairweather in the middle of winter,' she said. 'He'd surely have mentioned if he knew someone here.'

She also wondered if she should be concerned about a stranger, particularly a male stranger, living in such close proximity to them. Their little corner was very secluded, even if Fairweather was only a few minutes away. He hadn't come across as dangerous in the least, but you never knew. Harold Shipman, in any photos she'd seen of him, had looked like someone's genial grandfather.

She heard a soft patter on the window. She saw

the drops landing on the glass like little dots of quicksilver in the dark. The rain down for the night, wettest week they were having in a long time. Not cold enough for frost, thankfully – they'd have a skating rink out there if it was.

The cat hopped down from the chair then and came to brush against her calves, mewing. 'Hungry boy,' she said, and went to open a pouch for him. She used to wonder if he missed the family he belonged to, there one day and gone the next. Nobody left but Lil, and he'd been Hollie's cat. Did he miss the sounds and smells of next door, the familiar nooks and crannies of the house, the stairs he'd climb each afternoon to snooze on Hollie's bed? Maybe that was why he chose Lil's chair at the table, his cat's sixth sense pulling him towards the closest connection with his old life.

Inevitably, he wandered into the garden next door. Beth had spotted him rambling around in the long grass from her bedroom window. After field mice, no doubt. She should probably have mentioned that to the new tenant too. She should have warned him not to leave the back door open or the creature might wander in, force of habit. Hopefully it wouldn't be a big deal.

She'd found it cruelly hard, going back into Killian

and Maria's house after the accident. Not directly afterwards, not in the first week or two, so blinded by shock that she barely knew where she was, she and Lil drifting like ghosts from one house to the other. Not then but later, after Lil had moved in with her, unable to stay alone in the emptied-out house – and unable since then to return there, so it had fallen to Beth to go back in search of documents, needing dates and facts and figures because officialdom demanded it. So much red tape required to close off lives, to declare them over.

And she'd gone back two months after that to bag up their clothes and shoes, to take photographs off the walls, to remove all evidence of them. Too early, she knew it was, the loss of them still an open wound inside her, the grief still raw and rough-edged – but she did not want the place turned into a shrine. She absolutely did not want that, so she'd spent a week on the edge of tears, filling bags and boxes, wiping down shelves, closing doors.

And each time she entered it since then, each time she forced herself to turn the front-door key and cross the threshold to check that nothing was amiss, the silence, the hollowness of the house nearly killed her. No music, no radio, no light feminine laughter, no footsteps on the stairs. No Maria saying, I was just

going to run over and tell you to come to dinner. I'm
doing lasagne.

No more Maria living twenty steps away. The
fact of her only child being gone, the waste, the
utter *obscenity* of that still had the power to render
her senseless, to reduce her to nothing, to leave her
as dumb as Lil until she was able to gather herself
together again.

She was a mother no longer, and she'd stopped
being a wife thirteen years ago, when she'd lost
Gerry to emphysema. Now she was nothing but
grandmother to Lil – and she was tortured by the
suspicion that she was to blame for Lil's silence.

I'll go next door with you, Beth, the sergeant had
said, after he'd broken the news to her. I'll come with
you to tell Lil. You don't want to do it alone – but
she'd refused to let him, pig-headed as ever despite
her heart having blown apart at his quiet, dreadful
words, despite the loud buzzing that had started up
in her head, despite the squeezed-tight feeling in her
chest that was turning breathing into an effort.

I can do it on my own, she'd said, and she had
– but Lil, home for the weekend from college,
preparing dinner in the kitchen next door for her
returning parents, poor Lil, smiling at the sight of
her grandmother as Beth walked in, smile fading as

she took in Beth's devastated face, tragic Lil, her eyes widening, her mouth opening in horror at the words Beth had shot out too fast, needing to do it quickly, needing to get it over with – Lil, Lil, eyes filling and reddening, mouth wide open but nothing, no word, no scream, nothing at all coming out of it but an awful strangled, guttural kind of noise, her anguish terrible to witness before she let fall the bag of frozen peas she'd been holding, before her knees buckled and she sank to the kitchen floor too swiftly for Beth to catch her – why hadn't she sat her down first, why hadn't she even thought of that? – hitting the tiles with all her weight, the impact knocking out a tooth and causing the entire side of her face to darken into a bruise within hours, and jarring an elbow and an ankle as peas jumped and skittered and rolled in all directions.

The trauma had sent her to a place of silence, had left her unresponsive to Beth's repeated pleas, to doctors' careful urging, to friends' gentle coaxing to try to speak. The shock, the grief, lodging in her throat, allowing no sound to pass it.

There's no physical reason why she can't talk, Beth was told. As if she needed to be told that, as if she was stupid.

Will it come back?

It might, but it will take time.

What can I do?

Well, you could look into counselling – but that, it turned out, was something that Beth simply could not do, with Lil flatly refusing to consider any kind of mental therapy, remaining deaf to her grandmother's pleas. *I can't*, she'd write in her notebook, anytime Beth brought up the subject. *I just can't. Sorry.*

Best you can do is let things lie then, Beth was told when she'd reported her failure. Something might trigger a release, something good or something bad. Give her time, she was told – but was two years not long enough? Could Lil not learn to live with her sadness, as Beth had had to do? Sometimes Beth had to fight the urge to shake her, or shout at her, to call her selfish and uncaring, with no feeling for her grandmother – because what good would that do?

She'd also refused to return to college. Halfway through the third year of her business studies course, and loving it before the accident. Beth hadn't insisted, knowing she needed time before facing into the world again, but days had turned into weeks, and still she lay in bed till midday, and sat hunched and rocking slowly on the sitting-room couch after that, pale and hollow-eyed and interested in nothing, not in the books she'd loved, or the walks or swims she'd taken every day when she was home, or any of the outdoor activities she'd enjoyed with the others. They'd been such a team, the four of them. So close.

I want to reopen the library, Beth had said eventually. I need to get it going again for all the people who use it, but I'm not sure I can do it alone. Will you help me, Lil?

She could of course do it alone, she could run the place blindfold on her own, but her strategy had worked, and she and Lil had sat together for three and a half days of the week – winter hours, ten till five, closed Tuesdays and Thursdays, half-day Saturday – in the cabin at the end of the garden, and the locals began to drift back in when the news went around.

So careful everyone had been in the first few weeks. Tiptoeing into the cabin, as if any kind of noise might cause Beth and Lil to shatter. Asking Beth in hushed voices how they were, some of them unable to look directly at her, most of them ignoring Lil altogether. Oh, Beth knew it was out of embarrassment, and fear of getting it wrong, and bewilderment in the face of Lil's silence, of course she knew all that – but their clumsy attempts at kindness had made her so angry she'd wanted to throttle them. She'd wanted to thrust

Lil in front of them, to shout that her granddaughter was mute, not invisible.

Everything had made her angry, in the first few weeks and months. Anger had coursed through her, colouring everything and everyone she encountered, making fire of her grief, raging like a molten river through her dreams. She'd spoken little, fearing it might escape in cruel, sharp words. She'd hidden it behind short, clipped sentences, and they'd thought her cold because of it.

But time had passed, like it always did, and her anger had cooled slowly, and turned into loneliness and emptiness. Spring became summer and they were busier then, as they always were, and at the start of May they opened five and a half days a week, summer hours. Visitors to Fairweather, hearing about the library – and maybe also of the tragedy, the worst in Fairweather's history – had made their way to the cabin to leaf through the books and sneak glances at Lil or Beth, and talk in low voices and different accents and other languages.

In September, Lil had been just as insistent about not returning to her studies. *I want to stay in the library*, she'd written – and while her state of wordlessness continued, Beth could hardly insist. You can do the weekdays on your own then, she'd said, and I'll do Saturday mornings. Not quite ready at seventy to yield control of it, but sensing that Lil needed the extra responsibility if she were ever to pick herself up and move on.

It had been the wrong thing to do, of course. She could see that now. The last thing she should have done was to give Lil an excuse to hide herself at the bottom of the garden, knitting her days away. Thankfully, her love of books returned, along with her regular walks and swims – but was this really what her granddaughter planned to do with the rest of her life? Was she never to fulfil her academic promise and find a job that actually stimulated her, motivated her, made her feel useful in the world?

And what about her family home? Did she never envisage living there again? Letting it had been Beth's idea, not Lil's. Seeing the dust build on the surfaces, inhaling the stale air of the rooms each time she'd gone in to check on the place, the sad, hollow feel of the house had eventually driven her to suggest looking for a tenant.

It was a tactical move, another attempt to get Lil back on track. Maybe the thought of a stranger moving in would be the catalyst her granddaughter needed to return there herself – but Lil had put up no resistance to the notion, had seemed almost to welcome it, so Beth had had no choice but to follow through and advertise the house.

A six-month lease she'd decided to offer. Short enough for them to be able to tolerate an awkward tenant, long enough for Lil to see what it felt like to have the house denied to her.

She'd taken amateur photographs. She'd found an online marketplace, and put the ad up. She hadn't expected a lot of interest – Fairweather was a summer destination, with little to offer off-season – and sure enough, for several weeks nothing had happened. Her ad had got a few views, but no enquiry. And then, when she'd been almost ready to admit defeat, a message had come in.

Is the house still available?

Beth's reply had been equally succinct. *Yes.*

I'd like to take it.

Just like that, going purely by Beth's brief description and substandard photos, looking for no further information.

Do you wish to view it?

No. Too far away.

He didn't say how far too far was. *So you're happy to take it sight unseen?*

I am.

How many people?

Just me.

One person would be good. Not much wear and tear. *I would need a month's deposit and the first month's rent in advance.* She wondered again if she was charging too little or too much. She'd taken all the circumstances into account, and put what she'd considered to be a fair price on it – let him take it or leave it.

That's fine.

He was the only interested party. She'd decided to go for it. *It's yours if you want it.*

Thank you. How soon can I move in?

As soon as you like.

How about this Friday?

Day after tomorrow. Suddenly it had seemed to be happening too fast – but she couldn't back out now. *Friday will be fine. I'm attaching a lease with all the details, which I'll need signed and returned, and my bank details for lodgement of funds before Friday.*

Within an hour, the signed lease was back. *I've just done an online bank transfer*, he'd written in his accompanying message, and the money had landed in her account the following morning.

Too late, she'd thought of character references. She would just have to take her chances. Mark and Fred had separately offered to meet him with her: she'd turned them both down, not wanting to come across as a vulnerable female, even if that was precisely what she and Lil were.

The porch door opened just then, lifting her from her thoughts. A second later, Lil appeared.

'Hello, my sweetheart,' Beth said. 'Good day?' and her granddaughter nodded and smiled, her cheeks pink from the cold air, her waxed hat and jacket beaded with rain. She took them off and dropped them onto a chair, and came to wrap her grandmother in an embrace.

So tactile she'd become, one sense seeming to compensate for the loss of another. Twining Beth's fingers in hers as they watched *MasterChef*, trailing a hand across Beth's shoulders if she passed her chair, tucking an arm into Beth's when they went for a walk, resting a palm briefly against Beth's cheek sometimes, for no reason at all.

'I was in with Olive this morning,' Beth said. 'She's wondering if we have the new Banville. I said I'd ask you.'

Another nod. The little notebook appeared that Lil carried everywhere. *Martin dropped it in a few days ago*, she wrote. Martin O'Donnell, the family solicitor who'd drawn up an insurance policy for the library when it opened, and who'd been passing on all his reads to them ever since.

'Great. I'll set it aside in the morning.'

Lil handled all the cataloguing now, sorting the donations that arrived every so often. It was unique, their little enterprise. First, because of its location at the bottom of Beth's garden, accessible either through a small gate on the cliff path or down by the side of Beth's house, and second, because it wasn't a library at all, or not in the official sense of the word. It was a project that had succeeded, an act of rebellion born of frustration.

No library had ever existed in Fairweather, the closest one being in the town of Listowel, thirty kilometres away. The lack of it had always bothered Beth, who'd been a reader from the moment she'd learnt to make sense of written words on a page, but she'd never thought to do anything about it until her husband's death. In the aftermath of that, needing a distraction when she came home from work to an empty house, she'd begun a determined lobbying of her nearest councillor, whose office was in Listowel.

Fairweather needs a library, she'd told him. It's ridiculous that there's none here. She'd said it to his face, she'd emailed him, she'd phoned him. She'd kept up the pressure until she'd lost patience with his vague promises, and taken matters into her own hands.

Without looking for council permission – why

should she, when they had so little interest? – she'd installed the cabin at the bottom of her garden, just inside the wall that separated it from the cliff path, and kitted it out as best she could. She'd got a carpenter to fashion floor-to-ceiling shelving throughout. She'd arranged for electricity to be connected from the house, so they could have light and heat. On the wooden floor she'd spread a Turkish rug that had done service in her sitting room for decades. She'd added a desk behind the door, and folding chairs, and lots of cushions.

She'd cleaned out the old coal shed, a little way up the garden, and organised a toilet and a sink there, and stuck a stern notice on the door with regard to keeping it presentable – and by and large, people did.

After much thought about wording, she'd had a sign made for the door of the cabin that simply said *Welcome*.

When she considered it ready, she'd put out the call among her reader friends, and everyone had contributed books. It hadn't been enough, not nearly enough, so she'd taken out ads in the national papers, and found other ways to spread the word, and little by little, more books had started arriving.

Several boxes had come from a charity shop that was closing its doors. Owners of houses up for auction had donated a portion of their personal libraries. A fire-damaged bookshop had sent them salvaged but unsellable stock.

Just as in a regular library, the books were alphabetised on the shelves, with fiction separated from non-fiction, and a children's section along the end wall. As in a regular library, people borrowed and returned books – but there were two significant differences between Beth's library and all others.

First, books were handed out without recording who was taking them, and second, there was no time limit on the borrowings. A date *was* stamped on an outgoing book, but it was the date it was taken out, purely so Beth could see which books were in demand and which not – useful information when the time came, as it did every so often, to make room for new donations.

Moreover, the library was open to all, locals or not. Send it back when you finish it, Beth would tell visitors to Fairweather when they enquired, writing down her address and slipping it between the pages – and most if not all of the books did find their way back. When you trusted people to do the right thing, she found, the vast majority of them did.

For the first five years of its existence, while Beth was still working fulltime, the library was manned during the week by a rota of local volunteers, with Beth handling the Saturdays. After her retirement at sixty-five she took over, glad to have something to fill her time, to make her feel that she was still useful.

Residents of Fairweather and its immediate surroundings used the library all year round. It was also the venue for a book club Beth had started a few years ago. Its members met on the last Wednesday of every month, except July and August.

'The tenant has arrived,' she said now. 'He seems fine. I forgot to mention the library to him.'

Lil didn't react. She took the candlesticks from the dresser and set them on the table, and followed with placemats and cutlery. She was bound to feel conflicted, despite her lack of resistance to the idea of letting the house.

'I told him you don't talk. I felt he should know, to avoid awkwardness when you meet. I didn't go into any detail.'

Lil gave a tiny nod, putting out salt and pepper, finding clean napkins. Unable to speak, or unwilling: nobody but she knew which it was, the truth buried somewhere inside her. Beth switched on the radio for the news and took the casserole from the oven, and they sat at the table to eat, and after that their evening passed in the same quiet manner that all their evenings did.

Saturday morning was dry and sunny, a relief after all the rain. The library would be busy this morning, the crisp brightness coaxing people out. Beth hummed along to a tune on the radio, wondering how the new tenant had slept on his first night in the house. She would call over this afternoon and tell him about the library. Give him a leaflet with the tide times as well, in case he was planning to swim. Enquire if he'd found the takeaway, point him in the direction of a few other eating places. She would try to be accommodating.

She was alone in the kitchen, no sign of Lil yet. Lil could sleep till the middle of the morning on the days she wasn't on duty in the library. Beth had never slept late, even in her youth; she found it mystifying that some people could spend what she considered the best part of the day unconscious.

Fifteen minutes till opening time. She lifted cutlery from the soapy water and ran it under the tap to rinse it, composing that afternoon's shopping list in her head. Milk they needed, and tea, and vanilla pods, and more aloe vera gel. Her hands got so dry in the winter, even wearing gloves as she always did.

She became aware of a sound coming in through the window that she opened a notch when she got up, winter or summer. What was it? She dried her hands and turned off the radio, frowning. Yes, there it was, short metallic bursts, a kind of swishing – and suddenly, she identified it.

Clippers. Hedge clippers.

Lord almighty.

She hurried through the hall, face growing warm. She opened the door and stepped out – and right away, at the top of the dividing hedge, she caught the glint of clipper blades in the sun, and the new tenant standing behind them.

He was cutting the hedge.

He was *daring* to cut the hedge.

'Stop!' she called sharply. 'Stop that!'

The blades halted. He turned. She marched over and stood before him, rigid with anger. He was cutting the hedge with Killian's clippers. The invasion of it, the presumption of it, almost shut off her breath.

He looked surprised, the clippers still poised. He'd barely begun; the corner was all he'd cut. 'I was tidying it up,' he said. 'I thought—'

'You had no right!' she shot back, the words coming out too loudly, with a tremble beneath them. 'You had *no* right!'

He frowned. 'Sorry, I didn't think you—'

'You had no right!' she repeated, more forcefully. 'You are not to *touch* that garden, not to *touch* it!'

He lowered the clippers. He shrugged. 'OK,' he

said mildly, and she wheeled and went back inside, not trusting herself to say more. How dare he! How *dare* he!

And then, of course, over the next three hours in the library, when she regained her senses, when she calmed down, she was mortified. What must he think of her, attacking him like a fishwife for clipping a hedge that could badly do with clipping? What must he have thought, being ordered so peremptorily to stop? She'd practically shouted at him.

She must apologise. She must do it as soon as she closed up. She must also tell him of the accident, because it was the only way to explain her behaviour. She must steel herself, and do it.

The morning crawled by. The storytime at eleven seemed endless. The smile she conjured for those in attendance was wooden; she knew it, and was powerless to do anything about it. A few asked if she was alright: she told them she was, hearing how tense – and clearly *not* alright – she sounded. To her relief, nobody probed further. Nobody was brave enough.

One o'clock finally came. She bade goodbye to the last of the borrowers and locked up, and made her way towards the next-door house with a sinking heart. The sun still shone, the sky was still a milky blue, but now she saw none of it. What if he slammed the door in her face?

He didn't.

'May I have a word?' she asked quietly.

He regarded her for a millisecond, and then stepped back. 'Come in,' he said.

She followed him silently to the kitchen, where he offered her some of her own tea. 'I haven't got around to doing a shop yet,' he said, 'so it's tea or nothing, I'm afraid.'

He was being so polite, so civilised. Acting like the earlier scene hadn't happened. 'No tea, thank you. I just—'

To her horror, she felt the sudden onset of tears. She never cried. Hardly ever cried. She curled her hands into fists and clamped her mouth shut, and blinked rapidly.

'Please have a seat,' he said, so she did. The page she'd left him, with the bin collection days and the meter reading, was still on the table, still folded. She kept her eyes on it as she drew in a deep steadying breath, and another. Then she lifted her head and said what she had come to say.

'Lil's parents and sister were killed in a road accident, two years ago. Lil wasn't involved, she wasn't with them, she was here, but she stopped talking afterwards, and hasn't spoken a word since then. She also hasn't been back to this house since she moved in with me. She can't bring herself to come back.'

He stood by the sink, arms folded, unmoving and silent. She took another breath, and released another gush of words.

'I haven't touched this garden in two years, and I haven't let anyone else do it either. I'm not sure why, but I can't. So when I heard the clippers, I'm afraid I – overreacted. I was terribly rude to you, and I … apologise. I'm sincerely' – another falter, another catch in her breath – 'I'm sincerely sorry.'

She stopped, out of words. There, it was done.

'Please,' he said quietly, 'you have nothing to apologise for. It's my fault – I should have checked with you before I did anything. I'm so sorry for your loss.'

She got to her feet, completely unable for his sympathy, the look of pity on his face. 'I'll be off now,' she said, hearing how abrupt it sounded, how ungrateful for his understanding.

He followed her through the hall. He reached past her to open the door. She lifted a hand in silent farewell and left, relieved that he'd taken her apology with such grace. Back in her own house she found Lil making coffee. She briefly debated bringing him over a mug, along with a couple of biscuits – presumably he had yet to eat today. She could bring the tides leaflet too, and tell him about the library.

She decided to leave him alone. He'd had more than enough of her today.

Olive

Olive Purcell, née Wilson, knew Mark Purcell for years before she clapped eyes on his son. All through her childhood and adolescence Mark would pull up outside her family's corner shop every ten days or so, his van loaded with whatever supplies her father had ordered. He'd stack boxes on his trolley and wheel them through to the back, breaking off his whistled tune to call a cheerful greeting to whoever happened to be manning the till at the time.

How's the smartest girl in Galway? he'd ask whenever he encountered Olive. Have you won the Nobel Prize for brains yet? He was corny and lovely; you couldn't help liking him. He told her he was from a place called Fairweather, and let on to be deeply insulted when she told him she'd never been there. It's the jewel in Kerry's crown, he said. There's no place like it in Ireland. You'll have to check it out – and she promised him she would, some day.

And then his wife died.

Olive's father read out the death notice at the breakfast table one morning. *After a long illness*, he read, and Olive thought of how happy Mark always seemed, how she couldn't picture him without a smile on his face, and how he'd never told them he had a sick wife at home. Maybe he didn't care, maybe they'd fallen out of love – but the next time she met him, a few weeks later, it was clear that he was shaken by the loss.

How's Olive? he asked, a quieter, sadder smile on his face, no more whistling, and she said fine, and was too unschooled in death at sixteen to sympathise with him so she said nothing, and felt bad afterwards.

Children had been mentioned in the death notice. Two sons it said, no ages given but Olive figured they couldn't be adults. Mark looked about her father's age; his children were likely to be in their teens, like her. She wondered if boys missed their mother more than girls, or if it made any difference.

Years passed. Olive left school and went to study art in Limerick, and came home only once a month or so. For a time she didn't encounter Mark, who she knew still called into the shop. She heard news of him through her parents: one son gone to Australia, the other still around, working in a local pub – and then, one Saturday she was home, the shop door opened and Mark wheeled in his trolley, whistling his familiar tune.

Hello, stranger, he said. How's college treating you? He looked pretty much the same, if a little more solid, a little balder. I'm going part-time soon, he told her. The company's cutting back.

Sorry to hear that, she said.

Don't be a bit sorry, I'm delighted. I've just acquired a little rowboat – a buddy of mine was selling it, and I beat his price down. I'll be doing plenty of fishing in my spare time.

Sounds good.

I'm losing this route though, he added, and she said she'd miss him, and meant it.

You don't have to miss me – you promised to visit Fairweather, remember? If you come early some Saturday, I'll take you out to sea. Mornings are better to get the fish. We'll catch a couple of mackerel and you can bring them home for your tea. We can have lunch after in my son's pub – he's just taken over the place where he was working, and he's got himself a marvellous chef.

Deal – so she took the mobile number he offered, but she didn't really expect it to happen. She didn't drive yet, so a day trip to Kerry was unlikely. Maybe in years to come, she might look him up out of nostalgia.

More time passed. Towards the end of her first year

in the art college, she realised that she didn't have the talent or drive of her fellow students. She dropped out and applied to a teacher-training college, and was accepted. She'd always liked children, and planned to have a big family. Teaching should suit her. Her parents put up no objection, preferring the idea of a permanent, pensionable job to the more uncertain artistic life.

The summer before her final year, she and her boyfriend of a few months, also a student teacher, decided to spend a couple of weeks cycling part of the Wild Atlantic Way. The first day they covered the seventy kilometres that brought them around Galway Bay, through Clarinbridge and Kinvara, past the Flaggy Shore in County Clare and on to Ballyvaughan and the music-rich village of Doolin. They pitched their tent in the campsite there and fell asleep to the sound of fiddles and tin whistles from the nearby pub. The following day they took in the Cliffs of Moher, and stopped for lunch in Miltown Malbay, and fitted in an afternoon swim in Kilkee's beautiful horseshoe bay before setting up camp in nearby Kilrush.

On the third day they took a ferry across the Shannon estuary that brought them from Clare to Kerry – and within an hour of leaving Tarbert, where they'd disembarked, Olive saw a road sign for Fairweather, and thought immediately of Mark. It was outside their itinerary but she couldn't miss it, having come so close. Three years since she'd seen him, more than that. She imagined him sitting in his little boat, a fishing rod dangling over the side.

Let's make a detour for lunch, she said, so they took the turn and covered the eight kilometres indicated by the sign, and before long they were wheeling their bikes along Fairweather's bustling main street. It was lined with the usual mix of businesses: a bakery, a fishmonger, a chemist, a hardware shop with plastic buckets and spades hanging outside, a mini mart, a boutique, a butcher, the usual scatter of pubs. Olive searched the passing faces – plenty of tourists about – but saw no sign of Mark. His number was still in her phone, but it was too last minute to contact him now.

A sandwich board positioned outside one pub advertised the best pub grub in Ireland, so in they went. The barman, stocky and friendly, handed them menus and told them to find a table. I'll be over to take your orders, he promised. A fair-haired bearded man seated at the end of the counter glanced up from his newspaper and nodded a smile at them.

Ten minutes or so later, as they waited for the

seafood chowder they'd both opted for, the door opened and Mark walked in. He threw a glance around the room, missing her, before peeling off his yellow oilskin jacket and taking the stool at the bar that had been occupied by the bearded man, who was now moving about behind the counter.

He was tanned, weatherbeaten. He'd lost more of his hair, but looked otherwise largely unchanged. She saw him lift a hand to someone at the far end of the bar counter.

Their chowder arrived as she got to her feet. In the act of reaching for a slice of the brown bread that accompanied the soup, her boyfriend looked up.

I've just spotted someone I used to know, she told him. Back in a sec.

Mark's face broke into a wide smile at the sight of her. Olive Wilson, he said, rising from his stool to greet her. You made it to Fairweather at last.

I made it. I had to keep my promise.

Why didn't you ring me?

It was last minute, sorry.

Never mind, it's good to see you. And you found Fred's place.

Fred?

My son. He turned and beckoned to the bearded man, who approached them and was introduced. Olive and I go back a long way, Mark told him.

Nice to meet you, the younger man said. In his face she saw echoes of Mark. She reckoned him to be a few years older than her. Any friend of my father's, he said.

This is the boy making the money, Mark told her. The other one is having fun in Australia.

Don't mind him, Fred put in. The other one is the tycoon. I'm just a poor publican.

Olive laughed. I didn't think there was such a thing.

Now! Mark exclaimed, delighted. Olive knows what's what. Tell me, how are all your family?

She filled him in on the comings and goings of her parents and brothers as Fred left them to attend to customers. She told him about switching her college course; he approved. You'll never starve as a teacher, he declared. You won't make a million, but you won't starve.

And you? What's happening?

He told her he still worked part-time, but fished any chance he got. I've been out all morning – shame you didn't arrive earlier.

Next time.

For sure.

As they spoke, she kept his son in her radar. He had his father's easy way in his interactions with his customers, the same ready laughter, the same cheery banter. Every so often he threw a glance back in their direction.

In her direction?

She wondered if he was married. No ring, but that was no guarantee.

I'd better go, she said eventually. My lunch will be getting cold, indicating the table she'd abandoned, raising an apologetic hand to its occupant.

Mark followed her gaze. You didn't tell me you were with someone, he said. Is he your young man?

Being Mark, he got away with it. He's just a friend, she replied – because in that instant she knew that that was what he had become.

Well, give me a shout when you're around again. Ring the night before, and I'll be all set. You have to come out in the boat, discover the joy of fishing.

She wondered later if he'd had a plan. Years later she wondered, after she and Fred had got together, and then got engaged, and then got married. Had Mark seen something that first day between them, had he sensed the attraction she'd felt within minutes of meeting Fred?

Before the month was out she'd broken up with her boyfriend. She borrowed a brother's car and arranged to meet Mark on the Fairweather pier for a fishing trip, and afterwards they went back to the pub for lunch, and that was the start of it all.

'I can't do this sum.'

She lifted her head from the novel she wasn't reading. A frowning Nancy was holding out her maths workbook. 'Let's have a look.'

The teaching career hadn't happened after all. By the time Olive finished her final exams, a year after meeting Fred, they were engaged and planning to marry the following summer, and the butcher beside Fred's pub was retiring, and the place was up for letting, which gave Olive something new to think about.

She wasn't convinced that she was cut out to be a teacher. The practical weeks she'd done in schools hadn't really endeared her to the profession. She enjoyed her time in the classroom, but there was so much other stuff involved in teaching, so many lesson notes and reports to write up – and if she got an actual job she'd have to deal with yard duty and parent-teacher meetings and more. All things considered, she wasn't at all sure she liked the sound of it.

What if she were to take a year out? What if she followed in her parents' footsteps and opened a shop in Fairweather instead? Renting a property meant it needn't be a major commitment. She hadn't yet got her exam results, but she was a diligent student, and confident of a good outcome.

She talked it over with Fred. I'm familiar with how a shop is run, she said, and I think I'd like to give this a go. I know I change my mind a lot, but now I have my teaching qualification to fall back on if it doesn't work – or I will soon. What do you think?

If it's what you want, he said, go for it. I'd be good for a few bob to set you up. So much faith he had in her. She kissed him and told him she'd pay back every cent. What kind of shop though? he asked, and she thought about it for a week and decided on a gift shop that showcased local art and crafts. There were surely lots of creative people about the place who would welcome an outlet for their work.

Her parents, when she told them, were dismayed. You're changing your mind again? her mother asked.

I have my degree now, Olive replied. I have that security behind me.

You haven't got it yet, her father pointed out. You won't know that till August – but she knew and he knew that she had nothing to fear. It was the changing, the hopping about, that worried them.

Just one year, she said, to see if it's what I want. Shop work is in my blood, and I know how a shop is run – you've made sure of that. And anyway I'm marrying Fred, and Mark says the pub is a gold mine – and in the end she convinced them, and went for it.

While Fred negotiated a fair rental price with the landlord, whose son had been in school with him, she met with Fred's accountant, who agreed to keep an eye on her books. She and Fred painted the place, and local handyman Jimmy Talbot built shelving units while Mark, who knew everyone, put the word out around the community. Before long, she began talking to Kerry-based artisans, and soon she had more than enough stock to fill the new shelves.

Towards the end of August, a week after her exam results brought the news she wanted, she took a deep breath and opened Fairweather's first dedicated gift shop. It was the wrong time entirely, with the season nearly over, but somehow or other, through a combination of luck and brass neck, and much local support – and serendipity, which she firmly believed in – the business took root and grew strong. When she and Fred were married a year later, the shop was firmly established within the community, and last August she celebrated twenty years of trading, and nineteen of marriage.

They had troubles along the way, of course they

had. Within months of her and Fred's wedding Mark got a cancer diagnosis, a tumour in his lung that was thankfully caught in time and removed, and now with his seventieth birthday approaching he was in as good spirits and health as ever. Fred fell down the pub cellar stairs a couple of Christmases later and put himself on crutches for six weeks. A heart attack claimed Olive's father on a beautiful September morning, two weeks after her fourth wedding anniversary.

And the day after his funeral, she suffered her third miscarriage.

However hard she and Fred tried – and they did try, they did – they couldn't manage to make a baby. They could start them, five times they started them, but one by one they slipped away. Her best friend Maria Noonan, who was the chef in Fred's pub, and who'd had no trouble having her two daughters, held her hand while Olive cried all the tears in Ireland after every one of her lost babies.

'I hate long division,' Nancy said crossly, pulling her mother back to the present.

'I remember hating it too,' Olive told her. 'I don't think anyone likes it. And it's not as if you'll ever use it when you leave school.'

'So why do I have to learn it?'

'I wish I knew, sweetheart. Maybe it makes you a better person every time you learn something new.'

'It does *not*.'

Looking at her daughter's glowering pink face, Olive thought back to the realisation that she and Fred had come to, sometime before Olive's thirtieth birthday, that adoption might be the only way they'd ever have a child. By the time they'd cleared all the hurdles and taken possession of their infant girl, Olive had turned thirty-one. She remembered the flood of emotion that overtook her without warning when the little bundled-up scrap was placed in her arms for the first time. She might not have carried her for nine months, or given birth to her, but however she'd arrived in their lives, Nancy had become their daughter from that moment on.

And now she was eleven going on twelve, and Olive's forty-third birthday was just a couple of months away, and she had news to break. She waited until they'd muddled through the rest of the long division.

'Nancy,' she began then, 'I have something to tell you, lovey. Something really good.'

She'd thought early menopause when she'd missed the first period. Of course she had – what else could it be? Along with the decision to adopt, she and

Fred had also decided not to take any more chances, not when a conception invariably led to heartbreak. There was no way she could be pregnant, not with condoms *and* a diaphragm. No way.

Except that she was.

You're eleven weeks gone, Olive, her doctor had said when she'd finally taken herself off to his surgery to find out what she needed to know about the menopause.

She'd stared at him in total disbelief. Pregnant? You can't be serious.

I wouldn't joke about something like that.

It had been a bombshell, nothing short. Miles, I can't be pregnant. You know we use birth control. We're as careful as we can be.

I know that, Olive. He'd lifted his hands. What can I tell you? You're certainly defying the law of averages here. It's very unusual – but somehow you've managed to become pregnant again.

Everything was against it. Her age, her history, everything. I can't do this, she'd said. I'll lose it like I lost all the others. I can't go through that again. She'd felt panic rising in her, the old sadness and fright and frustration stirring into being. I just can't do it, Miles.

The doctor had nodded. Olive, I fully understand your reaction, really I do – but let me just say that your previous miscarriages have no bearing here. You know there was no medical explanation for them; you were just terribly unlucky. This pregnancy has begun in the face of impossible odds, and it's lasted eleven weeks so far. You're certainly due a bit of luck, Olive.

Eleven weeks. Longer than most of the others, but still she'd baulked, still she'd resisted. I can't, Miles. I just can't go there again. Honestly, I can't.

Well, the decision is yours and Fred's, and if you want to put a stop to it, I'll give whatever help I can – but you should at least let the news sink in, Olive. This is a huge decision, and you need to be sure it's the right one. Give it a few days, even one day. Talk it over with Fred. Sleep on it. Can you do that much?

Yes, Fred would have to be told. She couldn't take that giant step without him. He'd back her up though. He'd be of the same mind; she knew he would.

And again, she was wrong. He wasn't of the same mind.

Maybe it'll go right this time, he'd said. We can't deliberately end it, Ollie. We have to try again. Please.

How foolish his hope had sounded, in the face of all their tragedies. How ridiculous his faith, even still. It had sent impatience – no, anger – flooding through her.

Easy for you to say, she'd whipped back. It's not you who has to carry it, it's not you who has to let it bleed out of you – and straight away, seeing his face, seeing how her words changed it, she'd regretted them.

I'm sorry, she'd said. He'd suffered too, every time it happened. I'm sorry, Fred, but I'm just too frightened. I can't face it – and back and forth they'd gone until in the end she'd worn him down, and he'd grudgingly agreed to what she wanted.

But she'd reckoned without Maria.

We're going to go again, Maria had said, in one of the last conversations they'd had. We both want another child – and Olive had wished her well, and smothered the jealousy that had reared up at the thought that her friend could decide to get pregnant again, just like that. But then Maria and Killian had died, along with their first-born Hollie, before they'd had a chance to fulfil their wish, and now Olive was the one who was pregnant, and about to run away from it because she was too afraid to hope.

Don't lose heart, Maria had said that night, her voice clear in Olive's head as she'd lain in bed. Don't be afraid, Olive. You can do it.

'What news?'

Nancy's question snapped her back again. Here

goes, she thought. Her first time to say it aloud to anyone apart from Fred.

'There's going to be a new baby in the house,' she said. Because now it was nineteen weeks, and the life inside her was clinging on. Somehow she'd found the courage to hope, or maybe she'd lost the courage to go ahead with the alternative – had it been Maria, guiding her from beyond the grave? For whatever reason, she was still pregnant, and people would have to be told soon, or they'd guess, and Nancy had to be the first to know. 'Isn't that wonderful news?'

Her daughter's eyes widened. 'You're going to adopt another baby?'

'No, we're not adopting. I'm pregnant – imagine!'

Nancy looked puzzled. 'But you told me all your babies went to Heaven. You said that was why you got me, because you couldn't have children yourself.'

The innocent words brought a twist of pain. 'I did say that, lovey, and it was true – but now we've started another one, and so far it's staying put, so Dad and I are hoping we'll be lucky this time, and you'll have a new brother or sister.'

Nancy's frown travelled to Olive's abdomen.

'You can't see any sign of it yet, but soon I'll start to have a little bump.' The thought of a pregnancy bump, the outward sign of the miracle, sent a happy flutter through her.

'How come it's not going to Heaven like the other ones?'

Another knife, pushed innocently into her heart. She took a breath and carried on. 'I really don't know, pet. All I know is that it's lasting longer than any of the others, and it's getting stronger all the time, so fingers crossed.'

Nancy digested this, her face still full of uncertainty. 'So when will it be born?'

'June. It might even have the same birthday as Dad – wouldn't that be amazing?' Fred was the thirteenth; Olive's due date was the eleventh. 'And you'll be a big sister – imagine!'

Please let me hang on to it, to him or her. Please let nothing bad happen. Please let everything go right this time. All day long she offered up prayers, not one bit sure that anyone, even Maria, was listening. Her jury was out on whether there was a Heaven, or any place at all after this one, but better safe than sorry.

'So what do you think about a new sister or brother? You can help me get ready. It'll be fun, won't it?'

A shrug. 'If you want. I have to do my Irish now.'

Not exactly the reaction she'd been hoping for.

Never mind, she wouldn't make a big thing of it. Nancy was always a bit cranky at homework time.

That evening, she rang Beth.

'Just saying hello,' she said. 'Thinking of you both today.'

'Thank you, Olive. It's kind of you.'

'How's Lil?'

'She's good.'

'Anything I can do, Beth? Anything you need?'

'Not a thing, thank you.'

She searched for more to say, and found it. 'I presume your new tenant arrived.' She hadn't seen Beth since the morning of the day he was due, a week ago now.

'He did.'

'What's he like? First impressions?'

'He seems fine. He's quiet.'

'Quiet is good.'

'He could tidy himself up a bit.'

She smiled. Beth liked things to be tidy. Poor chap had probably worn brown shoes with navy trousers, or forgotten to comb his hair. Unlikely that he knew anyone local – wouldn't they have warned him off the Noonan house? Not so much for its sad history as for the fact that he'd have Beth as his landlady: her shell could be a little too hard for some to crack.

'What does he do?'

'A handyman, he says.'

'Really? That's interesting, with poor Jimmy gone. I suppose we'll all meet him soon enough, if he's looking for work.'

'No doubt. Well, I won't keep you, Olive. Thank you so much for calling.'

'Please pick up the phone anytime, Beth. I mean that.'

'I will, thank you.'

She wouldn't, of course. Beth Sullivan hadn't once, in the two years since her daughter had died, picked up the phone to ask Olive, her daughter's best friend, for anything at all. She did drop into the shop every so often, and she never left without buying something. A new diary, candles, writing paper. Giving Olive the custom, supporting her for Maria's sake.

The eighteenth of January, the second anniversary. The library would have remained closed today, a notice on the door. They'd have visited the grave, Beth skirting the town to get to the cemetery rather than driving through it. No desire for people around them, no wish to have anyone sympathising. Olive had found this out last year when she'd turned up at the house with flowers, and Beth hadn't let her past the threshold. She'd taken the flowers and thanked

Olive civilly, and told her they'd prefer to be left alone. Olive didn't hold it against her – after suffering an immeasurable loss, you did what you had to do to keep going.

'Two years,' she said to Fred, home early for once on a Friday night. 'Imagine.'

'I know.' Maria had been his chef from the start. She'd made the chowder that Olive and her boyfriend had ordered all those years ago, the first time Olive had set eyes on Fred.

On the morning of the accident Olive's phone had rung. She'd ignored it because she was driving to the shop after dropping Nancy to school. *We're on the way to the airport,* Maria's voicemail message had said. *It's raining here. We've had such a week. I'll call around tomorrow and fill you in.*

Olive hadn't returned the call. They'd be queuing in the airport, or going through security. They wouldn't need the distraction of a ringing phone. She'd talk to Maria that evening, when they were landed – but she'd never got the chance. Hours after the call Maria was dead, along with Killian and Hollie. All three killed instantly, a photo of the car on the paper the next day looking like a giant fist had crumpled it in a rage. And two years on the thought of it, the sudden loss of them, was every bit as shocking.

It had been months before she could erase that last voicemail. Months.

'There you go.'

She looked up, and took the mug of liquorice tea her husband had made for her. 'Don't ever die on me,' she said.

'I'll do my best,' he promised.

The January Book Club Meeting

Four minutes to seven, the library warm. On book club Wednesdays, Lil left the heat on when she closed up. *I just want to finish this row,* she'd written when Beth was leaving the house. She was knitting herself a pearl-grey sweater with a complicated pattern. She was a beautiful knitter, but Beth wished it didn't fill her days so much.

The cabin door opened. Mark Purcell halted in the doorway. 'Good evening to you, Mrs Sullivan.'

'Close the door,' she replied testily, 'unless you want us both to freeze to death. Aren't the others coming?' The three of them always travelled together.

'They're following on. They weren't ready when I called – some problem with the babysitter.' He took the chair next to hers. 'Cold,' he said, rubbing his hands briskly. 'Left my gloves at home. Where's young Lil?'

'On the way.'

Mark had been the one to keep the book club going. After she'd finally found the strength to reopen the library, Beth couldn't face the further challenge of recalling the book club without Maria and Hollie, who'd both been members. She'd wanted to put an end to it, but when she'd said as much to Mark, the first of its surviving members to reappear in the library, he'd been against it.

I think it would be a mistake, he'd said. You need distractions now, and so does Lil. I really think the book club would help, Beth.

She hadn't believed him, not for a second. He was as full of useless advice as all the others who had called to her door in the wake of the accident, all those who had drunk her tea and eaten her biscuits as they doled out platitudes she hadn't asked for and didn't want.

You can keep it going, she'd told him, but it will have to be without us – because she knew Lil wouldn't go on her own. Lil had yet to pick up a book again, and how could she participate anyway, with no voice? Recruit a few new members, she'd said to Mark. You can still use the library for your meetings.

Beth, it wouldn't be the same without you. It's your book club – it'll fall apart if you're not there.

That was nonsense, of course. The book club didn't belong to her, or to any of them. I'm not coming back, she'd insisted. Tell the others it's finished, if you don't want to carry it on – but she'd found herself wondering, as the last Wednesday of March approached, if she'd done the right thing.

She *did* need distractions. She and Lil needed all the distractions they could find. Maybe, after all, a sad, ripped-apart book club was better than no book club at all.

She'd broached the subject with Lil – and as she'd expected, Lil had been against it, but Beth had persevered. I think it might do us both good, she'd said. We need normality now, Lil. Remember how we used to enjoy the meetings.

That was when the others were there.

Lil, we have to go on. Our lives didn't stop. We can't just give up.

I can't read any more – and anyway, I couldn't take part.

You don't have to take part, just come along. Just show up. I don't want to go without you – I won't go without you.

She'd felt mean putting pressure like that on her granddaughter, but she'd also felt justified. Her motives were good – and finally Lil had very grudgingly agreed to accompany her.

She'd left it until the day itself to phone Mark, part of her hoping it was too late, that he and the other two had already signed up with a different book club.

If you still want to meet this evening, I'll come along, she'd said.

That's wonderful. I'm so glad to hear it, Beth. And Lil?

She'll come too, very much against her will. I haven't said it to the others. I don't know if they're still interested.

They are. I'll let them know, they'll be delighted.

So she and Lil had gone along, and it had been every bit as awful as she'd feared. Two voices were missing, three if you counted Lil's. The book club membership had shrunk overnight from seven to five. That first evening, all Beth could see were the ones who weren't there, and she knew the others were feeling their loss too. Olive in particular would be missing Maria – those two had been like twins separated at birth.

They'd reviewed the January book – a lifetime ago it felt like since they'd read it. Their contributions had been halting, with a new awkwardness among them. Lil had barely stirred, had spent the time hunched in her chair. Even Mark had been relatively subdued.

I can't do this, Beth had kept thinking. It's too hard. It had been the longest hour of her life. After the talk had petered out, Beth had taken from her basket the flask of tea she always supplied, and Fred had produced, almost shamefacedly, a tin. I brought some almond slices, he'd said, from the pub kitchen.

Maria had always been the one to bring the food. Beth had brought the tea, and Maria had supplied the food.

She'd stumbled to her feet, unable to endure any more. She'd pleaded a headache and left with Lil, leaving the other three to lock up when they were done, and to drop the basket and the key in the back porch on their way home.

Mark had phoned her the following morning. Thank you for coming, he'd said. It was brave of you.

It was terrible. I hated it.

I know you did. I don't think any of us found it easy, but I still think it was the right thing to do.

I'm not going again, Mark.

There had been a short pause. How about if you just keep it up until the summer, Beth? Just do the next three months, and if you still want to stop after June, we will.

Three more meetings, just as awful as last night's. She couldn't. I can't. I just can't face it.

I think you can. I think the others would want you to.

That had infuriated her. How could he possibly know what the others would want? On the point of hanging up, she'd stopped. He was trying to help. Everyone just wanted to help.

I think it would be good for Lil, he'd said.

Her anger had flared again. Lil? You saw how she was last night. I had to practically threaten her at gunpoint to come with me. Mark, this is not going to work. I know you mean well, but—

I saw how she was, Beth, and that's why I think we need to keep the pressure up. I know it's tough, but don't you think it might act as an incentive for Lil to try speaking again sometime?

She couldn't disagree with that. She had to find a way through to Lil, she had to keep trying. She wasn't convinced that the book club was the answer, but everything was worth a try – and if nothing else, it would keep him quiet.

Three months, she'd said.

Three months.

And if we want to stop after June, you'll say no more about it?

I promise.

So they'd gone to the April meeting, and to the May one. And despite having been convinced that nothing would change, something *had* begun to change, so subtly she was hardly aware of it. The painful loss of the absentees didn't abate, but each meeting became less of an endurance test. Fred continued to supply the eats, and Beth learnt slowly to accept it.

It took until June for Lil to begin reading again. The first Beth knew of it was when Lil had handed her, the day of the June meeting, a sheet of paper that she discovered was a review of that month's chosen book. *Will you read it out for me?* she'd written, and Beth did.

And here the five of them still were, two years later. Still coming together on the last Wednesday of each month, still reading, still arguing and debating and reviewing books. And Beth was forced to acknowledge that Mark had been right when he'd persuaded her to continue with the book club, and to bring Lil with her.

Not that she'd ever tell him.

The door opened again and Lil appeared, nodding a hello at Mark – and right behind her came the other two.

'Sorry we're late, Beth,' Olive said. 'I was just telling Lil that Nancy was in a bit of a mood. She didn't want to stay with Katy – we had to resort to bribery.'

Katy Fortune, a teen who lived nearby, came to sit with Nancy on book club evenings so both Fred and Olive could attend. 'I thought they were great friends,' Beth said. 'Didn't Katy help Nancy to paint her room before Christmas?'

'She did, and normally they get on fine.' Olive shucked off her coat and sat. 'But now Nancy has suddenly decided she doesn't need a babysitter any more. She's been funny lately – I'm putting it down to hormones.'

'Hormones?' Beth stared at her. 'The girl is twelve.'

'Actually eleven till May – but some of them can start the teenage stuff early, apparently. Hope she doesn't turn into too much of a monster.'

'Hmm,' Beth said. 'We should get started.' Hormones indeed. Someone had said boo to her in the school yard, more likely. Children these days could be such sensitive little things.

Afterwards, when all verdicts on the last choice had been submitted, and Fred, whose turn it was to choose the next, had given them a Niall Williams to read for the February meeting, Lil began pouring tea from Beth's big flask, and Fred produced a container of flapjacks.

'So how's your tenant doing?' Mark asked.

'Settling in well, as far as I know.'

She didn't know. She hadn't a clue how well or otherwise he was settling in. She hadn't gone near him since the day he'd begun to cut the hedge, nearly three weeks ago.

'Olive tells me he's a handyman.'

'Apparently. He claims he can turn his hand to most things.'

'Has he picked up any work yet?'

'None that I'm aware of. I assume he's looking.'

But was he? She hadn't seen any ad in the local paper, hadn't noticed a sign on the supermarket message board. How exactly was he getting the word out?

'Any sign of him in the pub?' she asked Fred. 'Tall, fair hair. Needs a cut.'

'No strangers at all, just the usual degenerates. Have you met him, Lil?'

Lil shook her head. Beth saw how their lack of interaction with the new arrival must look to the others. Lil had some excuse, of course, but they must consider Beth most unneighbourly. No doubt Olive would be inviting him to dinner every second night if she were his landlady – particularly if he lived right next door to her.

The truth, of course, was that Beth was deliberately keeping her distance, still mortified at how she'd attacked him about the hedge. But even though they hadn't spoken, or had any face-to-face contact since her apology, she *had* seen him.

He was a walker; that much she knew. Practically every day she caught sight of him from a window, on his way to or coming from the cliff path, and she'd spotted him, or heard him, going off in his ramshackle Jeep a couple of times too. Stocking up on provisions, presumably. What he did the rest of the time was anyone's guess.

Maybe she should pay him another visit, show some interest. She really must tell him about the library, which was literally on his doorstep. Of course, if he'd had any initiative he'd have made the acquaintance of some of the townspeople, who would, if he'd enquired, have pointed him in the direction of the library, but it sounded like he hadn't put himself about at all. Olive and Fred wouldn't be long hearing if he'd met any of the locals – they didn't miss much, with their two businesses, and Mark knew just about everyone in Fairweather.

After the meeting ended, the five of them proceeded together up the path, which was illuminated by the soft glow of solar lights set at intervals into the verge. On the way Beth glanced, as she could never avoid glancing, in the direction of the house next door.

She saw a light on in Killian and Maria's room, and felt the familiar heart-droop at the thought that they weren't there, and never would be there again.

She was glad she couldn't see the garden, hidden by the darkness, and the untidy hedge between them. She was ashamed of how overgrown it had become, how unkempt and neglected everything was. She felt guilty every time she saw the tenant making his way through the long grass down to the back gate, trying to locate the stepping stones that were all but hidden.

Maybe it was time to reclaim it. Maybe she needed to get over whatever stumbling block was there. It wasn't fair to the tenant, particularly when he'd attempted to put some shape on it himself.

Could she possibly ask him? He must have time on his hands now, since he clearly had no work to go to. And of course she'd insist on paying. He didn't look like someone with lots of money.

He'd be fully within his rights to laugh in her face – but recalling his gracious acceptance of her apology, she didn't think he would.

They approached the house, and the others said their farewells and took the side passage around to the front. Lil, ahead of Beth, entered the back porch. About to follow her in, Beth spotted a small bundle propped against the wall beside the door. She stooped and picked it up, and discovered it to be a newspaper cone, so weightless she wondered if it contained anything at all. She brought it through the porch and into the kitchen, and peered inside.

'Snowdrops,' she said. 'Someone's left us snowdrops.' A fat bunch of them, nestling together in their cone, still beaded with dew, or rain. 'Get a glass, Lil.'

Their pure white heads drooped prettily. Their stems and spear-like leaves were wonderfully green. She put her face into them and inhaled their delicate perfume. She arranged them in the glass and gazed at them.

She'd always had a soft spot for snowdrops. The first brave flowers of the year, able to withstand, despite their size, the harshest of winter weather. Pushing tiny heads above frozen ground, reminding everyone that spring wasn't far away. She'd seen them in the past few days, popping up along the hedgerows. She'd meant to pick a few and bring them home, but someone had beaten her to it.

They must have been left by the door while they were at the book club. Beth wondered again who might have been responsible. She tried to recall the boys in the group of young people who'd made up

Lil and Hollie's overlapping circles of friends. Beth would encounter them from time to time at the other house, but she'd never paid them too much attention.

Hollie had always been the more outgoing of the two girls, and coupled up happily with Pat Danaher since their schooldays. Lil was the gentler one, with a frail prettiness about her that had appealed to some of the boys. Maria would mention a name to Beth now and again, tell her that Lil was seeing him, but as far as Beth was aware, none of them had turned into someone special.

Her circle of friends had melted away after the accident – not unkindly, more out of bafflement in the face of her continuing silence, and her reluctance to mingle with them like before. They texted back and forth – at least Lil could still do that – but she rarely met them in person. Clearly someone was interested though. Beth hoped he found the courage to declare himself before too long more.

She stifled a yawn as she hung up her coat. Tired today, up at four in the morning making tea, her ability to sleep through the night diminishing as the years went by. 'I'm going to have an early night,' she told Lil, who hugged her and disappeared into the sitting room. She boiled the kettle and filled a hot-water bottle, and was about to exit the kitchen with it when her phone rang. What now?

She saw Olive's name on the screen and pressed the answer key. 'Olive? Everything alright?'

'Everything's fine, Beth. I just wanted to run something by you, and I couldn't bring it up at the book club. You have a few minutes now?'

'I do.' What on earth could she not say in front of the others?

'It's just that I had an idea about Mark's birthday.'

Beth waited, wondering what it had to do with her.

'You know he'll be seventy next month?'

'I did not know that, no.'

She knew he was roughly that age, but there had never been a reason for his birthday to register on her radar. Olive must be planning a big party for this one. A surprise, it must be, if invitations had to be issued without his knowledge. She cast about for a credible excuse.

'The thing is, he keeps insisting that he doesn't want a present, that he has everything he needs. You know what he's like, Beth – but of course we can't possibly give him nothing, and I've been racking my brains to come up with something a bit different, and today I thought of one thing he doesn't have and could definitely do with.'

Presumably she'd get to the point before Beth's hot-water bottle went cold.

'Now, Beth, I want you to promise me you'll say no if this doesn't appeal to you, or if you think it sounds like a daft idea, but you're the only person I know with the expertise and the experience, so I'm coming to you.'

Beth felt a stirring of alarm. 'What exactly are you asking, Olive?'

'Well, I was wondering if you'd consider giving him a few cookery lessons. One-to-one, I mean. Private lessons.'

'Cookery lessons? Me?'

'Yes, I thought maybe three. He hasn't a clue how to cook, and I really think he'd enjoy it. I'd happily feed him every night here – he's so good about picking Nancy up from school when I'm at work, and he won't take a penny for it – but he'll only come to us for Sunday dinner, so what can I do? I'd love to know he was getting a good meal every evening, but I suspect he's just opening tins, or living on takeaways.'

'Olive, the man goes fishing all the time. He's given me mackerel on occasion. Does he not eat any himself?'

'Would you believe he doesn't? He gives away whatever he doesn't throw back. He says he wouldn't fancy taking the insides out.'

'For goodness' sake.'

'I know, he's a disaster. Even if you just taught him three or four simple dishes that he could rotate – fish included, of course – I think it would make a big difference.'

Beth hardly knew where to begin saying no. 'You want me to teach him how to cook,' she said. 'You want me to teach Mark how to cook.'

'Well, I was hoping you'd consider it – and obviously I'd pay whatever you felt was appropriate – but please say no if you'd rather not.'

She was asking Beth to be his birthday present. She was asking Beth to give up her time, to bring this man into her home, not once, but three times. She was imposing on Beth to an unbelievable degree.

'I'm sorry,' Beth said. 'It's completely out of the question, Olive. I haven't taught cookery since I retired, and I've never given one-to-one lessons, least of all to adults. I'm sorry, but the answer has to be no.'

'Fair enough, it was just a mad idea I had. Thanks Beth, I'll think of something else.'

But after she'd hung up, Beth felt bad. Olive had been Maria's best friend practically since the day they'd met. She'd offered herself as surrogate godmother to Lil, whose original godmother, an aunt of Killian's, had died when Lil was still small. She'd always been so good, so generous, to both girls. Despite her own miscarriages she'd helped out with birthday parties and sleepovers, and had taken them to the cinema countless times, and done a hundred other things over the years without having to be asked.

And since Maria's death she'd been there for Beth and Lil, even when Beth didn't want anybody there. In the early days she'd called regularly with gifts – flowers, chocolates, toiletries – and had been content to sit silently with Lil when Beth had made it plain that she'd prefer to be alone. Please pick up the phone if I can do anything, she'd said, each time she left.

She'd done a lot, and Beth did feel ashamed of her refusal – but this was simply too much to ask. Olive should never have put her into that position.

Upstairs she undressed and washed, the matter still in her head, refusing to be banished. She remembered Mark Purcell in school, small and skinny and invariably to be found in the thick of things. Well able to say what he wanted, more than capable of standing up for himself in the yard, unlike other bigger lads.

And later, in his teens, always in the company of girls. Full of charm, making them laugh and blush. Not Beth: he'd had more sense than to try it on with her, knew she'd have none of it. He had plenty of older sisters, of course, so he was well used to female company.

And then he'd married Catriona Prenderville, both of them too young, the reason for the wedding obvious when Catriona began to show a month later. Lasted the course though, two sons and around twenty years of marriage before Catriona had made him a widower.

She couldn't say she had any real objection to him. They'd never been close contacts, but their social circles had butted up against each other over the years. They'd meet in the interval of a concert, say, or they'd find themselves at the same wedding or funeral. She'd encounter him on the street; they might sit in adjoining pews at mass.

The book club had thrown him more into her orbit, when Olive had signed up and brought Fred and Mark with her. Beth had been surprised to hear of Mark's interest – she'd known he was a reader from his frequent trips to the library, and his taste in books was far wider than hers, but she hadn't imagined a book club would appeal to him. He'd confounded her assumptions, and turned out to be a most able reviewer.

They had a sort of casual friendship, you could

say. They got on fine when he wasn't trying to act the clown. And obviously she could teach someone to cook a meal without thinking about it, having done it for over forty years as the domestic science teacher in the local convent school.

It was just … what? What was it? Why was she so reluctant to do this, to give this man a few hours of her time? He wasn't some random stranger, or some casual acquaintance – he was Mark Purcell, whom she'd known practically her whole life.

But he would be invading her kitchen, using her utensils, filling her house with his laughter and his clownish carry-on. And of course he'd tell half of Fairweather that Beth Sullivan was teaching him to cook, leaving the situation open to all sorts of speculation.

No. Out of the question. Impossible.

She got into bed. She opened her book and started to read, but before she'd turned a page her eyes grew heavy, and at length she gave up and turned off the lamp. She pulled close the memories that came into sharper focus with the absence of light, and little by little, as she meandered further into the past, she drifted to sleep.

FEBRUARY

Tom

A scratching at the back door roused him. He wondered how long he'd been staring blankly at the remains of his Weetabix. He got to his feet and stretched, yawning. For whatever reason – the sea air, the distance he'd put between himself and his past, the gratifyingly comfortable bed here – his sleep had improved in the weeks since his arrival. He'd taken to going to bed earlier, after a bath most evenings in the big claw-footed tub, and sleeping pretty soundly till morning.

He scraped the dregs of his cereal into the bin. He splashed a little fresh milk into the bowl and set it on the floor by the sink. He opened the door and the cat padded in. 'Morning,' he said, but as ever it ignored him and went straight for the milk.

He resumed his seat and watched it. Just shy of a month here, and apart from a walk most days, and a couple of trips to Listowel, he'd done a whole lot of nothing much. He told himself he was getting used to his new surroundings – but the truth was more like he was in a kind of no man's land, a place where time had stopped mattering.

It wasn't like him. Normally, he hated being idle. During his time at Joel and Sarah's he'd done everything he could find to keep himself busy, from painting to repairing to gardening. He'd been desperate for diversions, with his job lost, and his mind nearly lost too – but even before that, he wasn't one to sit about twiddling his thumbs.

Now it was different. Now he could sit for an hour or more at the kitchen table, his tea or coffee growing cold, his head empty of thought. He could lie in bed till noon some days, awake but drifting, content to watch how the light changed on the ceiling, and listen to the rain pelting against the windows. Fairweather, it turned out, was an unfortunate name for a place that was subject to sudden vicious storms, and long uninterrupted bouts of rain.

Evenings he spent watching whatever he could find on the limited TV channels, or hunting down YouTube videos. His phone data was patchy, but an Internet account, assuming his landlady allowed it, would be another monthly bill he didn't need.

He'd done nothing at all about looking for work. He must make a start, now that he could see the bottom of his bank account. Next week, for sure.

He wouldn't have minded a bit of gardening. He could have taken his time with it, whenever the rain held off – but that was before the grandmother had come storming over and ordered him to down tools. He'd been dumbfounded, and more than a little irritated – what the hell was her problem? He'd wondered if she might be mentally unbalanced.

But a few hours later she'd come back and explained precisely what her problem was. A family wiped out, apart from one member. He'd rented a house whose inhabitants had all died, bar one. I'm sincerely sorry, she'd said, and he'd seen the struggle she'd had to hold it together, and he was glad he hadn't retaliated when she'd blown up. She'd lost a child and a granddaughter, and a son- or daughter-in-law. If anyone was entitled to an angry outburst, she was.

He couldn't imagine what that must have been like, losing them so suddenly, so shockingly. Worse that they'd lived right next door, so she'd probably seen them every day, heard them coming and going – and then, just like that, they were gone. And how was it now, having a stranger living here? He was the first to inhabit the house since the accident – how weird and difficult that must be for them.

And Lil had to be a minor. She hadn't been involved in the accident, so injuries wouldn't have prevented her from living alone. She'd inherited a house that she was too young for, so she was being looked after by her grandmother until she matured.

He should have been told though, before he'd signed along the dotted line. Why the big secrecy? You'll hear it eventually, she'd said on the first evening – so why hadn't she been straight with him from the outset?

Ironic that he'd ended up in such a house, having chosen it so randomly. He'd have gone anywhere, as long as it was as far as possible from Dublin, with a price tag he could afford. Would it have changed his mind about taking the place if he'd known its history? It might have. Too late now, with the lease signed and money handed over.

He'd phoned Joel and told him what he'd learnt. I remember that accident, Joel said. It was on the radio. They were going on holidays, or maybe coming home. How do you feel about staying there now?

I'm not sure.

But really, what was the problem? They were dead, and the dead couldn't hurt him, not like the living had done. So he'd decided to stay put and hope the ghosts left him alone, and to keep his distance from his neighbours insofar as it was possible. He'd returned the hedge clippers to the garage and put the confrontation, and the explanation that had followed it, from his mind.

His daily walks were giving him a feel for the area. From the cliff path at the bottom of the garden he had a pleasant view of the town, off to his left. A gaggle of brightly coloured houses overlooked a beach and a long pier, with a church spire rising above them in the background, and tiers of other buildings of varying heights ranged around. Gently undulating hills served as a backdrop, patched in greens and purples and yellows.

He'd found the town's main supermarket on the afternoon of his first full day. He'd packed the Jeep with groceries and driven home, and then he'd walked back in by the cliff path. It had taken ten minutes for the path to reach a point where it descended to the beach, and he'd figured out the turns to make until he was back on Fairweather's main street.

He'd strolled the length of it, taking in the three pubs and the scatter of other businesses that lined it. He was glad to see a big hardware shop: hopefully it wasn't too pricey.

At the far end, the supermarket was flanked by a flower shop on one side and a credit union on the other. He'd wandered up and down various side streets, past a small department store, a post office and a bank, hair salons, charity shops, a chemist, a few restaurants and a few boutiques. A surf shop had a 'closed till May' sign on its door. Not too many surfers looking for kit at this time of year.

The cliff path, if taken in the opposite direction to the town, brought him in twenty minutes to another bigger beach, a long wide expanse of coarse grey sand and pebble that was interrupted every so often by large black slabs of rock worn smooth and shiny by the sea.

The sea.

He felt a pull towards it. He loved it in all weathers. He loved it on windy days, when the waves would crash onto the rocks, the spray flying up to slap his face. He loved it when the sun scattered it with shards of light that leapt and danced across its surface. He loved to see rain falling on it, puckering it with a billion tiny splatters. He could crouch for ages by a rock pool, watching its small inhabitants dart about in the salt water.

Up to this, his encounters with the sea had been fleeting. The odd family trip to a beach, a few adult holidays to foreign resorts. He'd never had it as a constant companion before, never lived with it on his doorstep. It had never flavoured his days and nights like it did now.

He'd seen swimmers on the more temperate days. Small groups of adults mainly, a young woman on her own a few times. He'd kept his distance, reluctant to engage with any of them. He supposed it must be exhilarating to plunge into water that had to be freezing. It must make the heart quicken, the blood pump – evidenced by the whoops and hollers he heard from some – but he still regarded them as completely insane to want to shed their warm clothing in February and submerge themselves in anything other than a hot bath.

Every time he visited the beach he filled a bag with driftwood. Shame not to use it, free fuel on his doorstep. He'd intended to try carving some new little houses with it, just to pass the time, but even that had seemed like too much effort, so into the fire it had gone.

He walked further. He discovered that if he followed the cliff path to the town he could cross the beach and pick up another path that eventually led him inland to any number of little grassy lanes bordered with hedgerows, and hill climbs that rewarded his efforts with wonderful coastal or pastoral views.

The only people he'd interacted with in the past month, apart from the brief episodes with his landlady, were supermarket checkout operators and the occasional fast-food server. His only company was the cat. Nobody rang his doorbell. Nobody phoned him apart from his brother. He continued to avoid the social media sites he'd spent so much time on in the past, going online now only to find a film or documentary that would pass an hour or two.

His bedroom was located over the kitchen, and like that room it had two windows, one that overlooked the back garden, another that faced the gable wall of the neighbouring house. It contained a double bed flanked by matching lockers, and a wall of built-in storage units with sliding doors, and a dressing table with an accompanying stool.

The two smaller bedrooms had stripped beds and wardrobes whose open doors showed them to be empty, and chests of drawers and lockers that he assumed were empty too. After a quick glance into both rooms on his first day, he kept their doors closed.

He was getting to know the rest of the house. A stair creaked near the top; a floor tile didn't quite match the others behind the bathroom door. Something had gone amiss with the mechanism of the whistling kettle, causing it to emit a series of bubbly beeps instead to announce boiling point. It was probably something he could easily put right, but he didn't bother.

A yellow mug with a green cartoon frog on it was a lone rebel among its plain white companions, and one he was drawn to because of its bigger size. Mismatched spoons lay in the cutlery drawer, along with an impressive number of knives and forks.

With the passage of time he'd grown accustomed to living in a house whose former inhabitants were mostly dead. He decided it wasn't haunted; he got no sense that he shared it with ghosts. Despite their traumatic and sudden end, it seemed that the family wasn't interested in disturbing his sleep, and were instead resting in peace.

It didn't stop him feeling mildly unsettled when he would come across, as he did every now and again, some evidence of their prior existence. *We were here*, it seemed to whisper. *Look, here we were* – and the sight of it would prompt a brief little shiver within him.

He'd traced with a finger the column of words that was scored into the surface of the kitchen table. *Toothpaste*, *coffee*, *bananas*, all perfectly legible. A shopping list written with too heavy a hand, the items accidentally immortalised in the pine.

The words could be sanded away, new wax applied

to the wood and buffed. All signs of the list could easily be obliterated. His landlady must have seen it, but had done nothing – and he certainly wasn't about to go near it. She would have recognised the writing, and for whatever reason had left it undisturbed, like the garden.

Another time he'd found a book that had slipped between the sofa cushions in the sitting room. It was a copy of *The Catcher in the Rye*, the pages dog-eared, the back cover missing. He hadn't ever read it but he'd heard of it, a mixed-up teen trying to negotiate his way through adolescence. Hadn't a copy been discovered in the coat pocket of John Lennon's killer?

He'd opened it and found *Property of Hollie Noonan* written in green ink on the flyleaf, doodles of birds and hearts covering the rest of the page. He guessed Hollie was the sister of Lil, killed along with her parents.

He couldn't remember the last book he'd read. Books had taken a back seat to girls, somewhere in his early teens. He used to love reading – he was a serious bookworm when he was younger. He recalled his mother taking him to the local library every week. He'd read all the Harry Potters, devoured them one after another – and he'd loved Roald Dahl too, and Anthony Horowitz, and a few others. He'd had such a hunger for the written word; maybe he should try to revive it, now that he had time on his hands.

He'd placed *The Catcher in the Rye* on the empty shelves in the sitting room, where it looked as lost as his one and only jacket on the hallstand. He had an idea it was aimed at a younger reader than him, but he might just give it a go, one of these days. He hadn't spotted a library in Fairweather; he'd enquire next time he was in the supermarket. No way could he afford to buy books right now.

For a while he'd puzzled over a series of short horizontal pencil lines drawn at irregular intervals along the hinged edge of the bathroom door. They began about four feet from the ground, with the highest just about level with his armpit. He peered closer, and made out a tiny pencilled L or H next to each of them. L and H might be, must be, Lil and Hollie – but why there?

A few days after that discovery he'd found a photo when he'd crouched to retrieve a dropped pen that had rolled under the fridge. His probing fingers had touched the corner of the snap: he'd slid it out, and regarded what had to be the family.

The parents looked older than him. Mid-thirties he reckoned, the father dark-haired and sallow and stubble-chinned, the mother plump and blonde.

Two girls around eight and ten, with their mother's fair colouring and their father's dark eyes, one curly-haired, the other straight. Grouped at the end of the same kitchen table he sat at now, parents flanking their seated children. A cake with lit candles, *Happy birthday Hollie* inscribed on the top. Everyone smiling, everyone happy – and as he'd pondered it, it had come to him: the markings on the bathroom door had to be a record of their changing heights. He'd wondered if the grandmother had taken the birthday snap, and how recent it was.

In the garage were two bicycles and four surfboards, a huddle of folded garden furniture, an electric lawnmower, a wheelbarrow propped on its end. Hanging on the wall were the hedge clippers he'd briefly used, and a pair of secateurs, and various other gardening tools.

A tower of cardboard boxes was set against one wall, along with a folded-up trestle table that might well come in handy. There was also a metal bucket, a watering can, a collection of paint tins and a stack of plastic flowerpots ranging in size from teacup to child's sandcastle pail.

Gardening gloves sat in a basin, their stiff material holding the shape of the hands that had last worn them. The air in the garage was so cold he could see his breath, but there was a double socket in the wall shared with the kitchen, and a two-bar heater on the concrete floor beside it.

He refilled his coffee mug while the cat lapped milk. It had turned up on his third day, scratching at the back door until Tom had gone to investigate. He reckoned it belonged here, or used to. He'd come across signs of it about the house: scratched furniture legs, a chewed blind cord end, a little plastic ball with a bell in it that he'd uncovered when he'd moved one of the couches closer to the fire. And the cat, tiger-striped with a white patch on its breast, and eyes that looked golden, was well used to human contact, pushing its head into Tom's palm when he bent to stroke it, twining around his calves when he straightened up.

He wished it could talk. He'd ask it what they were like, the people who'd lived here. He'd ask it about Lil, the surviving child who didn't speak any more. He had yet to spot her about the place, but he'd seen someone else. A few days after moving in he'd glanced out the window as he pulled his bedroom curtains apart one morning, and he'd caught sight of a figure making her way down the path in the next garden.

Taller than the woman he'd met. More slender

too, the shoulders narrow in the padded red jacket she wore. A sea-green scarf slung around her neck, twined a few times so the lower half of her head was swaddled. Hair pale in colour and long, a thick plait emerging from under the scarf to trail halfway down her back. Blue jeans tucked into fur-rimmed ankle boots. She held the handles of a cloth bag in one hand; what looked like a leather satchel hung from her other shoulder.

He assumed she was heading for the large wooden cabin at the bottom of the garden, the one he'd seen looming in the darkness on his first evening – but instead she walked past it to the little gate, similar to the one at the end of his own garden. He imagined she was going out for a walk, as he did so often – but again he was mistaken, and the gate remained closed. There she stood, still as a statue, facing out to sea.

He wondered who she was. She couldn't be Lil: even from his limited view of her, it was obvious that she was no child. Another member of the family then, living nearby, or possibly an employee of some sort. A cleaner maybe, or a tutor for the girl if she was being home-schooled after losing her voice – but what would any employee be doing wandering alone in the garden?

After a minute or so she turned slowly – and it

seemed unnervingly to Tom that she looked directly up at his window. Too far away for her to see him, he was sure – her face was no more than a pale blank oval to him – but still he stepped back hastily.

Since then he'd caught sight of her several more times, coming and going from the wooden cabin, or passing it to exit onto the cliff path, and turn in the direction of the beach. He never got a clear view of her features, her lower face and hair wrapped as they usually were in a scarf. She was long-limbed and slender, that much only he could be sure of, and she moved with the swift grace of a dancer.

He thought he'd encountered her on his walks a few times too. He was fairly sure it was the same woman. She would dart a glance at him in passing – he got an impression of dark eyes – but never gave a greeting, or returned his.

She puzzled him, and so did the cabin next door. What exactly went on there? From his upstairs window he spotted various people entering and leaving it, some of them approaching it from the cliff path, others making their way down to it through the neighbouring garden, having parked in the lane. On Saturday mornings, people brought children there – and on that day he'd seen the grandmother emerging from it too.

One evening he'd heard a low murmur of voices outside as he was washing up his dinner things. He'd peered through the kitchen window – the sound came from next door's garden – but his view of the speakers was blocked on this level by the dividing hedge. Was a light on in the cabin? He thought so, but couldn't be sure.

He considered various possibilities, and settled on a treatment centre of some kind. The young woman, he decided, was a yogi or a masseuse, or some other kind of therapist. She might stick pins in people, or hypnotise them – or maybe she read palms or tarot cards, telling people what was in store for them. He wondered why his landlady had made no mention of it, since whatever was on offer was clearly open to the public. Maybe it was only for locals, and he didn't qualify.

The doorbell rang, startling him. His first visitor. He couldn't imagine who it might be. A meter reader? A parcel delivery? Hardly a political canvasser, with no election upcoming. He scooped his empty cereal bowl from the floor and set it in the sink. He left the cat washing itself.

'I meant to give you this.' It was his landlady, thrusting a pamphlet at him. No good morning, or good anything. 'The two beaches are safe, but it's best not to swim alone.' The same clipped, neutral tone that he remembered from the day of his arrival. The hedge incident, and her subsequent apology and explanation, might never have happened.

'Thank you.'

Tides tables, he read on the front of the pamphlet, above an image of waves rushing to shore. He wondered what a tides table was. How piercingly blue her eyes were, not in the least faded with age. Today she was in a navy coat and hat. Her lipstick was red.

He was acutely conscious of his own dishevelled state in comparison. His uncombed hair, his stubble of more than a week – when had he shaved? At least he was dressed. He should probably ask her in, but with unwashed dishes in the sink and the cat still about, he thought it best not to.

'I'm not much of a swimmer, to be honest,' he told her. 'Especially at this time of year. I like the beaches though, especially the one out of town.'

'You've been walking.'

It wasn't a question. She'd seen him, like he'd seen her and her female companion. 'I'm getting to know the area,' he said.

'Are you a reader?'

She liked her sudden shifts of topic. He got the

direct gaze again. 'I used to be. I'm thinking of getting back into it.'

'Well, if you do, there's a library at the bottom of my garden.'

A library, not a treatment centre of any kind. 'I saw people coming and going from it. I wondered what went on there.'

'It's not official. I set it up myself.'

He didn't doubt it. She struck him as someone who could do anything she put her mind to.

'It opens Mondays, Wednesdays and Fridays in the winter, ten to five, and Saturday mornings too, although it can be busy then. You can use the gap in the hedge to get to it.'

The gap was there, he understood now, to facilitate the dead family's access to the library. He thought of the book he'd found between the sofa cushions: maybe they'd all been readers. 'Thanks. I'll check it out.'

'So how are you settling in?'

'Fine.'

'You have everything you need here?'

'I have, thanks.'

He wondered if he should offer her the photo he'd found under the fridge. No, best say nothing in case the sight of it caused upset. He'd stowed it on a shelf in the utility room: let her come across it after he'd moved out.

'Have you picked up any work yet?' she asked.

'Not yet, no.'

'May I ask how you're advertising your services? I've seen no indication anywhere.'

He felt like a schoolboy caught smoking by his mother. 'I haven't actually advertised yet.'

Silence. Her silences spoke volumes.

'I've got business cards. I'm planning to hand them around the shops.'

'When?'

She didn't let up. He was half-amused, half-annoyed. 'Today. I was just about to get ready to go out.' That should get him off the hook.

'Start with the gift shop on the main street. It's called Treasure Trove. Tell Olive I sent you.'

'Right, thank you.' Now he'd have to follow through, in case she checked with Olive.

'So you have time on your hands.'

'I do.' He wondered what was coming. Maybe she was going to order him to find a hobby.

There was a small pause. 'I was thinking,' she said, a different note entering her voice, 'of asking if you'd reconsider tidying up the garden.'

He wasn't sure he'd heard her right. 'Pardon?'

She touched a coat button, dropped her hand. 'I was thinking I shouldn't leave it in this state, now that someone is living here. I thought I'd ask you first, since you were prepared to do it before.'

She had some neck. He wondered what had prompted the change of heart. 'What exactly are you looking for?' Better not risk another attack.

'The lawns, back and front. There's a lawnmower in the garage, although I'm not sure if it will cope with the length of the grass now. The hedges could be brought down quite a bit, a foot or more, and the shrubs need cutting back too. I know it's not the best time of the year for gardening, but I thought you might consider it.'

He shrugged. 'I'll do it.' It would pass the time. Bit rich, though, to be making an unpaid gardener out of him.

'And I thought rather than pay you by the hour, it would be easier if you skipped your next rent payment.'

He hoped the surprise didn't show on his face as he pretended to consider. 'That seems fair.' He had no idea how long the job would take him, but he figured a month's rent would cover it nicely. 'What about hedge clippings, grass cuttings? Where do I put them?'

'There's an old compost heap at the end of the garden, in the corner.'

'OK.' He hadn't noticed it, so overgrown everything was.

'My son-in-law,' she said. 'He was the one who did most of the outdoor work. He cut my grass too, after my husband died.'

Her tone was softer now, like it had been when she'd returned to apologise after attacking him about the hedge. Less distant, more human. She'd had a son-in-law, which meant she'd lost a daughter. The more he learnt, the more sympathy he had for her.

'I'll leave it at that so,' she said. 'Thank you for agreeing to do it.' She turned and was gone. He was getting used to her abrupt arrivals and departures. He closed the door and returned to the kitchen, and pondered.

A month without rent would stretch his savings nicely. He still needed to find work, but the pressure was off – except that he'd told her he was handing out his cards today. Who had she said to call on? The names of both the shop and the owner had slipped from his head, but he remembered it was a gift shop. He thought he'd spotted one, across from the hardware.

He'd go. He'd get it over with. She'd given him

the kick in the backside he needed. As he finished washing up his phone rang, and he saw his brother's name. Joel never missed their weekly conversation.

'Hey there.'

'Tom. How are things?'

'Fine. Good. How's Sarah?'

'She's in top form. She says hello.'

'And the lads?'

'All good, no worries.'

No worries in Joel's life. A wife he loved, and who seemed to love him back. Two little kids, one of each. His own business that paid the bills, a house in Kildare that they'd bought at the right time. Tom should be jealous, or at least envious, of him, but neither was possible. Joel had saved him, had pulled him out of Hell six months ago when Tom had fallen in – or been pushed.

'The small people miss you.'

'I miss them too.' He did. 'Hug them for me.'

'Will do. Any sign of work yet?'

He always asked, every week – and for the first time Tom wasn't saying no. 'Actually, my landlady has just offered to let me off next month's rent if I tidy up the garden here.'

'Hey, that's great.' A little too enthusiastically. 'You need money, Tom?'

The question, another regular, never failed to

sting. His London job had earned him double Joel's income. 'No, I'm OK.'

'You sure?'

'Sure.'

'That's good.' Pause. 'Tom, listen,' Joel said, a new note entering his voice, 'there's something we think you should probably know.'

His grip tightened on the phone. 'Joel—'

'No, Tom, will you just listen? Please?'

He waited, jaw tight. Everything on high alert.

'It's Vivienne, she's—'

He jabbed at the disconnect button. He dropped his phone with a clatter onto the worktop. He glared at the cat, which had halted its grooming to regard him warily. 'Get out!' he yelled. 'Get the hell out!'

It streaked through the door, seconds before Tom slammed it shut. He scrubbed his head hard, hearing the echo of his outburst, waiting for the beats of his heart to quieten.

Never mention her name, he'd told his brother. Never mention either of them again. They're dead, they're both dead to me. And he'd meant it, every word. He didn't care whether they lived or died, the two people who'd been everything to him. And Joel had sworn he wouldn't talk about them, and now he had.

He stomped up the stairs and into the bathroom,

where the mirror showed him exactly how much of a mess he was. He ran a hand wearily through hair that should have been cut months ago. A wonder his landlady didn't order him to tidy himself up. Probably dying to.

He shaved and brushed his teeth. In the bedroom he stood at the window and looked down on the jungle of a garden he'd agreed to tame, in exchange for four free weeks in a house he no longer wanted to live in.

He closed his eyes and rested his forehead against the cold glass. His anger was gone, leaving emptiness behind. He badly needed to get his act together. He needed to feel good about himself again.

He shouldn't have hung up, not on Joel. Eight years older than Tom, Joel was the big brother he'd shadowed as a kid until he grew old enough to want to do his own thing. Their school years couldn't have been more different, Joel struggling with the books and happiest on the sports field, and Tom making the top three in every class test, but clueless and clumsy in the gym or on a playing pitch. Never rivalry between them though: the gap in their ages took care of that, with Joel starting secondary school the year Tom had walked for the first time into the junior infant classroom.

Different strengths, different ambitions, but both ending up where they wanted, Joel with his own flourishing company after years of hard work, Tom taking a fast track out of college to the heights of the computer world.

Should have known it wouldn't last.

Enough. He straightened up, opened his eyes. He'd hand out the business cards, every last one. He'd smile and joke with every shopkeeper in Fairweather if he had to. And he'd get his damn hair cut too.

He shucked off his slippers and got into the boots Joel and Sarah had given him for Christmas, feeling the resolve build in him. Back downstairs he pulled on his jacket and shoved his rubber-banded bundle of cards into an inside pocket. He left the house and strode towards the town on the cliff path, heedless for once of the sea below him, the saltiness in the air.

He located the gift shop on the main street. It was painted orange, and set between a pub and a flower shop. Treasure Trove – yes, that was what she'd called it. He tried again to think of the name of its owner, and couldn't.

He regarded the window. It was crammed with colourful teapots and knitted tea cosies, and prettily wrapped bars of soap, and bundles of candles tied with raffia, and framed artworks, and fountain pens in little brown boxes, and more. The display was haphazard, the items looking thrown together rather than carefully arranged, but still it drew the eye. It aroused curiosity for what lay within.

He pushed open the door, causing a small bell to ping. His first impression was of heat and clutter. The randomness of the window was echoed inside, with goods piled anyhow on shelves and display units, or spilling from painted crates on the floor. He saw door stoppers and bookends and jigsaws and sketch pads, painting-by-numbers sets and tea caddies and draught excluders and rolled-up socks. Every inch of visible wall space was covered with a painting or a clock.

A clothes rail held patterned silky dressing gowns. A basket of calendars had a *50% off* sign propped against it. A miniature Punch and Judy looked out from a tiny puppet theatre. Woolly hats of every colour were pinned to a corkboard. Model aeroplanes and mobiles hung from the ceiling. There was a heady, spicy scent to the place that tickled his throat.

'Hello there!' a woman's voice said brightly. He looked beyond the chaos and found her behind a desk at the far end, holding a teapot aloft and smiling warmly at him.

'Morning.' He advanced towards her, pasting on a returning smile. Smoke twining up from a joss stick by the till explained the scent.

'Still raining?' she enquired. 'I can hardly see out with all this clutter.'

Glasses shoved up into her tousled auburn hair. Face bare of makeup, as far as he could tell. Freckles, covered with them. Older than him, younger than his landlady. Somewhere in the middle.

'Stopped raining,' he told her.

'Chilly though,' she said. 'Wintry.' Lifting the teapot an inch higher. 'Care for a cup? Made this very minute.'

He was caught off-guard. She didn't even know his name. 'Um, I'm OK, thanks.'

'Go on,' she said. 'It'll hot you up.' Reaching as she spoke into the press behind her for a second blue mug. 'I always make enough for two – someone is sure to wander in. You take sugar?'

Looked like he was getting tea. 'No sugar.'

'Milk?'

'Please.' He wondered if everyone in Fairweather, apart from his landlady, was this friendly.

'I'm Olive,' she said, setting down the pot and extending her hand. 'Proprietor of this establishment, and wife to Fred of the pub next door.'

'Tom,' he said. 'Sorry, cold hands. I've been walking.'

In response she caught his hand and rubbed it briskly between both of hers, which were wonderfully warm. 'Other one,' she ordered, and did the same with it. 'You need gloves,' she said. 'It's always colder by the sea. Are you passing through?'

'Staying a few months.'

'That's nice.' She blew on her tea before taking a sip. 'Feel free to have a look around,' she said. 'If I can help you with anything, give a shout. Bring your tea. I'll trust you not to spill it.'

'Thanks.'

He felt obliged, after accepting the tea, to show some interest in her wares. He could splash out on something small, after the arrangement he'd made with his landlady – but what?

Gloves, that was what. He found a collection of them in a wooden box. Waxy outsides, fleece lined. *Warm and waterproof*, the accompanying sign said. *Made locally by Claire Comerford*. Thirty euro was more than he'd planned to spend, but at least he'd use them.

'I hope you didn't feel you had to,' she said, ringing them up, glasses on her nose now. 'The tea wasn't a bribe.'

He smiled, disarmed by her easy warmth. 'That

never occurred to me. You needn't bother wrapping them.' While she was making change for him he pulled out his business cards. 'Could I ask you to find a spot for a couple of these? Would you mind? I'm trying to get the word out.'

She took one and read it aloud. '*Handyman available, punctual and reliable. Maintenance, repairs, decorating, woodwork, minor plumbing and electrical. All jobs considered, interior and exterior. Free quotation. Rates reasonable.*'

She looked up, shoving the glasses away again. 'You're Beth's tenant.'

'I am.'

'I was wondering when we'd get to meet you. Beth told you about the accident.' Her smile dimming.

'She did.'

'They were lovely people. Maria was my best friend.'

'Beth's daughter?'

She nodded. 'Her only child.'

'I didn't know that.'

'She worked for my husband; she was the head chef in the pub. She was married to Killian, and they had two daughters, Lil and Hollie. Hollie was the older girl.' A small pause slipped by while she drank tea. 'Have you met Lil yet?'

'No. Haven't even seen her.'

'Lil was always the quieter of the two girls. Dreamy, you know? But clever too: she was in college when it happened, studying business. Doing well.'

He frowned. 'College? I thought she was a child.'

'No, she was twenty-three last month.'

So he *had* seen her, lots of times. He'd thought her an employee of some sort, but she wasn't. 'She manages the library at the bottom of the garden,' he said.

'She does, most of the time. Beth does the Saturday mornings.'

More things slotted into place. She never returned his greeting on the cliff path, because she couldn't. She was also, he thought, the lone female swimmer he'd noticed a few times at the beach. He pictured the four surfboards in the garage. They must have been into their water sports.

'She dropped out of college after it happened,' Olive said. 'She moved in with Beth – but you already know that.'

'That was what confused me. I assumed it was because she was too young to live on her own.'

'Not too young, too sad. And she stopped speaking.'

'Yes.'

'It's tragic. She's cut herself off from – well, from everything, really. She walks and she swims, but always alone. And she spends the rest of her time in that library, reading or knitting. You haven't called in?'

'Not yet. I only heard about it this morning.'

'We're very proud of it in the town – but it's no place for a young woman to spend her days. Are you a reader?'

The same question his landlady had asked. 'I used to be. I got out of it in my teens. I'm thinking I should go back.'

'You should. I couldn't imagine life without a book – and you'll get to meet Lil there. She's a sweetheart.' She turned her attention back to his business card. 'Actually,' she said, 'it's interesting you're a handyman. Our old one died a few months back.'

'Really?'

'Poor Jimmy, a big loss to the town. He could do anything. Fell off a ladder, broke his neck. Only seventy-eight, fresh as a daisy.' She regarded Tom thoughtfully. 'It might be a sign,' she said.

'What might?'

'You coming here now, just when we need a new handyman.'

He didn't believe in signs. He had no faith in anything he couldn't see, couldn't touch. He said nothing, not wanting to offend her.

She laughed. 'Don't mind me – I'm a bit all over

the place right now, with one thing and another. Hot drop?'

'No thanks.' Having made a start, he was anxious to get rid of the rest of the cards, and maybe do a bit in the garden, if the rain held off. He returned his mug. 'Thank you – that *did* warm me up.'

'You're most welcome.' She indicated his bundle of cards. 'Why don't you leave those with me? I can pass them around.'

'What? No – I couldn't ask you to do that.'

'You didn't ask, I offered. It's not a problem, and it won't take me long at all. I know every trader in town, and if you're half as good as Jimmy was, you'll find plenty of work. The cards will help to get you going, but word of mouth is alive and well in Fairweather.'

'Good to know.' So tempting, not to have to traipse from shop to shop. 'Well, if you're sure you don't mind …'

'Not in the least.' She stowed the cards under the counter. 'I'll hand them around at lunchtime.'

'Thanks so much,' he said, pulling on his new gloves. 'You've been a big help, on several fronts.'

'Not at all. Call in anytime for a cuppa, now that you know the way. I open every other weekday in winter, and Saturday mornings.'

'Same as the library.'

'That's right. Same as a lot of the places around here, actually. We're very seasonal in Fairweather. Oh, and make sure you introduce yourself to Fred when you go into the pub. He's the handsome chap with the beard.'

'Will do.' But he didn't intend going into a pub, Fred's or anyone else's. On the point of leaving he hesitated, struck by a new thought. 'There's one more thing,' he said.

'What's that?'

'I do a bit of woodcarving.'

'Do you now? Tell me more.'

'I carve houses.'

'Houses?'

'Small houses.'

'How small?'

He used his hands. 'This size. And they're all a bit ... off.' He stopped. He'd never make it as a salesman.

'What do you mean, a bit off?'

'Off-centre, skewed. Walls not plumb, chimney tilted, windows wonky. That kind of thing.'

'Ooh, I love the sound of them. Do you paint them?'

'I do. They're quite colourful. I could bring you in

a few, see what you think. No problem if they don't grab you.'

'Bring them in,' she ordered. 'Bring in your three favourites, next time you're in town.'

'OK.' She might hate them. She might take one look and tell him no way. But she mightn't. 'Last thing – where would you recommend I go for a haircut?'

'Best barber is up the street, first turn left. Say I sent you. Here, take back a few cards.'

He found the place easily. It was tiny, wedged between a bakery and a chemist. Short Cuts, it was called. He must have walked past it on his wanderings, but he didn't recall it.

There was a single barber's chair positioned in front of the mirror, and benches set against two walls. A woman was sitting in the chair, reading a magazine. She got to her feet on his entry. 'A customer,' she said. 'Hallelujah.'

She was older than him, around Olive's age, and attractive. Dark eyes, full mouth painted reddish-orange. Her shoulder-length hair was dark brown and shiny, with a pure white streak on one side, whether by nature or design he couldn't say. She wore a short green dress, beneath which blue patterned leggings emerged. Chunky legs, navy ankle boots.

She took his jacket and hung it. 'What are you looking for?'

'Short,' he told her. 'As short as you want.'

'Wet or dry cut?'

'Dry.' He was never fully comfortable with someone else soaping his head. 'Olive from the gift shop recommended you,' he added, taking the chair she'd vacated.

'Did she now?' She flapped out a large black cape and put him into it. 'You a friend of hers?'

'Just met her.'

'New in town.' Meeting his eye in the mirror, hands resting lightly on his shoulders.

'For a while, a few months.'

'I'm going to hazard a guess,' she said, 'that you're renting the house beside Beth Sullivan.' Securing the cape at the back, picking up a large, wide-toothed wooden comb.

'That's right.' He wondered if there was anyone in Fairweather who didn't know that Beth had let the house.

'Have you a name?'

'Tom.'

'I'm Denise, best barber in town.' She followed the remark with a sudden grin, and he saw a small gap between her front teeth. 'Me and Olive have the odd cocktail,' she said. She ran the comb through his hair, stopping to untangle as she went. 'A while since your last cut.'

'A while,' he agreed. His last cut had been in London, a month before the bank-holiday weekend in Dublin that had ended everything.

The cut after that was to have been for his wedding.

She got to work. Silence fell. Beneath the snip of her scissors he made out a faint wheeze at the top of her inhalations. Classical music played softly, an air he recognised but couldn't name. He smelt coffee on her breath. No offer of a cup here.

'I suppose Beth told you what happened to the Noonans.'

'She did.'

She made a few more snips. 'Poor Lil, the only one left. Tell her I said hello.'

'I will.'

Denise. He must remember the name. Denise and Olive, and Fred in the pub. He tried to recall the name of the previous handyman who'd obligingly bowed out before his own arrival in the town, but couldn't. Paddy Something? Jimmy Something?

'Good hair,' she said. 'Strong.' She tilted his head a little to the left, snipped around his ear. 'So what do you do to earn a bob, Tom?'

'I'm a handyman.'

'Are you now?'

'I have a few cards. You might help me spread the word.'

'Sure I will. Might be calling on you myself – my husband can't change a light bulb, and I'm as bad. We had a great handyman, Jimmy. Fell off a ladder in the autumn.'

'Olive told me.'

Every so often she would rest a palm briefly against his head, or tilt it one way or another with a gentle push of a finger. Impersonal though it was, he found himself welcoming this physical contact. Apart from his sister-in-law's hugs, he'd been a long time without any kind of feminine touch.

He marvelled at the volume of hair dropping soundlessly to the floor. How could it have grown so much? He could have got it cut in jail – a barber came in every few weeks – but he hadn't bothered. Interest lost in everything, his appearance the least of his concerns. Should have attended to it when they'd let him out, but again he'd lacked the will.

'Close your eyes,' she ordered, and he felt the whisper of hair on his face. Eventually she took up a spray bottle and dampened what was left. She drew her fingers through it, her reflection frowning at his.

She gave another few snips around his ears, tilting him again. Finally she laid aside the scissors.

'All done,' she said, showing him the back view in a mirror, brushing hair from his neck. 'A big improvement, if I say so myself. You'll need to get yourself a woolly hat to keep the heat in – you'd be surprised how much you lose through your head.'

She'd cut the back and sides close, and left just enough on top for it to be pushed in one direction or another. The style made his face seem more familiar. It was the face he remembered from when he was making serious money and spending it just as fast. He didn't regret those days, but he didn't mourn them either. He was different now. He wanted different days.

When she untied the cape and shook it away he saw a small unravelling in the shoulder of his sweater. He was reminded again of the time when he wore suits that had put a sizeable dent in his wages. He took out his wallet and handed her the business cards Olive had returned to him. 'Thanks. What do I owe you?'

'Eight euro, if you please,' she said.

He must have heard it wrong. It was a fraction of what he'd paid in the past. 'How much?'

'Eight.' She smiled. 'Not too dear, I hope.'

'Hardly.' He gave her a tenner and told her to keep the change. 'I'll be back,' he said, pulling on his jacket.

'I hope you will. Nice to meet you, Tom – take care now.'

A cloudburst accompanied him on his return journey, a downpour that soaked through his clothes in minutes: so much for an afternoon of gardening. He hopped over puddles on the cliff path, his hands in their new gloves the only parts of him that weren't wet, until he saw with relief the cabin that told him he was approaching home.

As he pushed open the small gate he dislodged something that fell to the ground. He picked it up and discovered it to be a square of tightly folded paper. He shoved it into his pocket and sprinted up the garden to the house. In the kitchen he shook off his gloves and unfolded the paper carefully. It was wet from the rain, but its many folds had kept it from disintegrating. One edge was jagged, a page ripped from a pad. He read the single unsigned sentence.

We'll try to make sure the cat doesn't bother you again.

He read it a second time, his heart sinking. They'd heard him shouting at the cat, taking out his anger on a defenceless animal. Bloody hell. He looked at the note again. It hadn't been written by the grandmother; the handwriting was different. This must be from Lil, the silent orphan. Maybe she'd been the only one to hear him on her way to open the library. Yes, it would have been shortly before ten.

He removed his boots and stuffed them with newspaper and propped them by the radiator. He hung his sodden jacket on the end of the banister and trudged upstairs. In the bathroom he stripped off the rest of his things and stood under the shower until he warmed up. On his return to the kitchen, dried and dressed, he spotted the phone he'd abandoned after Joel's call. He saw *1 missed call, 1 new voicemail* on the display.

Tom, I'm sorry, I shouldn't have mentioned her. It won't happen again. Give me a ring over the next few days, will you?

He slipped the phone into his pocket. He'd return the call in a while and make his peace.

He picked up the note and read it a third time. Their first proper encounter was to be his apology to her. Ironic, after the grandmother had already issued *him* an apology. Were the three of them to spend the rest of his lease saying sorry to one another?

The rain had lightened. He sprinted over the stepping stones and stopped at the gap in the hedge, remembering the feeling he'd had on his first night that something, or someone, was there in the shadows. He stepped through and glanced up at the neighbouring garden, familiar to him by now from his sightings of it through his bedroom window. A biggish rockery set in the centre of a neat lawn, a small shed adjacent to it, a bare rotary clothesline beyond that. An oil tank, a boiler house further up. A crazy paving path led all the way from the patio to the cabin.

He turned and regarded the cabin door, to which a wooden sign had been screwed. *Welcome*, it read. He wondered if he'd be welcome, after his abuse of the cat. He listened to the familiar roll and suck of the sea, the cliff path just metres away from where he stood, and the always urgent-sounding cries of gulls in the sky, but nothing at all, not a whisper, came from within. Maybe nobody was there. Maybe it was closed, even though today was Monday.

He brushed beads of rain from his newly shorn hair. He pushed down on the handle: it yielded, and he stepped inside.

Books, floor to ceiling. A few chairs positioned randomly, more folded by the wall. A large rug, its floral design faded, covering most of the floor, cushions in primary colours scattered about the far end. Wall heaters located in the gaps between the bookshelves. The three windows he'd seen on his first night. Spotlights, and a skylight, set into the roof.

The place was empty apart from a young woman in a green jacket who sat behind an old desk that faced the door. A book lay open in front of her. A cloth bag dangled from her chair back. A red scarf hung on a nearby hook. She regarded him solemnly and warily. She must know who he was. She must have seen him coming and going, as he'd seen her.

His first close-up look at her. Hair the colour of straw, curling and twining past her shoulders. Side sections drawn up and captured around the back by something he couldn't see. Striking dark eyes, high cheekbones. An uptilt at the end of her nose, a small mouth with a full bottom lip. A light flush to her skin.

Elfin came to mind. Pretty, not in an obvious way. He was glad nobody else was there to witness his apology.

He would get this over with. He would be charming. He smiled. 'You must be Lil,' he said. 'I'm Tom. Good to finally meet you. Thank you for letting me stay in your house.' He put out a hand, and after a split second of hesitation she accepted it.

She wore grey woollen gloves that left most of her fingers uncovered. Her skin was cool.

'I got your note,' he went on. 'I presume it was yours.'

She continued to regard him gravely, gave a small careful nod.

'I didn't mean to yell at the cat. I was … angry about something else. I shouldn't have shouted, and I'm sorry.' He took a step back, conscious of his height, the way he towered above her.

She didn't react, didn't blink. So dark, those eyes. Almost black. The same candid stare as her grandmother, but a gentler element to it, he thought. Maybe it was because of her silence.

His smile had long since stiffened. 'I hope you'll accept my apology. I wouldn't like us to get off on the wrong foot.'

She gave another slow, solemn nod. It would appear that he was forgiven. He found it tricky, being the one doing all the talking. He also felt compelled to go on doing it.

'I don't mind it coming into the house. I actually like cats.' The last was a stretch – he'd never owned one, or lived in a house that contained one. He was ambivalent about them at best. 'It's very friendly. Nice colouring too.'

Still nothing. Just as he was about to give up she opened a drawer in the desk and drew from it a pen, and a notebook whose size suggested that her message to him had come from there. She wrote briefly, then turned the notebook in his direction.

Him, he read. Just that, just the single word. Communication at least, but its meaning beyond him. He looked up, shook his head. 'Sorry, I don't understand.'

The cat is male.

'Oh … I see. And is it yours? I mean, is he yours?'

A quick tiny nod. Her eyes flicked from his face to his shoulder and back again.

'So he used to live … in my house – I mean, your house.'

Another nod.

'Does he have a name?'

Skimbleshanks.

He thought it an odd name for a cat, or for any creature. 'Right … well, please don't feel you have to keep him away from me. I promise not to shout at him again.'

And that, finally, got the tiniest of smiles, causing a dimple to faintly indent a cheek. He'd always had a soft spot for dimples.

On the point of leaving, he remembered his

resolve to give reading another go. 'I might have a look around, as long as I'm here. Do I need to sign up, or anything?'

In response, she pulled out the desk drawer again and produced a laminated card, and handed it to him.

Welcome to our community library. We operate it on a trust basis without membership. Please help yourself to a book or two, and return when read. We'll stamp them with the date you take them out, just to keep a record of borrowings, but there's no time limit. Visitors to Fairweather should feel free to bring home an unfinished book, and return it at their convenience. Donations of books in good condition are always welcome.

No membership, and no return date on books, which meant no fines for late returns. Just help yourself, and off you go. Probably didn't hurt that most of the borrowers would be known to them, but still extraordinarily trusting. He wondered what percentage went astray – particularly during the summer months, with English-speaking tourist readers no doubt taking away a book to help them pass the flight home.

He handed back the card. 'Thanks. I'll have a look.' He moved off and began to explore. The stock, he discovered, was a mix of old and recent publications, with hardbacks and paperbacks nestling side by side. Fiction to his right, non-fiction to his left. At the far end was a small children's section.

Everything was neat and orderly. Everything alphabetised, and in its rightful place. The books weren't wrapped in plastic sleeves, like most books in a conventional library, but despite this he found no tatty editions, no dog-eared pages. Wouldn't be tolerated here, not if Granny had anything to do with it. He imagined a reader accidentally leaving a coffee ring on a cover, and trying frantically to wipe away the evidence before the book could be returned.

Hard to calculate how many volumes the cabin held. His very rough estimate put the total in the region of two thousand. How on earth had she rounded them all up? Whose arms had she twisted? What powers of persuasion had she used? *We're proud of it*, Olive had said, and he could see why.

As the seconds and minutes ticked by he became acutely conscious of the silence in the cabin, emphasised by the steady drum of rain on the wooden roof. Every small sound he made – a sudden sneeze, muffled in his sleeve; the scrape of his trainers on the floor; the slide of a book from a shelf; even the turning of a page – seemed greatly magnified. Now he wished for someone else to arrive, but nobody obliged. Was it always this quiet, or had he picked a slow time?

She'd resumed her reading. He glanced in her direction now and again, saw the book held in her gloved hands, the straightness of her back, the tiny tilt to her head. He thought of how she walked, how the sway and grace of her stride had put him in mind of a dancer. Maybe she'd taken classes before her life had changed.

He wondered what she'd been like before, when she could speak. Her silence made her something of a curiosity, a mystery.

He sneezed again. He doubted it was caused by dust – it wouldn't dare hang around in here. So many duckings he'd got since moving to Fairweather, damp clothes constantly draped over radiators, boots never getting a chance to dry out fully. Only a matter of time before he picked up his first Kerry head cold. The haircut probably wasn't helping – must get his hands on a woolly hat, like Denise had recommended.

Eventually he settled on a Bill Bryson whose first page made him chuckle, and a Jo Nesbø that sounded like it would pass a few dark evenings. He brought them to the desk.

'I'll take these two then, if that's OK. I'm trying to get back into reading – no excuse, with a library pretty much on my doorstep.'

Another small smile. She took them from him, and stamped and returned them. He should go now.

He didn't go.

'What are you reading?'

She lifted it to show him the cover, and he read *This Is Happiness*. The title struck him as ironic, given the reader. 'Any good?'

She nodded.

'Might try it after you then.' He sneezed again while she wrote.

I'll keep it for you.

'Thanks.' He looked for more to say. Why was he looking for more to say?

'I got my hair cut this morning. I think that might be what's making me sneeze. The woman who cut it told me I should get a woolly hat.' Christ, she didn't want to hear this rubbish – and yet, it seemed he couldn't stop. 'I met Olive earlier, in the gift shop. I presume you know her.'

A wash of pale pink spread across her face. *She was my mother's best friend.*

Of course she was. Olive had told him that, and he was the idiot who forgot everything – and now she'd mentioned her dead mother, and he would have to make some expression of sympathy, or be thought heartless.

'I'm sorry,' he said, 'about what happened to your family. Your grandmother told me.'

Her gaze slid away and came to rest somewhere around his chest. Her hands crept together on her notebook, fingers interlacing.

'My mother died too, but she got cancer, so at least we had some warning. It was still hard, but …'

He trailed to a stop. He should go. He tucked his books under his arm. 'Nice to meet you,' he said. 'I'll see you around.' He lifted his hand in a wave that somehow came out dismayingly like the little waggle the queen gave. He left the cabin, feeling clumsy and foolish. Why hadn't he just taken the books and gone? Where had this compulsion to talk come from? She'd run a mile next time she saw him on the cliff path. She'd avoid the moron who blurted out rubbish, and who waved like a British monarch.

The rain stopped as he boiled two eggs for lunch, his intermittent sneezing continuing. Afterwards he took the clippers from the garage and resumed work on the hedge he'd begun a month earlier, but within a short time he became aware of an ominous drag in his muscles, a weariness descending that slowed his progress. He plodded on until he was forced to admit defeat, out of energy. He raked the clippings together, limbs leaden, and bundled them into the wheelbarrow and left it by the hedge, unable to take it further.

Back in the house he made himself a generous hot whiskey, hoping to head off whatever was coming before it took hold. He brought it into the sitting room and cradled the glass in his cold hands, relishing the warmth that coursed through him with every sip. A fire would be good, but last night's ashes were still in the grate and he couldn't face the trek to the shed.

He drifted into a doze, lying awkwardly on the too-short couch. He awoke with a stiff neck and a sour taste in his mouth. The light was fading in the room, colours dimming, outlines blurring. He hoisted himself with some difficulty from the couch and went to the window to close the curtains – and a flash of something white by the small gate caught his eye.

He went out and made his way down the path, every muscle protesting stiffly. He picked up the object, which was wrapped in a plastic bag and which felt like a book. He brought it into the kitchen and opened it.

It *was* a book. It was a volume of poems about cats by T. S. Eliot. It appeared, from the colourfully illustrated cover, to be a children's book. Inside, he saw the glued-on slip and the stamped dates that told him it belonged to the library.

He checked for an accompanying note, but found none. It must have been left there by whoever had borrowed it – but why? Why not bring it to the library, if they'd come that far to return it? Why leave it at the gate of the house next door?

He put a pizza into the oven, not at all sure he wanted one but thinking he should probably eat. He sank into a chair and leafed through the book – and he found, quite by chance, 'Skimbleshanks the Railway Cat'.

And then it made sense.

It had come from Lil. It must have been Lil who'd left it there, after their conversation. It did seem a roundabout way of telling him where the cat's name had come from – couldn't she just have written it while he was there?

Then again, her taking the time to do this meant, didn't it, that she hadn't been put off by his prattling, and also that she'd forgiven him for his treatment of the cat? He imagined her hunting for the book on the shelves and packing it up, and bringing it with her when she left the library. He pictured her leaving it by the gate while he slept on the couch.

After wolfing the pizza – turned out he was hungry after all – he opened the first of his borrowed books, but within an hour the tickle in his throat had morphed into a proper phlegmy cough, and a soft but insistent ache began to push against his temples. He skipped his usual bath and went straight to bed, where he hacked and sneezed his way through the night, and got virtually no sleep.

He stayed put for most of the following day, huddled beneath the duvet, switching the electric blanket on and off as he froze and sweated by turns. Every cough hurt, the jolt of every sneeze brought a corresponding stab of pain to his temple. His throat felt like it was lined with gravel. He suspected he had a temperature, but without a thermometer he couldn't confirm it.

With the return of evening, he climbed wearily out of bed. He stripped it and balled up the damp sheets, and found fresh ones in the hot press. He remade the bed, shivering, and peeled off his pyjamas and replaced those too. After that, thirst drove him downstairs. As he stood gulping water at the sink, trying to summon up the energy to make toast or peel an orange, there was a tap at the back door.

He opened it to find his landlady standing there, holding a covered pot. 'Lil heard you coughing in the night,' she said. 'This is chicken noodle soup. You're not vegetarian, I hope?'

'… No.' It came out as a croak. He accepted the pot. Its sides were warm. 'Thank you.'

'Heat it up and take as much of it as you can. Do you need more bedding? I could let you have another duvet.'

'No, I'm fine.' The air coming in was icy: he clenched his aching muscles to stop himself from shivering.

'I see you've been clipping the front hedge, but please don't dream of doing anything more until you're well again.'

'Right.' He hadn't brushed his teeth all day. He was probably giving off a sweaty waft. At least he looked halfway presentable in fresh PJs.

'You got your hair cut,' she said. 'Much better. Give me a call if you need anything else.' She pulled the door closed and was gone.

She'd made him soup. He set the pot on the cooker. He lifted the lid and saw shredded chicken and various other things – noodles, peppers, carrots, celery – floating in a thin liquid. He heated it until it simmered, and then ladled some into a mug. He found it to be comforting and delicious, with a wonderful kick. She must have chucked in a few chillies. As he sipped, he felt the clogging in his head begin to loosen.

Lil heard you coughing in the night.

For some reason, there was comfort in this too.

Three Years Earlier

'It's great,' he said. Its split-level space held two good-sized en-suite bedrooms, both with double beds, a kitchen, and a spacious living room whose patio doors led to a deck overlooking the Thames. It was tastefully put together, all taupe and cream walls, and pale furnishings with pops of colour – teal cushions on the oatmeal couch – and decent kit in the kitchen, no rubbish. 'It's really great.'

It would want to be great. The rent was scandalously high. Even with the generous raise in salary his new job afforded, paying his two-thirds each month would make a nice dent. Two-thirds, because Vivienne earned considerably less than him in her marketing job – he had no problem with that. Of course, they could have

got someplace a lot cheaper than Hammersmith, he
wouldn't have objected to that either, but she'd been so
excited on the phone that he'd said nothing.

'Tom, it's amazing. Everything about it is perfect:
the location, the size, the furnishings, just everything.
I went for a two-bed, so your father can stay when he
comes over. You can't see it until you're here. I want it
to be a complete surprise.' So she'd sent no photos, and
hadn't given him the address. 'You'll adore it,' she'd told
him, and he'd known he would, because she did.

She was his first real love. He was pretty sure she'd be
his last. Everything about her was wonderful. He loved
the way she sang off-key. He adored the mole she hated
inside her upper arm, and the cluster of tiny tattooed
stars above her right ankle. It delighted him that he
could pick out her laugh in any crowd. He loved the
curve of her calf, the downy hair on her neck, the way
she slept with a hand tucked under a cheek. He even
learnt to love television in the morning – or at least
tolerate it, for her.

It frightened him sometimes, how important she had
become to him. He lived in constant fear of losing her.
He watched his friends jealously when she was around
them, and worried silently about her glamorous work
crowd, even if most of the males in it were gay.

He'd transplanted himself to London, giving up his

job of less than two years just to be close to her, to live with her all the time instead of only at weekends and holidays, to wake up every morning with her. Who cared how much it cost, if he could have that?

'You're sure about this?' his father had asked. 'It's a big move.'

'I'm sure. And you like her, don't you?'

'Of course I do. I think she's great.'

They'd been together since the wedding, eighteen months previously. He'd stayed in her hotel room that night, buzzing with champagne, and with the excitement of having ended up in her bed. Since then they'd alternated their weekends between Ireland and England, sharing with Tom's father in Dublin and with Vivienne's two female flatmates in London, but he'd hungered to be with her all the time, in their own place. One of them would have to move – and with Vivienne wanting to stay where her mother was, he'd been the one. It was no great sacrifice: London had so much to offer, so many opportunities.

Finding another programming job had been easy. With his qualifications, and a reluctant but glowing reference from Google, he'd had his pick of London companies. His only regret had been leaving Dad on his own in the house. Joel and Sarah lived in Kildare, and with both of them working full time, and a small baby to cope with, they weren't exactly frequent callers. Then again, Dad had never been a hermit. He had no shortage of friends – and a lot of them were female. Like Tom, he had little difficulty in finding a woman to keep him company. Since Mum's death seven years earlier, he'd had plenty of company.

Not surprising, Vivienne said. *He's good-looking and loaded and available. He's probably the most eligible man in Dublin. No wonder they're all gagging for him.* Tom was glad she and his father got on so well, glad the idea of a spare room for him in London had come from her.

'So,' she said, 'you approve of my choice?'

'I approve.'

It was Friday evening. They had two whole days together before he started work. He was exactly where he wanted to be, gainfully employed and sharing a beautiful space with the woman he loved.

They would never live apart again; the thought brought a rush of elation. They'd be together for the rest of their lives. He stepped closer, slid an arm around her waist. 'I feel we should check out the bed though, just to be on the safe side.'

She gave her wonderful laugh and began unbuttoning his shirt. 'Thought you'd never ask,' she said.

Beth

'I wanted to tell you my news,' Olive said. 'I wanted you to know' – and from the look on her face Beth instantly knew, she was certain of it, but waited out of politeness for it to be said.

'I'm pregnant, Beth. I'm over four and a half months gone, due in June. Can you believe it?' Smile wide, face practically glowing with happiness, delight colouring her voice – and Beth had to smother the memory that sprang up at the words, and offer her congratulations, and call it wonderful news, marvellous news, and say that Fred and Nancy must be thrilled, and find an excuse as soon as she decently could to leave the gift shop without the photo frame that had brought her in.

She returned to her car. She drove past the supermarket she'd planned to visit, and kept driving until she'd left the town behind her. After eight kilometres she turned onto a smaller road that twisted and climbed to the top of a hill. She pulled in at a lookout point and sat in her car with the Atlantic ocean spread out like a blanket below her, and she didn't see it. Instead, she unrolled the memory that Olive's news had poked awake …

First holiday on our own since our honeymoon, her daughter said. Can you believe it?

I can well believe it. You and Killian both work far too hard. Where are you going?

Paris, just for a week. We've found a gorgeous little hotel – well, it looks gorgeous on the website – not too far from Notre Dame.

I hope it won't be noisy.

It shouldn't be – it says the street is quiet.

It was ten days before Christmas, and the two of them were in Beth's kitchen. Beth was rolling out almond icing on parchment paper, and Maria was brushing melted apricot jam onto the top of the rich dark fruit cake. An annual tradition: Beth baked the cake and they iced it together. It was destined for Maria's house, Beth not being a fan of fruit in cakes. The warm scent of Jamaica rum hung in the air, the base of the cake having been pricked a few minutes earlier to allow a generous drizzle of the alcohol to permeate it.

Mam, there's something else, Maria said then.

What's that?

We're thinking of going again.

Beth looked at her. Going where? A second holiday?

Maria smiled. We're thinking of having another baby, Mam.

Another baby, with Lil, their younger daughter, soon to turn twenty-one. Beth digested the information silently. She shook icing sugar through a sieve onto the slab of marzipan. Another pregnancy, with Maria into her forty-third year. She flipped the slab over, her movements deft after years of practice.

Say something, Mam.

She gave the icing a few final swipes before setting aside the rolling pin. She wiped her hands on her apron. Careful now. Choose your words wisely.

I'm surprised to hear it, Maria.

You think I'm too old.

She gave a small sideways twist to her head. Not agreeing, not disagreeing. You're not young, dear.

Her daughter made a sound, a mix of impatience and resignation. Beth was familiar with that sound. Silence followed, interrupted only by Maria's slap-slap of jam onto the top of the cake.

When are you off to Paris? Beth asked, wanting to pull back the calm contentment of a few minutes before.

The eleventh. Her tone cooler, flatter.

Well, I hope you and Killian have a lovely time. You deserve it.

No response.

Maria, you know I always speak my mind.

Oh, you certainly do that. Maria dropped the pastry brush into the pan of jam and went to the sink. She ran the tap, keeping her back to her mother. It would just be nice if you considered people's feelings once in a while.

For heaven's sake – I'm concerned, that's all. You'll be forty-three in March. It's trickier when you're older.

It might be tricky if it was a first baby. Women are having babies in their forties all the time.

Fine, I'll hold my tongue then. Beth lifted the cake and placed it upside down on the rolled-out icing. Maria turned off the tap and dried her hands in silence.

Beth trimmed the excess marzipan, swept it aside. You'll want a drive to the airport. I'll do it.

No need. Mark is taking us.

That stung. Mark Purcell already knew about the holiday Beth had just been informed of. Mark knew because Maria would have told his daughter-in-law Olive, which meant that Olive's husband Fred knew too. Was Beth the last to be told?

And of course Olive would also be aware of Maria's wish for another baby. Those two shared everything.

She slid a hand under the parchment and eased the cake right side up. She peeled off the paper carefully. She would not allow herself to feel hurt, when she knew no hurt had been intended.

What about when you get home? Have you Mark lined up for that too? Careful to keep her tone light, not to allow a hint of resentment to colour it.

Maria reclaimed the cake and began brushing the sides with jam while Beth gathered the icing into a new ball. Well, I'm sure he wouldn't mind, but I wouldn't like to ask him to collect us as well.

I'll do it then.

That would be good. A half-smile came and went. Thank you, Mam.

The subject of another baby wasn't mentioned again between them. Christmas Day came, with everyone dining in Beth's house as they always did, and the New Year celebrations passed, and Lil's birthday party, three days after that. On the day the holidaymakers were departing, Mark arrived to ferry them as he'd promised to the airport. Beth took in his mud-spattered car, and thought the least he could have done was to give it a wash.

How are you, Beth? You had a good Christmas?

I did, thank you – and you?

His face fell. I was hoping you wouldn't ask. I got the bag of coal again, still on the naughty list.

Silly man. But he was kind to bring the holidaymakers to the airport, so she smiled.

She and Lil waved them off, Hollie having left for work an hour earlier. See you in a week, Beth told them. Text your arrival time and I'll be there – but on the day they were due to return, Hollie offered to collect her parents instead.

I've got the afternoon off, I don't mind, she said, so Beth agreed, glad to be spared the hour-long journey in the filthy winter weather, rain falling steadily since early morning. Take it easy on the roads, she told Hollie, and her granddaughter promised she would, and she was a careful driver, she was – but the next person to come to her door was the sergeant, braced to tell her the worst possible news.

She hadn't baked a cake for the past two Christmases. She and Lil didn't really celebrate the day any more. Beth roasted a turkey breast, and they exchanged gifts, and that was it. No tree, no crib, no crackers, no decorations. Just two of them, when they'd been five.

And oh, all the what-ifs that persecuted her still.

What if she'd gone to collect them, like she'd

planned? What if she hadn't taken Hollie up on her offer? They'd all still be alive; they'd still be living next door. There might be a new baby in the house, or maybe a toddler now, learning to say 'Gran', and she would love it every bit as much as the other two.

What if she'd held her tongue in the kitchen that day in December, or stifled her concerns and told her daughter that she was glad, she was delighted they were trying again, and she'd be thrilled to have another grandchild, and she'd help out as much as she could? What if she'd done that instead?

If she could just take Maria into her arms one more time and hold her tight, if she could just do that. If she could have the chance to tell her that her mother was proud of her – because she had been, she had been, she had been, so proud of the woman and mother Maria had become.

If she could only make it right. If she could have one minute, half a minute, of her daughter's life back, to tell her that she meant the world to her, and that nothing she could ever do would make her any less loved. If she could only have that much, she'd willingly walk through the gates of Hell afterwards.

If she could only have her back. She just wanted her back.

Time heals, people had told her, but they were

fools. Time didn't heal: it only pulled lost ones further away. It dimmed the memory of their faces, it muffled the sound of their voices, but it didn't *heal*. The anniversaries hurt just as much, the remembered conversations and laughter and arguments and reconciliations stabbed with a poignancy just as fierce. Time didn't dig out the loneliness that death planted in the bereaved, far from it. Time, it turned out, didn't give a damn.

But Maria had known, hadn't she? Beth and Gerry's only child must have known that she was loved. Maria, from the day of her birth, had become the focus, the hub, of her contrary mother's life. Not that Beth could ever show it, not in gentle words or soft smiles or warm embraces – she wasn't *built* like that, she didn't have it in her – but Maria would have known.

She would have tasted it in her mother's cooking, in the melting butter on a spoonful of mashed potato, in the slice of roasted chicken breast cut carefully into pieces for a small mouth. She would have felt it in the pretty cotton dresses Beth had made for her, hunched in the evenings over the sewing machine inherited from an aunt, tired from her day's teaching but able to do it, wanting to do it.

Maria knew. She must have seen beyond the curt

words, she must have known the love that was always, always there.

Beth remained sitting in the car, lost in her sadness. The rain that had dried up around noon began again, running down the windscreen, blurring the sea. Doing her crying for her, it felt like. She sat until the light began to drain from the day, and the cold gnawed at her feet, and her watch told her she needed to move. She drove back to the town and stopped for the groceries on her list. As she pushed her trolley along the aisles, hoping to God that for once she wouldn't meet anyone she knew, she thought of Olive counting down the days and weeks, full of hope for the frail life inside her. Over four and a half months gone. Halfway there.

Olive was forty-two now, the age Maria had been when she'd told her mother she wanted a third baby. This would be Olive's first time to give birth, if all went well. She'd be forty-three when it was born.

'Beth!'

She turned from the jars of honey to see Mark Purcell advancing towards her, a wire basket on his arm, a grin on his face. Sausages, she saw in the basket. A white sliced pan, devoid of nutrition. A six pack of crisps, tins of beans, a jar of instant coffee. Not a single piece of fruit, not a sign of a fresh vegetable.

'Olive told you her news,' he said. 'I was just in with her.'

'Yes. Congratulations.' All going well, he would acquire a new grandchild in June. 'You must be delighted.'

'I'm over the moon.' He laughed. 'I feel like dancing a jig!'

He'd do it too, given the smallest bit of encouragement. Wouldn't care who saw him.

'Will you say a prayer, Beth?' he asked then. 'She needs all the prayers she can get.'

'Of course I will.' Not that Beth had faith in prayer any more, not since God had done what he had done to her. She began to edge away, not able today for any more talk of babies and useless prayers. 'Please give Fred my best wishes,' she said, and hurried off before he had a chance to do more than send goodbye in her wake.

The sight of him reminded her of Olive's recent request for cookery lessons as a birthday present to him, and her own refusal. Standing at the checkout, she tried to recall if Olive had mentioned the actual date of his birthday. Sometime in February was all she remembered. Olive hadn't mentioned it since the phone call. Hopefully she and Fred had come up with a more sensible gift for him.

The first thing she saw when she got home was a small tissue-wrapped bundle by the front door. Beneath the wrapping she found a little lavender tea light, the kind Olive sold in her shop. Lil's admirer again, her diffident beau.

Olive had told her she could pass on the news to Lil so she did, as soon as her granddaughter returned from the library. 'They're over the moon,' she said. 'So exciting for them.'

When? Lil wrote.

'June, sometime in June – and look,' showing Lil the little tea light, 'I found this at the front door.' She set it on the table. 'Get a match, Lil – and let's have a glass of wine. We should celebrate the good news.'

Because that was what you did, wasn't it? You found reasons to be happy, reasons like a pretty candle left at a door, or news of a much-wanted baby on the way, or the image of Mark Purcell suddenly dropping his wire basket that was full of the wrong kind of food and launching into a jig in the middle of the preserves aisle.

Silly man. Ridiculous man.

After dinner she found Olive in her contacts, and placed a call before she could change her mind.

'Beth, lovely to hear from you. Is everything OK?'

'I'll do them,' she said. 'The cookery lessons. If you still want them. If it's not too late.'

'Oh, *would* you? It's not too late, thank you so much – I really appreciate it, Beth.'

'When did you say his birthday was?'

'This Saturday. He'll be thrilled. Think about a price and let me know. I just hope I'm not putting you under pressure.'

'You're not.'

All the pressure was coming from Beth herself – because this was her way, wasn't it, of making amends to her daughter? This was her way of saying sorry to Maria, this favour she could do for Olive, who was pregnant in her forties, like Maria had wanted to be.

'One condition,' she said. 'I'd appreciate it if this didn't get out, Olive. I'd rather not have Fairweather knowing my business. Can you ask Mark please to be discreet, and not to broadcast it?'

'Of course I will. Don't worry, I'll make sure he doesn't breathe a word.'

'I'll be in touch with him over the next while,' Beth said. 'I'll make arrangements with him directly.' The fewer involved in the negotiations, the better.

'Thanks again, Beth. You're a darling.'

A darling she most certainly was not, and never had been. 'Another thing,' she said. 'I may have been a little abrupt in the shop today, when you told me your news.'

'Oh, I didn't—'

'I wouldn't want you to feel I'm not happy for you, Olive. I *am* happy, I'm truly happy for you and Fred, and I really hope everything goes well. It was just … it reminded me of something I found upsetting, and I needed to get away and be alone.'

'Oh, Beth, I'm so sorry.'

She knew, Beth was sure of it. She had guessed, or she would guess later, when she thought about it, what had upset Beth. Maria would have told her best friend how her mother had reacted when she'd revealed that she wanted a third baby.

'By the way,' Olive said – wanting as much as Beth did, no doubt, to steer the conversation away – 'I finally met your tenant. He came into the shop last week with his business cards.'

'I'm glad to hear it. I thought he'd never get around to looking for work.'

'And I *love* his carvings.'

'Carvings?'

'Maybe he didn't tell you, Beth – he makes the most beautiful things, the sweetest little houses. You should call in and ask to see them. He carves them out of wood, and they're quirky and charming, and

I adore them. He brought me three in today, and I put them straight into the window, and I just know they're going to be a big hit.'

'Well, that's good.' Quirky houses sounded peculiar. She thought it might be safer not to ask to see them; she wasn't good at pretending, and she didn't want to offend.

She hadn't spoken to him since she'd delivered the chicken broth. He'd left the empty pot by the back door a few days later; she'd lifted the lid and found a scribbled note of thanks. The following day he'd resumed work in the garden: she'd been glad to see that he was on the mend.

'How's Lil?' Olive asked. Always concerned for her.

'She's doing well.'

'I got lovely new notebooks into the shop – I thought of her as soon as I saw them.'

Yes, these days the sight of a notebook would probably call Lil to mind for a lot of people. Never without one, to write what she couldn't say. How many more notebooks would she go through before she found her voice again?

The following morning, which was Valentine's Day, Beth came downstairs to find a red envelope on the hall mat. Addressed in block capitals like the previous one, but again without a name on it. Maybe it would finally contain a clue as to his identity, or even reveal it.

It didn't. When Lil opened it in some bemusement, she found a card that read *Love is the sweetest thing* above an image of an open box of chocolates – and inside, no message whatsoever below the sentimental printed verse, nothing but a single x. Just like before.

He could have been a little more informative, for pity's sake. He could at least have named Lil on the envelope. Beth was beginning to lose patience with this anonymous beau. Was he never intending to declare himself?

Gerry had given her tulips every Valentine's Day, every single year. No card, a bouquet of tulips instead, which she'd been perfectly happy with. She'd lived to regret it, of course, in the wake of his death, when she had no bundle tied with a ribbon that she could untie and read again.

Lil left her card sitting on the table when she went out for a walk. Hardly surprising she was showing little interest in it, with the sender remaining so elusive. Beth returned it to its red envelope and slipped it into the drawer of the dresser that held her shopping-list pads and notelets, and last year's card.

She'd keep them safe, just in case.

Olive

He looked so much better since the haircut. Two weeks later, she was still marvelling at the difference it made to have that mop gone. *I couldn't take it off fast enough*, Denise had reported. *Not a bad-looking man, is he?*

He wasn't. That lean and hungry look, and that lovely eye colour, somewhere between blue and green. Full of a headcold when he'd dropped in the houses, poor thing – even now, she could hear the trace of huskiness in his voice, the remains of a rattle in his chest when he laughed.

'I've finished the garden,' he said, and pulled off the gloves he'd bought from her to show his blisters, matching ones at the base of each thumb, more on his palms. It was two o'clock on a Friday afternoon, and he'd become a regular visitor to the shop.

'Ouch – didn't you wear gardening gloves?'

'No. There was a pair in the garage, but I didn't feel I should use them.'

Of course he didn't. A dead man's gloves wouldn't sit right, not with the dead man's mother-in-law liable to see them if she stopped by to check on the work.

'Bathe in warm salty water,' she instructed, 'and apply Sudocrem. Here' – she rummaged in her bag and brought out her tiny tub – 'take this.'

'But that's yours – I'll get my own.'

'Oh stop – it cost me all of a euro. I'll pick up another on the way home. So how did it go, the gardening?'

'Fine. The lawn was a bit of a challenge, it was gone so long – but I got there in the end.'

'I can't wait to see it. What did Beth say?'

'She seems happy enough.'

'That's good. I'm so glad she asked you to tidy it up. I hated seeing it becoming such a wasteland. Killian always kept it so nice, and Maria planted flowers in the front every summer. I offered to send Fred and a couple of his friends over, when it started to get overgrown. I said they'd be happy to do it. Beth wouldn't hear of it though – as much as told me to mind my own business. I suppose I deserved it.'

He smiled. 'I started to cut the hedge, the day after I moved in. She came out and asked me to stop – well, ordered me to stop. She was … quite upset.'

'Oh, no, poor you – and you thinking you were doing the right thing. And poor Beth too.'

'She did apologise later. That was when she told me about the accident.'

'Well, I'm so glad she had second thoughts. And before I forget,' handing him an envelope, 'your latest earnings.' Eighty per cent of the selling price she was giving him, instead of the usual sixty she handed over to her suppliers. Something told her he might need it, and she could handle the reduced income. They'd live comfortably on Fred's takings alone; anything the gift shop made was a bonus.

She was thrilled that his little houses were a hit. She'd known they would be, the minute she'd seen them. Brightly coloured, full of character. Perfect on their own, equally sweet when grouped together to make a quaint, lopsided street.

Bring me more, she'd ordered, even before she'd put the first three in the window. Bring them all to me – and he had, all twenty of them, and so far eight had sold, and she was quite sure the others would quickly follow. Wait till the summer, she'd told him. You won't have time to be a handyman, you'll be too busy making houses.

'So how's the work going?' she asked.

'Fine.' He talked of replacing cracked floor tiles, and assembling a flat-packed chest of drawers, and stripping a stairs of its carpet before sanding and staining, and she rejoiced that he was finding his place, and settling into life in Fairweather.

Still that darkness in his eyes though. Still hadn't managed to chase that away. She'd been struck by it the first time he'd walked into the shop. The air of melancholy that hung about him, the sense that something bad, not good, had brought him to the town. She wished she knew his story. He might tell her, if she gave him time.

His little houses reflected him, she thought. Something wrong, something skewed, but still lovely.

'I've met Lil,' he said. 'I called to the library.'

'Well – what do you make of her?'

He grimaced. 'Hard to know, when she doesn't talk. Hard to figure her out.' He paused again, crossed his arms. Didn't meet her eye. 'She gave me a book. Well, she left it at the gate.'

'A book? What book?'

'Poems about cats. T. S. Eliot wrote them.'

This was getting interesting. 'Nancy has that – she got it a few years ago for her birthday. Why would Lil give it to you?'

He unfolded his arms and scratched at an ear. 'I, um, well, I shouted at her cat.'

'You *shouted* at Skimbleshanks?' She couldn't imagine him shouting at anyone.

He shrugged. 'It's a long story. I was … angry about something else, and I took it out on him. He was in the kitchen at the time.'

She wondered what had angered him. 'Skimbleshanks was Hollie's cat; she got him as a kitten. He used to sleep on her bed. I'm sure he forgave you for shouting at him.'

'He did, we're friends again – but the thing is, Lil overheard me.'

'Oh no – was she cross with you?'

'Not exactly. She stuck a note into the back gate that just said they'd keep the cat away, but I was sort of mortified that she'd heard, so I went to the library to apologise.'

He'd felt the need to say sorry. There was something sweet about that. 'I'm still wondering where the book comes in.'

'I asked Lil what the cat's name was, and she told me, but she probably saw that I didn't get the connection, so she left the book to explain.'

'Of course – I'd forgotten the name came from there.'

Sounded like they'd had quite the exchange. Maybe, she thought suddenly, the Fates had sent him to Fairweather for Lil, rather than as a replacement for poor Jimmy. Maybe Tom would be the one to bring Lil back to them. If she said that to Fred he'd tell her to stop hallucinating, but it wasn't outside the bounds of possibility.

And the fact that Tom had signed a six-month lease was neither here nor there. Look at her – cycled into the town for lunch one day, ended up packing her bags for Fairweather.

'So what do you think of our little library?'

'It's good. I was impressed.'

'Have you gone back to reading then?'

'I have.'

'We're in a book club,' she told him, 'Fred and myself. We meet in the library on the last Wednesday of the month. Fred's father is in it too, and Lil. Beth set it up, about five years ago.'

He nodded slowly. 'I heard some people going down there one evening. I wondered what was going on.'

'Yes, that would have been us.'

Maybe they could let Tom into the club. Give him an outlet, something to put in his diary. Another opportunity for him to be in Lil's company too, if he wanted it. She might propose it to the others next week, at the February meeting.

Later that afternoon she was alone in the shop, trying to remember if there were mushy peas at home. Fish and chips for dinner, and Nancy loved mushy peas with them. She'd stop at the supermarket and pick up a can, just in case.

She stirred milk into her umpteenth cup of tea, wishing for a chocolate biscuit. These days she was trying hard to be good, trying to do everything right, but some days she would just kill for a chocolate biscuit. She still bought them for Nancy, the fingers they both loved. Hide them, she would tell Nancy. Put them somewhere I won't find them. Trying to coax a smile from her daughter, trying to pull her out of the sulk she'd been in for a while, but Nancy wasn't playing along.

Ignore it, Fred said. She's just looking for attention, with the baby on the way. Easy for him to say, behind the bar of the pub five nights out of seven, only seeing Nancy at breakfast some days. Easy for him to ignore the moods, the glowering looks, the monosyllabic responses to questions, when he was safely out of the way at work.

She sipped her tea and turned her attention to the happier subject of Beth Sullivan and her father-in-law. She wasn't wrong. She knew she wasn't. Of course she had no idea how Beth felt, but Mark she could read like a book from Beth's library. The clues were there: she'd picked up on them some time ago.

How he found a way to pull Beth's name ever so casually into a conversation, how his face took on a certain look if Olive happened to mention her. Men were so transparent when it came to matters of the heart.

She knew he'd got married because Fred's brother Paul was on the way. He'd done what had been expected of all men at the time who'd found themselves in his situation. Maybe he and his wife would have got married anyway: she remembered her father reading out the death notice all those years ago, and the sadness in Mark's face when she'd met him after. Hopefully their marriage had been a happy one, even if it had been thrust upon them.

And Beth had married too, and she and Gerry had always seemed content to Olive – but that was then, and this was now, when Mark and Beth were both alone again, and Olive had thought to try her hand at a little matchmaking. She'd been disappointed, but not altogether surprised, when Beth had turned down the idea of the cookery lessons. It had been a long shot, a mad notion – but now, for whatever reason, they were going ahead, and she was delighted. She'd bought Mark a new oilskin jacket as a birthday gift from her and Fred after Beth had said no, but never mind that. Now he'd have two presents from them instead of one.

Or ... maybe the cookery lessons could come from Beth, not from her. Maybe she could give Mark that impression when she told him. She'd have to do it in such a way that if the truth came out she'd be able to convince him that he'd simply picked her up wrong.

She'd said nothing about the plan yet to Fred, knowing he might not take too kindly to her trying to fix his father up, but if he thought it was Beth's idea to teach Mark to cook, he couldn't possibly object. Yes, that was probably the way to go. She'd have to think about how to put it.

As she set down her mug she felt a queer little leap inside her. Not a leap, more a kind of twitch. What? She sat quite still, every sense tuned inwards. Please, she thought. Please.

It came again. Not painful, not in the least. A little tremor, it felt like. A little flutter. Or ... a little kick. A tiny limb, connecting with the wall of her womb.

She waited, palms resting against the bump that was getting more substantial by the day. For ten minutes she didn't move a muscle. She sat while her tea cooled, praying for once that no customer would appear – and then it came again, the same peculiar little flip, or jolt, or whatever it was. Once, twice.

And nothing bad followed. She felt no cramp, no pain, no feeling of dislodgement, no warm gush of anything. None of the signs that had signalled an end in the past.

Twenty-five weeks pregnant yesterday, and horribly afraid up to this because Miles had said it would be possible to feel movement anytime after sixteen weeks, and she hadn't, she'd felt nothing at all – until now.

She picked up her phone. She pressed Fred's name.

'Ollie – what's up?'

'It kicked, Fred. I think it kicked' – and before she could stop them, a flood of tears erupted out of her, and she had to hang up then because she couldn't say another word. She was incapable of forming a single other word because she was bawling in a most unladylike manner, and for once she was thankful for no customers, no witnesses to what could only be described as complete and utter hysterics.

Before a minute had passed the door flew open. 'Ollie—'

He dropped to his knees by her chair, cradling her head, telling her it was going to be OK, it was going to be fine, while she cried all the tears in Fairweather.

'Oh, boy,' she said, blotting her hot face when she finally ran dry. 'Oh, Fred.'

'It kicked,' he said. 'Our baby kicked, Ollie,'

and she saw that he was filled with the same pure happiness, the same sense of wonder. He was also on the verge of his very own tears.

'Don't you start, Fred – you'll get me going again.' She found him a tissue and he blew his nose while she blotted the damp patch she'd made on his shirt. Their baby had kicked. It was a marvel, a miracle. It was all the good in the world packaged up. Their baby had kicked.

He kissed her forehead. 'I love you.'

'I love you back.'

He got to his feet. 'I'd better move – I left Seamie Hogan with half a pint.'

'Don't tell anyone, Fred. Don't breathe a word. Tell Seamie I thought I saw a mouse.' Still afraid, despite the encouraging signs, to take anything for granted, still terrified that it might all go wrong.

'Tell me if it happens again. Ring me the minute it happens.'

'I will.'

In bed that night, she brought up the subject of the cookery lessons. It was well past midnight when he got to bed, like it always was on the nights he closed up. After the drinkers had been waved off and the glasses collected, after he'd driven home and showered the smell of the pub off him.

'She's going to teach him how to cook,' she said. 'Isn't that kind of her?' Laying the ground work – because he'd have to believe it was Beth's idea too.

'*Beth* offered to do that?' His voice full of the disbelief she'd expected.

'Well, she *was* a cookery teacher for years. I suppose it shouldn't be surprising.'

'I wouldn't have thought she'd be giving him any present at all.' He rested his palm on her bump, something he'd taken to doing lately. She liked it. Looking after his child even before it was born. 'I mean, they're not exactly bosom buddies, are they?'

'No, but they've been friends for years. And they get on great at the book club.'

'Well, yes, but she's not coming to the party.' Finger food and cake in the pub on Saturday night for anyone who fancied it. Mark in his element, a speech planned.

'No, because you know as well as I do that she's not a party person. She'd only have found an excuse if I'd asked her. But I happened to mention his birthday lately, just in passing, and I suppose she wanted to do something to mark his seventieth. I thought it was a lovely gesture.'

'I suppose so …'

'But don't be saying it in the pub, Fred. She doesn't want it to get around, in case there's talk.'

He gave a soft laugh. 'What – she's afraid people will think they're an item?'

'Of course not – it's just that she's a private person. She doesn't like people knowing her business, and we have to respect that. Whatever you do, don't mention it at the book club.'

'Does Dad know he's getting lessons from her?'

'Not yet. I'm to tell him on the day, and she's going to ring him after that and set them up.'

Another laugh. 'Maybe I should warn him.'

'Warn him? What do you mean?'

'Oh, come on, Ollie – do you really think he'll look forward to that? Would you fancy having Beth as your cookery teacher? She'll slap him with the wooden spoon if he adds too much salt.'

'She will not. I'm sure he'll be delighted. I'd say he'll really enjoy them.'

But would he? What if she'd got this all wrong? She was forcing them together three times, just the two of them, based purely on a conviction she had that Mark was interested in Beth.

She wasn't wrong. She was sure of it.

Well, maybe not exactly sure. She was reasonably confident. Fairly confident.

She turned on her side to curl into her husband. 'Tom was in again today,' she said, and yawned. 'Beth's tenant.'

'I'm beginning to think he doesn't exist. He hasn't come near the pub.'

'Well, there could be any number of reasons for that, Fred. Maybe he doesn't drink. Maybe he's a recovering alcoholic. Maybe he's watching the money.'

'Did he know anyone in town before he moved here?'

'Not a soul.'

'Isn't it a bit weird though? Turning up on his own in Fairweather, in the middle of winter?'

She'd come up with a few theories. 'He might have gone through a bad break-up, or a bereavement. Or maybe he lost his job, and wanted to make a fresh start. Who knows? Anyway, why shouldn't he choose Fairweather to live in? Mark told me once that it was the jewel in Kerry's crown.'

Another low laugh in the dark. 'Yeah, sounds like something he'd say.'

'Why don't you find a job for him, Fred? You'll meet him then.'

'What kind of a job?'

'Anything. He can do any kind of repairs, or

painting … or maybe he could make something for the pub.'

'Like what?'

'Fred, I have no idea. But he makes the little houses, so he could make something else. What about a clock?'

'A *clock*? He's not a clockmaker. Anyway, I have a clock. You gave it to me.'

'Oh, that old thing – I can't believe it's still going. I bet Tom could make you a fabulous new one.'

'Ollie, a clock has a mechanism in it. You need to know what you're doing to make one. You'll be telling me next he could carve me a new van.'

'Fred, your problem is you have no imagination. A handmade clock would be a real feature in the pub – I'd love one myself.' She yawned again. 'I like him, Fred. I feel he's – I don't know, a bit lost, or something.'

'Lost?'

'I can't explain. There's sadness there. Something bad happened to him.'

'It did. He got Beth for a landlady.'

'Stop that.' She yawned and closed her eyes, and went to sleep before he had a chance to make her cross.

She rang Tom the following week to tell him that

three more of his little houses had sold. It wasn't something she made a habit of – if she were to ring a supplier every time she made a sale, she'd never be off the phone, but Tom brought out the mother in her. She wanted to sit him down and feed him something delicious, and ask him if he had any friends. She wanted to ring him with happy news, just to put a smile on his face. She wanted him to be run off his feet with work.

She might have known Fred wouldn't go for her clock idea. Sadly, Fred didn't really have an eye for the unusual. He might find something else for Tom to do though. He usually came through, after he'd had a bit of time to mull things over.

'I hope you're making more houses,' she said to Tom.

'I am. I have six new ones for you. I carved them out of driftwood.'

'Perfect – bring them in soon.' And then, because she'd felt the little kicks again, because they were happening now with reassuring regularity, and because it wasn't raining for the second day in a row, and she was feeling hopeful and joyful, she said, 'I'm pregnant, by the way,' and laughed at the silence it was met with. 'Sorry, that was totally out of context. I have no idea why I said it.'

'Hey, no, that's great. That's really great. Congratulations.' And he sounded like he meant it, and she thought, *Yes, I like this man.*

She must introduce him to Mark. They'd get on, she was sure. Well, everyone got on with Mark. He could take Tom for a drink in the pub, or a coffee if a drink wasn't his thing. He could introduce him to a few more locals.

You're such an organiser, Maria used to say, and it was true. Olive liked managing things, sorting people out, fixing problems. Some might look on it as nosiness, which showed how little they knew.

That evening, a familiar problem presented itself. Not such an easy fix.

'Aoife's having a sleepover on Friday night,' Nancy said. 'I told her I'd go.' Looking at her mother in defiance, daring her to take issue, so Olive counted silently to ten, and then obliged.

'You mean you said you'd ask your mother's permission.'

'It's only a *sleep*over. Everyone's going.'

'Who's everyone?'

A shrug. 'All my friends.'

'All your friends? They're all going to fit in Aoife's bedroom? Is her mother putting on an extension for the night? Is she hiring a marquee for the occasion?'

Nancy raised her eyes to Heaven, something she'd taken to doing lately. Olive resisted the impulse to throttle her. 'Nancy Purcell, you're going nowhere on Friday unless you lose that attitude this minute.'

'What attitude?'

'Don't what-attitude me. You know full well what attitude.'

Nancy threw her a mutinous look. 'I bet *Dad* would let me.'

'I bet he wouldn't, if he knows what's good for him. If you ask me nicely I'll consider it' – and Nancy immediately adopted a simpering, wheedling tone: '*Please* may I please go to Aoife's sleepover, please, Mother *dear*?'

What on earth was the matter with her? What was causing this ridiculous carry-on? Was it insecurity, with a new sibling on the way? Was she afraid of being shunted aside? Olive had tried her best, when Nancy's behaviour had begun to veer towards the rebellious, to put any fears that might be causing it to bed. She'd sat her daughter down and told her she had nothing to fear, she was loved by her parents and would continue to be loved by them, no matter how many other babies came along.

She'd trotted out all the stuff the so-called experts said you needed to tell children at this time, and

Nancy had listened silently with a blank face. Can I go now? she'd asked, when Olive had run out of reassurances, and off she'd gone, and it hadn't made an ounce of difference.

It would all change when the baby came. Nancy would love it just as much as her parents would. She'd realise it posed no threat to her, and she would be a wonderful big sister.

Say it often enough, Olive told herself, and you might just believe it.

The February
Book Club Meeting

The talk, after Fred's book choice had been reviewed and the next put forward by Lil, was of babies – or rather, of one baby in particular. They toasted Fred and Olive with tea. Possible names were tossed around. Lil liked Emma or John; Beth favoured Kathleen or David. Mark, true to form, suggested Mark – 'Mark Purcell the Third, to give him his full title' – and didn't put forward any girl's name, saying he was full sure Olive was having a boy.

'We're going to wait till we see it,' Olive told them. 'We're not even thinking about names in advance.'

In case it didn't make it, Beth thought. In case it went the way of all her other lost babies. Poor Olive, her history and her age both against her. She must be afraid to breathe these days. She looked tired too, a drawn aspect to her features, the skin beneath her eyes smudged with shadow. Over five months gone, plenty more tiring times ahead.

Still in good spirits though, still smiling and

joking. Still kind, bringing along a leopard-print hair clip for Lil this evening. Every woman needs some leopard print, she'd said.

She must have told Mark about the cookery lessons, his birthday come and gone at this stage. It looked like she'd taken Beth's request on board and warned him to say nothing, because thankfully he'd given no sign at all that he knew about them.

But as long as she'd promised, she would do the best she could. She'd start with mackerel, since that was what he caught. She must begin by teaching him how to gut and clean one; she imagined he'd have plenty to say about that.

'Beth, a word.'

Olive's voice brought her back. Fred and Mark had begun to pack up the tea things, leaving the women members still sitting. 'Yes?'

'I was just wondering if we might invite Tom to join the book club.'

'Tom? From next door?'

'Yes. I thought it might be nice for him, for the few months that he's here. He might be glad of it, just as a social thing, since he doesn't really know anyone.'

Beth had spotted him leaving the library one afternoon, a week or so ago. When questioned, Lil had told her that he'd been in a few times. You never mentioned it, Beth said, and Lil had shrugged a shoulder, and volunteered no further information. Beth was glad he'd begun to use the library – but asking him to join the book club was another matter. No attempt had been made to fill the vacancies the others had left, and now Olive was wondering if they could bring in a complete stranger.

Well, not quite a complete stranger. And he was leaving in July, so only four meetings would be affected.

And he'd transformed the garden. There was that to consider.

'I took the liberty,' Olive went on, 'of running it by Fred and Mark on the way over here, and they have no objection, so if you and Lil are in agreement ...'

Beth looked at Lil, who lifted hands in a noncommittal way.

'You wouldn't object?' Beth asked, and she shook her head.

'If you'd rather not,' Olive added, no doubt seeing the indecision in Beth's face, 'then of course we won't ask him.'

But it would seem churlish, wouldn't it, when none of the others had an objection? It would seem mean not to include him, just for the few months.

'Very well,' she said. 'I'll mention it to him.' He might turn it down, of course: just because he was borrowing from the library didn't necessarily make him book club material. Still, they could give him the option.

Lil rose and began folding chairs. 'He tidied the garden,' Beth told Olive. 'I asked him.'

'He said it to me. I'm so glad. I'm dying to see it in the daylight. Are you pleased?'

'I am.'

But pleased didn't begin to cover it.

He'd done as she'd asked. He'd clipped and pruned and mown, he'd cleared away all the horrible briars. It had taken him a couple of weeks, in between rainy afternoons and showery spells, and the other work he was getting now. She'd witnessed his struggles with the back lawn from her window, how he'd strained to get Killian's mower through the grass, how often he'd had to stop to clear the blades.

She'd seen how many times he'd had to make the trip to the end of the garden with a full grass box, and again with barrow loads of hedge clippings, and all the time she'd felt terribly conflicted about seeing anyone apart from Killian doing such work.

But as she'd followed his progress, as he'd brought it slowly back to how Maria and Killian would want it to be, it had felt like a weight was lifting. It had felt like her two years of neglect were being written out, and she knew she'd done the right thing in asking him.

He had also, without being asked, repaired the small gate at the front so it didn't stick any more. I hope you don't mind, he'd said. It was easy enough to put right. He'd swung the gate open and closed to show her. She couldn't recall a time when it hadn't stuck.

Thank you, she'd said. She was ashamed that he'd have thought she might mind him repairing it. You've done a good job, she'd told him. On balance, she was glad Olive had suggested inviting him to join the club. He wouldn't be replacing anyone, just bringing a new voice to the meetings for a few months.

Later that evening, while Lil read in the sitting room, she scrolled through her phone contacts and found Mark's name.

'Beth?'

'I'm ringing about the cookery lessons. I assume Olive mentioned them to you.'

'She did indeed. It's very kind of you, Beth.'

Not kind at all, purely a business transaction. She let it go. 'Also, I want to wish you a belated happy birthday.'

'Thank you. I believe I'm now officially over the hill.'

Not exactly a tactful thing to say to someone who was two years older, but she let it pass too. 'I was thinking,' she said, 'of the thirteenth, for the first lesson.'

'The thirteenth ... of March?'

'Yes. I thought we should wait till the weather softened, and the days got a little longer.' She was putting it off, of course. Delaying what she really wasn't looking forward to. 'It's a Wednesday. Fred is off early on Wednesdays, isn't he? To look after Nancy, I mean.'

'He is. Wednesday would suit. And what time were you thinking?'

'Half past four.'

'Half four it is. At your house, yes?'

'Yes.' Of course at her house – where else?

'And should I bring anything with me at all?'

'No, I'll provide whatever's required.'

'Will I need to take notes?'

Was he laughing at her? 'Notes?'

'Yes, so I remember what we do. The old memory isn't what it used to be.'

'No need for notes. I'll have a copy of the recipe for you.'

'That's perfect. I'll see you then. Thank you again, Beth. Very generous of you.'

'Goodnight,' she said, and hung up. He'd been

uncharacteristically civilised. She wasn't altogether sure it suited him.

She saw a light on in the other kitchen. Twenty past nine, not too late for a house call. Might as well put the book club invitation to him now, while it was in her head. She pulled on the coat she'd taken off and took a torch from the drawer.

She looked into the sitting room. 'Just popping next door,' she said. 'Won't be a minute.'

She'd go around the back, since he was in the kitchen – but as she approached the door it opened, and he emerged with a smoking frying pan. He stopped dead at the sight of her.

'Sorry,' he said. 'I'll replace it.'

'What?'

'The pan. I forgot it.'

'What did you burn?'

He held it out, and she saw four blackened somethings. 'Sausages,' he said. 'Dinner.'

Four sausages for his dinner. It saddened her, how careless people could be about nutrition. And twenty past nine was far too late to be eating. 'Come back with me,' she said. 'I'll give you another pan. That one will probably be fine with a good scrub, but take one of mine in the meantime.'

He left his burnt dinner at the door and returned

with her to the house, where she gave him her third best pan and the remains of the ham and mushroom pie that she and Lil had eaten earlier. He demurred: she insisted – and it was only after he'd gone that she remembered the book club, and her reason for going over. He must have wondered why she'd shown up.

The tenth of July his lease was up. He'd be leaving then unless Lil decided she still didn't want to move back into her house, and Beth offered to extend the lease for another six months, and he accepted. Lots of unlesses there.

By the tenth of July, all going well, Olive would have given birth, and would be a mother of two. She'd made no mention of Nancy tonight; either the child had got over whatever had caused her previous sulks, or Olive had stopped fretting about them.

By the tenth of July, summer would be well under way. Fairweather businesses that closed completely for the winter – the ice cream shop, the surf equipment store, the periwinkle cabin on the prom, the tiny pizza parlour, the smaller of the two beauty salons – would have pulled up their shutters and would be back in business.

Fred would have dusted down the sandwich board he displayed on the path outside the pub from May onwards. Mark would be offering tourists an hour's fishing in the harbour. The days would be long, the temperatures kinder. The beaches and shops would be full, the restaurants and pubs busy and thriving.

By the tenth of July, Maria and Killian and Hollie would have been gone just under two years and six months.

She shook away the thought and filled the kettle for her hot-water bottle.

MARCH

Tom

'Fred Purcell here,' the man said. 'Olive's husband. I think she told you I have the pub next door to her shop.'

'She did indeed.' He watched the cat playing with the laces of the boots that were drying out after yet another wet walk. 'Sorry I haven't been in, I'm … not much of a drinker.' Let him take what he wanted from that.

'No problem. I'm ringing to see if we could have a chat, sometime you're free. I don't know if you'd be interested, but I have this mad idea I'd like to run by you.'

A mad idea sounded interesting. More interesting than a sash window with a broken cord, or a tap spindle that needed replacing, or a blocked drain. The work was coming in steadily, and he was grateful for it, but he'd welcome something that veered away from the usual handyman tasks. 'I'm dropping by the gift shop this morning; I could swing by the pub if you're around.'

'I would be. I open at noon, but I'm there from

eleven on. Or we could meet someplace else, if you prefer.'

In case Tom was a recovering alcoholic who didn't care to cross the threshold of a licensed premises. 'The pub would be fine. Say eleven thirty?'

'That sounds good, but say nothing to Olive – I'm planning this mad thing as a surprise. If she comes to the door when you're leaving, pass the pub and double back when she's gone in. Give a knock on the window.'

'Will do.'

Intrigue in Fairweather. He hoped the double-back wouldn't be necessary, with local shopkeepers liable to witness the manoeuvre. The new handyman acting suspiciously in the vicinity of the main street. Loitering with intent, shortly before noon. At the very least he'd get the name of being a drinker, knocking on a pub window before opening time.

He hung up and went to the garage for his latest batch of carvings. The driftwood was proving a good medium, having been weathered and softened by its time in the sea. Some of it had been too long in the water, and crumbled and collapsed under his tools, but more of it was fine, malleable and quickly shaped, and his houses emerged in all their imperfections.

The very first house he'd made was imperfect by

accident. Despite his best attempts his walls had remained stubbornly skewed, making the house wider on top than on the bottom. Try again, his teacher had suggested. Start another one – but Tom was not in a mood those days to listen to suggestions, so he'd kept doggedly on with his first.

He'd put a slight tilt in the roof, thinking to make it look more in keeping with the walls. He'd angled the chimney and carved a knocker on the front door that was slightly left of centre, and positioned the upstairs windows at different levels. If it was going to be flawed, let it be properly flawed.

He'd been equally reckless with the colours. He'd painted it sky blue, with a yellow door and scarlet windows and a grass-green roof, and the others in the class had had a good laugh at it, but he hadn't cared. He'd be the master of crooked houses. He'd make it his trademark. Nobody outside the class would see them; nobody else would have a chance to laugh at them.

He'd kept going, he'd persevered – and somewhere along the way, the imperfect little houses had begun to grow on him. He'd found himself thinking up new quirks to give them. A back-to-front number on the door; a drainpipe that ran diagonally; a balcony without a window behind it. He would line up his peculiar, tipsy little houses and admire their idiosyncrasies, and feel a kind of satisfaction. Flawed like himself, every one of them. Rejects like himself – but made by him. Dreamt up by him, and turned into reality by him.

When he was released he'd taken the houses with him, in the box his teacher had found for them. He'd felt curiously attached to them, unwilling to leave them behind – but he'd shown them to nobody, not even Joel. Just bits and pieces, he'd said when Joel, who had come to pick him up, enquired what the box held. Nothing important.

It had stayed shut in the months following his release, while he'd pretended his way through Halloween and Christmas in Joel and Sarah's house, and hunted online from their small spare room for someplace to live, someplace to hide away while he tried to find himself. The box had travelled with him to Fairweather, again because he couldn't bring himself to abandon its contents, but he'd had no plans for them, none at all.

And look what had happened. He'd taken a chance with Olive, and she hadn't laughed, and the odd little houses had found favour. People were happy to pay for them, and Olive kept ordering more. Who would have imagined it?

And Fairweather, like his imperfect houses, was growing on him.

His old job and his current situation could hardly be more different. Then, his tools were his laptop and his brain, his workspace a sizeable desk in a comfortable, temperature-controlled open-plan office. Now he spent his days taming a jungle of a garden, or up a stepladder painting a ceiling, or shoving rods into a blocked drain, or whatever else he was called on to do. People were friendly and welcoming; he'd heard the sorry tale of Jimmy's fall from the ladder half a dozen times at least. You came at the right time, he was told, over and over. Great to have someone to call on again, they said.

And on days when nobody needed him, he made more little houses from driftwood, surrounded by a scatter of shavings, and occasionally joined by a cat called Skimbleshanks.

And he couldn't say he was unhappy here. Still a long way from happy, nowhere near that yet, but he felt he might be on the right road to get there.

There were things he missed, of course, from his old life. He missed the excitement of programming, the buzz of the race to outdo the competition, to come up with the most ingenious app, the most efficient operating system, the most user-friendly search engine. He missed the camaraderie and banter with his colleagues, the after-work drinks, the office celebrations when things went their way.

He missed other things too, like having someone to listen if he wanted to offload, someone to tell him to cop on when he needed to be told, someone to share his jubilation when things went well.

He missed being held, being kissed. He missed reaching for a warm body in the dark, or being reached for. He missed love, and all it had brought with it, before it had betrayed and destroyed him.

He was still ambushed, now and again, by memories of what had happened. They would descend without warning, always accompanied by a mix of shame and anger. They reminded him of why he'd fled, why he'd felt the need to distance himself from everything familiar.

But on the whole, he was doing OK in Fairweather.

He felt his landlady was warming to him. The work he'd done in the garden had gone down well. He could see the mix of emotions in her face when she'd come over to thank him, and he thought he could understand it. He figured it had stirred memories for her, seeing it come back to how it used to be.

Embarrassing to be caught that time he'd burnt the sausages though – he could have set the house on fire. She'd had good reason to bawl him out of it then but she hadn't said a word, and the pan had scrubbed up fine.

Cat wasn't too impressed with the sausages. He'd taken a sniff when Tom had offered them the following morning, and walked away.

He'd been back to the library a few times. He was rediscovering the joy of a good book after his years of no reading, but that wasn't the only reason he found himself returning frequently to the wooden cabin.

He'd brought back the poetry book, a few days after she'd left it by the gate, when the worst of his cold was over.

I found Skimbleshanks, he'd told her.

She'd smiled. *Are you better?*

Yes, all better now, thanks to your grandmother's excellent soup.

She makes it when anyone's sick.

My mum would tear up a slice of white bread and mash it into hot milk with brown sugar whenever we were poorly. Goody, she called it. Sounds weird but I loved it, real comfort mush.

Another time: What are you knitting?

A wrap for Olive. Her birthday is next month.

I thought a wrap was something you roll around

chicken. He knew what the other wrap was, but he missed no opportunity to make her smile.

I'd like to get Olive a present for her birthday. What do you suggest?

Ferrero Rocher. She loves them.

Another time: That Niall Williams book was good. My grandmother came from that part of Clare. We used to go on holidays there when I was a kid. I remember her telling us about when they got electricity in the village.

Gran remembers when it came here.

With each exchange, he felt like he was inching closer. Standing at a bookshelf, pretending to read, he would watch her bent head and the flash of her needles from the corner of his eye. The wool was the colour of green apples, the ball of it stowed in her cloth bag. Every now and again she'd pause to tug out a little more, and then the tiny click of metal on metal would resume.

He continued to encounter her occasionally on the cliff path. Hi, he'd say, and she would give her shy smile but never stop, and he would catch a drift of her peppery scent as she passed. Once, about to step onto the long beach from the path, he spotted her emerging alone from the sea in a red swimsuit, and bending to pick up a blue towel that was waiting with the rest of her things on the sand. He turned back, reluctant to approach her, sensing she might not welcome an encounter there.

If she could talk. If she could just talk to him. If he could just hear her voice.

She would wander into his head at odd moments, when he was bent over his carving, or guiding a roller full of paint along a wall. Whenever it happened, he let her in. She prompted his curiosity. She intrigued him. That was all. He wasn't looking for love. He didn't think he'd ever be capable of that kind of trust again.

Sometimes the cat showed up in the evenings and joined him on the couch as he read; other times it left him alone. He caught it padding upstairs once, and followed it, and found it sitting at the closed door of one of the other bedrooms. He opened the door and it walked in, and sniffed about in the corners before leaping onto the unmade bed.

After that he left the door of the room open, and it came and went from it. He remembered Olive telling him that it used to sleep on Hollie's bed. He wondered if cats knew when people died. Weren't they supposed to have some kind of psychic sense?

He and Joel still spoke regularly on the phone. It was Joel's birthday on the seventh of April, which fell this year on a Sunday. Joel had suggested meeting up on the day, somewhere between their two locations.

We could get lunch, he'd said, and Tom had agreed, but they had yet to decide on a venue.

Time to get moving, if he was to fit Olive in before his meeting with Fred. He pulled on his boots, not fully dried out since their last wetting but his only alternative was a pair of ancient runners that would be useless if it rained again. He really must invest in waterproof footwear, but he needed to get steadier work before that could happen.

He should have saved more when he'd had a chance. He'd thought he'd be working in tech till he retired, a fat salary landing in his bank account each month. More than he needed, far more, but he'd spent it as fast as he'd made it. An apartment in one of London's most expensive boroughs, designer suits, luxury holidays. In the aftermath of the nightmare the apartment was surrendered and the fancy suits went to charity, and the holidays stopped. His car, all £70,000 worth of it, was reclaimed by the boss who couldn't see him clear his desk fast enough.

He took his jacket from the hallstand. He packed up the latest houses and shooed the cat out the back door ahead of him. He'd long since given up locking the house when he left it – if a place like this wasn't safe, nowhere was.

He made his way down the garden on the stepping

stones that were now clearly visible, the stones he'd scrubbed clean with a wire brush he'd found in the garage. A man he didn't recognise emerged from the library as he passed the gap in the hedge. Tom called a hello, and it was returned. He debated briefly dropping in on Lil, and decided against it. He should at least have a book with him, pretend he had a reason for appearing.

He strode along the cliff path, trying to ignore the cold dampness in his feet. A woman came towards him in a blue padded jacket, her pace more leisurely than his. Out for her constitutional. She smiled up at him as she passed. The tip of her nose was pink. 'Morning,' she said. 'Chilly one.'

'It is,' he agreed, but this kind of day he didn't mind, with no rain or wind, and the sea like glass below him.

Olive was alone in the shop, looking very pregnant in her yellow sweater. Was her face beginning to look a little puffy too? 'How are you doing?'

'Couldn't be better,' she told him cheerfully, 'if you don't count heartburn, and running to the loo a dozen times a day, and a craving for salami, and liquorice tea. Oh, and wanting to throw up if I get even a whiff of coffee – Fred is banned from drinking it in the house. Other than that, I'm flying it.'

'Glad to hear it.' He handed over his latest carvings.

'Oh good.' She lifted out a house from the bag and turned it upside down – checking, he knew, for the signature she'd insisted on. You must sign them, she'd said, it gives them extra status – so now he etched a small *TMcL* on the base of each one. He felt a bit foolish doing it, but she was the boss.

She set them one by one on the counter. 'I don't know how you do it, Tom. The only time I take up a block of wood is to throw it on the fire.'

'Well, I'm sure there's plenty of stuff you can do that I can't. I'd be a hopeless shopkeeper, for one.'

'I grew up in a shop in Galway,' she told him, arranging the houses in a curve. 'A little family-run corner shop, part grocery, part newsagent, part deli. My brothers and I helped out from an early age. Mam finally retired last year – Dad died a long time ago – and one of my brothers took over. What do your parents do?'

The question caught him off-guard. 'My father was a doctor,' he said quickly. 'My mother was a teacher. Both dead now.'

It wasn't exactly a lie. His father might as well be dead.

'Oh, I'm so sorry to hear that. They must have died young.'

He nodded. 'Cancer.'

'Both of them? How sad.'

He needed to change this subject. 'So you moved to Fairweather when you got married?'

'A bit before that. The shop came first, twenty-one years ago this autumn. We were engaged at the time, and we got married the following year, but I'm still considered a blow-in.'

The door opened just then with its usual tinkle, and a man entered. 'God save all here,' he called cheerily. Older, sixties or more. Weatherbeaten face beneath a grey knitted hat. Yellow oilskin jacket, trousers tucked into green wellingtons. Carrying a newspaper-wrapped bundle.

'There you are,' Olive said. 'I was hoping you'd show up. Tom, you're finally getting to meet my lovely father-in-law, Mark Purcell. Mark, Tom is the handyman I told you about, renting Noonans' place.'

'Ah, yes.' The man offered his hand. 'Your fame has gone before you. And you're the one who makes those quare things too,' indicating the houses.

'I am.'

'You're very welcome to Fairweather. You chose the best part of Kerry – didn't he, Olive?'

'He certainly did.'

He winked at Tom. 'Did she tell you she's a foreigner from Galway?'

'She did, just now.'

'We're thinking of granting her citizenship.'

'Get away – you've been telling me that for the past twenty years.'

'And one day it will happen.' He passed her his bundle. 'Two for the pan.'

'You're as good.' She got to her feet. 'Mackerel,' she told Tom. 'He's Fairweather's most enthusiastic fisherman. Hang on till I put them in the fridge.' She disappeared behind a door, leaving the men alone.

'You fish from here?' Tom enquired.

'I do. I have a little red rowboat at the pier. I don't take her out far, just around the harbour.'

'I've seen that boat. Do you go out a lot?'

'Most mornings for a couple of hours, unless the weather's too bad. You like to eat the mackerel?'

'I do, but I've never taken a whole one apart. I'm a fan of the fishmonger's fillet that I can just throw on the pan.'

'Ha – same here. Wouldn't know what to cut out and what to keep from the lads I pull up.'

'He lives on beans on toast,' Olive called from the other room. 'Imagine, and a world of fresh fish for him to eat. Only time he has a proper dinner is when he comes to us on Sundays.'

'Excuse me – I'll have you know that I have spaghetti hoops on toast every other night.'

'Oh, shush. You're a disgrace.'

The easy affection between them was evident. Tom thought of the bond he'd enjoyed with his father. They'd been close, as close as a father and son could be. Closer after Tom's mother died.

He hadn't had a conversation with his father in months.

Never mention him again. He's dead to me.

'You're welcome to join me any morning.'

He pulled himself out of his past. 'Sorry?'

'On the boat,' Mark said. 'Any morning you feel like it. Take my number, and give a shout when the mood is on you.'

'Thanks, I'd like that.' He added the new contact to his phone. 'Do you have a spare rod?' He thought he might enjoy a bit of fishing.

'Sure do – I take the tourists out in the summer, earn my beer money. I head out early, around eight.'

'Fine by me.'

'I'm putting the kettle on,' Olive called. 'Tea in a minute.'

Tom checked his watch. 'I'll pass, thanks. I have

a few things to do.' Time to check out her husband's secret mad idea. 'I'll take you up on that offer sometime,' he told Mark.

'Do that. Be seeing you.'

'See you soon,' Olive echoed.

He hated that he'd lied to her about his father having died. The lie nagged at him like a toothache. He shouldn't have said died, he should have said estranged, or emigrated, or anything less final than dead.

Through the pub window he saw a man sitting on a stool at the far end of the bar, an open newspaper spread out before him, a mug at his elbow. Tom rapped on the glass, and the man looked up.

A bolt was slid across, the door opened. 'Tom?'

'That's right.'

'Fred Purcell. Thanks for coming.' Bearded. Smiling. Big nose. He slid the bolt back into place. 'Have to keep it locked, or the mob will descend. Grab a stool.' He indicated his mug. 'Can I get you a coffee?'

'I'd love one, thanks. Olive tells me she's banned it in your house.'

'She has. I'm a deprived man.' He fed a pod into the machine.

'Congratulations, by the way.'

'Thanks.' He poured milk into a small jug and

placed it and a stainless-steel dish full of sugar sachets before Tom. 'We have an adopted daughter,' he said, adding a serviette and a spoon. 'Olive probably told you.'

'She did.' She'd mentioned the daughter, but not the adopted part.

'She'll be twelve in May.' He set the coffee before Tom and resumed his seat, lifting his own mug to cradle it in both hands. 'We haven't a great history. Ollie lost five when they were on the way.'

Tom stared at him. '*Five?* Jesus.'

'She didn't tell you that, no?'

'No. Sorry to hear that. Must have been tough.' Her first baby, after – how many years of marriage had she said? Around twenty, he thought. 'Hope all goes well.'

'Thanks. This one's lasted the longest, so fingers crossed.' He folded his newspaper, ran the side of his hand along the fold. 'You got kids yourself?'

Tom shook his head. 'Only a niece and nephew, my brother's.'

'You're young. Time enough.'

Vivienne hadn't wanted children. Tom had secretly hoped to change her mind, once they were married. He lifted his mug too quickly, causing a small splash that he blotted with his serviette.

'So what brings you to Fairweather, Tom?'

The anticipated question. 'Fresh start,' he said, like he'd been telling anyone else who'd asked. 'Broke up with a woman, was made redundant, all in the one week. Wanted to get away.' All technically true, and roughly a quarter of the full story.

'You know anyone before coming here?'

'Not a soul.'

'Settling in?'

'Yeah, I like it.'

'Coping with Beth?' A raised eyebrow, a crooked grin.

'She's fine. Her bark's worse than her bite.'

'True for you. Underneath that crusty exterior she's got a good soul, and Lil's a sweetheart.'

Her name conjured up hair that curled, and dark eyes, and a tiny careful smile, and the dimple it created. Olive had called her a sweetheart too.

Fred tapped fingers on the counter. 'Good to have that house lived in again. I'm sure Beth was looking after it, but a house needs people in it.' He got to his feet. 'Right, before I hit you with my big idea, I need a refill. How are you doing?'

'I'm OK.'

While he waited, Tom had a look around. The pub wasn't big. A square space with dark red padded benches against two of the rough whitewashed walls. Half a dozen tables, a scattering of stools.

Cushions set into the two wide windowsills. A pine floor, mellow with age. A stone fireplace at the end with a coal fire already alight, a beam set into the wall above it for a mantelpiece, a large clock above that. A framed sports jersey in the Kerry colours hanging off to the side.

Fred reclaimed his seat, added milk and sugar to his mug. 'OK, here's the thing. Olive's birthday is next month, the twenty-first of April – actually falls on Easter Sunday this year – and I was wondering if you could make her a clock.'

'A clock?'

'Yeah. I was thinking of a grandfather clock.'

Tom laughed.

Fred smiled. 'Yup, I had a feeling that was what you might say.'

He couldn't be serious. 'You do know I'm not a clockmaker, right?'

'I do, yes. It's just that Olive has always had a thing for clocks. She got me that one' – pointing – 'and our house is full of them, one in every room, two in some. I was trying to come up with an idea for her present, and I want it to be a bit special this year, because of the baby, and she made some remark one night … You know how she loves your small houses?'

'Well, yeah—'

'And the way they're all a bit – sorry, but a bit wonky.'

'They are. The first was an accident, and after that I just kept it up.'

'Fair play. Well, I thought you might be able to translate that into a clock. A kind of giant house, except not a house.'

'Not a house, a clock.'

'Exactly.'

'Not a tiny house, a giant clock.'

'That's it. A giant wonky clock.' He smiled. 'I warned you it was mad. I have no idea what's involved in making a clock, but I thought since you're creative, you might want to give it a go.'

Tom lifted his mug, lowered it. As ideas went, it was pretty insane. He'd never made a clock, large or small. He could cut a shelf to fit an alcove. Thanks to Joel, he could fashion a simple piece of furniture – a free-standing bookshelf, a blanket or toy chest, a bench. He had no problem putting a flat-packed whatever together, but this was entirely different. This was a clock, a working clock, from scratch. Insane.

And yet … it was for Olive, who was pregnant after five tragedies. And she had a thing about clocks, and her birthday was approaching.

'I might,' he said slowly.

'You might give it a shot?'

'I might.'

It would be a challenge, a new endeavour, and one he found himself willing – no, *wanting* – to explore. He'd always been a quick learner – why couldn't he learn this? He felt the same buzz starting up inside him that he remembered from his tech days, when a fresh assignment was presented to them. He felt something unfurl that had lain dormant inside him for half a year. *Just because you've never done it doesn't mean you can't.* Something his boss had often said to them, a kind of mantra.

How hard could it be to make a clock? He could look up videos on YouTube – everything was on there. He could make a sketch, hunt down whatever materials he needed. Carve a numbered face and hands, and a pendulum. Put a frame of sorts together, misaligned but somehow stable – he'd have to figure out that part too.

And if he pulled it off – he *would* pull it off – he'd paint it in bright colours. She liked bright colours.

'Leave it with me,' he said. 'I'll have a think. I'll do some research.' He drained his mug and stood up. 'Give me a few days to figure out if I can do it. What date did you say her birthday was?'

'The twenty-first of next month.'

Roughly six weeks. Enough time to make a few mistakes along the way. 'I'll get back to you as soon as I can.'

'Brilliant.' Fred glanced at his watch. 'Another coffee before you go?'

'No thanks – I need to get moving.'

'One more thing,' Fred said at the door. 'If Olive asks, I'll have to say I met you – that woman can smell a lie from miles off. I'll tell her you dropped in for a coffee this morning, so you can say the same.'

'Will do. Good to finally meet you.'

'Likewise. Thanks, Tom – I'll live in hope.'

Making his way back down the street, he began to plan it, began to see it taking shape in his head. Already committed, already determined to make it happen.

On this cold day, there were few about. A man standing cross-armed in the hardware-shop doorway nodded at him. An older woman passed with a little grey dog. A younger one wheeled a bike, on the rear of which perched a tot in a wicker seat, swaddled in a padded outfit and fleecy hat. Winter in Fairweather, the long quiet lull before summer cranked the town back into life.

On his return to the cliff path, stamping his feet to warm them, he passed a shop with sportswear in the window, along with a big red *Sale* sign. On impulse, he pushed in the door.

'Swimming shorts,' he said to the skinny teen behind the counter, and was directed to a rail at the rear of the store where only a handful hung, all reduced to a fraction of their original cost. Last summer's leftovers, not in big demand in March. He went through them and chose the only pair that looked like they'd fit. They were navy, and under a tenner.

'You want to try them on?'

He shook his head and paid. Why was he even buying them?

She'd worn a red swimsuit.

He was still convinced that swimming in Ireland in March was barmy, but for some reason he was feeling reckless.

She'd come out of the sea and reached for a blue towel.

He'd barely left the shop when the rain came. He wished again that his jacket had a hood as he turned onto the lane that led to the small town beach.

From the cliff path he saw Mark's little red boat, bobbing by the pier. The rain grew heavier while he plodded along resignedly. Definitely rained more in the west. He broke into a slow jog as he neared the gate.

He left the new shorts on the kitchen table. He shrugged off his jacket and draped it over the radiator. He towelled his hair dry and shoved it sideways with his fingers. He found the two books he'd borrowed five days earlier, one read, the other having lost him after twenty pages. He tucked them under his arm and ran through the rain to the library.

She sat at the desk as always, again the sole occupant of the cabin. She set aside her book at his entrance. Her hair was loose. She wore a light grey sweater that made her eyes look darker.

'Hi.' He set his two volumes on her desk. 'Bringing these back. I failed with that one, I'm afraid, but the other was good.' He always felt obliged to report his progress to her.

She picked up her pen. *No jacket in the rain?*

'It's too wet. It got drenched on the way home from town – and it's the only one I have.'

No hat?

'No. I keep forgetting to get myself a hat. Does it always rain so much here?'

Not always.

'Well, that's good to know. I'll live in hope.'

You want another Jo Nesbø?

She remembered he'd taken one out on his first visit. Maybe she remembered what everyone read. 'Sure, if you have one.'

In response she went to the shelves and found it, and held it out for his approval. 'Great, thanks.' While she stamped it, he indicated the open book on the desk. 'What's that?'

She lifted it, and he read *The Catcher in the Rye*, and he thought of the book he'd pulled out from between the couch cushions in her house. *Property of Hollie Noonan.*

'Any good?'

I like it. It's for a book club – and he recalled Olive telling him about the club that met in the library. He'd wondered, when she'd said Lil was a member, how she could participate without a voice.

'I met Fred this morning,' he told her, 'and Mark. Mark's offered to take me out in his boat.'

You should go.

'I will. I bought togs today too. I have a mad notion I'd like a swim.'

You don't normally swim this time of year?

'No – but there's a first time for everything, right?'

Very cold if you're not used to it.

'Duly noted.'

She was writing again. He waited.

Gran says you might help with my new phone.

'What's up with it?'

I can't figure out how to transfer things from my old one.

'They didn't do it for you in the shop?'

I bought it online.

Of course she did. No face-to-face if she could avoid it. Must make life tricky.

'No problem, I can sort it for you. Do you have the two phones here?'

She shook her head. *I'm charging the new one in the house.*

He was about to suggest that she drop them over to him when he remembered the grandmother telling him that Lil hadn't been inside her family home since moving next door. She can't bring herself to come back, she'd said. He remembered the note stuck into the back gate, the book of poems left by the front gate. It seemed she was incapable of even entering the garden.

'I could come by this evening.'

That would be great.

They ate at six, the grandmother had told him. 'Around seven?'

Perfect, thank you.

Back in the house he changed into dry clothes and went off to replace a broken socket, and put up a TV bracket. Jobs done, he returned home and lit the fire and opened *The Catcher in the Rye* – and at seven o'clock precisely, having dined on fish fingers and beans, he presented himself at the neighbouring front door.

Beth answered. 'Tom, thank you for doing this. I'm afraid neither of us is very technically minded. Lil could have got someone else to help, but since you were right next door I suggested she ask you. She's in the kitchen, through there.'

The hall had an old wooden floor that continued into the kitchen. He saw a dresser, and copper pans hanging from a rail, and Lil in the act of plugging in a kettle. At the sight of him she held up a teapot and a cafetière. Her two years of silence had taught her how to get her message across without words.

'Coffee would be great, thanks.'

Two phones sat side by side on the table. He went to work as she moved about. It was warm in the room. He caught a lingering savoury smell, and guessed their dinner had been a lot more appetising than his. There was a white cloth on the table – yes, this house would have a tablecloth – and a pair of silver candlesticks holding the stubs of cream candles. A pale blue china cup and saucer were placed before him.

Waiting for an app to load, he watched Lil take a jug from the fridge. She caught his eye for an instant before dropping her gaze. He felt a charge, small but definite.

No. Not going there. Couldn't go there.

'Nearly finished. Want me to add my name to your contacts, in case you have any issues?'

A nod, so he did. A new connection between them. She poured coffee as he wiped data from the old phone. A plate of biscuits appeared that looked homemade.

'Who's the baker?'

Gran. She was a domestic science teacher.

Made sense. She'd have no problem keeping a class in line. The coffee was good, the biscuits gingery. He slid both phones across the table. 'All done.'

She smiled her thanks and picked up the new phone and began tapping. As he drained his cup and got to his feet he heard a ping in his pocket.

Thank you, she'd texted. *What do I owe?*

Bill's in the post. He sent it back and got another smile. She took biscuits from the plate and packed them into a small freezer bag and offered them to him.

'Thanks, don't mind if I do.'

He wished her goodnight and left. He added her to his contacts. *Lil Noonan*, he typed, and then deleted the surname. She was the only Lil he knew.

Two days later he came back from a job and found a bag hanging from the small front gate. He opened it and took out a hat – woolly, turquoise – and a slip of paper fell from it.

Your bill never arrived, so I made this instead. Hope it fits. Hope you like the colour.

It fitted. He liked the colour. *Thank you for the hat*, he texted. *Just what I needed* – and a minute later his phone pinged.

You're welcome, Tom.

Tom.

Two Years Earlier

The eighteenth of August. Three years to the day since they'd met. Joel and Sarah were throwing a party in their back garden to celebrate their third anniversary. A small crowd was assembled: Tom and Vivienne, Tom and Joel's father, Sarah's sister and her husband, a couple of Sarah's teaching colleagues, a few neighbours.

The sun shone. Joel and Sarah's son Harry, a year and ten months, dozed on a blanket under a beach umbrella that had been stuck into the grass. Sarah, heavily pregnant with their second child, sat on a nearby garden seat, nursing a glass of fizzy water with a slice of lime in it. Joel manned the barbecue and drank a can of beer with his father.

Vivienne was in pale pink, a simple cotton shift dress that showed off her tan. They'd returned the previous day from a ten-day holiday in Jamaica, flying out from London but back to Dublin so they could take in this event. They were staying with Tom's father as usual.

On this occasion Tom would have been happy to book a hotel room for them in Kildare, but Vivienne had insisted they stay where they always stayed. You know I love that house, she said, and George enjoys having us around.

She did love the house. She was charmed with its old elegance and exclusive location. People didn't move out of their square; houses were handed down through the generations, and Tom knew every family. He wondered if Vivienne was hoping his father would leave the property to them, and then he felt disloyal for the thought. He'd love it himself – but of course he and Joel would inherit it equally. Not that they were going to be orphaned anytime soon – at sixty-one, George McLysaght was a man in his prime.

Life was good. Work was challenging, with long hours and frequent travelling, but the rewards were gratifying, from the salary to the company Porsche to the annual leave. He would happily have spent all his holidays on their deck in London – he travelled enough with work – but Vivienne liked her sunshine and *balmy seas, so they'd spent the last two Christmases in the Caribbean, and the previous summer they'd flown to Mauritius, and he'd sat in the shade with crosswords and his iPad while she'd flicked through magazines and sipped cocktails on her sunbed.*

They rowed, like every couple. She flirted with his friends, and occasionally even with his father. When Tom pulled her up on it she'd laugh, insisting there was no harm in it. It's just a bit of fun, she'd say, but still he wished she wouldn't.

She complained about his frequent business trips, and his occasional Thursday nights out with work colleagues. She called him stingy when he baulked at paying more than thirty pounds for a supermarket bottle of wine.

She never did the washing-up. She constantly left taps running. Her hair clogged the shower drain. He would find her clothes strewn on the bedroom floor, and used makeup-remover pads on the side of the bathroom sink, and half-empty water bottles everywhere. Once, a rogue mascara wand in the laundry basket made it into the wash and ruined two of his shirts.

She took the Porsche without asking him and scraped the side of it against a low wall, and sulked when he got mad. She moved in with her mother for two days when he made the mistake of renewing her gym membership as a Valentine's Day present.

But on the whole it was fine. They were fine. They were more than fine: they were great. After three years she still coloured his days, gladdened his heart. He missed her when they were apart. She floated often into his head at work, and brought a leap of joy with her. He was the luckiest man in the world.

And today the sun was shining, and he was buzzing nicely with beer, and she was beautiful in her pink dress, with matching polish on her toenails, and three years ago to the day he'd looked behind him in a church and seen a lime green hat.

And today he was going to do it.

He set his beer can on the low wall that separated the patio of Joel's house from the rest of the garden. He edged away from the little group – Sarah's sister, the couple from next door – who were chatting with Vivienne, and he went inside and found his jacket, and took what he needed from the pocket.

He became aware of his heartbeat, suddenly thumping in his ears. This was it.

He returned to the garden and retrieved his beer and resumed his position beside Vivienne. She was telling the others about the Jamaican resort they'd stayed in, their bungalow with its private infinity pool. He waited for a break in the conversation, for a pause that would let him in. Over Vivienne's shoulder he could see his father, now in conversation with one of Sarah's teacher friends. Making her laugh, reaching to swat at something – a bee? – that was hovering around her.

He zoned back to his group. 'Sorry,' he said, into the middle of someone's sentence. 'Sorry, can I interrupt?'

They looked at him. He dropped to one knee too abruptly, knocking it painfully against the ground. Someone drew a sharp breath. He produced the velvet box, opened it with a hand that had started to shake. 'Vivienne Chambers, will you marry me?' he asked, presenting the box to her. Another indrawn breath. He was dimly aware that every conversation had halted, and all eyes were now on him and Vivienne.

She didn't react, didn't move. She looked from him to the box, and back to him, her expression blank. For a few seconds that felt like years, he was gripped by terror. His knee throbbed. She was going to turn him down.

And then she smiled.

'Yes,' she said simply, and he got to his feet and took out the ring that had cost him a small fortune, the ring he'd brought with him to Jamaica and home again, and slipped it on her finger. And everyone clapped, and everyone hugged them and admired the ring, and he was filled with elation as he found her other hand and held on.

Beth

'Alright for you?' the girl asked, holding up a mirror to the rear of Beth's head, tilting it this way and the other. 'Happy with that?'

'Fine, thank you,' Beth said crisply. She had never understood this palaver of mirrors, the back view of her head being of no concern whatsoever to her. She endured the soft brush that was whisked over her face and neck, the performance of her cape being removed, the production of her coat and hat, the pantomime of getting her into both. The girl hoping for a tip, of course, which Beth duly handed over. Two euro, more than enough for this young replacement for Beth's usual Ann, who'd called in sick that morning.

'Ah, you're too good,' the girl said, slipping the coin into the tiny bag whose strap crossed her body. Her close-fitting top left nothing to the imagination, her swollen belly proclaiming her pregnancy to the whole of Fairweather, the protruding knob of her navel clearly outlined through the fabric. At least Olive was a little more discreet.

Crossing the street outside, she wondered why

some people felt the need to fill every second with talk, as if they were terrified of a bit of silence. That girl, Cynthia – or was it Christine? – had been irritatingly chatty, prattling on about the weather, asking nonsensical questions about Beth's holiday plans – holiday plans, in March! – talking about some film she'd seen that Beth hadn't the slightest interest in. Ann knew better, just laid a stack of magazines in front of Beth and left her to them.

To the butcher next, for pork chops and chicken fillets that would go into the freezer for later in the week. She wasn't a big fan of pork, but Lil enjoyed a chop with some apple sauce. 'How much?' she asked the butcher, and tutted a little before paying up. How expensive everything had become.

Not that she couldn't afford it. Thankfully, Gerry had made some very prudent investments that were still reaping benefits, and she was also paid a perfectly adequate pension from her years of teaching.

Lil had no financial worries either, with her father having made a small fortune just two years before his death, when he'd sold the online estate agency he'd launched a decade earlier. The profit had paid off their mortgage, and he was left with a substantial sum that was earmarked for his and Maria's retirement, but which Lil had instead inherited.

Might be better, Beth often thought, if her granddaughter was forced to find a salaried job to make ends meet, but as it was, Lil could stay earning nothing behind the desk in the library for as long as she chose. It gave her something to do, it put a shape on her days – but Beth so wished it were otherwise.

She proceeded from the butcher to the fishmonger for two mackerel. 'Want me to prepare them for you?' the lad behind the counter asked.

He was new, easily known. 'I've been preparing fish since before you were born,' she replied, perhaps a little more tartly than was warranted. Her father had shown her how, when he was nurturing her love of cooking in her teens. A good sharp knife and a steady hand, he'd said, all you need.

The boy wrapped the fish silently and took her money with muttered thanks. Offended by her sharp tone, no doubt – young people were so easily put out now. To soften the air between them she asked if he was a brother of a girl she'd taught. He had to be: the similarity was remarkable.

'She's my mother,' he told her, and Beth felt every one of her seventy-two years. Could it really be that long since Laura McDermott had been her student? Evidently it could, the years merging together all too readily as she left them behind.

'Tell her Mrs Sullivan says hello,' she replied, and felt his eyes on her as she left the shop. Laughing with his mother later, probably, when he reported Beth's mistake. Laura, now that she thought about it, had been a right smart little madam at times.

Back on the street she halted outside the gift shop. She needed notelets, and more candles. No dinner table was complete without candles, and she liked the beeswax ones Olive sold. She was about to go in when her tenant's little houses caught her eye in the window.

They were certainly colourful. Olive had lined them up in a tipsy row of eight. *Handmade locally by Tom McLysaght*, her accompanying sign said. The price had caused Beth to raise an eyebrow the first time she'd seen it, but evidently people were prepared to pay it. Flying out the door, Olive had reported.

Beth had never been drawn to such knick-knacks, but Hollie would have adored them. Mad about stuff like that, any little miniature. Arranged on every surface, covering every horizontal space in her room. Collected since childhood, friends adding more on each birthday, new shelves put up to house them.

Nightmare dust-collectors, drove Maria mad. After the accident, Beth had packed them all into boxes and brought them to her house, not knowing what else to do with them. Not wishing to display them, but unable to part with them. There they still were, in an unopened stack on top of the spare-room wardrobe.

She entered the shop and saw nobody behind the counter, so she found what she wanted and thumbed through a basket of trinkets – key-rings, badges, tiny notebooks – until Olive appeared.

'Beth – you got your hair done. It's lovely.'

'Thank you. How are you feeling?'

'I'm fine,' Olive replied brightly. A little too brightly. 'All good,' she said, wrapping the candles in yellow tissue paper. 'Well, nearly all good.'

'What is it?'

'Oh, it's nothing – well, it's Nancy, she's still being difficult. I was hoping it would sort itself out, but it hasn't. She's moody and sulky, and downright insolent at times, which isn't a bit like her.'

'Perfectly normal, just a bit of jealousy. I remember Hollie kicking up when Lil came along.' But Hollie had been two: this little madam was nearly twelve, for Heaven's sake – and the baby had yet to arrive.

'I know, you're right. I'll just have to ignore it till it passes.'

'How is she with Fred?'

'Fred? He sees none of it – I'm with her a lot more

of the time.' She gave a small laugh as she took Beth's money. 'Oh, don't mind me – I'm probably a bit hormonal.'

Of course she was. Hormonal, anxious, seeing a problem where none existed.

She handed Beth her change. 'Have you invited Tom to the book club yet?'

Beth had completely forgotten. 'I called over to ask him, the night of the last meeting, but I got distracted – he'd burnt his dinner, he needed another frying pan – and it went out of my head. I'll see if he's there when I get home.' Her pan had been left by the back porch door a day later, which she'd taken to mean that he'd either rescued or replaced the other.

'He's a big hit,' Olive said. 'Several people have said good things about him.'

'So I believe.' He fixed my Hoover, Sally Furlong had told her in the library the previous Saturday. Didn't take him long at all. He's nice, isn't he?

She drove home feeling relieved and not a little surprised, that no mention had been made of this afternoon's cookery lesson. Either Olive hadn't been told about it, which Beth thought unlikely, or she'd decided to make no mention of it, which would be uncharacteristic. Olive had many good points, but discretion wasn't one of them.

After stowing her purchases she went next door and rang the bell, and got no reply. She was on the point of leaving when she became aware of music coming from the garage.

She crossed to the big door and rapped sharply on it with her key. After a second or two, the music stopped. She waited some more, and rapped again when nothing further happened. 'Hello?' she called. 'Are you in there?'

Footsteps approached from within. The big door rattled up slowly. 'Hello,' he said. He wore a jacket and a scarf and a blue-green woolly hat she hadn't seen before. His nose was pink-tipped. 'Sorry,' he said. 'I wasn't sure if I'd imagined your knock.'

'What are you doing in there?' she asked sharply. 'It's like a fridge. Are you trying to catch another chill?'

'I'm working,' he replied. 'I have to do it here.'

She frowned. 'Working? You mean making those little houses? Can't you do them in the kitchen?' Behind him she could see that he'd set up Killian's trestle table, and filled it with various bits and pieces. She saw little heaps of sawdust on the floor, and lengths of wood stacked by the wall, next to the surfboards that she hadn't been able to let go. The sight of them caused a squeeze in her chest. Lil hadn't surfed in over two years.

'No, this isn't the houses. I've been asked to … make something else. It's too big for the kitchen, and too messy.'

'For goodness' sake – you'll catch your death in there.'

'I've got layers on.' He lifted his jacket and pulled up the end of a sweater to reveal another beneath it. 'And I have heat.' He indicated a pathetic little heater plugged into the wall.

'That's not nearly enough. You look frozen.'

He tucked his hands into his armpits. 'The thing is, I've agreed to do this job, and there's really no other place I can work on it.'

'I have a fan heater I can let you have. Come back with me now and take it. Are there two sockets, or do you need an extension lead?'

'No, there are two, but—'

She didn't wait for buts. 'Come with me,' she ordered, and he accompanied her next door, where she retrieved from a shelf in the back porch the little heater she used for her feet when she did duty behind the desk on chilly Saturday mornings. His need, she felt, was greater than hers. She'd wear two pairs of socks under her boots, and nobody would be any the wiser.

'Make sure you use both heaters,' she instructed. 'You need to keep warm.'

'I will, thanks.'

She wondered suddenly if he had family, people he kept in touch with. She wasn't aware of anyone having been to visit him since his arrival. What if he had an accident, or became seriously ill while he was here? She wouldn't have a clue who to contact. She knew so little about him.

'I should have a number,' she said, 'in case anything happens to you. Someone I could call in an emergency.'

A beat passed. 'I can give you my brother's number. I'll text it to you.'

'Do.' At least he had someone. She suddenly remembered the reason for her visit to him. 'There's a book club; a few of us meet once a month in the library. We were wondering if you'd care to join us.'

'A book club,' he repeated, the colour rising a little in his face. 'Well – thank you.'

He looked a little trapped. 'Olive is a member,' she said. 'It was her idea to invite you. She thought you might like it.'

'OK … thanks.'

Was that a yes or a no? 'We're reading *The Catcher in the Rye* for the next meeting, Lil's choice. Have you read it?'

His cheeks went slightly pinker. 'Yes,' he said, 'I finished it a couple of nights ago.'

'That's convenient. So you'll join us then? This day fortnight, seven o'clock.'

'Yeah, OK, I will. Thank you. And thanks for this,' indicating the heater. He turned to leave, and stopped. 'It was kind of you,' he said, 'to bring me the soup that time. I'm not sure I thanked you properly.'

'It was nothing,' she said. 'Nothing at all.'

'It wasn't nothing,' he replied. 'Not to me.'

She saw him out and watched him returning to his cold garage. She wondered what he was making that was too big to work on in the kitchen. A few minutes later, her phone beeped with a text message.

My brother is Joel McLysaght, he'd written, and followed it with a number. She copied the details into her phone – *Tom's brother Joel* she called him – and turned her thoughts to half past four.

She still regarded it as bordering on ludicrous, teaching a man of seventy to cook. She had no expectation that he would ever put what she taught him into practice. He'd treat it as a big joke, like he treated everything. He'd let it all in one ear and out the other, and go back to his convenience foods. Still, it would please Olive, and that was enough.

She hoped her tenant wouldn't see him pulling up

outside, and come to the wrong conclusion. She also hoped fervently that Mark Purcell wouldn't think she'd got her hair done because he was coming – and he'd better not bring flowers, or any of that nonsense.

He didn't bring flowers. He brought a book.

'It belonged to my grandfather,' he said. 'I thought you might like it.'

It was worn and battered, with a cracked brown leather spine and a faded pattern of maroon and gold swirls front and back. Its parchment pages were rough-edged, and mottled with age. Its red woven bookmark was darkened and threadbare, but still intact. Even without lifting the volume to her nose she could smell the wonderful musk of it. She smelt wood smoke and candle stubs and port wine and tobacco and camphor and boot polish. She smelt history, and yellowed newspapers, and the inside of a very old mahogany desk.

Its title had worn off the spine. She opened it and saw that it was *Little Dorrit*, and that it had been printed in 1857.

1857. The year *Little Dorrit* was published.

She looked up. 'This is a first edition.'

'Is it?'

How could he not be aware of that? She thrust it back at him. 'I can't possibly accept it: it's far too

valuable. There was no need to bring me anything.'
It killed her, just killed her, to return it.

'It's just a thank you, in return for doing this.'

She couldn't take the credit. 'If you want to thank anyone,' she said, 'thank Olive. It's her birthday present to you. Didn't she explain that?'

His expression changed. 'It's *Olive's* present? I thought ...'

'What did you think?'

'Well,' he said slowly, 'I thought this was your idea, to be honest.'

He thought Beth had offered to give him cookery lessons. He thought it was her gift. He must have taken Olive up wrong. Suddenly, seeing the effect they'd had on him, she wished the words unsaid. 'Well, it was Olive's idea, but I'm happy to do it.'

His frown stayed in place. 'May I ask if she paid you, Beth?'

Guilt washed over her. Why had she opened her mouth? 'I'd rather not go into that,' she said, which of course answered his question. 'Mark, please take back your book. I appreciate the gesture, it's very kind of you, but it's much too generous.' He'd offered it to her as a thank-you, when he'd thought she was gifting him the lessons – how could she possibly keep it?

Still he made no move to take it. 'I'd prefer you to keep it, Beth. It's wasted on me – I'm not that big on Dickens, whatever edition it is, and it's clear you'd appreciate it a lot more.'

How stubborn he was. She wanted to protest, still feeling as if she was taking it under false pretences. She also wanted badly to keep it. She fought a brief inner battle.

'Beth, it's not a big deal. Just take it. Go on.'

She weakened. She gave in. 'Thank you,' she said. 'It's beautiful.' How inadequate the words were. How undeserving of it she felt. How chastened.

'You're very welcome. I'm glad it's gone to a good home. Now, as long as I'm here, I suppose we'll go ahead.'

'Of course we will.' She sent him upstairs to wash his hands. While he was gone she ran her fingertips over the worn cover, imagining all the hands that had touched it since 1857. She adored Dickens. She loved the richness of his language, and the humour and pathos of his stories, and his memorable characters, his rogues and his villains and his heroes. She'd read and reread them all, and returned regularly for more.

The book was possibly the best gift she'd ever got. She'd set her current book to one side – *The Catcher in the Rye*, not her kind of thing at all – and make a start on this one tonight.

His face though. How it had fallen. How she had made it fall. She wished more than anything for that not to have happened. She wished she knew how to be less outspoken, and more thoughtful.

He was kind, she realised. He was so much kinder than her.

He returned, his sleeves rolled. 'I washed my face too,' he said solemnly, 'just to be on the safe side,' and she had to laugh. She'd try to make it up to him, make the lessons as enjoyable as she could.

'Now pay attention,' she told him, careful to keep her tone light. 'You catch fish, which is one of the healthiest foods you can eat, but you need to know how to prepare it. Once you have that done, you could just fry it on the pan, but I'm going to show you how to make fish cakes, so you have another option. I have two mackerel here. I'll prepare the first, and you can do the second.'

'Fair enough' – and he did pay attention, and he made a pretty good attempt when it was his turn, and he promised to invest in a knife like Beth's, and practise until he got it right. Maybe, after all, he was taking it seriously.

Together they diced and fried onions, and she

showed him how to poach and flake the fish, and he peeled and chopped the potatoes she'd steamed that morning. And it was quite pleasant, she found, to step into the role of teacher again, particularly with a student who showed such an unexpected willingness to learn.

And as they worked, he talked. Of course he did.

'I should have made more of an effort to cook after Catriona died. The boys could have done with healthier meals, but I was still out on the road, and I used that as an excuse. I'm afraid we lived mostly on frozen pizzas and takeaways when it was just the three of us, although I did rise to the odd mixed grill on my days off. And after they both moved out, there didn't seem to be any point in doing dinner for just me.'

Beth tipped the chopped-up potatoes into the bowl that already held the rest of the ingredients. 'There's always a point. After Gerry died, I went on making dinner every night. You have to eat proper meals to stay healthy. Remember that you got cancer – your poor diet may well have contributed to that.'

'True, but I bounced back. You know what they say, Beth – only the good die young.'

And after that there was silence, and she concentrated on turning the mixture over and over.

Potatoes and onions and fish tumbled about while the clock on the wall seemed to tick more loudly. 'Can you get me the salt and pepper? They're by the cooker.'

He handed her the cellars. 'I'm sorry. Truly I am, Beth. You know I'm always talking nonsense.'

She looked up and saw the remorse in his face. 'You should think,' she said quietly, 'before you speak. It might be nonsense, but it can still hurt.' And even as she was saying it, she thought again of his face falling earlier, of her own words that had caused hurt.

'I know. You're right. I'm so sorry. What an awful thing to say.'

And because she wasn't blameless, and because they'd been having a pleasant time up to then, and because he'd presented her with a beautiful book, she decided to go a little easier on him.

'It's Maria's birthday next week,' she said. 'It always makes me more sensitive.'

'Ah,' he said softly. 'So it is. A month before Olive.'

She added salt and pepper silently. She mixed it in and set down her spoon. 'That's ready now. Can you pass the breadcrumbs?'

He didn't pass the breadcrumbs. He didn't move. 'I remember them going out to dinner together every year,' he said. 'Olive and Maria.'

'Yes …'

She remembered it too. Exactly a month between the birthdays, Maria's the twenty-first of March, Olive's the same date in April. Maria the older by a couple of years, which hadn't mattered a jot to them. They'd pick a day in between, usually the first Saturday in April. They'd get dressed up and head out, just the two of them. They never missed a year, even when Maria's girls were small, even after Nancy had come along.

'Remember when they decided to do an overnight,' he said, 'instead of just dinner? They wanted to really treat themselves.'

'It was Maria's fortieth. They booked into a hotel in Dingle. No, it wasn't Dingle.'

'Killarney,' he said. 'They went to Killarney.'

'That's right. And Olive got food poisoning.'

'She did. And the time they went to that Italian restaurant—'

'And there was a kitchen fire, and everyone was evacuated. I'd forgotten that.'

Silence fell again. A different silence.

'I don't know how you cope, Beth,' he said. 'If anything happened to either of my boys I don't think I could go on.'

'Of course you'd go on. You'd have to, for the one

who was left.' She wiped her hands on a cloth. 'Now, where are those breadcrumbs?'

And after that, things were better. Things were alright after that.

'I've met your tenant,' he told her. 'He was in the gift shop a while back when I dropped in. Seems like a nice fellow.'

'He's coming to the book club.'

'That's good. I was admiring the garden when I arrived. He did great clearing.'

'He did.' She scooped up a handful of the mix and showed him how to shape it into patties, and dip them in flour, then beaten egg, then breadcrumbs. 'I should never have let that garden get so out of hand. They'd have hated to see it like that.'

'You did the best you could, Beth. It's all we can do.'

He had a smudge of flour on his chin. There was a small splash of egg on the front of his shirt. His patties were rougher looking than hers, but she held her tongue. He'd improve with practice.

When he wasn't acting the clown, he was really rather nice.

They were frying the first batch of fishcakes when Lil returned from the library. A favour to Olive, Beth had told her. I felt I couldn't turn her down. She hoped she'd made it perfectly clear to her granddaughter that this hadn't been her idea.

'You might set the table,' Beth said to her. 'It won't be long now,' and Lil obediently began putting out placemats and cutlery.

Mark stayed to eat with them, of course. You could hardly teach a man how to cook a dish and then not let him taste it. In all the years Beth had known him, it was their first time to share a table. She realised with a small shock that she couldn't remember the last time she and Lil had had anyone to dinner – and he certainly made an entertaining guest.

'You wouldn't believe,' he said, 'what I've pulled from the sea. I could open a shop.' He reeled off a list that went from bicycle wheels and wellingtons to skateboards and heads of cabbage and baby buggies and a typewriter. Beth suspected he was making half of them up, but it didn't matter.

He told them how he'd met Olive when she was just a young girl, and he described her family's shop in Galway. He gave an account of a long-ago incident when a farmer had aimed a shotgun at him, after Mark had approached to ask for directions.

'Once he knew I wasn't planning to rob him, he was fine. Turned out he'd been robbed a few times, so he was taking no chances. He apologised and brought me into the house, and his wife made me tea. It gave me a terrible shock, though – I honestly thought I was a goner. I wasn't right for the rest of the day. Beth, these fishcakes are works of art, if I say so myself.'

'You'll have another.'

'I will so.' He told them other tales from his life on the road, tales of burst tyres and cranky shopkeepers and strange hitchhikers and damaged orders. It made a nice change to have company, a new speaker at the table. It was good for Lil too, to have someone else to look at, and listen to.

He offered to help with the washing-up. 'I promise to pay for all breakages,' he said, so she left him in the kitchen with Lil and climbed the stairs to brush her teeth, listening to the rumble of his deep voice, and the eruption of his laughter.

'Thank you,' he said when he was leaving. 'I've had a really nice time.'

'You'll get that knife?'

'I will, I promise. They'll come from miles away for a taste of my fishcakes. I may have to set up a stall on the prom.'

He was joking, of course – but she could see it. She could see the little stall, and his sign, and his patter that would have them queuing up. 'Are you free next week for the second lesson?'

'Are you sure?' he asked. 'Are you sure you want to do it, Beth?'

Her fault. Her and her careless tongue. 'Of course I'm sure.'

'In that case, what day suits you?'

'Wednesday again?' The day before Maria's birthday. She could use a distraction.

'Wednesday again. Same time?'

'Same time.'

Beef burgers, she was thinking, with blue cheese in them for the kick. She thought he'd like a burger. No bun, a colourful salad on the side instead, and maybe homemade chips. And he'd stay to eat it with them again.

'Thank you for the book,' she said. 'I truly appreciate it.'

'You're more than welcome. See you this day week.'

But he didn't. He didn't see her on the following Wednesday, because the second cookery lesson didn't happen then. What did happen was that he tripped as he stepped into his boat early on Wednesday morning, and he thumped his head on one of the seats, and knocked himself unconscious.

That was what happened.

Olive

The fright of it. She didn't need frights like that, not now. Not for the next two and a half months.

'Dad had an accident,' Fred said, turning up at the gift shop not half an hour after Olive opened it. Looking like he was about to faint, so drained of colour was his face. 'He's been brought to Tralee hospital. I'm going there now.'

Mark. She felt a swoop of fright, a wash of shock. Mark. 'What happened?'

'I'm not sure, he was in the boat … I'll ring you from the car – I need to go.'

'I'm coming,' she said, grabbing her bag, switching off the kettle. Flipping the sign on the door to *Closed*, turning the key. 'You want me to drive?'

'No – I'm OK.'

In the car he told her what he knew. It emerged in jerky little bursts as she squeezed her hands together. The news had come to him from Jack Dalton, who had a small café near the pier.

'Jack saw him passing on his way to the boat, around eight o'clock.'

She breathed in, breathed out. Let him be OK.

'He was found a little before nine, lying in the boat. It was still moored. A man going out to a trawler spotted him. He was unconscious.'

If the boat was still moored, whatever had happened had happened soon after eight. For the best part of an hour he'd been lying in his boat. Olive tried not to dwell on that, tried not to think of all the possible reasons – heart attack, brain haemorrhage, stroke – that might have led to this, but they were all her traitorous mind kept presenting to her, kept parading through her consciousness.

Heart attack. Brain haemorrhage. Stroke. And probably several more possible causes that her addled pregnant mind couldn't come up with.

They lapsed into silence. Fred turned on the radio, turned it off. The forty-five-minute journey to the hospital seemed endless. A pale sun shone. There had been frost in the night: the hedgerows still twinkled with it. She felt the hot lurch of heartburn, which had begun plaguing her in the last couple of weeks.

Heart attack. Brain haemorrhage. Stroke.

Aneurysm: there was a new one. Their next-door neighbour Beattie had died of an aneurysm when Olive was eight or nine. She remembered the huddles of people in Beattie's garden the following afternoon, when Beattie was being waked. She remembered her private fear for ages afterwards that one or both of her parents would suffer the same fate, would be fit and healthy and smiling like Beattie one day, and gone the next.

The hospital car park was full. They drove around for ten minutes before finding a space, Olive's fear blooming, filling every spare inch inside her. Nails pressing into palms, sweat prickling uncomfortably on the back of her neck, the familiar pressure on her bladder.

'He's having a CT scan,' a nurse told them, after they'd finally parked, and Olive had found a toilet, and they'd negotiated miles of corridors, an eternity of them, and eventually located the section he was in. 'We'll know more then.'

'How long will that take?' Fred asked.

'Not too long,' the nurse replied, which told them nothing at all. They were directed to wait on chairs that were uncomfortably hard in a corridor that was bright with skylights, and had lemon walls that featured, every so often, various dispensers of hand sanitiser or gloves or aprons, and in between the dispensers were white doors with frosted-glass panels in them.

Fred called Sean, his second in command in the

pub, and told him what had happened. 'You might have to do without me today,' he said. 'I'll give a shout later on when we know more.'

'He's only seventy,' Olive said when he hung up. 'Seventy isn't old, not these days. And he's healthy. Apart from the cancer, he's never been sick.'

The idea of anything happening to him was unimaginable. He was as close to her, it felt like, as he was to his two sons. They were father and daughter in everything that mattered.

He'd been there every time life had pulled the rug from under her, all the bad times – and all the good ones too. She remembered his elation when she and Fred told him they were getting married, and his speech on their wedding day that had caused tears and laughter. She recalled his delight and wholehearted support when he heard they'd decided to adopt, and how thrilled he'd been when they'd broken the news of this pregnancy to him. Thrilled, yes, but she'd seen the apprehension too that had mirrored her own.

He'd always been there. Always.

Fred got to his feet. 'I need to move,' he said. He paced to the next bank of chairs and back again, shoulders hunched, hands dug into his pockets. He didn't want to hear how young and healthy his father was; she knew that. She was saying it to fill the air with sound, that was all. Putting out words to keep the fear from clawing at her.

'I could use some tea,' she said, although the brew that spurted from those machines was as different from a pot of proper tea as it was possible to be, and would cause even more trips to the loo. But it would give him a job, some other place to walk to. It might distract him for a few minutes.

The tea was delivered, and she endured it. Shortly afterwards she went in search of another toilet, and found one. They sat some more while rain drummed on the skylight above them.

A quarter past eleven. He'd be up from the boat now, making his way to the shop for tea like he did most Wednesdays. Never arriving without something – a custard slice or a KitKat to split between them, or a bag of the jelly sours they both loved, or two small fudge bars, one each.

People padded past in dressing gowns and slippers. Women in navy uniforms and comfortable-looking shoes pushed trolleys loaded with trays of food that left a smell of cabbage in their wake. Male and female doctors in white coats hurried by with stethoscopes and files. She thought they looked like they knew where they were going, but didn't particularly want to get there.

Just as Olive was beginning to think everyone had forgotten they were there, double doors swished open at the end of the corridor, and a dark-haired man approached them. 'Mr and Mrs Purcell?'

Good-looking. Two pens poking from the top pocket of his white coat. Olive hung on to Fred's arm as she searched the man's face for clues, and found none. He introduced himself as Doctor Something; she wasn't listening to that part. He shook hands with them.

'The news is good,' he told them in a Cork lilt. 'He has sustained a linear fracture of the skull, but it's a nice clean break, and no sign of bleeding or pressure in there. He has a fine bump on his head, again not anything to worry about, and a cut that we've stapled up, and a broken ankle that'll put him out of commission for a while. We've given him painkillers, and we'll hang on to him for a few days, just to keep an eye on him, but he's had a lucky escape. Can I ask his age?'

'Just gone seventy,' Fred said. 'What happened? What caused him to fall?'

The doctor lifted his hands. 'Hard to be sure. He has no memory of it, and presumably there were no witnesses, but I would guess that he just tripped on the edge of the boat getting in. There's no sign of anything else.'

'So he didn't have a heart attack? Nothing that would have caused him to collapse?' Thinking along the same lines as Olive, both of them afraid to give voice to their fears.

'No. His heart is sound, actually. We'll give him a DEXA scan while he's in with us to check out his bone density, and do a few other tests, but apart from the injuries I've just outlined, from what I can see he's in very good nick for a man of seventy.'

Olive wanted to kiss him. She wanted to reach past her baby bump and rest her palms on the sides of his handsome face and look right into his brown eyes and plant her lips on his. Probably best not to, under the circumstances. 'Can we see him?'

'Sure. He might be a little woozy from the pills, but otherwise he's fine. Don't stay too long – he needs to rest. And you might stop by the nurses' station to fill in a registration form for him before you go.'

He directed them to a ward with four beds. Mark was just inside the door, a sheet pulled up over his lower half. He'd been undressed down to a rather grubby thermal vest, from the stained neck of which grey curling chest hairs crept. There was a white bandage above his left ear, and an egg-shaped bump on that side of his forehead. His face was frighteningly pale for one who spent so much of his life out of doors, breathing in the clean sea air.

She hated how exposed and vulnerable he appeared. When had his wrists become so bony? In spite of the doctor's reassuring words, she thought he looked every one of his seventy years, and more. She wanted to wrap him up in something soft and cosy, and sing him to sleep like she'd done for Nancy as a baby.

He fluttered his fingers as soon as he saw them, and made a sound she didn't catch. She sat on the side of his bed and took his hand: how cold it was, despite the heat in the ward. She leant towards him. 'Did you say something, dear?'

'Beth.' Little more than a whisper.

Her heart sank. 'I'm Olive,' she told him. 'Your daughter-in-law. You had a fall, you're in hospital.' What if he never recognised any of them again?

He gave a smile, a poor, watered-down version of his usual one. 'I know you're Olive,' he said, the words slurring into one another. 'I was supposed to go to Beth's house today for … something, I can't remember.'

He hadn't lost his senses: the relief – but the lack of energy in his voice terrified her. She told herself it was just the painkillers – the doctor had said he'd be woozy, hadn't he? Mark never took a pill if he could avoid it: these ones must have gone straight to his head, pretty much knocked him out.

'Don't worry about Beth,' she said. 'I'll ring her. I'll let her know you're in hospital.'

Was it the cookery lessons? Were they finally getting under way? She'd vowed not to get involved, since Beth had said she'd handle them. It had nearly killed her but she hadn't asked him anything about them, and he hadn't mentioned them. It must be the lessons – what other reason would he have to call to Beth's house?

'What happened?' Fred asked. 'What made you fall?'

His forehead puckered. 'I can't remember. I don't remember falling.'

'Do you remember being in the ambulance?'

'... No.'

So quickly it could occur. One minute he could be fine, turning up at the shop with treats, or coming to Sunday dinner with a box of Ferrero Rocher. The next minute he could be gone, snatched from them as quickly as Maria and her family had been.

She rubbed warmth into his hands. 'Don't ever give us a fright like that again. I want this baby to grow up with at least one grandfather – you hear me?'

The same diluted smile. 'I hear you. Message received, loud and clear.'

'You'll have to teach him stuff, like ... catapults, and marbles. I don't know. Conkers. Climbing trees.

No, not climbing trees. No tree climbing allowed.'
She was babbling. She stopped.

'I'll be back in a while with your pyjamas and
things,' Fred told him. 'They're keeping you in for a
few days, just for observation.'

He yawned. His eyelids fluttered closed. His
breathing deepened. They watched him sleep for a
bit. Olive saw his chest rise and fall beneath the awful
vest. They checked the tiny metal wardrobe by his
bed and found the rest of his clothes. The woolly hat
Lil had knit for him made her want to cry. His phone
and wallet and keys were in a pocket of the oilskin
jacket they'd given him for his birthday. They went
to the nurses' station as they'd promised and filled in
a form, and then they left.

On the way home Olive rang the mother of
Nancy's best friend, and filled her in. 'Could you
collect her from school and keep her for the night?'
she asked. 'Tell her Gramps is OK, he'll be home in
a few days and she'll see him then. Tell her he'll be
staying in our house for a while – she'll like that.'

He might protest – no, he *would* protest, not
wanting as usual to be a burden on them – but Olive
would insist. She'd use emotional blackmail if she
had to, tell him she'd be too anxious if he was alone
in his house, and she shouldn't be anxious right now.

And it might be good for Nancy to have him with them: it might distract her from her hatred of her mother.

Fred glanced at her after she'd hung up. 'Why did you ask her to keep Nancy?'

'I need a night off,' she told him. And maybe Nancy needed a night away too. Maybe they both needed a break.

'You can drop me back to the shop,' she said. She wasn't in the mood to work, but she'd only mope if she went home. 'I'll call into the pub before I open up. I'll tell Sean he'll have to manage without you for the rest of the day.' Wednesday nights were quiet, especially off-season.

'Thanks, Ollie.'

It would be nice, just the two of them for the evening. She couldn't remember the last time they'd been on their own, other than in bed at night, and it had been quite some time since she'd had the energy to take advantage of that.

'Don't forget to get his phone charger from the house, and a few books – and his pack of cards if you can find them. Tell him I'll be in to see him tomorrow. Maybe say nothing for the moment about him coming to stay with us – we'll wait till he's a bit stronger.'

'Right-o.'

'And stop at a garage on the way back and pick up a big bottle of Cidona and the paper – and a bag of jelly sours if they have them. Bring him a biro too, for the crossword. And for God's sake bring home that vest he's wearing when you get it off him – I'll bin it and buy him a few more.'

Fred found her hand without taking his eyes from the road, and gave it a squeeze. 'I love how you look after him.'

She smiled out through the windscreen. 'That's what daughters do.'

When he dropped her she went inside and used the loo, and then called to the pub and sorted things with Sean.

'Give him our best,' he said. 'Tell him we'll keep his stool warm.'

He was popular in the pub. He was popular everywhere. She picked up a cheese sandwich for her lunch and brought it back to the shop. She put on the kettle and pulled out her phone.

'He's alright?' Beth asked. 'You're not keeping anything from me?'

'No, honestly I'm not. He was dopey from the painkillers they gave him, but otherwise he's OK. The doctor says there's nothing to worry about, that he's in good shape for his age.' Oops, maybe not the most tactful remark to make to a woman who was a little older.

'How long are they keeping him in?'

'A few days, they said.'

'And after that?'

'He'll come to us, for as many nights as I can persuade him to stay. He just doesn't know it yet.'

'I think that's wise, Olive.'

'Beth, he had it in his head that he was supposed to be going to your house today. He couldn't remember exactly why.'

Silence.

'Hello?'

'That's fine. Please tell him not to worry. We can reschedule when he's well enough.'

The cookery lessons, had to be. 'I'll let him know.' A pittance was all Beth would accept for them, however Olive had tried to make her take more. The price of the ingredients was all she wanted, she'd said, but Olive had doubted they'd cost so little.

'Do pass on my best wishes when you see him.'

'Of course I will.'

Tom's phone rang repeatedly. She was about to hang up when he answered. 'Sorry,' he said, 'I'm in the garage. I had the radio on full blast.'

'What are you doing in the garage?'

'… Just working on something.'

'Really? What?'

Pause. 'Just a … repair job on a piece of furniture, nothing interesting.'

He sounded curiously cagy, but she didn't have the energy to pursue it. 'Is it warm enough in the garage?'

He gave a laugh. 'You sound like Beth. I'm fine.'

'That's good. I'm actually ringing with some news about Mark.' She filled him in.

'God, sorry to hear that. Will he be OK?'

'They've told us he'll be fine. He'll be on crutches for a few weeks. I'm going to kidnap him and force him to stay with us.'

'He's lucky to have you. Give him my best.'

'Actually, he was talking lately about painting the outside of his house. It's a bungalow, and he's always done it himself. Can I suggest that he asks you to do it? A paying job, obviously.'

'Sure, I'd be happy to.'

'Great – thank you. How are things otherwise?'

'Everything's fine. I've been invited to join your book club. I believe it was your idea.'

She'd forgotten all about it. 'Oh, that's good – I hope you said yes.'

'I did. I don't think I'd have the nerve to say no to Beth.'

'Oh, stop – but are you happy about coming? I'd hate you to feel under pressure.'

'Ah no, I was chuffed to be asked. I just hope I can keep up with the rest of you. I've never been in a book club before – I'm not sure what's expected.'

'Don't worry, we're very casual. Just basically say what you thought of the book, and nobody will judge you – not even Beth. Fred and Mark are members too, and Lil. We've all been in it from the start.'

'Yes, I wondered about Lil. How does that work?'

'She writes her review, and Beth reads it out.'

'Right.'

'So I'll see you next Wednesday night then, if not before.'

'You will. Take care.'

After the call she laid her arms on the counter and rested her head on them. She closed her eyes, her mind replaying the happenings of the last few hours. It felt like a week since she'd gone to work, thinking it was going to be like any other Wednesday.

She heard the kettle clicking off. As she rose heavily to her feet she felt again the small stirring, the little nudge that told her it was still there, still growing. Still kicking its mother.

All would be well. All would be well.

She made the tea. She unwrapped the sandwich and ate it. They could have a curry for dinner, herself and Fred. She could pick it up on the way home. Korma they both liked, nothing too hot.

The door opened. The bell pinged. She put on her shopkeeper smile.

The March
Book Club Meeting

It wasn't the same without him. It felt wrong without him. In five years he hadn't missed a single meeting. He'd been an enthusiastic member right from the very first Wednesday night. His and Beth's reading tastes didn't often coincide – some of his suggestions she found challenging, like the biography of a Russian spy he'd put forward in November, and she was sure he'd say the same of some of her choices – but that was the nature of a book club, wasn't it? You read what was chosen, and sometimes you enjoyed it and discovered a new author, and more times you moved on.

And now, for the first time, they were meeting without him. He was missing, and his absence created a void far greater, it seemed to her, than the space he would have occupied if he'd been there.

'He's doing well,' Olive reported, 'but he's still a bit shaky on the crutches, and I didn't want him coming out in the cold. I'm determined to hang on to him for a week at least – I know he'd be taking chances if he was on his own.'

'Nurse Ratched,' Fred murmured, and got a look.

He'd been discharged from hospital on Monday, just two days ago, and he'd gone straight to Olive and Fred's house. Beth had rung him that evening. How are you feeling?

Better, he'd said. Got a right wallop on the head, and the crutches are slowing me down big-time, but I'll get there. Can't keep a good man down.

Still at the jokes, but she'd been dismayed at how weak he'd sounded. I dare say we won't be seeing you at the book club.

I'll play that one by ear, he'd replied. I'd hate to miss it – but he *was* missing it.

'Is Tom coming?' Olive enquired. 'I tried ringing him earlier, but I got no answer.'

'I'm expecting him,' Beth replied. 'He said he'd be here' – but as yet, ten minutes past seven, there was no sign of him. Could he have forgotten? Should she have reminded him? Or had he had second thoughts, and decided to skip it? As she was debating whether to give him a call, there was a light tap on the door.

'It's open,' Olive called, and Tom appeared, looking apologetic at the sight of them all assembled.

'I wasn't sure,' he said, 'if you started on the dot.'

He brought a blast of cool air in with him. He

wore the only jacket he seemed to possess, and a navy scarf knotted at his throat, and the same nice blue-green knitted hat she'd seen on him lately. It matched his eyes, a good colour choice. It was similar to the ones Lil knitted for Olive's shop – maybe he'd got it there.

There was a small dark stain just above the knee of his jeans, about the size of a one-cent coin, and splattery about the edges. On his feet were grey runners that looked like they were about to fall apart.

'You're welcome,' she told him. 'Do have a seat.' He took the vacant chair between Fred and Lil. She got a waft of soap, or maybe shampoo, as he passed her. She saw him throw Lil a quick grin, saw Lil return it with a brief smile. 'Olive and Lil you know,' she said. 'Have you met Fred?'

'Yes, we've met. No Mark this evening?'

'He's not up to going out yet,' Olive told him.

'Shame. Is he still staying at yours?'

'He is, for the next while.'

'How is he?'

'On the mend. He'll be fine.'

They got started. Round the circle they went as they always did, Beth setting the direction so Tom was left till last.

When it came to his turn, he crossed his arms and

stretched out his long legs in their awful runners. He looked around the small circle, his eyes briefly meeting Beth's.

'My first book club,' he said. 'Thanks for asking me. I hope you won't regret it.'

'We hope so too,' Fred replied, and got a nudge from Olive.

'I used to read loads as a kid,' Tom went on, 'but I gave it up when I hit my teens. I've only just got back into it – thanks to this place, really.' Another darting look at Lil. 'It would never have occurred to me to join a book club though. To be honest, I thought it was something only women did.' He grinned at Fred. 'Seems I was wrong about that.' Another pause. 'So, *The Catcher in the Rye*.'

For one who had never reviewed a book, he did well. He admitted that it hadn't grabbed him, but he was fair too. 'I didn't hate it, but I suspect I'd have liked it a lot more if I'd read it as a teen. I think it would have struck a chord, all that angst and insecurity.'

He outlined the book's strengths and weaknesses. It was clear he'd put a bit of thought into his review. He wasn't shy about the attention being focused on him either. He'd struck her as an educated man the first time they'd met. She'd bet anything he'd been to college, and wondered again what had led to his putting himself about as a handyman.

After he'd finished there was the general book talk that usually followed the individual contributions. While this was going on, Beth caught Tom glancing once or twice in Lil's direction. Wondering if she felt left out, maybe. The others had been like that too when she'd first stopped talking: uncomfortable, almost guilty that they could argue and toss ideas about, and she couldn't. Now they took her silence in their stride, which was understandable but also sad.

Eventually the talk petered out, and Beth gave them her choice for April, an autobiography of a well-known Irish chef that she'd picked up out of curiosity, and found to be enjoyable. She'd selected it for the book club with some mischievousness, suspecting that it wouldn't be to Mark's taste. Already she looked forward to his review next month.

As ever, Lil moved to the desk to pour the tea. 'I need the loo,' Olive said, and Beth insisted she go to the house rather than stop at the more basic toilet facilities in the shed. Fred went to accompany her up the path, leaving Beth and Tom alone – or as alone as they could be, given Lil's proximity.

'I hope you enjoyed your first meeting,' Beth said.

'I did, thanks. It's been interesting. How long has it been going on?'

'Coming up for five years.' She darted a glance at Lil, lowered her voice a notch. 'My daughter and Lil's sister were members.'

He shook his head slowly. 'That must have been difficult – going on with the book club, I mean.'

'It's still difficult, but life continues. We have to leave the past behind. We have to move on.'

'Easier said than done,' he replied quietly, so quietly she barely heard – and just then Lil approached, and the topic was dropped.

Her first impression of him had been right. He was trying to free himself from some sad history. She hoped he managed it.

The other two returned, and Fred passed around a tin of shortbread. 'He brings treats from the pub,' Olive told Tom. 'He steals them from the kitchen.'

'Hardly stealing from my own premises,' Fred pointed out, 'but if your conscience is at you, darling, you needn't have any.'

'What has my conscience go to do with it? I'll have another – I'm eating for two.'

They left soon afterwards, Olive anxious to get back to her patient. 'You might fold the chairs and stack them against that wall,' Beth said to Tom. She moved around switching off heaters while Lil packed away the tea things.

'Here,' Tom said, 'I'll take that,' and Beth watched Lil surrender the basket to him.

'You two go ahead,' she said. 'I have a call to make.'

Lil looked questioningly at her. 'I won't be long,' Beth told her. She stood listening to the ticking of the cooling heaters above the diminishing sound of their departing steps. She pictured them walking side by side up the path to the back porch.

Tom might have suited Lil very well. They might have suited one another. The thought came unbidden – but wasn't there truth to it? Lil deserved better than some anonymous admirer who looked like he might never do anything more than leave her trinkets, and who hadn't the wit to give some clue to his identity in a Valentine card. The Lil she knew, the Lil she'd always known, was bright and gentle and thoughtful, and so very deserving of love.

And Tom, the stranger who'd come among them, running from whatever had put that haunted look in his eyes – what about him? Whatever his history, didn't he need love too? Wasn't he as deserving as anyone? If he and Lil had met before the accident, who could say how it might have gone? He might have saved Lil in the aftermath; they might have saved one another.

She caught herself, and shook her head. Saved one another: what a fanciful thought. Exactly the kind of soft, romantic notion that Olive would come up with.

She found Mark's number, and rang it. Quickly, before Olive and Fred got home.

'Beth?'

'I was wondering,' she said, 'how you are.'

'Send help, Beth,' he said. 'I'm being kept here against my will. You may have to pay a ransom, but I'm worth it.'

His voice was stronger. Definitely on the mend. She'd never imagined she'd be relieved to hear his nonsense. 'Olive tells us you'll be there for another while.'

A heartfelt sigh. 'I imagine I will. Don't get me wrong – I'm being treated like royalty, and it's lovely and comfy here, but I'm pining for my own bed.'

'Well, you'll just have to be patient. You won't be fishing for a while either.'

'No, not till I'm off the crutches – and I can't drive, but I can potter. I'll be doing plenty of pottering once I get home.'

'Did you get a chance to make the fishcakes?'

'Not yet, but I got the knife. I got that far.'

'Well, that's a start. Tom came to the book club.'

'Did he? How did he do?'

'He did very well.'

'Good. Olive wants him to paint my house. I suppose she has a point – I could hardly do it with one and a half legs.'

'Of course you couldn't. Have you asked him?'

'Not yet. I'll give him a bell when I'm back at base.'

'I was thinking,' she said then, 'about the next cookery lesson.'

There was a pause. A definite pause. 'Yes?' In the single word she heard a new note of caution, his jollity gone.

'How about if I come to your house when you're home, since you can't travel?'

More silence. She waited.

'Beth,' he said, 'we don't have to do this.'

'Well, if you'd prefer to wait until you're more mobile—'

'No,' he said. 'I mean you don't have to teach me to cook. It was a nice idea of Olive's, and it was very good of you to agree when she asked, but I think we should leave it at the one session. Olive doesn't need to know. I'll say nothing.'

Her turn to be silenced. He'd asked her if she wanted to keep going after the first lesson, and she'd told him that she did, but now he seemed unsure again. Or maybe he really didn't want them. Maybe he was dreading the next two as much as she was.

Except that she wasn't dreading them. The first one had been fine – mostly fine. She had no reason to believe that the next two would be any different.

'I made a promise to Olive,' she said stiffly. 'I never go back on my word.'

'I just feel I'm a burden to you, Beth.'

'You're not a burden, not in the least. I thought you enjoyed the first one.'

'I did, of course I did. It was very pleasant.'

'And we'd made arrangements for the second. It was all organised.'

'Yes, that's true. But ... I suppose I've had a bit of time to think, and I'm just conscious of the commitment it is to you, Beth. I don't want to be taking up your time.'

This had gone on long enough. 'Nonsense. I'm coming to your house, and that's that. I'll bring what's needed, ingredients and cookware. I take it you have a working oven, and a hob?'

A further little pause occurred. 'Yes,' he said. 'I do have those.'

'That's settled then. Let me know when you're home, and we'll set a date.'

'It looks like you're determined.'

For Heaven's sake. She couldn't believe she was the one practically ordering him to allow the lessons to continue. 'I made a promise,' she repeated.

'In that case, I'll give in gracefully, and gratefully. You know where my house is?'

'I do.'

She'd never been inside it, but she knew where he lived. A kilometre or so beyond Fred and Olive's house, on the far side of town. A red-roofed one-storey cottage set back from the road, rhododendrons climbing over the rough stone garden wall.

'Can I set a condition?' he asked.

Lord above. 'What condition?'

'That you'll stay to eat it with me.'

'I was rather taking that for granted.'

'Good.'

Another brief silence fell. 'I'll say goodnight then,' she said. 'You'll let me know when you're home.'

'I will. Take care, Beth.'

She was conscious, after hanging up, of an unsettled feeling. Had she foisted herself on him? Had she bullied him into agreeing? Could he actually be *dreading* the occasion? Surely not. Olive would never have asked her to teach him if she thought he wouldn't enjoy it.

But maybe Olive had got it wrong. Not all gifts were welcome.

It might just be that he was reluctant for her to see his house. Maybe it was a mess; maybe his oven hadn't been cleaned since Catriona's time. Maybe that was all it was. Did he think she couldn't cope with an oven that needed a good scrub? Lord knows she'd risen to greater challenges.

But it could also be embarrassment. She recalled how his face had fallen when she'd blurted out how the lessons had come from Olive, not from her. It could be that, still niggling him.

She shivered in the rapidly cooling cabin. She must put the matter from her mind: it didn't merit all this deliberation. She locked the door behind her and walked slowly up the path, a feeling of disquiet remaining stubbornly with her. She looked ahead to the house where she'd lived all her married life.

After Gerry died she'd felt so lonely there, so alone, even with Maria and the others living right next door, in the house they'd built on the plot Beth and Gerry had given them as a wedding present. Despite this, Beth had felt the pang of her solitary state every time she closed her front door. Their home had still echoed with memories of him, reminders of their years together. She had loved him, even if she'd rarely told him so.

She'd been widowed at fifty-nine. Still healthy, still employed, and certainly young enough to marry again, plenty did at that age – but the idea hadn't interested her. She didn't want another husband, she wanted a project, something to distract her in the lonely hours after she finished work – and so the quest for a Fairweather library, and her subsequent decision to provide it herself, had become her focus.

And it had worked out. The library was a success, and everyone was happy to have it – but sometimes you wanted more than *books*. You wanted more than make-believe people living made-up lives. You wanted things to happen that were *real*.

She reached the house. She opened the porch door and stepped inside, wishing she could shrug off a mood as easily as a coat.

APRIL

Tom

He washed up his breakfast things and thought about the book club.

He'd been wary in advance of the meeting. Despite Olive's reassurances he'd dreaded making a fool of himself, but he thought he'd done OK. Nobody had laughed, or looked pityingly or impatiently at him. Contrary to his expectations, he'd found it interesting. He'd enjoyed it.

Wait till he told Joel he was in a book club.

Wait till he told Joel a woman had knitted a hat for him.

Or maybe he wouldn't tell him that, because that would cause questions to be asked, and he had none of the answers.

What if he and Lil had met by chance, under different circumstances? What if there'd never been a Vivienne, and he'd met Lil instead? Would a spark have ignited? Would one of them have taken a step towards something, and waited to see if the other would follow?

Because it wasn't just curiosity he felt towards her.

It wasn't morbid fascination with the woman who'd lost her family, the woman who didn't speak. It was more than that. He was drawn to her, to the way she looked, the way she moved, the glimpses he got of her personality from their interactions. He was drawn to her stillness – and maybe to her sadness. Maybe his sadness was reaching out to hers. When she smiled at him, it caused a contented little blip inside him.

He was visiting the cabin more often than he needed to, returning books he'd never intended reading, asking if she had others in stock, just to inhabit her space for a few minutes. On the days the library was closed he hoped to encounter her, however fleetingly, on the cliff path – and when he did, they were good days.

After Vivienne, he'd resolved never again to leave himself vulnerable to the loss and pain that love was capable of causing – and yet here he was. His heart, it would seem, was impervious to resolutions, wanting only what it wanted.

Not that anything was going to happen between them. He knew this. Even if he found the courage to walk that path again he wasn't mended enough, and neither was she, from the damage their pasts had done to them.

And anyway, he was only passing through.

Fairweather was never meant to be more than a stepping-stone in his recovery. One day he'd pack up and leave, either in a few months when his lease was up here or later, if he opted to find another place and hang around a bit longer. However it panned out, the house he was renting, the garden he'd reclaimed, the cliff path and the beach beyond it, the book club members and the others he'd met here, all of it would move eventually into his past, and fade and diminish over time.

And one day he would try to recall her face, and he would fail.

He'd carved her a miniature library in return for the hat. It was all he could think of to do. He'd taken furtive photos of it and replicated the structure. He'd tried to make the walls true and straight, unlike his little houses. He'd lined up the three windows, and put the welcome sign on the door, and levelled the pitched roof. He'd brushed a pine stain on the sides and painted the top dark green, trying to mimic the real thing as closely as he could.

When the paint was dry he'd turned it this way and that, and had seen only its flaws. It looked drab; he should have made it more colourful. The windows should be higher on the wall, the door closer to the corner. It was all wrong.

He hadn't given it to her. He'd left it on the

sitting-room bookshelves, beside Hollie's copy of *The Catcher in the Rye*, and instead he'd got her a three-pack of the roll of mints he'd seen on the library desk, and she'd accepted his gift with a puzzled smile and written *No need.*

He'd been back to Denise for a second haircut. I got a cold, he'd told her, after you cut it before, and she'd laughed and said it wasn't the first time she'd heard it, and she hoped he wouldn't sue. Settling in OK? she'd asked, and he'd said yes. Plenty of work? she'd enquired, and he'd said yes to that too. All good, he'd told her, and it was. It was all good.

But what had happened was still there, still painful. It seemed he couldn't shake it off – and the thought of anyone here learning about it made him shudder. They could find out easily: anyone handy on the Net could Google him and discover what had happened, with the newspaper accounts of the trial up there for anyone to read. He just hoped nobody was interested enough to do that.

The lie he'd told to Olive about his father being dead continued to nag at him too – but what could he do about it? How could he explain it without sounding like an idiot? The only way he could redeem himself was to tell her the full story, and that wasn't going to happen. He hadn't told the guards, or his solicitor. Nobody knew apart from Joel – and Sarah, who'd been sworn to secrecy, and whom he trusted to keep her word.

He didn't think Vivienne would have told anyone. He imagined she'd just said they'd split up – maybe that she'd been the one to finish things – and left it at that.

He put away the dishes and dried his hands. He took his phone out to the hall as he scrolled through his contacts and found Fred's number.

'It's done,' he said. 'I'm looking at it right now.'

'Really? Brilliant. Are you pleased?'

'I am – pleasantly surprised that I managed it. Just hope Olive likes it.'

'She'd better. Are you sure you're OK to hang on to it till the twenty-first?'

'Not a problem.'

'Great. Was it tough going?'

He laughed. 'Let's just say it was a learning curve.'

'That's a yes then. Look, I really appreciate it, Tom. Swing by when you're in town and I'll settle up – or I can drop it out to you if you prefer.'

'It'll do when you collect it, no rush.'

He'd trawled through images of grandfather clocks online and made preliminary sketches, lots of them. When he had a design he was happy with he'd gone on a new hunt and eventually located a clockmaker in Yorkshire who'd sent him a kit that included a clock movement, a pendulum arm and a chime mechanism.

The movement is operated by an electromagnet that sends a pulse to a magnet on the arm, he'd told Tom. This is what gives the pendulum its sway. The movement must be properly level for the pendulum to operate. When the pendulum stops swaying, it's giving you a warning that the clock battery needs replacing.

I'd like to make my own pendulum, Tom told him. I want to carve it.

Fine – but you need to get the weight right. It needs to weigh precisely the same as the one I'm sending you. It might take a few tries.

It had taken more than a few tries. It had taken several tiny adjustments to the position of the movement and several changes to the size and weight of the pendulum before he finally got it to sway, and to keep swaying. That was before he attached the clock head to the housing that he'd painstakingly put together – and found, to his dismay, that he needed to make fresh adjustments. It had kept him from sleeping for a week, his head filled with measurements and calculations.

None of that mattered. It had all been worth it. Every time he looked at the clock, his very first working grandfather clock, he was filled with deep satisfaction. He couldn't remember the last time he'd felt this sense of achievement. Each little house gave him a kick when it emerged in all its weirdness, but the houses didn't compare to this. This was something he was truly proud of.

It stood five and a half feet tall, or thereabouts. It was asymmetrical, with no opposite sides quite parallel. It was narrower at its top than at its end, and wider on one side than the other. There wasn't a single true right angle to be found on it. It had taken all his maths expertise to figure out how to get the panels to align and assemble.

The clock face was somewhere between an oval and a circle. The numbers were in the right positions, but a few were backwards. The pendulum was triangular. He'd deliberately set the chime mechanism out of kilter, so it sounded too many times for some hours, and too few for others.

It was wonky in the extreme. It had refused to stand upright until he carved a pair of long clown shoes from driftwood to anchor it, drilling out small holes carefully so he could thread real laces through.

He'd painted the body orange. The clock face was

blue, with yellow hands and numbers. The pendulum was yellow too, and housed behind a little glass panel. The clown shoes were blue, with red laces.

It was a clock you'd love or hate. Even though the making of it had nearly killed him, or maybe because of that, he'd grown to love it. He was tentatively hopeful that Olive would love it too.

He'd made virtually no profit on it. The estimate he'd given Fred hadn't taken into account the hours of work he'd spent on it. The materials would be covered, with a tiny remainder – but he wasn't bothered. What the experience had taught him was invaluable, and thanks to other jobs he'd fitted in along the way, he was pulling in enough money to get by. And it was for Olive, so he'd happily have made it for nothing.

But if he ever made another, he'd know exactly what to charge for it.

He'd taken photos at every stage of its production. He'd emailed the final one to the clockmaker in Yorkshire. Thought you might like to see where your innards ended up, he said. Thanks for your help. That is some clock, the man replied. My wife has sent the snap to all her friends. I'm terrified she'll want me to make her one. I might have to pass on the order to you.

But Tom had really taken the photos to show Joel. Besides PE, the only school subject his brother had shone at was woodwork. From the start he'd taken to it, bringing home picture frames and trinket boxes, and later a stool and a little shelving unit, telling anyone who'd listen about dovetail joints and butt joints, asking for tools and materials as birthday gifts, so he could do more of it at home.

His passion had lasted. After securing a mediocre Leaving Cert he'd announced that he wanted to become a carpenter, and so he had, working his way through a foundation course, following that with two years of apprenticeship with a furniture maker. At the age of twenty-four he'd started his own small company, which he'd nurtured slowly and carefully over the years. Eleven years later, just before last Christmas, he'd taken on his thirtieth employee.

Tom's break-all-the-rules clock was a million miles away from the meticulously crafted items of furniture that Joel and his workers produced. He'd made no mention of it in their phone calls, wanting to see Joel's unfiltered reaction when he looked at the photos and saw what his little brother had created.

The lunch they'd been planning was happening a few days from now, on Joel's thirty-sixth birthday. They'd settled on a small hotel on the outskirts of

Nenagh. Even when Tom had been living in London, he and Joel had met up at least once a month, so this was the longest they'd gone without seeing one another.

The doorbell rang. He edged around the clock and opened the door, and saw his landlady with a jar in her hand.

'I'm sorry to bother you, Tom,' she said, 'but I can't open this, and Lil is out. Would you mind?'

'Sure.' It was a jar of wholegrain mustard. He twisted it open and handed it back. As she was thanking him, her face changed. 'What on earth is that?'

She'd spotted the clock. He didn't think it would be her thing. 'It's just something I made,' he said, 'for a customer.'

'You *made* it? May I see it?'

He could hardly refuse. He stepped back and she entered the hall, and stood silently before the clock. He waited for the first verdict on it.

'Well, it's certainly colourful. It must have taken you some time.'

'A few weeks, in between other jobs.'

'This is what you were working on,' she said, 'in the garage.'

'That's right. I moved it in here when I finished it.

I thought it might be better to bring it in from the cold. It's not being collected for a while.'

She tilted her head at it. She smiled. 'It's like the little houses you've given Olive,' she said. 'Eccentric.'

'Yes.' Eccentric was a good word.

'I wasn't aware that you made clocks.'

He laughed. 'Neither was I. This was my first attempt.'

'Really? And it keeps good time?'

'It does, so far.'

'Well done. It's very ... unique. You're a talented man.'

'Thank you.' It occurred to him that she might mention it to Olive. 'It's actually a surprise birthday present. Fred asked me to make it for Olive.'

'Really? How thoughtful of him. It's the kind of thing she'll love.'

'Hope so.'

She turned then to look at him. 'May I ask you something, Tom?'

That direct, searching gaze again. He folded his arms, steeled himself. 'Sure.'

'Did you go to college?'

'... I did.' He could hardly deny it, and it gave nothing away.

She turned the jar slowly between her hands. 'I

hope you won't think me forward,' she said, 'but when I met you on that first day I felt something was troubling you.'

He didn't react, didn't respond. Telling her without telling her that she wasn't wrong.

She nodded as if he'd spoken. 'I hope things are getting better for you now. If there's anything I can do to help, please let me know.'

'Thank you.'

'Will you go back? To … whatever you did before?'

'I don't know. I'm not thinking too far ahead just now.'

She shifted her gaze back to the clock. 'Lil was in college. She was doing a business course. She was in her third year.'

He was relieved by the change of focus. 'Maybe things will change,' he said. 'She might just need more time.' But even as he spoke, he could hear how hollow and clichéd it sounded.

So could she. 'Yes,' she said, and he caught the resignation in her voice, the polite acceptance of what he'd said, and what she didn't believe.

He replayed their conversation after she'd left. Her offer of help was unexpected, and generous in the face of her own challenges.

How he'd misjudged her. It must be lonely, living

with a granddaughter who couldn't speak to her. We have to leave the past behind, she'd said at the book club meeting – but every day she was reminded of it, with Lil's continuing silence.

Joel's birthday dawned bright and sunny. Going out to collect the ash carrier after breakfast, he was surprised by the mildness in the air, the first truly spring-like day of the year. Seventh of April, about time. As he stood there breathing it in, the cat appeared through the gap in the hedge and ambled up the lawn.

'Morning,' he said. 'You missed breakfast,' and it pressed against his leg, and twined around him. Skimbleshanks the Railway Cat. He looked down at the cabin, the half of it he could see over the hedge he'd clipped in February. She wouldn't be there today, not on a Sunday.

He spent the morning in the kitchen, painting a new batch of houses. He left the back door open to let in the spring. The radio played tunes his foot tapped along with; the cat dozed on the chair it had taken to occupying. He was aware of a feeling of contentment as he chose colours and brushed them on. The past might still rear its head from time to time, but the darkness was lifting. Little by little he was mending, coming back to himself.

When noon approached he cleared away his paints and rinsed his brushes. He washed his hands and got into his jacket. 'See you later,' he told the cat, scooping it up and setting it on the back step. He took a box from the worktop – the box his clock parts had come in – and left the house.

As he drove slowly down the lane he found himself thinking back to the rainy Friday afternoon in January when he'd driven in the other direction for the first time. Three months, just under, since he'd negotiated the rutted surface, wondering what was ahead, in every sense. It felt longer.

Traffic was light. He arrived at his destination with fifteen minutes to spare. He circled the car park slowly and found no sign of Joel's red Skoda. He parked and sat for a while with both windows open, looking at the sunlight slanting onto the immaculate lawns.

Eventually he got out, tucking the little box under his arm. As he approached the revolving doors he became aware of an odd sense of foreboding. In his life as a programmer he'd been in and out of hotels all the time, for conferences and seminars and awards ceremonies and dinners. He'd entered them without a thought, checked in and checked out as a matter of course. Now, as he stepped into the door's chamber, as it rotated slowly to deposit him in the lobby, he waited for a hand on his shoulder, an order to vacate the premises. Ex-jailbirds had no business in hotels.

No hand descended. Nobody even glanced at him. Get over yourself, McLysaght. He chose a corner seat and let out the breath he'd been holding.

It being Sunday, the place was quiet, but he recalled lobbies filled with sharp-suited, clean-shaven men and tailored, manicured women. Types he'd recognised, because he'd been one of them. Sipping coffee, flipping open laptops to tap on keys, leaning forward to converse in low, earnest tones with their companions. Clients, or prospective clients. He remembered well how it all worked, even if it felt like a lifetime ago.

A youth approached. White shirt, black trousers, circular tray under one arm. 'Can I get you anything, sir?'

No sign on his face that Tom was out of place, that the 'sir' was ironic. 'I'm OK, thanks. Just waiting for someone.' He still felt that he should have made more of an effort. Ironed his one decent shirt, chosen a less worn pair of jeans, one without the paint stain on the knee.

'Hello, stranger.'

He looked up at the face he'd known all his life.

He got to his feet and shook his brother's hand, and was pulled into a rough back-slapping embrace. They never used to hug; it had begun only after Tom had fallen apart. It had come from Joel, this physical gesture, this assurance of support and solidarity, and Tom had been glad of it, had literally clung to it, and was happy for it to continue.

Joel wasn't in a suit either; he only ever wore them when he had to. 'It's good to see you,' he said, peeling off his jacket.

'You too.' After his months of solitary living, it *was* good to see his brother. 'Happy birthday.'

'Thanks. Got the hair cut, I see. Takes years off you.'

'Found a good barber.'

'Excellent. Come on, let's grab some food, and you can tell me the latest gossip from Fairweather.'

They located the bar and ordered cheeseburgers from the menu. Over a beer Tom recounted his most recent jobs: a skylight replacement, the reroofing of a shed, the installation of a shower screen, new bath taps.

'You're flying it. You ever miss the programming?'

How many times he'd asked himself that question. 'I miss parts of it, but not as much as I thought I would.'

The thing he'd realised, sometime after leaving that world, was that computers were ultimately soulless things. Pushing out the boundaries of electronics was challenging and exciting, but it had never got under his skin the way the clock had. And working with even basic tools, bringing something physical into being, seeing it take shape and come together, was a whole other excitement. 'I'm in no rush back to programming.'

'Then don't rush back. Do whatever makes you happy, Tom.'

Joel had done what made him happy. Joel, who'd never shone in school, who'd scraped a pass in every exam, had got it spot on, while Tom had flown to the moon and come crashing down in flames.

They moved on. Joel told him of Sarah's promotion to deputy principal, and a friend's wedding they'd attended the weekend before, and the break in Donegal they were planning at Easter, and an offer of interest from a Danish furniture store.

'That sounds promising.'

Joel lifted his hands, let them drop. 'Might be. Someone's coming over next week. We'll see.'

Making his fortune had never been high on Joel's list. He worked for the love of it, to feed his passion and hone his skills. Despite confiding to Tom at

Christmas that the company was making a steady and growing profit, he paid himself just enough to keep the family afloat. Most of their holidays were spent at the mobile home in Wexford that their father had given him and Sarah as a wedding gift. His modest car was eight years old. He put the bulk of the profits back into the business that one day Harry and Emily would inherit.

'They miss you,' he told Tom. 'They wanted to come today when I said I was going to meet you.'

After Joel and Sarah had installed him in their spare room on his release from jail, while Tom was attempting to get his head together and figure out his next move, two-going-on-three Harry would clamber onto his lap and nuzzle in like a little kitten, smelling of shampoo and biscuits and demanding a story, and Emily, just gone one, would give him a placid gummy smile when his mother handed her over to her uncle. Their childish hearts seeing no wrong in him, making no judgements, offering him their innocent acceptance.

'I've got something for them,' he said, taking his offering from the chair beside him and setting it on the table. 'And for you and Sarah. It's really your birthday present, but I think you'll have to share, so I'm giving you four.'

'What's this?' Joel opened the box and took in the

contents. He lifted out a house and studied it. He sent a puzzled smile to Tom. 'You made these?'

'I did.' He told him then of the classes in the jail, and the houses that had come out of them. 'I didn't think they were any good. I have no idea why I even hung on to them.' He spoke of his impulse to offer them to Olive, and her reaction to them, and the steady sales that had given him the confidence to go on making them.

Joel scrutinised them in turn. 'They're brilliant,' he said. 'The kids are going to go wild for them – Sarah too. Are they driftwood?'

'They are. The first lot were pine or walnut, but the driftwood is free, so …'

'Amazing. And great that you're making money on them.'

'Well, not a whole lot, but I enjoy doing them. And there's something else I want to show you.' He took out his phone and found the photos of the clock. 'This is something I finished a few days ago, a commission I was offered. Scroll through. '

He kept his eyes on his brother's face as Joel went through the photos, conscious that to some extent he was muscling in on his brother's territory. The hotshot computer kid had strayed into the place that Joel had made his own. Maybe he'd resent it.

He didn't. He flicked back and forth between

the photos. 'You made a grandfather clock. I can't get my head around this, Tom. You actually made a grandfather clock from scratch. There was I, thinking I was the only furniture maker in the family.'

No trace of resentment in his voice. Tom could hear only astonished delight. 'There's a world of difference between your furniture and mine. I made a lopsided plywood clock with clown's feet. It took me an eternity to figure out how to make it go, and stay going.'

Joel shook his head as he passed back the phone. 'You can put it down all you like, but it's a heck of an achievement. I shouldn't be surprised – you could probably do anything you put your mind to. I'm really impressed, Tom.'

He was touched and gratified. His big brother had always had his back, even when he didn't need it. The gap in their ages – or just Joel being Joel? 'Glad you like it. It's a surprise for Olive's birthday, from her husband. She loves the houses, so I think she'll be happy with it.'

'For sure. Send me on those snaps, will you? Sarah would love to see them.' He speared a chip with his fork and dunked it in ketchup. 'She asked me to ask if you've met anyone nice in Fairweather.' He threw it out with a half laugh, and Tom said no, even as Lil's face flashed briefly into his head.

To his relief, Joel didn't pursue it. 'You like living by the sea?'

'I do. Did I tell you I bought togs?'

'You did. Have they got an airing yet?'

'No. I haven't been brave enough – but I have high hopes.'

'Today mightn't be a bad day to try.'

'Might not. I'll see what it's like when I get back.'

They finished the burgers and ordered coffees, and then – because he could wait no longer, because he had to know, for better or for worse – Tom asked the question.

'What were you going to tell me about Vivienne, that time on the phone?' The time he'd hung up the second he'd heard her name, and yelled at an innocent cat immediately afterwards.

Joel stared at him. 'You really want to know? Are you sure?'

'No – but tell me anyway.'

Their coffees arrived. Joel added milk and stirred in sugar. Working his way around to it, whatever it was. Choosing his words, wary of Tom's reaction maybe. Tom waited, wanting to hear, and not wanting.

But the wanting was stronger. 'Tell me, Joel.'

His brother met his gaze. They had the same eyes, and different everything else. Different heights, with Joel a head shorter; different builds, Tom lanky, Joel broad. Different hair colour, different noses, different chins.

'She's engaged, Tom.'

He should have expected it. He *had* expected it – that, or she was pregnant, or seriously ill, or dead. Since Joel's mention of her name, his mind had tossed around every possibility it could come up with – but the words still hit him, still stung him. Engaged, less than eight months after she'd sent back his ring.

'Anyone I know?' Not sure if he'd be able for the answer, if it was the wrong one.

Joel saw the unspoken fear in his face. 'Nobody you know,' he said quickly. 'An American, apparently. We haven't met him.'

As Sarah's cousin, Vivienne was still in their lives, whether they wanted her there or not. We don't have anything to do with her any more, Joel had told him, and Tom believed him – but still it was inevitable that news of her would filter through to them from someone in the family.

And now she was engaged for the second time, Tom's ring having been returned to him in a registered padded envelope addressed to Joel's house, two weeks after he'd seen her for the last time. No note had accompanied it. When he'd been released from jail he'd taken it from the envelope and pocketed it.

He could have got money for it. Could have put it up for sale online, or offered it to a jeweller. Could have done with the money too – but instead he'd gone for a long walk and thrown it off a bridge that spanned the motorway. Two thousand euros' worth of platinum and diamonds, hopefully crushed beneath the tyres of at least one articulated truck.

They finished their coffees. The subject wasn't mentioned again, but he was aware of a dropping in his mood. Still she could affect him. Still she could stir him up.

'Mam's anniversary next week,' Joel said. Tom hadn't forgotten it. She'd died aged fifty while Tom was in college, a victim of the cancer he'd told Olive had claimed both his parents. He hadn't been to her grave in Dublin since her last anniversary. It was out of bounds to him now: too dangerous to risk going there for fear of an encounter he wasn't prepared to have. Couldn't have.

'Why don't you join us in Donegal at Easter?' Joel suggested. 'I know Sarah and the kids would love it.'

Tom thanked him, and turned him down. He had no plans for Easter, but Joel and Sarah both worked hard enough to deserve a break without him barging in.

While Joel went in search of the Gents Tom paid

the bill. 'Forget it,' he said, when his brother returned and protested. 'It's done. The clock paid for it.' Just about.

At Joel's car he was hugged again. His brother looked searchingly at him. 'You OK, Tom?' Sensing the mood change too.

'I am. I'm fine.'

'Let me know if you need anything. See you soon. We'll do this again.' He climbed into his car, and Tom waved him off. The day was staying fine, the sun still in the sky, a few clouds to the west but so far, so good. As he turned the Jeep in the direction of Fairweather, his thoughts inevitably wandered back to his ex.

He remembered the rage that had coursed through him at the start, so strong he could almost taste it – but even as he'd wanted to hurt her, to hurt both of them, his anger had battled with the desire he stupidly still felt for her.

Would he have forgiven her, if she'd asked him to? So many times he'd thrown this question around in his head. If she'd begged him to take her back, if she'd sworn it would never happen again, would he have given her a second chance?

Maybe. He might have, even though it would have forced a terrible choice on him – but it had never been an option. She'd made no attempt to contact him. Nothing had passed between them but the anonymous padded envelope. She'd never said sorry, never shown remorse, never looked for his forgiveness.

She was twenty-five now, three years younger than him. Twenty-three when he'd popped the question, and she'd said yes. They'd settled on a wedding date in September of the following year. No rush, she'd said. Plenty of time. He remembered wondering afterwards if she'd ever intended becoming his wife. Maybe she wasn't going to marry this new guy either. Maybe she just liked being someone's fiancée for a while.

By the time he got back to Fairweather the day was deteriorating. The clouds were thickening, the sun vanished. Still mild enough though, still dry and calm. Before he could change his mind, he bundled his new shorts into a towel and struck out on the cliff path.

The beach wasn't busy. Two adults and two small children tossed a ball between them on the sand. A man threw a stick into the sea for a dog that raced joyfully after it. Two teens walked hand in hand by the water's edge.

He went beyond them and found a quiet spot.

He quickly pulled off his sweater and T-shirt. He wrapped the towel around his waist and wriggled as best he could out of the rest of his clothes, and into his shorts. The sand was cold on his bare feet. His skin prickled with goose bumps. He had second thoughts.

No. Come on. You can do this. He left his things in a pile and trotted to the shore. He dipped a cautious foot into the water – and gasped at the cold of it. Very cold if you're not used to it, Lil had told him, and she wasn't wrong. He advanced, wincing, praying that nobody was looking in his direction. From the corner of his eye he saw the dog bounding again into the sea.

Come on, do it. The water was up to his calves. Already, all feeling in his feet was gone. He pushed on, gritting his teeth. The iciness stung his skin, each step harder than the one before. How did they manage it, the year-round swimmers? He was knee-high in the water when a small wave approached, prompting another gasp as it smacked into his thighs.

No. Enough. He turned and strode back to the shore, and sprinted up the sand to his clothes. He scrambled into them and bundled his dry shorts into the towel. He left the beach, not meeting anyone's eye in case he saw smirking, and galloped home as his toes returned slowly to life.

On the back step he pulled off his socks and shook sand from them, and rubbed heat back into his feet. So much for his first Fairweather swim: wait till he told Joel. The early evening beginning to feel chilly, he lit the sitting-room fire and piled on a heap of coal.

He checked his phone and saw three missed calls and three voicemail messages waiting for him. The first two were from people looking for job quotes; the third was from Olive.

Tom, I'm ringing to ask if you'll have Easter Sunday lunch with us. Mark will be there, and I'm inviting Beth and Lil too. I hope you can come – I know Nancy would love to meet the man who makes the little houses, so if you have no other plans, please say yes. I'll see you in the meantime, but I wanted to put the invite out there nice and early. Talk soon.

Easter Sunday, two weeks from today. Her birthday. The day Fred was to come and collect the clock. Why not? He dialled her number.

'Hey – sorry I missed you. I attempted to go for a swim.'

'What? In April? Have you lost your mind?'

'I thought it might be warm enough, but the water was like ice. I got as far as my knees and chickened out.'

'I'm very relieved to hear it. Those year-round

swimmers are a hardy lot; you need to wait till much later. You could have given yourself a heart attack!'

'Well, I'm even more glad I turned back then.'

'Put that togs away till June at least. Will you come to lunch?'

'Sure. I'd be happy to come.' She didn't know he knew it was her birthday. He'd say nothing.

After hanging up, he found Lil's name and opened a text box.

I heard today my ex is getting married, he typed. *She used to be engaged to me.* He looked at the message, and deleted it. Of course he wasn't going to send her that. *I attempted a swim just now*, he typed. *I failed miserably, and narrowly avoided hypothermia. Hope you're having a good Sunday.*

He sent it off. Less than a minute later, his phone pinged.

Poor you. Wrap up warm. See you in the library. L
And after it, a single *x*.

Last Summer

The plane was full – par for the course on the Friday of a bank-holiday weekend. His neighbour, smelling of whiskey, fell asleep as the plane taxied down the runway.

Tom looked out the window as they left London behind, as the huge grey and green expanse of the capital got smaller and smaller and finally vanished below a cloud. So hot and muggy the city became in August. He looked forward to fresher weather in Dublin.

He was following Vivienne, who'd flown ahead of him that morning to road-test a hair stylist and a makeup artist in advance of the wedding. He'd stayed behind in London to attend a work get-together, intending to travel the following morning, but the night out had been postponed at the last minute when the head of department's wife had gone into early labour, so Tom had changed his flight and rushed home to pack a bag. If they landed on time, and traffic was light from the airport, he should arrive at his father's house, where Vivienne was staying, in plenty of time for dinner.

September the second they'd settled on for the wedding, four weekends from now. They were getting married in the church in rural County Kildare where Vivienne's parents had tied the knot. The choice of venue had surprised Tom, with her parents' knot having been untied after eight years, and with both parties now in second marriages, but Vivienne had set her heart on the old stone church, which he had to admit was charming.

The reception afterwards for their two hundred and

fifty-four guests was taking place in a Dublin hotel. The venue was fifty kilometres from the church, but it would facilitate the newlyweds' flight the following morning to Dubai, a place Vivienne had always wanted to see. It's our day, she'd insisted. We can arrange it any way we please. People won't mind travelling.

He'd have done it differently. He'd have had a small wedding, like Joel and Sarah's. He'd have kept it low-key, with dinner after the ceremony in a venue close to the church, and a honeymoon in the Cotswolds, or maybe Scotland. He loved a party normally, but for some reason he'd have welcomed a gentler, quieter introduction to married life.

He hadn't argued though. Vivienne had told him, on the plane back to London after his proposal, that it had disappointed her. *Sarah and Joel's back garden isn't my idea of romantic,* she'd said, *especially not on their anniversary.*

I chose the day because it was our anniversary too, he'd pointed out, but it hadn't really washed with her. He figured that after a disappointing proposal, she was owed whatever wedding day she wanted, so he'd put up no objection to the lavish plans.

It didn't matter. What mattered was that she'd said yes, that she'd promised to spend the rest of her life with him. What mattered was that in a few weeks they'd be husband and wife.

He'd debated phoning his father to let him know the change of plan, and swearing him to secrecy, but then he'd decided against it. If dinner wouldn't stretch to feed a third, he'd order a takeaway.

His luck was in. The flight landed ahead of schedule. He retrieved his hand luggage and hurried through the various checks to the taxi rank. Within fifteen minutes of touching down he was on his way into the city.

'Home for the bank holiday?' his driver enquired. The taxi smelt strongly of garlic.

'I am, yeah.'

'Working abroad?'

'Yup, London. OK if I open a window?'

'Fire away.'

It was misting lightly. He stuck his head out and drank in the cooler, fresher air he'd been craving. They could stroll to Leeson Street for a drink after dinner; he wouldn't mind a few Dublin Guinnesses. He'd wait and see what she wanted.

They arrived. He paid off the driver and bounded up the steps to the front door and let himself in quietly. He dropped his bag on the rug in the hall and stood for a moment. He'd always loved his family home, with its high ceilings and sweeping staircase, its spacious rooms and solid, familiar furniture.

There wasn't a sound. He could smell no dinner cooking. He walked through the hall, opening doors and finding empty rooms. He climbed the stairs, his hand sliding up the polished wood of the banister, past the framed family photos that climbed with him. Eight-year-old Joel holding his infant brother in his arms. Mam and Dad on honeymoon in Wales. Tom at three or four, sitting solemnly on Santa's lap and clutching a wrapped box.

She might still be in town. She might have arranged to meet friends for dinner. But where was Dad? Surely not still at work at this hour on a Friday?

He entered the bedroom they used when they visited. His old room, a double bed having replaced the single several years earlier. Vivienne's heady scent hit him when he walked in. Her weekend case was open on the bed, clothes spilling from it. Her phone was on the pillow, her jacket thrown across a chair. Her black stilettos were on the floor, one tipped over, exposing its red underside.

She wasn't gone out, not without her phone. He dropped his bag and looked through the window. There was nobody in the back garden. He checked the bathroom, also empty. Where was she? He stood on the landing, thinking — and then he heard a sound coming from his father's room.

A laugh.

Vivienne's unmistakable throaty laugh.

He didn't stop to think. He walked across the landing and threw open the door – and there they were. There they both were in his father's bed, heads whipping around at Tom's entrance, her laughter cutting off abruptly.

'Tom—' His father threw back the sheet and scrambled out of bed, his nakedness, here, now, so horrific that Tom turned and took the stairs two at a time, three at a time as his father called after him to stop, please stop. He didn't stop. He ran through the hall and wrenched the door open and stumbled down the steps, almost losing his footing in his haste to get away, unaware of the rain that had worsened while he was inside.

He kept going, kept rushing away from them, his mind racing as fast as his body, everything whirling madly about, nothing making sense, nothing able to be processed, nothing possible for him to do but keep going, keep going, don't stop, don't stop.

He left the square behind and blundered on, heedless of direction. He collided with people. He skirted a bin on the path but didn't quite miss it, sending it wobbling away from him to crash down on its side. He banged his knee on the handle of a baby buggy. He leapt over someone's suitcase, barely clearing it. He heard 'Hey!' and 'Watch it!' Horns blared as he crossed streets without looking. He didn't react to any of it, didn't stop, his only coherent thought to keep going, get away.

And eventually, of course, he stopped. He stopped, breathless, at the counter of a bar he didn't know and he took out his wallet with trembling hands and found two fifty-euro notes in it, and he ordered a whiskey, something he rarely drank. 'Large,' he said, and downed it in two burning swallows that knocked what breath was left out of him.

'Another,' he said, when he could talk again, and another came after that, and soon time became too slippery to hang on to, and all he could see was Vivienne's look of astonishment, the tumble of her hair as she lay unclothed in his father's bed, and he had to blot it out. He had to keep drinking until he couldn't see it any more.

And somewhere along the way, when he was hardly able to stand, when faces and voices were sliding away from him, he lurched against a man at the counter, who turned and pushed him roughly in the other direction and snarled at him to fuck off – and that was all he needed. That was all it took for his fuzzy tormented brain to crack.

He came back and landed a drunken punch that would probably have done no damage at all if the other *man hadn't been in the act of turning away with a full pint. The drink went flying; the man, taken by surprise, slipped and crashed down, banging his head on the pub's stone floor.*

And he stayed down while someone bent over him, and someone else, two someone elses, pinned Tom to the counter, and someone else phoned for an ambulance and the guards.

Beth

'I'll be back by seven at the latest,' she said. 'Probably earlier.'

No rush.

'Don't forget to put a match to the fire when you get in from the library.'

I won't.

'And remember to take the salmon out of the fridge while the oven is heating up, and then put it in for twenty minutes, middle shelf, a hundred and eighty degrees.'

I will.

'The potatoes just need to be reheated for ten minutes, and there are peas in the freezer. If you have any problems, anything at all, ring me – I mean text me.'

Lil just smiled at that. Beth was fussing; she knew she was. Lil didn't need her grandmother issuing a raft of instructions. It was no bad thing that she would be dining alone this evening – on the contrary, it might be an idea for Beth to find a reason to be missing for dinner on a regular basis, so Lil could get used to her own company at mealtimes.

But of course it wasn't Lil who was turning her into such a fusspot. She was cross with herself, with how jittery she felt. She was only going to Mark Purcell's house to give him his second cookery lesson, for Heaven's sake. It didn't merit an ounce of this nervousness.

Except ... recalling their last phone conversation, and his seeming reluctance to continue with the classes, she wondered again if she should have insisted on going ahead with them. She'd find out, this afternoon, the real reason for his hesitancy. She was going to ask him outright, first chance she got. She would demand the truth, and if genuine lack of interest was behind it, she'd call the whole thing off and offer Olive a refund. She wouldn't go where she wasn't wanted.

When Lil left for the library Beth washed up, and swept and mopped the kitchen floor, and vacuumed the entire house. She cleaned windows and dusted surfaces and wiped down skirting boards, compelled by ridiculous nervous energy to keep moving.

Lunchtime came and went. Tomato soup and crackers, followed by a pear and a wedge of cheese. Afterwards she pulled on the old shirt of Gerry's that had become her gardening coverall, and spent a couple of hours digging weeds from the rockery and coaxing more out from between the patio bricks, taking advantage of the lovely weather they were currently enjoying. A bit too soon for it in April though – would they pay later with a wet summer?

Eventually she returned her tools and gloves to the shed and went inside to clean up. Showered and changed, she filled her shopping basket with the ingredients that waited in the fridge. She added a grater in case he didn't have one, and a chopping board, and her knives. She brought the basket to the car and returned to the kitchen. She looked at the carrot cake she'd made early that morning, sitting now on the worktop.

Should she bring it? He might not even like carrot cake.

She twitched a shoulder, impatient with herself. For Heaven's sake, he could pass it on if he didn't like it. She found a tin for it and set it on the car's passenger seat.

She went back inside for the second time and climbed the stairs. She looked into the bathroom mirror and gave herself a talking-to. She brushed her teeth and applied a fresh coat of lipstick and blotted it. She straightened her skirt and pulled down the sleeves of her cardigan, and pushed them up again.

For Heaven's *sake*.

Before leaving the house she checked the windowsills front and rear, and found nothing. Lil's secret admirer appeared to have lost interest, no little anythings left in weeks, no communication since the Valentine card that had told them nothing. She decided she was relieved it had come to an end – what was the point of him shilly-shallying around, never having the courage to come forward and declare himself?

A quarter past four. She should get going. In the hall she collected the canvas bag of books she'd put together for him and left the house for the final time – and as she put the bag into the boot she thought she heard a sound from the front garden next door. She crossed to the hedge that divided them and saw her tenant on his knees by one of the flowerbeds, Killian's wheelbarrow on the path beside him.

'Tom,' she called, and he looked up, and she saw that he was holding a trowel.

'They were coming back,' he said. 'The weeds.'

'You don't have to do that. I wasn't expecting you to maintain it.'

'I don't mind, I like it. I hate to see them coming back.'

'In that case, please keep track of your time, and let me know at the end of the month how long you've spent.'

He shook his head. 'I don't need payment, Beth.'

It was the first time he'd used her name. She was glad he hadn't called her Mrs Sullivan. 'I pay the boy who mows my lawn in the summer,' she pointed out. 'I can't have you working for nothing.'

He lifted a shoulder. She was probably coming across as bossy again, but she couldn't make an unpaid gardener out of him. She looked at the beds that had always been Maria's territory. It had sickened her to see weeds filling the spaces where flowers had been, but now they were clear again, and he wanted to keep them clear.

'She planted flowers there every summer,' she said. 'My daughter. There wasn't room for a weed. My son-in-law did everything else in the garden, but those flowerbeds were her territory.'

She saw them again, Maria's favourites. Geraniums, begonias, busy lizzies, colourful little flowers marching along on both sides of the path, accompanying visitors from gate to front door.

'You want me to plant something new?' he asked.

She shook her head. She wasn't able for that. It was hard to see it bare now, but new flowers would be too painful.

'Thank you for offering,' she said. 'Thank you for looking after it, the house and the garden.'

'No problem.'

'Olive tells me you're going to lunch on her birthday,' she said, suddenly remembering.

'That's right.'

'Lil and I have been invited too.'

The invitation had come as a surprise. Maria and the girls had called to Olive every year with birthday presents, and since the accident Beth had felt she should carry on the tradition, so for the past two years she and Lil had dropped in gifts, but hadn't stayed for longer than was necessary to wish Olive a happy birthday, despite her urging. This year, though, it was going to be different.

Because it's falling on Easter Sunday, Olive had explained, I'm pushing the boat out. At first, Beth had demurred. You shouldn't be putting that work on yourself, she'd scolded, not at this stage in your pregnancy – but Olive had assured her that she was going to no trouble at all. Fred has booked a caterer from Listowel, if you don't mind, so I'll be twiddling my thumbs before you arrive, painting my nails and that. Do come – so Beth had accepted, for both of them.

'Perhaps we could travel together,' she said now.

He nodded. 'Sure. I'd be happy to take you both.'

She'd meant him to sit in with them – his Jeep looked a little … serviceable – but she thanked him and went off. Driving down the lane, she remembered her mixed feelings about him at the start, her reluctance to have anyone, any stranger living in Killian and Maria's home, and her misgivings when she realised that she'd forgotten to ask him for references, or for any information at all about his previous circumstances.

Now, three months on, she'd become reconciled to his living there, more than reconciled. He'd rescued the garden and was still looking after it, and he'd helped Lil with her new phone. He was polite and approachable, and a nice addition to the book club.

In fact, if she'd hand-picked a tenant, she thought she could hardly have done better.

She pulled up outside Mark's cottage just after half four. His car was parked around to the side, leaving plenty of room for hers. The place was neat, a row of terracotta pots lined up outside the front wall, each holding a different-coloured heather. As she switched off the engine, the white front door opened.

'I heard you coming,' he said. 'You're welcome, Beth.'

She regarded him in dismay, her first sight of him since his mishap. Frail was the word that came to mind. Despite his smile he looked alarmingly wan, and older than when she'd last seen him. His ankle was in a cast, a crutch wedged under each armpit. His temple had a new scar. He'd lost weight.

'Please go in and sit down,' she said. 'I can bring everything in.'

'I'd rather wait here. You don't know where the kitchen is.'

Stubborn as ever. As if she wouldn't be able to locate a kitchen. She popped open the boot, feeling suddenly dejected. She shouldn't have come. She should have respected his wishes, and not insisted.

She followed him silently into the house. It was tidier than she'd been expecting. No clutter, no mess in the small hall, his oilskin jacket hanging with a few others on a rack, the cream floor tiles spotless, a smell of polish in the air. His kitchen was equally fuss-free, the sink and draining board empty, the worktops holding just a toaster and a kettle. The round table in the centre was bare. The window was uncurtained. A glass door looked out on a small neat garden.

He leant his crutches against a chair and sank

down. 'I can chop and peel,' he said, 'if it's needed. My hands are still in working order, and I've just washed them.' He held them out for her inspection.

She paid no attention to them. She set her basket down on the table. 'You look terrible.'

For some reason, this made him smile. 'Thank you.'

She didn't smile back. 'Are you taking care of yourself?'

'I don't have to. I have great neighbours who pop in every day, and Olive has put enough food in my freezer to see me out. There's fear of me. You're allowed to sit down, and to smile,' he added.

But she didn't sit, and a smile was beyond her. 'I'm sorry,' she said. 'I should have listened to you. I shouldn't have come, if you didn't want me to. I'll go if you'd rather I left, if you don't feel up to this. It's not a problem.'

He drew back his clean hands and folded his arms and looked levelly at her. 'First of all, I do feel up to it. I might appear a bit shook, but I assure you I'm fine. Second of all, please don't ever think that I don't want to see you, Beth. The only reason I had reservations about this is that I feel your heart isn't in it. I suspect Olive talked you into it – I know how persuasive she can be – and that makes me uncomfortable.'

Beth took a seat then, her coat still on. She pushed the basket aside so she could see him properly. Honesty was called for here. She would be honest, as she always was, because she didn't know how else to be. She would be forthright as ever.

'I turned her down when she asked me first. It was the last thing I wanted to do. I thought the whole idea was ridiculous, giving cookery lessons to a man of seventy. I'm not saying seventy is old: you know I'm more than that, and I don't feel old. I just felt that you wouldn't be interested in changing your habits now – and I was also afraid that you'd treat it like a big joke, and tell all your friends, and they'd have a great laugh at my expense.'

She stopped. He didn't attempt to speak. His expression gave nothing away.

'But I changed my mind, and it wasn't Olive talking me into it. I changed my mind because it was Olive asking me to do something for her, it was Maria's friend asking me.' She blinked quickly. 'I got it into my head that if I did this for Olive, I'd be doing it for Maria too. I can't explain that, so don't ask me to.'

His eyes remained on her face, silently taking in the words.

'I still thought it a foolish notion, mind, and I

wasn't exactly looking forward to the first one. I
didn't think I'd enjoy it, but I did. I'm sorry I said
what I did about it being Olive's present, not mine
– I could see that made you uncomfortable, and
I felt bad about it. And I know you respected my
wishes not to broadcast what we were doing, and I
appreciated that. I'm happy to keep going with them,
but only if you are too. Do you want me to stay?
Please be honest.'

'I do,' he said simply, so she took off her coat and
hung it in his tidy hall, and put on her apron and
washed her hands and began. He peeled and chopped
an onion and grated a carrot as instructed, and she
did the rest as he looked on. He talked, not as much
as he normally did. The fall had taken its toll. She
hoped it wasn't permanent: it felt wrong not to have
him chattering as usual.

She chipped potatoes and tossed them in a little
oil before spreading them out on a baking sheet.
'Much healthier than deep frying,' she told him. She
mixed the grated carrot and the onion with minced
beef and crumbled in blue cheese, and seasoned it
with salt and pepper.

'Can you shape it into patties, like the fishcakes?'
she asked.

'Certainly.'

While he was doing that she heated the oven

and prepared a salad, and told him about the consignment of books that had been delivered a few days earlier to the library from a factory in Wales, following an employee's visit to Fairweather the previous autumn. 'She got all the workers to donate one book each, over fifty of them, and persuaded the management to cover the shipping cost.'

'Wasn't that marvellous. She must have been impressed with the library.'

As the meal was cooking he told her of his mother's apple crumble cake. 'A cake with a crumble topping. She never used a recipe, just guessed everything. It never failed.'

'Cake,' she said, 'I forgot' – and she went out to the car and brought in the tin.

'Just a little something,' she said. 'A get-well gift.'

He opened it. He dipped his head and sniffed. 'Spicy.'

'It's a carrot cake. There's cinnamon and nutmeg in it. If you don't like it you can pass it on.'

'Beth, the cake hasn't been invented that I don't like – and homemade is twice as good as shop-bought. This was thoughtful. Thank you.'

'And books,' she said, presenting the canvas bag. 'I asked Lil to put a few aside – although Fred and Olive are probably keeping you stocked up.'

'A man can never have too many books,' he

declared, and she thought of the first-edition of *Little Dorrit* he'd given her, just handed over that precious thing, and of how much she loved turning those old yellowed pages, how Dickens's words seemed to belong there, how they sounded even richer there.

When the smell of the food began to fill the room she set the table. He directed her to cutlery and serviettes and tablemats, and plain white crockery. 'I like things simple,' he told her. 'No frills. Nothing fancy.'

So did she. 'I didn't expect your house to be so neat,' she admitted, and he laughed with some of his old vigour. 'Don't be so quick to judge, Mrs Sullivan. I believe in a place for everything, and everything in its place.'

'I do too.' Who'd have thought they would have that in common?

Over dinner, she told him of Tom weeding the flowerbeds. 'It was kind of him. He didn't have to.'

'He's a good lad.'

'He is. He offered to plant new flowers, but I said no.'

Mark studied her. 'He tidied up the garden, and you were glad. Maybe it's time for more flowers. What ones do you like?'

She told him freesias, for their magnificent

scent. 'And sweet peas, for the scent too, and yellow roses. And I love fuchsia, and snowdrops.' She was reminded of the snowdrops that had been left at the back door in a newspaper cone, and the other little offerings. She debated telling him about them, and then thought better of it. Lil might not like her sharing it.

After the burgers – she'd coaxed him to have two, feeling the need to build him up – she made tea in his big brown pot, and they cut the carrot cake, and she asked if he'd been in touch with Tom about painting his house.

'Not yet. I must give him a ring.'

She washed up, ignoring his protests. She stowed his white crockery in its press, his cutlery in the drawer. She packed away her things but left him the cake tin, telling him she had plenty more. 'It will keep fresh in that for a week or so,' she said. 'I can let you have the recipe, if you like,' and he said yes, he would like.

'I won't promise anything – I never made a cake in my life, but I'll have great intentions. And I'll give the fishcakes a go too, as soon as I'm a bit more mobile. I told you I got the knife.'

'You did.' She put on her coat. 'So you're happy to go ahead with the last lesson?'

'Absolutely,' he replied, 'as long as you don't mind coming here again. I have three more weeks on the crutches.'

'Will we say next week so?'

'Next week is fine.'

'Same day, same time?'

'Perfect.' He reached for his crutches and hauled himself up to standing.

'What are you doing? Don't get up.'

'I'd like to see you out.'

'For goodness' sake, there's no need.'

'Too late, I'm up now,' he said, so she stopped wasting her breath.

'Thank you,' he said at the door. 'I enjoyed that. And thanks again for the cake.'

'My pleasure. See you next week.'

On the way home she found classical music on the radio and listened to Vivaldi without hearing him. Chicken, she thought. She had a nice simple recipe for Tuscan Chicken with spinach and Parmesan. Maybe not the healthiest, with a generous helping of cream, but he needed the calories right now.

And another cake, definitely.

Olive

'You're quiet,' she said.

'Ah no.'

'You are though. Are you feeling OK? Is your ankle at you?'

'No, it's coming right.'

Something was up. She knew him too well. She opened his fridge and found space for the eggs and milk and butter she'd picked up for him at the supermarket. She put on the kettle and took out two mugs, and reached for the biscuit jar.

'There's cake,' he said, pointing. She hadn't noticed the yellow tin, sitting in a corner of the worktop.

'Who brought you cake?'

'Beth. She made it.'

She turned to look at him.

He looked back at her. 'Carrot cake,' he said. 'Very tasty.'

She brought the tin to the table and prised off the lid, and lifted out what was left. 'Looks lovely.' She cut two slices and got plates for them. 'So Beth was here?'

'She was, a few days ago.'

She scalded the teapot and spooned in tea, and thought about the fact that Beth had been into the shop yesterday and had made no mention of the visit.

'Actually,' he said, as she brought the pot to the table, 'maybe there's something I should get off my chest.'

'Oh yes?' Oh no. He knew.

'I wasn't going to, I was going to leave it off, but maybe it needs to be said, Olive.'

She took milk from the fridge and got sugar from the press. His house was far tidier than hers, everything put away. In her house the sugar bowl and butter dish never left the table, or the salt and pepper.

'Why don't you sit down?' he said.

Here it came. She pulled out a chair and sat, and braced herself. He knew. He'd figured it out, or Beth had told him.

'The cookery lessons,' he said. 'They weren't Beth's idea, they were yours.'

'That's right. I thought I told you that.'

'You paid Beth,' he said mildly, 'to give me cookery lessons.'

He'd found out about the payment. Beth must have told him.

'You led me to believe,' he said, 'that they were Beth's idea.'

'Well, no, I—'

'Please,' he said. 'Olive,' he said, and she stopped. 'You put me in an awkward position, and Beth too. She assumed I knew you'd paid her.'

She felt awful. Cornered. Ashamed.

He lifted the teapot and filled both mugs, and added milk and sugar to his. 'It's alright,' he said. 'We won't fall out over it. I'm sure your motives were good, but I would have preferred if you'd been straight about it, that's all.'

'I'm sorry,' she said. 'Mark, I'm really sorry. Did I ruin things between you and Beth?'

'Not at all, we sorted it out.'

'And ... have you had the lessons?'

'I've had two out of three.'

She waited for him to elaborate, but he ate his cake and said no more.

'Am I forgiven?'

'Of course you are. Eat your cake.'

She took a bite. It was delicious. Of course it was delicious: Beth had baked it. 'My intentions *were* good,' she said.

'I don't doubt it for a minute.' He licked icing from his fingers. 'And thank you, the thought was kind. But you know you don't need to organise everyone's life.'

'I know. I'm sorry. It won't happen again, I promise.'

'I'm delighted to hear it. Now – tell me what you want for your birthday.'

She sighed. 'A healthy baby in June, Mark. That's literally all I want.'

He covered her hand with his. 'And that's what we all want for you, my darling girl. How are things going?'

'Well, I'm so happy to have hung on to this one that it feels wrong to be complaining at all, but I'll be very glad when the nine months are up, and I stop feeling like an elephant, and I can see my toes again.'

'Complain all you want. Catriona was killed from carrying the two boys. How's Nancy?'

'Still like a weasel, but I'm ignoring it – most of the time. I'm just glad you didn't see it when you were staying with us.'

'I didn't see a bit of it. She saves it for the one she's closest to. I've told her I'm planning a boat trip for the two of us, once this cast is off and I'm on my feet again.'

'Well, let's not plan too much. I hope you won't be rushing back to that boat.'

'I won't rush,' he said. 'I'll walk with great care.'

'Mark, I'm serious. I'm nervous about you going out in the boat, after the fall.'

'You needn't be a bit nervous. I'll take good care – and if Nancy is with me, you can rest assured I'll be doubly careful.'

'In that case, feel free to bring her off for a sail around Ireland – and take as much time as you need.'

He laughed. 'I was thinking more of a little spin around the bay for her birthday, with a picnic on board.'

Her birthday was the middle of next month. 'That sounds wonderful. I know she'd love it. Let's see how you are when the time comes.'

The days must seem endless to him, stuck in his house unless someone called to take him out. Still too cold to sit in the garden for any length of time, no matter how bundled up he was. Not able to get much beyond his front gate on the crutches, so he was pretty helpless. He had his books, of course, but nobody could read solidly for six weeks.

They did what they could. Fred collected him for dinner each Sunday and dropped him home again, and either he or Olive dropped by every few days. Various friends called around to play cards with him, and on Friday nights someone brought him to Fred's for a pint – but for all that it must be frustrating for him to be without the means to leave the house under his own steam. Still, he was on the mend, and for that she was grateful.

'Tom was here,' he said.

'Was he? When?'

'Yesterday. He's going to paint the house for me, as soon as it gets a bit warmer.'

'That's great.'

She was torn by the news. Glad he'd accepted that he couldn't do it, sad that he'd had to hand it over. Would he ever be hale enough to climb a stepladder again with his brushes and bucket of paint, and put her heart in her mouth until it was all finished? Hopefully he'd get stronger, come back to his old self.

'Tom isn't happy,' she said.

'He isn't?'

She shook her head. 'There's something troubling him. I've thought so from the first time I met him.'

'Have you asked him about it?'

'No. I don't want to pry.'

'Really, Olive?'

Dripping with mock disbelief. She decided to ignore it. 'You might be able to draw him out when he's doing the painting. You know, man to man.'

He laughed. 'You don't give up, do you? Trying to sort everyone out.'

'I'm afraid not. I'm programmed that way.'

When she got home, before she could think about it and change her mind, she rang Beth.

'Good morning, Olive.'

'Beth – hello.' She crossed her fingers. 'I'm ringing to apologise.'

'Whatever for?'

'I'm afraid I was deliberately … um, vague, when I told Mark about the cookery lessons. I was afraid he might not want to go if he thought I'd set them up, so I, well, I sort of insinuated that they were your idea.'

There were a few seconds of silence. 'I see.'

'I'm sorry.'

'I assumed the mistake had been on his part. I thought he'd simply misunderstood you.'

'I'm afraid not, Beth. I'm very sorry. It was wrong of me to mislead him like that, and I shouldn't have done it.' She plunged on. 'It's just that I know how highly he thinks of you, and I knew he'd be delighted if he thought they were your idea.'

'But they were *not* my idea. In fact, you'll recall that I said no when you asked me. You really had no right to take matters into your own hands like that, Olive.'

'I know. I'm sorry.' She uncrossed her fingers. They weren't helping. 'Beth, I don't blame you if you're angry. You have every right.'

'I *am* a little annoyed, Olive. It was embarrassing for both of us, and it shouldn't have happened. However, you've apologised now, so let's not dwell on it.'

'Thank you. And you and Lil are still coming to lunch on Sunday?'

'Of course we are. We're travelling with Tom.'

'Great. Thanks, Beth, I'll see you all at two then.'

She hung up, chastened. The end of her short-lived matchmaking career – but at least both parties were still talking to her, and to each other. And the lessons were going ahead, two out of three down.

And Beth had baked him a carrot cake. Maybe all was not lost.

'Gramps says hello,' she told Nancy later. 'He misses you. He'll see you on Sunday for my birthday lunch.'

Nancy glanced up from her drawing. 'OK.'

'We'll have a great day.'

Nothing. She gave up.

The days passed and Sunday dawned. She awoke to find Fred gone from the bed, and another dry, blue-sky day looking in at her from the pulled-apart curtains. She thought, as she always did now on birthday mornings, of Maria ringing first thing to sing down the phone to her.

She focused on the positive. Today she was one day closer than yesterday to being a birth mother. Eight weeks to go, the new life reassuringly heavy inside her, the gynaecologist happy with her progress.

You're doing great, he'd told her at her last check-up, just over a week ago. Baby's heartbeat is strong; all looks fine. You've gained a little more weight than you need, so maybe ease off on the treats, and keep moving as much as you can. Any questions? And she'd told him no, no questions, because she knew he couldn't answer the only one she wanted to ask. Doctors by and large were wonderful, but they couldn't predict the future.

The bedroom door opened and Fred appeared with a tray. 'Birthday breakfast,' he announced, setting it down on her locker's book pile. 'Do you need me to haul you up?'

'Yes please.'

He'd poached her an egg. It was perched on a slice of toast that was buttered right to the edges. How well he knew her. Propped against the little teapot was a pink envelope.

'Happy birthday,' he said, giving her a kiss. 'Your present will come later.'

She poured tea. 'Because you forgot to get me something?'

'No.'

She added milk. 'Because you ordered it online and it hasn't arrived?'

'No.'

She stirred. 'Because you hid it somewhere and now you can't remember?'

'No. Wait and see.' He straightened the book pile. 'Listen, don't go mad – I have to make a quick run to the pub.'

She looked at him in dismay. 'What, this morning? Ah, Fred – you said you took the day off.'

'I did, but I have an awful feeling I forgot to lock the safe last night, and I want to check it.'

'Can't Sean check it when he gets in?'

'He won't be there for another couple of hours. I can't relax until I know, Ollie. I won't be long, honest.'

'Is Nancy up?'

'She is, watching telly. Don't take the tray downstairs – I'll do it when I get back.' He gave her another quick kiss and was gone, leaving her to eat her egg and open her card, and take a call from her mother, who'd flown to Tenerife for Easter a few days earlier with two other widows.

'What did you get from Fred?'

'Nothing yet – he says it's coming later.'

'Ah, he forgot. Don't be too hard on him. How are you?'

'Fine. Feeling grand.' Her mother had carried three babies to full term: no need to go into the highlights of the third trimester for her.

'And Nancy?'

'In top form.' No point in going there either, giving her something to worry about on her sunbed.

'How's Mark doing? Is he still on the crutches?'

'He is for another while, but he's bearing up. He's coming for lunch today.'

'Give him a hug from me.'

'I will.'

Olive had considered trying to get those two together, before she'd become aware of Mark's feelings for Beth. Her mother was mad about him, and Olive had thought they'd suit one another. Maybe more so than Mark and Beth, who could hardly be more different. No accounting for the heart though, and the goals it set itself.

Of course, if nothing came of the cookery lessons, if Mark's affections weren't returned, Olive might reconsider her decision to give up the matchmaking, and start to invite her mother to come and stay more often. The new baby would be the perfect excuse for that. The two surviving grandparents could take it out for walks.

She showered and put on the royal blue maxi dress she'd bought for a tenner at a market in Lanzarote, shortly before they'd taken possession of Nancy. It was as wide as a tent, acres of polyester dropping without interruption in voluminous folds from its embroidered neckline to the ground. In Lanzarote she'd worn it loose, loving the freedom of it, and the full swirl of it every time she moved. During cooler Irish summers she'd tied various belts around her waist to give it some shape; now, with her waist having gone into hiding, she found a narrow red scarf and secured it beneath her bust. She slipped on a white cardigan, and added a silver necklace that she'd instructed Fred to give her last Christmas.

She stood in front of the mirror. Not quite a Greek goddess, but close. Disregarding Fred's instruction, she carried her tray down the stairs carefully – all she needed was to trip on her hem and go flying – and washed up. She put her head around the sitting-room door. 'Good morning, honeybun,' she said.

Nancy was stretched on the couch, bundled into

a throw. 'Morning,' she said, without taking her eyes from the cartoons on the screen.

'Happy birthday to me,' Olive said, stepping into the room. 'Look, I have my birthday dress on.' She did a slow twirl, letting the dress billow out.

Nancy glanced over. 'Happy birthday,' she said, eyes sliding back to the television.

Last year she'd got Olive two scratch cards and a chocolate orange. Olive had won a tenner on one of the cards. She'd told Nancy to cash it and keep the money, but Nancy had returned to the shop and exchanged the winning card for five more. She'd refused to scratch any herself, insisting they were still part of Olive's present, and Olive had waited to scratch them until Nancy had chosen a bicycle as her reward if they had a big win, and not one of the new cards had yielded a cent.

This year was looking a little different.

'Did you have breakfast?' Olive asked.

'Yeah.'

'Right. I'll be in the kitchen.'

Sitting alone at the table she filed and painted her nails, and plucked her eyebrows, and checked the time. Forty minutes since Fred had left. The pub was twelve minutes away in the car on a Sunday morning unless he hit the mass-bound traffic, but he was too early for that. He must have stayed on for an illicit coffee, which she couldn't object to.

Fifteen minutes later there was still no sign of him. As she picked up her phone to call him it rang, and she saw her neighbour's name on the screen.

'Morning, Evelyn.'

'Olive – listen, I hate to bother you, but could I ever borrow Fred for two minutes? There's an enormous spider in the kitchen.'

Evelyn's terror of spiders was legendary. She lived alone, so either Fred or Aidan Gogarty on the other side were called on every so often to banish one from her house.

'Fred's not here right now, Evelyn. What about Aidan?'

'I've tried but there's no answer. I'm sorry, Olive – I hate to be a nuisance.'

'Not at all.' Olive looked down at her dress-tent. Fine for swanning around the house on her birthday, not the ideal garb for hunting down a spider. But she didn't fear them, and Evelyn had stepped up since Mark's fall to take Nancy after school on the days Olive was working. 'I'll come over.'

'Oh, I hate to trouble you, Olive, in your condition.'

'It's no trouble. I'll be there in a jiffy.'

She returned to the sitting room. 'Just going to

Evelyn's to get rid of a spider, won't be long. Dad should be back any minute.'

'OK.'

She threw on a jacket and hurried around to the back of Evelyn's house, and opened the door that was never locked. The kitchen, as she'd expected, was empty.

'Evelyn?'

'I'm in the hall. Thanks for coming, Olive.'

'Where did you see it?'

'Above the sink, on the ceiling.'

She looked up. She scanned the entire ceiling and saw no spider. She opened presses and peered inside, moving tins and packets about. She pulled saucepans and frying pans from their positions. She lifted each jar in turn from the spice rack, and searched around the kettle and toaster and bread bin.

She shifted the radio from its position on the windowsill, and shook out a bundle of newspapers that was on the table. She sat and hooked up Evelyn's slippers one by one with her foot, and peered into them and found nothing.

When she ran out of places to look she stood in the middle of the kitchen floor and let her gaze roam slowly about the entire room, and detected no movement at all.

'Evelyn,' she called, 'there's no sign of it. I've

looked just about everywhere. I think it must have moved on.'

'Oh no – I hate when they disappear like that. Did you try all the presses, Olive?'

'I really did.'

'What about under the table?'

'Yes, there too. And it's not in your slippers.'

A phone rang. 'Just a sec,' Evelyn called, and Olive took a seat again and waited, and wondered if Fred was home yet, and if he'd remembered to eat a mint after he'd finished his coffee, so his breath wouldn't make her want to retch.

The hall door opened. Evelyn entered, smiling widely. 'Olive, you look gorgeous. Happy birthday, and many more. That was Fred. He says it's safe for you to go back home now.'

Olive stared at her. 'Fred? Safe for me to go back? What's he on about?'

'He asked me to distract you while he brought in your present.' She laughed. 'Sorry about the lie.'

'You mean there was no spider?'

'Not this time. Fred said it was the only thing that would be sure to get you to come over. He knew you wouldn't let me down in my hour of need.'

It wasn't often he got the better of her. 'So I'm allowed back now?'

'You are, and I'm dying to know what he got you. Will you send me a snap?'

'Come on over' – so the two of them returned next door, where Fred was waiting with Tom in the kitchen. Tom?

'Happy birthday, Olive,' he said, handing her a box of Ferrero Rocher. 'You look nice.'

'Thank you.' She introduced him to Evelyn, thinking fast. What was he doing here so early? Lunch wasn't for another three hours.

'Your present's in the hall,' Fred told her, so she went out and they all followed – and there, standing by the wall, was a clock.

Not just a clock. The most wonderful clock she'd ever seen. The most glorious creation she'd ever set eyes on.

She stepped towards it slowly. It was her height. It was colourful, so colourful. It had feet with shoes on them, and real laces in the shoes. Its tick was steady. Its triangular pendulum swung in perfect sync. As she took it all in there was a soft whirr, followed by five chimes.

It was eleven o'clock, not five o'clock. She smiled. It was perfect.

'It's perfect.' She looked at Tom. 'You made it.'

'I did, on Fred's orders.'

'Tell me the wrong chime is deliberate.'

'I'm afraid so.'

She turned to her husband, reached for his hand. 'You got me a grandfather clock,' she said. 'You got Tom to make me a completely unique and very lovely grandfather clock.'

'I did. You gave me the idea.'

'I love it,' she said. 'It might just be my best present ever.' She hugged him as well as she could hug anyone right now, and after that she hugged Tom for making it, and then she hugged Evelyn so she wouldn't feel left out. 'What do you think?' she asked her, and their neighbour said she'd never come across anything like it, which probably meant that it wasn't to her taste. Evelyn was a dote, but she was more a staying-inside-the-lines kind of person.

'Has Nancy seen it?' Olive asked Fred.

'Yeah, she checked it out. She said it was cool.'

Cool. High praise from an almost twelve-year-old.

'Where do you want it?' Fred asked. 'I held on to Tom so we could move it.'

'Let's leave it right here for now,' she said, so Tom went away till lunchtime, and Evelyn went home, and Fred and Olive played Scrabble in the kitchen until it was time for him to go and pick up his father.

In due course Olga the caterer showed up, and

while she was setting out her food the other three arrived, all together in Tom's Jeep. Beth brought bath oil that Olive knew was expensive, and Lil gave her a soft wrap in a beautiful apple green shade.

Tom, on being introduced to Nancy, handed her a package.

'It's not my birthday,' she said.

'No, but your mum told me it's next month, so this is an early present, in case I don't see you,' and Olive marvelled at his thoughtfulness. She's acting up, she'd told him a while back. I've threatened her with no birthday party in May – and he'd remembered.

Nancy looked at her father, and then at her mother, and back at her father again. 'Will I open it?'

'It's up to you,' he told her. 'You can open it today or keep it till your birthday, but you should probably say thank you to Tom now.'

'Thank you,' she said, and ripped it open, and found a piece of driftwood that read *Nancy's room*. He'd painted every letter a different colour, and none of the letters were backwards, and Olive knew it was because he hadn't known if Nancy would appreciate that kind of thing.

Lunch was salmon in pastry, and asparagus with hollandaise sauce, and baby potato salad. By special request, the caterer had provided a small pizza for

Nancy, who would live on pizza if she had a choice –
and who, to her mother's relief, behaved impeccably
throughout the meal. And who might just be
developing a small crush on Tom, if her glances in
his direction were anything to go by.

And if she didn't once address her mother, or join
in the singing of 'Happy Birthday' that accompanied
the arrival of the candle-decked chocolate cake, Olive
refused to let it bother her.

And afterwards, after Nancy had been excused
to go to her room, and the others had been ushered
into the sitting room to eat cake and drink tea at
the fire, she asked Tom if he'd like to see the garden.
And when they were out the back, and he was
looking politely at the space that didn't deserve to
be called a garden, she said, 'Listen, I just wanted to
say something to you.'

He shot her a look. 'You brought me out here
under false pretences?'

'I did. I wanted to get you on your own because I
wanted to say thank you.'

He gave her a quizzical smile. 'For what?'

'For all you've done. For being kind to Nancy,
because you know we're going through a tricky
time. For agreeing to paint Mark's house, which has
put my mind at rest. For bringing back Maria and

Killian's garden – you don't know how much that meant to Beth. For creating those adorable little houses. For joining the book club, and giving us a bit of fresh input. And last but not least, for making that magnificent clock. Tell me honestly: did it break your heart?'

'It was tricky – but I enjoyed the challenge.'

'Would you hate the thought of making another?'

'Not really, now that I know I can.'

'Well, if you do, I'll be happy to sell it.'

'Really? You think it would sell?'

'In a trice. Was I wrong about the houses?'

'No, but the houses—'

'But nothing. Be sure to keep an account of what you spend on it, and your hours. I'm sure Fred didn't pay you half enough, but I'll put a fair price on the next one. Now I'd better bring you in, or they'll think we've absconded.'

He stayed put. 'There's one thing,' he said, 'I need to tell you.'

His face changing, all trace of a smile gone. She waited.

'My father. He's not dead. I told you he died, but he didn't.' He stopped, started again. 'He – we … fell out, last year. I can't say any more about it, but it was bad, and we haven't spoken since. I'm sorry I lied to you, Olive.'

Glory be. He looked so anxious she wanted to reach out and hug him, but she didn't. It mightn't be the right time for a hug. 'Tom, that's OK. I'm sure you had good reason.' But what reason could there possibly be? How badly must they have fallen out for him to say such a thing?

'If you ever need to offload,' she said, 'you can. Believe it or not, I can keep a secret.'

'Thanks.'

But he said no more, so they went back to the others. By four they were all gone, Tom taking Mark along with the other two. After they'd waved them off, Olive and Fred stood in the hall, she leaning into him.

'We had the book club to lunch,' she said. 'It didn't hit me until this minute.'

'So we had.'

A beat passed.

'Tom likes Lil,' she said.

'Ollie,' Fred said warningly.

'I'm just saying. Did you see how he kept shooting looks at her, all through lunch?'

'Leave it alone, Ollie.'

'I'm just making an observation, Fred.' Although it sounded like Tom had a lot more on his plate than a crush on Lil, and poor Lil had a pretty full plate too.

'What about those cookery lessons for my father?' he asked. 'Did they ever go ahead?'

'They did, two of them at least.'

'He never mentioned them to me.'

'That's because Beth wanted them kept low-key, I told you.'

'I'm his son,' he protested. 'I'm not the town gossip.'

'You also run a pub. He probably didn't want to take any chances.'

'So he can cook now?'

She laughed. 'I have no idea. He didn't tell me anything either; I kind of found out by accident.' She doubted that even Beth could turn him into a cook, but maybe he was picking up a few pointers. Maybe he'd make a bit more of an effort now.

'So you like the clock?'

'I love it so much. I still can't believe you thought of asking Tom. I asked him if he'd consider making another one to sell in the shop. I think he could definitely make a living from them.'

'I probably didn't pay him half enough.'

'I'm pretty sure you didn't. I'm also thinking he might like to fix up our garden sometime.'

'What garden?'

'Stop that. I thought it would be nice to have someplace pretty to sit in the summer.' She looked at him. 'With the baby.'

He squeezed her hand.

'Come on,' she said, 'I think there might be some cake left. You put the kettle on while I go to the loo.' She'd make no mention of the lack of a present from Nancy, not wanting to bring him down.

But when she went upstairs later to change into pyjamas and slippers, she found a wrapped package on her bed, with *Happy birthday from Nancy* written in biro on the wrapping. Not forgotten after all.

She opened it and found a framed photo of the two of them. A day trip they'd taken to Galway last September, to visit Olive's mother. They were on the prom at Salthill, and the sun was out, and Nancy was laughing at something, and Olive was smiling at her, and her mother had caught it perfectly on her phone, and sent the snap to Fred so he could see how happy his two girls were.

She looked at the photo. Fred had organised it, of course. It was exactly the kind of thing he would have done. He would have asked Nancy if she needed help getting a gift, or maybe offered to take care of it altogether. Doing what he thought was best, trying to smooth things out between them.

He'd got it wrong, of course. He'd chosen one of Olive's favourite photos, but the very last one Nancy would have picked right now to put into a frame for her mother. He'd done it for the right reason though, and she loved him for it.

She'd say nothing. She'd thank Nancy for her gift, and tell her she was delighted with it. She'd find a space on the wall and hang it up – and whenever Nancy decided that she loved her mother again, they'd both enjoy looking at it.

The April
Book Club Meeting

'Welcome back,' she said. 'It's nice to have you with us again.'

He still wore his cast, but he was down to one crutch. She told herself he looked stronger. Did he?

For the final cookery lesson they'd made the creamy chicken dish, and the little savoury scones Beth always baked to accompany it. While it was cooking she'd talked him through the steps of an omelette, and he'd written it down on the reverse of the carrot cake recipe she'd brought along – and after dinner, over coffee and slices of the lemon cake she'd also brought, he'd challenged her to a game of gin rummy, and beaten her.

Three nights later, he'd rung. I made blue cheese burgers, he'd told her, sounding exceedingly pleased with himself. They broke up a bit, but they tasted fine. The next time he phoned, a few nights after that, it was to tell her that Tom had made a start on the house painting. The next call was to ask if he could use cooked sausages in an omelette. The time after that was to confess that he'd mislaid the fishcakes recipe, and could she please drop another copy in to Olive next time she was in the shop.

He must be bored, still stuck in the house most of the time. He was probably phoning everyone in his contact list.

'Your cast will be off soon,' she said now.

'Another week. Can't come quick enough.'

'I hope you won't be in a hurry back to that boat.'

'I need to get the sea air into my lungs, Beth. I need it to revive me.'

'You could do that with a short walk on the prom.'

'I could, but being on the water is in my blood. I think I should have been a sailor, or a fisherman. I missed my calling.'

'A bit late for that now,' she said, and he told her it was never too late for anything. She didn't contradict him, but it seemed to her that seventy was too late for at least some things.

'I need to make up for lost time,' he said. 'Anyway, I've promised Nancy that we'll take a little boat trip, just the two of us, for her birthday – I can't let her down.'

No talking to him, as usual. To be fair, once she'd

set her mind on something she wasn't easily swayed either. 'Well, please be careful.'

'I will. There's something else,' he said. 'Something I wanted to ask you.' Shooting a quick glance at Olive and Fred, who were showing photos to Lil at the desk.

'I was wondering,' he said, turning his voice down a notch, 'if I could tempt you to come back to my house for dinner once my cast is off.'

'Dinner?'

'I want to try out one of the dishes on you. I need a guinea pig before I inflict my cooking on the wider world. I need to make sure I'm doing it right, and you're the obvious person to be the judge of that.'

He was inviting her to dinner. No mention of Lil, just Beth. Visiting his house to give him a cookery lesson was one thing; having him cook for her and her alone was entirely a different matter. Going to dinner in his house without the excuse of a lesson was, in essence, a date.

Nonsense. It was a trial run, just like he'd said. No need to make a song and dance about it – and if it encouraged him to keep putting what she'd taught him into practice, she could hardly refuse. 'I'd be happy to,' she said. 'Let me know when you feel up to it, and we can decide on a day.'

'Excellent. I might even tempt you to another game of gin rummy.'

'You might.' She suspected he'd cheated last time. She'd have to keep a sharp eye on him.

Tom arrived just then. Seats were taken, and the meeting got underway. Beth's choice of the chef's autobiography got a better reception than she'd been expecting, with even Mark giving it a mostly positive review. 'Good to see another side to the public face,' he said, 'although you'd wonder about some of his stories. Very far-fetched.'

A little rich, coming from him.

It was Olive's turn to suggest the next read. She gave them a new detective story from an author they'd often read. Olive tended to stick with the tried and trusted.

'Hopefully you'll make the meeting,' Beth said.

'Oh, I will – I won't be due for another two weeks. I was thinking of going out on maternity leave that day actually, so I'll be a lady of leisure.'

After the meeting ended the six of them left together, goodbyes exchanged as usual at the top of the garden. While Lil was hanging their coats, Beth pushed up her sleeves and turned on the tap to rinse the mugs – and as she did so, something pale caught her eye on the outside sill. She opened the window and took in a packet of flower seeds. Sweet pea seeds. Lil's mystery man was back, after several weeks of no deliveries. She didn't know whether to be glad or sorry.

Sweet peas. Hadn't the subject of flowers come up in conversation with someone lately? She'd grown them for years in a planter on the patio, so that she and Gerry could enjoy them when they sat out there in the summer. She would coax the plants through a section of trellis as they grew, and they would bloom and fill the place with their beautiful scent.

She'd stopped planting them after Gerry died. She'd kept the rockery going, further down the garden, but she'd given up on the sweet peas. She missed them in the summer, but somehow it seemed wrong to plant them, knowing he couldn't enjoy them with her. The trellis was ripped from the wall in a storm, a few years after his death, and she saw no point in replacing it. And after Maria and the others were taken, flowers of any kind were the last thing on her mind.

But now she had a packet of seeds. It was like a gentle prod, a small nudge. She thought again of Tom's offer to plant new flowers next door. She looked at the soft jewel colours of the sweet pea flowers. She could almost catch their sweet aroma.

She closed the window and turned off the tap. She'd visit the garden centre in Tralee that she often used. She'd go tomorrow. She'd see what they had in stock. She wouldn't replicate the past, wouldn't try to reinstate Maria's beds. She'd choose different flowers, maybe some of the old cottage garden ones, lupins and hollyhocks and foxgloves – and a rambling rose by the front door would be lovely. All gone out of fashion now, but she still loved them.

And she'd pick up more trellis at the garden centre, and Tom would fix it to the wall for her. The old planter was still in the back porch: she'd sow these seeds in it, and thread the shoots through the trellis like before.

Mark was right. It was time for flowers again.

MAY

Tom

'You've done a fine job,' Mark said. 'As good as I'd do myself – and that's high praise.'

'Glad to hear it.' Tom got out of his overalls. He put his brushes into a plastic bag and replaced the lid on the final bucket of paint. 'You've a quarter left in this. Will I drop it into the shed?'

'Do. I'll put the kettle on.'

Mark's small rear garden was simply laid out. Bushy plants bordered a paved central area that had a clothesline running along one side of it. Budding nasturtiums filled a narrow raised bed close to the back door, with a cast-iron garden seat next to it.

A tiny wooden shed in a corner had recently been varnished – Mark's doing maybe, before his fall. Tom found order within: tools hanging, a pair of wellingtons by the door, a watering can and paint tins on a shelf.

As he was wiping his hands on an old cloth, Mark reappeared.

'Tea or coffee for you?'

'Coffee would be good, thanks.'

The day being fine they sat out on the garden seat, and ate cake with chunks of apples in it and a crumbly topping. 'Made it myself,' Mark said. 'You needn't be spreading that around – my reputation would be in tatters.'

'You're a secret baker so?'

'Would you believe this is my very first attempt? I was telling someone about a cake my mother used to make, and she only went and found me a recipe for it, so I felt obliged to try it out.'

'It's tasty.'

'It's not bad.' He sat back in the seat and gave a contented sigh. 'Wonderful to have that blasted cast off. Life is good, isn't it?'

Life used to be good, Tom thought. It used to be great.

Mark glanced at him. 'Not so good with you?'

'… It's getting better.'

'You've had troubles.'

It didn't feel like he was prying. It felt like an observation, with no curiosity in it. 'I have.'

Mark set his mug on the card table he'd brought outside. 'I've had regrets in my life, Tom. Sometimes they were caused by things I did, and other times by things I didn't do, and should have.'

Tom ate his cake, and kept quiet.

'And I think, at the ripe old age of seventy, I've

finally realised that regrets serve no purpose at all. Regrets give you licence to let things fester that you might be better served trying to sort out. I know that mightn't always be possible, and sometimes things find their own resolution, but sometimes they don't, and then it can be hard to move on.'

He stopped and lifted his mug. Tom felt he was waiting for something, some response.

'I *am* moving on,' he said. He was. He'd realised, after the news of Vivienne's engagement had sunk in, that it had served to draw a line under their story. It had allowed him to turn the page, and finally leave her behind. She was part of his history now, unable to hurt him ever again – but of course there was something else, something that was not yet resolved. Something that was still festering inside him – and resolving this was a big ask. An almighty ask.

When he got home he took his painting gear from the Jeep and returned it to the garage. He shook out his overalls and cloths and draped them over the upended wheelbarrow. He washed brushes and set them out on the patio to dry. In the utility room he emptied the washing machine and pegged the damp clothes on the line outside. He returned to the kitchen and stood in the middle of the floor.

Could he do it? The very thought of it made him

feel sick – but Mark was right. He must do it, if he was ever to be happy again.

Before he could talk himself out of it he got his phone and dialled a number. Not in his contact list, gone from there, but still in his head.

He pressed call.

It was answered almost immediately.

'Tom … Tom?'

The familiar voice, although he'd been expecting it, jolted him into silence. The voice he'd heard say his name a thousand times caused a dart of pain. He couldn't do it.

'Tom, are you there? Is that you?'

He lowered the phone. He couldn't.

He must. He raised it slowly to his ear again.

'Tom … I'm sorry, I'm so sorry. I'll spend the rest of my life being sorry.'

Another long silence made its way from one phone to another. Tom stood, head bowed, searching for words that wouldn't come. Why had he thought he could do this?

'Tom. Talk to me. Please.'

And then something released within him, and the words spurted out in a hot angry rush. 'How could you do it?' he demanded. 'How could you hurt me like that? How could you?'

'It wasn't – I didn't set out—'

'I don't want excuses!' he yelled. 'I don't want to hear them! I wanted to kill you, do you know that? I wanted to *kill* you, and her!'

'I'm sorry—'

'Don't tell me you're sorry! What good is that now? I wanted to destroy you, like you destroyed me!'

A sound then, a low moan. 'Tom, if I could only undo it, if I could only turn the clock back—'

How many times had he wished the same? How many times had he backtracked in his head, tortured himself with a reimagining of that day? If he hadn't changed his flight, if he'd waited till the next day, if Vivienne had stayed with her sister instead. If, if, if.

So much he had wanted to know, so many unanswered questions. How it had started, and who had begun it, and how long it had been going on, and if love had come into it, and why neither of them had thought of him, and considered what it would do to him if he found out.

So much he'd hungered to know, all the questions that had tormented him afterwards, all the questions he'd almost asked Joel so many times – but what did it matter now? What difference did any of that make, now that it was all over?

As quickly as it had come, his anger ebbed. He

shut his eyes and listened to his father's soft sobbing at the end of the line until it diminished.

And then, gathering his courage, he forced himself to speak again.

'I forgive you,' he said. Three words, every bit as powerful as 'I love you'. Three words that offered resolution. 'I can't do this any more. I can't carry around this hate any more, so I have to forgive you.'

More silence. He heard the echo of his words in the silence – and then a long, shredded breath came down the line. 'Thank you, Tom. Thank you, son. You don't know what that means.'

'I don't want to see you,' he said. 'Not now. Not yet, and maybe not ever. But I wanted you to know that you're forgiven.'

He ended the call, unable for more. More would have to wait. He dropped his phone onto the worktop – and he felt, finally, at peace.

At peace.

He was at peace.

For the first time in months there was no quiet but insistent torment in his head, no hovering darkness. It was unfamiliar, this absence of turmoil. He was afraid to trust it.

He needed to do something. It was still only the middle of the afternoon, and while he could be getting on with the clock for Olive's shop that waited, half finished, in the garage, he needed to find something more physical, something that would take him over in his entirety, get him out of his head and focused on his body while he let this new sensation bed in. If he was a runner he'd run, but he wasn't – and walking wouldn't be enough.

And suddenly it came to him.

He took the stairs two at a time. He grabbed his swimming shorts from the wardrobe and rolled them tightly into a towel. Back downstairs he swiped his jacket from the hallstand and left the house. He strode along the cliff path, offering a nod to other walkers, none of whom he recognised – and with every step he took he was aware of a new energy, a new drive beginning to pulse through him. The day was continuing fine and dry, the sun weak but there, the clouds few.

By the time he reached the beach he was buzzing. He sat on a large rock and pulled off his boots and socks. He snatched them up and marched over cold sand and pebbles till he was just yards from the water's edge. At the far end of the beach he made out a few figures, and some running dogs, but there was nobody at all at his end, and nobody in the water, which was still and calm on this May afternoon.

He undressed quickly, his skin prickling with cold as the air hit it, conscious all the time of the euphoria, or adrenalin, or whatever it was that continued to surge through him. He felt more focused, his head clearer than it had been in a long time.

He could do anything. Anything. And the sea should be warmer than the last time he'd dipped into it, nearly a month ago.

He pulled on the shorts. He dropped his towel and walked to the shore and stepped in. The water felt no warmer. The cold of it drew a sharp intake of breath like before, but this time he didn't break his stride. He kept going, almost relishing the shock of the sea as it hit his warm skin.

At waist level he inhaled and plunged down with a yelp, submerging his shoulders, his neck and face, his ears, his head, the muffled roar of the sea taking over when he went under, the cold making his heart hop as he forced himself to stay below the surface for one, two, three seconds.

He gave a great leap upwards, skin burning and tingling. He waded further out and ducked again, and rose again. He continued in this way until he was chest deep, and then he launched into a clumsy breaststroke.

After a bit his body adjusted to the temperature,

and it got a little easier. He ploughed on, thrashing and kicking for what felt like an impressive length of time but which was probably a couple of minutes. When he ran out of breath he turned and floated back to his starting point, propelling himself with circling arms and scissor kicks until he spotted his bundle on the sand.

He waded panting from the sea and towelled himself dry. Exhilarated, triumphant, tingling, alive. He pulled on clothes and pushed fingers through damp hair and bundled up shorts and towel. He struck out for home, a blaze of heat inside him, fresh buoyancy in his step. He beamed at other walkers. 'Lovely day,' he said, and they agreed.

He arrived at the small gate. In his elation he decided to bound over it – but his back foot didn't quite clear the top, and he let out a startled yell as he came crashing down on the other side, his chin and chest taking the brunt, the impact winding him.

He lay where he'd fallen and waited for his breath to return, moving limbs cautiously to assess damage. Thanks to his grassy landing, nothing seemed to have been knocked askew. He massaged his stinging jaw, picturing the spectacle he must have presented as his great optimistic leap ended in an ignominious sprawl.

The image made him laugh aloud. He imagined startled witnesses rushing to his aid, and this brought new hoots of laughter. The more he laughed, the more it fed his merriment. He lay sprawled in the grass, guffawing helplessly, surrendering himself to the experience. So long since he'd laughed like this.

When it finally abated he pushed up to hands and knees, still grinning. As he got to his feet he saw Lil rounding the gap in the hedge and hurrying towards him. She must have heard his yelp as he went tumbling – or his hyena-like braying afterwards. If she hadn't thought him an idiot before, she definitely would now.

'I'm OK,' he said, stooping to retrieve the towel and togs he'd lost mid-flight. 'I tried to jump over the gate, but I didn't quite make it. I'm fine, nothing hurt but my pride.'

He walked back with her as far as the gap, bursts of residual laughter escaping. 'I've just been for my first swim here,' he explained. 'I think it went to my head a bit.'

She shook her head, smiling, and turned for the library. 'See you later,' he said, and chuckled all the way back to the house.

In the kitchen he rinsed the salt water from his shorts and squeezed them out, and added them to the clothesline with his towel. Now that he knew he could do it, he must go again soon. If he wasn't careful, he might be in danger of joining the ranks of the daily swimmers.

He spent a couple of hours working on the clock in the garage, the radio on, the big door wide open, a lone bee wandering in to float about. At six he shooed out the bee and returned to the kitchen, where he opened a can of beans, humming. When had he last hummed? He sliced bread and slotted it into the toaster. He threw sausages onto the pan. He was starving.

His phone rang as he was bringing his plate to the table.

'Joel.' He forked up a sausage. 'How's life in Kildare?'

'Dad phoned,' his brother said. 'Tom, he's so happy. It's terrific, what you've done. I'm proud of you.'

That served to sober him up. He took a bite of sausage. 'Wasn't easy.'

'I know it wasn't. Will you meet him?'

'I might, sometime.'

'I'm really happy you made that call. You feeling OK?'

'I am. I'm feeling good. I went for a swim.'

'You did?'

'I did. Only a few minutes, but still. It was bloody cold.'

They spoke of other things as he wolfed his dinner. Joel told him of the contract he'd signed with the Danes, and passed on the news that Sarah's sister was expecting twins in the autumn. Tom told him of his attempted leap over the back gate that had ended badly – and all through the conversation, which was peppered with laughter, his and Joel's, he was aware of a feeling of relief, and release. Nothing festering inside him.

His phone rang twice more, both new enquiries for work, and he took addresses and made appointments to drop by in the morning. He left his dishes on the table and sat with a can of beer on the back step while the clouds moved slowly across the sky. Getting on for seven o'clock, and no hint of the light fading. The stretch in the evening was wonderful to see. He thought he could smell summer in the air.

He wandered back through the events of the day, from his arrival at Mark's that morning to the phone call he'd finally made, and the words he'd found the strength to speak. He thought of the dip in the sea afterwards that had left him elated, and the failed leap over the gate that had afforded him such merriment.

On the whole, it had been a good day. On the whole, it had been his best day in a long time.

He tuned in to the low sound of the ocean at the bottom of the garden. He'd miss it when he moved on. He'd miss a lot when he moved on. As he finished the beer, he heard his phone ping. He went inside and found it.

Any bumps and bruises after your tumble? Lil

He smiled. Pressed reply.

All good. No bruises. Hide of an elephant.

A minute passed, and then another. He slipped his phone into his pocket and took a second can from the fridge. He popped it open and leant against the door jamb, not wanting yet to go inside. He saw the first tiny star wink on, and faint smudges of orange and pink appear in the sky, just above the horizon. Another fine day tomorrow, with any luck.

His phone pinged again.

Goodnight Tom x

Goodnight Lil x

Last Autumn/Winter

One punch he'd swung, a single drunken punch that had connected with its target against all the odds, nothing going for it but the element of surprise. When the man, none too sober himself, had crashed down onto the stone floor, the impact had fractured his skull and caused internal bleeding and concussion.

He was known to the guards, with a string of petty crime convictions and a prison record. This was of no benefit to Tom, because the pub had been full of witnesses who'd seen Tom knock him to the floor, and nobody at all, not a single person, had come forward to say they'd witnessed the first angry shove.

And Tom offered no explanation in the aftermath. Throughout his questioning, he refused to say what had led him to be in the pub in such a state.

'You must tell them,' Joel urged, turning up at the garda station the following day, the only person Tom could bring himself to call. Joel had heard what had happened, not from Tom, but from their father. 'You have to tell them, Tom,' he said. 'It'll help your case.'

'I'm not telling them, and you're not either.' He couldn't bear the thought of this being made public, of everyone knowing what had happened. He imagined the reaction of his friends, his work colleagues, his extended family. He imagined the pity he'd be shown, the nudges and whispers they'd hide from him. 'Tell nobody,' he'd ordered Joel. 'Swear you'll tell nobody.'

'Dad wants to come and see you.'

'Tell him he's not to show his face here. Never mention him again. He's dead to me. They both are.'

He was remanded in custody till Tuesday. The bank-holiday weekend was an endless nightmare, during which time he continued to offer no information, to the guards or to the solicitor Joel had found for him. He didn't sleep, apart from the stupor he'd fallen into on the night of his binge. He ate little of the food that was brought to him, unable to stomach it.

All he could think about was crossing the landing and opening his father's bedroom door, and the scene that had met him in the room. Again and again his treacherous mind returned to it, every detail cruelly sharp. In contrast, his memory of the pub was hazy, full of uncertain snatches. Had the barman spoken to him at one stage? Had someone asked him the time? Had he dropped coins on the floor, and scrabbled among shoes and boots to retrieve them?

On Sunday he was told that the man he'd hit had been put into an induced coma. 'If he dies,' the guard said, 'his death will be on you.' If he died, Tom could be facing a manslaughter charge. Horror piled upon horror, when he'd thought no more was possible.

On Monday he asked Joel to ring his boss in London. 'Tell him I'm sick,' he said — but when Joel rang, it was to learn that the story of the assault, having been reported in a local paper, had already made its way across the Irish Sea. 'He fired you,' Joel reported. 'All very civilised; he'll give you severance pay and a good reference. I'll take a trip over there and sort things out, collect your stuff and whatever.'

Tom gave him a key to the apartment, and told him where to find the car keys so he could return them. He asked him to contact the letting agents about cancelling the lease, and to find out how many unused months his severance pay would have to cover.

Vivienne's name wasn't mentioned by either of them. He figured she'd have moved out by the time Joel got there. Despite ordering his brother not to mention her, his contrary heart hungered for any scrap of information about her, but Joel didn't refer to her on his return, and Tom bit his tongue and didn't ask.

He alternated between bouts of rage and periods of despairing loneliness. Had she ever loved him, like she'd said? Did she know what had happened to him after he'd discovered her in his father's bed? She must know; someone would have told her. Did she care, even a tiny bit? Was she sorry?

On Tuesday he was brought to court, where he was formally charged with assault and sentenced to three months in jail, the sentence subject to review pending the outcome of the man's condition.

He served two of the three months.

Two months of sharing a cell with a man who chewed the skin around his fingers incessantly, and spat what he bit off onto the floor of the cell. Two months of keeping his head down, of speaking only when spoken to. Two months of weekly visits from Joel, and letters from his father that he tore up unread.

Six weeks of woodwork classes, which he finally signed up for when the idleness threatened to drive him insane, and which turned out to be the one bright spark in his week, the place where he learnt to make strange little houses.

On what should have been his wedding day he stayed in his bunk and told the guard who came to let them out for food that he wasn't hungry, and mercifully he was left alone.

The man in the pub regained consciousness. When Tom was told the news he felt nothing. What did it matter how long he spent in jail? Wasn't his life effectively over anyway?

On his release in early October he moved into Joel and Sarah's home, having nowhere else to go. Over the following weeks he painted all the rooms, one after the other, and washed up after every meal, and fixed a door that was sticking, and repaired a broken radio, and replaced all the tap washers, and took the tumble drier apart when it acted up, and got to know his little nephew and niece.

And every day he tried very hard not to fall apart.

Don't think about it. Don't think about them. It was his new mantra. He'd become a nail-biter in jail. His ability to sleep through the night had vanished. His hair was badly in need of a cut; he ignored it. Since August he'd lost over a stone, going from slim to thin. Thanks to Sarah's cooking he regained some of the lost weight but still he felt brittle, liable to snap in two if a single other bad thing happened.

Tears came easily. Emily's rosy sleeping face could bring them on, or the sight of Harry's tiny wellingtons by the back door, or the bag of fudge Sarah brought him home from the supermarket one day. She put her arms around him when she saw his face change. 'It's OK,' she whispered. 'You're OK, Tom. Everything's OK now.'

She was wrong, of course. Nothing was OK. Nothing would ever be OK again.

Time marched on. As the end of the year approached he felt he'd leant on them long enough, and began quietly searching online for rental properties. He considered going abroad, but quickly dismissed it. He'd stay in Ireland, but he'd get as far from Dublin as he could. He'd go where he knew nobody, and nobody *knew him. He'd keep to himself, live alone. And if the first place he picked didn't suit him, if people started asking too many questions, he'd move on.*

His money was dwindling, thanks in the main to what he'd had to shell out for the unused months of apartment rental. He might as well have flushed it down the toilet, or thrown it into the Thames from the wooden deck, but the fact remained that he would soon be in need of an income, so he'd have to find work.

Not programming, despite the lucrative earnings such work afforded. It would be too painful a reminder of all he'd had, and lost. He needed to look elsewhere, get right away from that environment.

Joel offered to take him on, train him up. Tom was tempted – such an easy option, and the classes in jail had given him a taste for working with wood – but in the end he turned down the offer. Joel had done enough: it was time for him to take control.

He didn't want an office job. He wanted to work for himself, set his own hours. Maybe he could become a handyman, a jack-of-all-trades. There was always a demand for that, especially if you were willing to do the smaller jobs.

Joel and Sarah would probably protest when he found someplace he could afford and told them he was going, but he was fairly sure they'd be secretly relieved.

As long as he lived, he would never be able to repay them.

He clicked into a new website, a marketplace that dealt in everything from used cars to kitchen dressers to rental properties. House to let in Fairweather, Kerry, he read. Fairweather. *The name rang a faint bell, although he didn't think he'd ever been there.*

He opened the ad and looked at photos of the property, and skimmed the brief description – by the sea, quiet location, working fireplace, central heating – and noted the low rent. The ad had gone up weeks ago so it was probably gone, but he figured it was worth a try.

Is the house still available? *he typed.*

Beth

He made the blue cheese burgers, and accompanied them with the homemade oven chips – and baked beans, because old habits died hard, he said, and he wasn't really a salad man.

'You've done well,' she said, when they'd finished. 'The burgers were slightly dry, so make them a little thicker next time, but otherwise that meal was perfectly fine. I'd prefer a salad to the beans, but you're the cook. And beans are a good source of protein, so they're not unhealthy as part of a balanced diet.'

'You're full of knowledge, Beth.'

'Not in the least. I would have been a poor domestic science teacher if I hadn't known about nutrition.'

'True. How are you finding the longer week in the library?

'Fine.' They'd resumed the summer schedule at the beginning of the month, with Beth manning the desk on Tuesdays and Thursdays, in addition to her Saturday slot. 'It's nice to have Lil to share the load.' She said no more, not wanting to bring down the mood.

But he said more. 'You'd prefer it were otherwise. You'd prefer she wasn't hidden away at the bottom of the garden.'

'Yes.' She hoped he wouldn't offer platitudes.

He didn't. He got to his feet and gathered their plates. 'Let me get dessert.'

'You've done a dessert?'

'Not exactly.' He produced a block of vanilla ice cream and a packet of wafers. 'Best I could do. Remember these?'

She remembered them, the wafers of her childhood. Costing from tuppence to sixpence, depending on how generously cut you wanted it to be. 'They were a Sunday treat after mass. You had to eat them quickly in case they dripped onto your good coat.'

'I had no such problem,' he said. 'I never had a good coat.'

'Oh dear.'

As they ate the wafers they conjured up other childhood treats. The bullseyes, the slab toffee, the clove drops. She called to mind her mother's sherry trifle on Sundays; he recalled his mother's lemon meringue pie, any day of the week.

She commented on the freshly painted house. 'Tom did a nice job.'

'He did indeed. I was very pleased with him, a

good worker. And that reminds me ...' He showed her what was left of the apple crumble cake he'd made. 'Tom was well impressed.'

'And so am I. There'll be no stopping you after this.'

'You'll have a small slice with the tea?'

'A very small one.'

'I'm reunited with my boat,' he told her. 'Went out yesterday, and again this morning. It's good to be back. And before you ask, I'm being very careful. If I had another fall, I wouldn't put it past Olive to sink the boat, or pay someone to do it. As it is, she's iffy about letting me take Nancy out for her birthday.'

'When is it?'

'Friday week.'

'And do you honestly feel you're able?'

'I do. Don't you think I look better?'

She had to admit that he did. It was good to see him returning to his old self. 'But I'll help Olive to sink the boat if there's any more nonsense.'

He roared with laughter. 'I can picture it. With the two of you ganging up on me, I'm definitely going to have to behave. Now – what would you say to a gin rummy?'

He cleared the table and produced his deck of cards, and when she beat him he insisted on another game. By the time she eventually thought to check her watch, she was surprised at how late it was.

'I must go. Lil will be wondering.'

'We should do this again,' he said. 'I want to try out the fishcakes.'

She fixed him with a look. 'You want me to come to dinner again.'

'I'd really appreciate it, Beth. I just feel I need more practice.'

'Anyone would think you were planning to open a gourmet restaurant.'

'Beth, like I always say, it's never too late. How's next Wednesday for you?'

'I believe I'm free.'

Driving home, she wondered if he really thought he was fooling her. Needed more practice indeed. A woman could always tell if a man was interested, even if it hadn't happened in a very long time. The fact was, however he tried to disguise it, Mark Purcell was wooing her.

He was seventy, she was two years older. Old enough to know better, both of them – but not old. Not by a long shot.

It was true they were very different. In a lot of ways they were diametrically opposed – but was that such a bad thing? She might have regarded him as a clown in their youth, but she'd never seriously objected to him. His sons had both turned out well, always a good measure of a parent. He could be annoying if you weren't in the mood for his antics, but he could also be sensitive and tactful. Behind the gregarious comedian, there was a man with a good soul.

It's never too late, he'd said – but was it? Was it too late to take a chance on this, to see if anything came of it? Did she want it to?

She thought about that. She thought about the safe, comfortable life she'd led, the marriage that had also been safe and comfortable. Gerry had been the most dependable of husbands, and an excellent father – but surprises had never been his thing. Unpredictability had never been his thing.

They'd booked holidays through the same travel agent each year, and travelled to destinations that were – well, safe and comfortable. The Lake District, the French Riviera, Florence, Capri, Madeira. Her birthday and Christmas presents were always perfectly thoughtful, jewellery and perfume for the most part, until Maria became old enough to help him choose a handbag.

In all the years that Beth had known her husband, she couldn't recall a single time that he'd raised his voice to her, or she to him.

He'd proposed on Valentine's Day, for Heaven's sake.

There was comfort in all this, of course there was. She knew wives who'd kill for the safety of it – but perhaps there was also a time for ... the unknown. Perhaps there was a case to be made for abandoning the beaten path and striding out into what lay beyond it.

Maybe she did want to take a chance on Mark Purcell. Maybe she was a little curious as to where it might lead.

She was seventy-two, and the object of a man's affections.

Never too late.

She smiled as she turned the car into the lane.

Olive

'I've got a deejay lined up for Saturday. He's not an official one, he's our neighbour Evelyn's nephew, and he's in transition year. He's planning to study music technology or something in college. I asked if he'd like to earn thirty euro for two hours, and naturally he said yes. I know he'll be a hit – I mean, a sixteen-year-old boy with twelve-year-old girls. He could sit in the corner and make a daisy chain, and they'd be charmed.'

'So he'll play music, and they'll dance?'

'Well, who knows about the dancing? They might just sit around and try to look cool. But I imagine he'll bring some kind of gizmo loaded up with Spotify playlists, or whatever. I've told him to keep it clean, and keep the music fast. There are a few boys coming too – don't want them getting any ideas.'

'Sounds good.'

'Well, it's hard to know with girls of that age – and since Nancy has decided that I'm public enemy number one, it's impossible. When I ask what she'd like for her party I get a shrug, or a "Whatever." The whatever makes me want to throw something.'

'She's still acting up?'

'She is. I take no notice.'

'Probably best. What about food?'

'Sorted. They're having pizzas delivered, and the freezer's full of ice cream, and I've got popcorn for the movie, so they're all set.'

'There's a movie?'

'I've told Nancy they can watch a PG on Netflix. I figured that would give me a window of peace.'

'Sounds like you've thought of everything. Is the boat trip going ahead?'

'Yes, I've decided to risk it provided the forecast is OK, and so far there's no sign of bad weather. They're going on Friday, which is her actual birthday. Mark is picking her up from school, and they'll be out for an hour or two. I think she's looking forward to that more than the party.'

She shifted position on the chair that had become, in the last week or so, impossibly hard, despite the extra cushion she'd added. She was crossing off days on the kitchen calendar: thirty-two to her due date. 'Enough about Nancy. How's the new clock coming on?'

'Nearly done. I should have it with you on Wednesday.'

'Wonderful. Will it fit in the Jeep?'

'It will.'

'Lil would help you carry it out, I'm sure,' she said, and he shook his head.

'Lil won't come inside the gates of the house.'

'Maybe she would if you asked.'

'I won't ask,' he said. 'I wouldn't like to put her in that position. I'll manage the clock myself.'

It was there. It was plain to see. The new alertness when Lil was mentioned, the careful look that came on his face, as if he was afraid he'd give something away. Leave it, Fred would say. None of your business, Ollie – but Fred wasn't here. Anyway, she wasn't going to do anything.

Well, not much.

'Poor Lil,' she said. 'My heart breaks for her.'

He made no comment, just fiddled with the turquoise hat he'd pulled off his head when he'd come in. Not really necessary any more, with the weather staying mild, but he was still wearing it. Lil had knitted it for him, of course. Olive hadn't asked, hadn't needed to. She stocked Lil's hats in the shop; she was familiar enough with the girl's knitting to recognise it.

'I just wish she had someone – I mean a romantic partner – but there wasn't anyone special when it happened, and now ...' She let it trail off. 'I think you two might have been suited, actually.'

'Olive,' he said, shaking his head.

'What? You're both creative. You're both readers, and walkers. You've just begun swimming here, and Lil is like a fish in the sea.'

'I hardly know her.'

'I know. I know you don't.' And still he liked her. She knew he did, she was sure of it. 'So have you asked Beth if she'll extend the lease?'

'Not yet.'

'You should. If Lil still won't go into the house they're going to want you to stay. You do want to stay, don't you? You're not making secret plans to move away?'

He laughed. 'No secret plans.' He pulled his hat back on. 'I'll see you first thing on Wednesday with the clock – I'll be on my way to a job.'

'Don't forget to have a price ready for me.' He wouldn't charge half enough. She'd fix that.

Fred called in later, on his way to the pub. 'My father phoned. He's getting his magic stuff ready for Saturday.'

'Lovely.'

Not lovely at all. Mark was a terrible magician, unwittingly giving away the secret to every trick. Up to this, Nancy had been happy to play along and pretend she hadn't spotted the mishaps, but Olive suspected that this year she'd have to bribe her daughter to look impressed. She might hint to Mark afterwards that maybe Nancy was getting a little old for a magician.

'A funny thing,' Fred said.

'What's that?'

'I reminded him about the table quiz on Wednesday.'

'Yes?'

'He was all set to come when I mentioned it a couple of weeks ago, but now he says he's got something else on.'

'Something else? Like what?'

'That's the thing. He didn't say. I thought he was a bit cagy, actually.'

'Really?'

Mark loved the occasional table quizzes in the pub, never missed them if he could help it. He'd get a gang of four together, and they'd install themselves early at a prominent table. They never came close to winning, but they kept everyone entertained with their comments on the questions. What could have kept him from this one?

'He sounded OK?'

'Yeah, fine. Just thought it a bit odd.'

That evening, she rang Mark. 'Just checking in,' she said.

'All good here.'

'Fred says you won't make the table quiz.'

'No. I have a prior engagement.'

A prior engagement? In all the years she'd known him, she'd never once heard him use the phrase. 'That's a shame. I know how you love the quizzes.'

'Ah, there are more things to life, Olive.'

He wasn't going to tell her. He was being cagy with her too. She puzzled over it for the rest of the evening. The fact that he hadn't said what was keeping him from the quiz was, she felt, highly significant. Could it be Beth? Was her wishful thinking running away with her? Possibly. It had a habit of doing that.

She remembered the wishful thinking she'd indulged in, the first time she'd discovered she was pregnant. Her baby would be the envy of other mothers, sleeping through the night, feeding by the clock. It would grow up to be kind and terribly clever, and would probably – no, definitely – win some big award for something or other. A Nobel prize, or an Oscar. Olive would be at the awards ceremony in a stunning new hat.

Wishful thinking. Look where it had got her. Now she'd take a baby who roared around the clock and spat up every feed.

She'd keep an eye on Beth and Mark, all the same. She'd watch for signs from either of them. She'd do that much.

NANCY'S BIRTHDAY

Tom

He woke with a headache, a dull but insistent throb in his temples. He ate breakfast with the back door wide open, hoping the sea air would shift it, but it didn't budge. The weather was strange today, a kind of leaden stillness about the place. The birdsong had lessened too: even the gulls, their cries normally so plentiful, were more subdued. Odd.

After breakfast he set off for the gift shop. He couldn't believe the clock he'd delivered on Wednesday had sold that same day, particularly when Olive had pretty much doubled the price he'd given her. He'd been convinced it would sit in the shop gathering dust – but as he was peeling potatoes that evening, she'd rung in great excitement.

It's sold! Your clock is sold! John Grimes bought it; he has a hotel on the prom. His wife was in earlier and sent him a snap. He's planning to put it in the lobby, where everyone will see it. You'll need to get yourself a new business card, Tom – you're going to be a clockmaker!

Clockmaker. He liked the sound of that. And he

was discovering that he liked making clocks. Into the second one he'd put a crescent-shaped pendulum, and chimes that behaved themselves, and a pair of hobnailed boots on the feet. He'd reined in the colours a bit too, using toning shades – cream, tan, terracotta, olive green – rather than Olive's more colourful palette. Now, along with planning new quirks for his little houses, he found himself thinking up variations for the clocks as he fell asleep.

Wizard's shoes, he thought, on the one for Harry and Emily he was going to make next. Long blue pointy shoes with gold stars stamped onto them. And he'd follow the theme with a star-shaped pendulum, and the hands would be magic wands. And he'd add the means to attach the clock to a wall, to make it more secure.

Ideas were flying about in his head. Everything, it felt, had suddenly come into sharper focus. Despite his busy work schedule – new requests coming in all the time – he'd been back in the sea twice in the past week, both dips leaving him wonderfully buoyed up, with the kind of mindset where everything felt possible.

Or maybe not everything.

He wondered if Olive had seen him glance once too often in Lil's direction during a book club meeting, or at the birthday lunch at her house. Had she seen it, and drawn conclusions?

If she had, she was wrong. He might be more open, since his call to his father, to something starting between them, but Lil still felt out of his reach, locked away behind her silence.

When he got to the gift shop he found Olive looking tired, and very pregnant. 'I have to say I'm feeling particularly gargantuan this morning, Tom.'

'Poor you. How long more?'

'Twenty-eight days – not that I'm counting. Not that I'm crossing them off every morning on the kitchen calendar.'

'Of course not. Why don't you finish up this weekend? Lie on the couch and read till the baby comes.'

'Not a hope – I'd go mad at home for a month. No, I'll stick to the plan and keep going till Wednesday week, book club day. I'm better off here, as long as no one expects me to do much more than sit and wrap things.'

'You know best. How's the birthday girl?'

She made a face. 'We had a row on the way to school, too silly to go into. Mark is picking her up afterwards for the boat trip, so I won't see her till dinner time. I'm cooking all her favourites – cocktail sausages and fried onions and potato croquettes – and Fred and I have got her a voucher for her favourite shop in Listowel. I'm doing everything I can think of.'

On the one occasion Tom had met her, the day of Olive's birthday, Nancy had seemed like a nice enough kid, but by the sound of it she was giving her mother a hard time. Puberty had a lot to answer for – and puberty and pregnancy might not be a great mix either.

He collected his earnings from the sale of the clock and took his leave, a job waiting. 'Wish Nancy a happy birthday for me. Hope the party goes well tomorrow.'

'Thanks, Tom. See you soon.'

The job didn't take long, a faulty toilet cistern that he'd seen from a quick look yesterday simply needed a replacement float seal. Fifteen minutes later he was on the way to the next job, a broken key in a lock. By the time he'd sorted that out, it was past noon.

He'd go to the library before lunch. He'd return his books and tell Lil about the clock for Harry and Emily. He'd show her photos on his phone of his little nephew and niece. He'd tell her of Harry's talent for drawing, and Emily's attachment to an old sock of her father's, and the ant farm Joel had constructed for them. He'd talk too much as usual, wanting to fill her silences, wanting to prolong his time with her.

Eight weeks, give or take, till his lease was up. Would he stay if a new one was offered, or would he go? He'd begun to find his feet here. His customer base was growing, and he had Olive's support for his carvings, and now for his clocks too, if he chose to go in that direction. He had the book club, and the friendship of its members. He had the sea, and the swims that were becoming part of his life here.

And there was Lil. There was the elusive Lil to consider.

As he approached the library a woman and a small child emerged from it, the child clutching a bundle of books. The woman looked familiar.

'How's Tom?' she said, and he remembered an upstairs sash window needing a new cord a few weeks back. The house higgledy-piggledy, coats heaped on the bed in the room where he'd been working, stacks of books on the stairs. Two cats asleep on the kitchen table, another on the draining board. A faint smell of cat from the notes she'd paid him with.

'Funny weather,' she said. 'Might be a storm coming.'

'You think?'

'Wouldn't surprise me. You take care now, Tom,' she said, ushering the child ahead of her onto the cliff path.

'See you.' He entered the library – and for the first time, Lil wasn't behind the desk on Friday.

'Hello,' Beth said. 'Lil is at the dentist, so I'm doing duty.'

He smothered a pang of disappointment. He dropped his books on the desk. 'Just need something to tide me over for the weekend.' He chose a John Connolly, and waited while she stamped it. He'd return it on Monday, and see Lil then.

'You got the flower seeds,' she said.

'I did. I've put them down.'

'Thank you, Tom.'

She'd posted them through his letterbox, along with a note explaining that she'd changed her mind, and would like to take him up on his offer to plant them. He wondered if she'd chosen the same flowers her daughter used to plant, or gone for new ones.

Back at the house he fried rashers and placed them between two slices of buttered bread. He ate the sandwich sitting on the back step, his preferred spot when the weather obliged. He listened to the news, which told him of a hike in petrol prices, and more bombing in Syria, and a fire at a disused warehouse in Cork. He watched a plane travel across the milk-white sky, conscious of the soft thump that persisted in his forehead.

It was after one by the time he returned to the garage to resume work on the new clock. Time passed as he sawed and carved, radio on full blast, outside world cut off. When he eventually downed tools and snapped off the music, he was surprised to hear the hammering of rain on the flat roof of the garage, and an intermittent rattle of the big door from what sounded like strong gusts of wind. Seemed the woman earlier had been right with her prediction of a storm.

What time was it? He'd left his phone in the kitchen. On returning there, he was struck by how dark it had grown outside. It wasn't that late, was it? He switched on the light and saw 4:28 on the wall clock, just a few hours since he'd sat on the back step, eating his lunch and marvelling at how calm and still the day was.

Rain pelted against the windows. Wind whipped at the shrubs. As he stood there, a bright flash lit the room, followed a few seconds later by a loud clap of thunder.

His headache was gone. He always got headaches before a thunderstorm.

Two missed calls, his phone told him. Both from Olive, one after the other, twenty minutes before.

Olive, he thought. Calling him twice, when he'd been in with her that morning.

Nancy, gone in the red boat with Mark – *Jesus*. They were never out in the sea in this.

He pressed the key to return her call, but before it had a chance to connect his back door flew open – and Lil, wet through and looking utterly terrified, burst in.

'My grandmother!' she cried. 'Please, come! Please! Hurry!'

Lil was speaking – no, Lil was shouting. Before he could take it in, before he could respond, she had snatched his arm and was dragging him out into the storm. He had no option but to accompany her, the gale pushing against them, the downpour drenching him almost immediately, another flash, another loud boom of thunder – and instead of bringing him next door, as he'd expected, she was pulling him down the garden, and he remembered Beth had been in the library, and he was hardly able to see with the heavy rain, and they had to battle against the wind, and she was making for the gap in the hedge – and as they went through it, as they struggled to push on, he stopped dead, and grabbed her to make her stop too.

'No, Lil, you can't!' he yelled. 'We can't!'

The library was moving.

It was tilting crazily, it was sliding away as they watched, as Lil screamed and struggled to escape his grip. The library was slowly sinking, slowly collapsing, the ground seeming to swallow it, and he could see nothing beyond it, no little gate, no cliff path, no fence on the sea side – was it all gone, or just hidden by the sheets of rain?

And as they watched, as he pulled Lil back, afraid that more ground would give way, as she continued to cry out, to shout for her grandmother, to thrash and strain in his arms, as the storm raged around them, the library gave a final terrible lurch and disappeared from view, and they heard it crashing and hurtling down towards the sea as Lil gave a final long, despairing wail.

Olive

'For the last time, no. And please don't ask me again, because the answer will still be no.'

'Gillian Fennessy has seen it.'

'I don't care if Gillian Fennessy has seen it. Everyone else in your class could have seen it and I'd still say no, because it's an over-sixteen film, and you're twelve.'

Nancy folded her arms. 'I *hate* you.'

Olive sighed as she changed gear. 'So you keep telling me. But the good news is you only have to put up with me for six more years, and then you can leave home.'

'I can't *wait*.'

Her resentment was almost palpable. It filled the car, clouded the air between them. 'Look,' she said, 'let's not fight on your birthday, sweetheart. There are so many other lovely films you can watch with your friends tomorrow. Why don't we choose one this evening?'

'I don't want *you* choosing it.'

Deep breath. Count to ten, or even three. 'OK,

you can choose it. As long as it's a PG, you can watch whatever you like. That's fair, isn't it?'

She'd woken up feeling cranky, which wasn't helping. The baby seemed to have lodged somewhere different, causing a new ache in her back, and a sickish feeling in her stomach. She hoped it didn't last: even with Fred around to help out tomorrow, she needed to be in top form for ten youngsters, a teenage deejay, an inept magician, and a sulky birthday girl.

'Aren't you looking forward to going out on the boat with Gramps? I know *he* is.'

A shrug of one hunched shoulder.

'Make sure you wear your lifejacket. Promise me you will.'

Silence.

'Nancy. Promise me.'

Big sigh. 'I *promise*. He always makes me, anyway.'

'I'm glad to hear it. I don't know what I'd do if anything happened to you.'

Silence.

'And I'll have your favourite dinner when you get home, and your surprise from me and Dad will be waiting.'

'Hurrah.'

Ignore it. She pulled up outside the school, behind the shiny red Volvo of Carmel Fennessy, who didn't seem to give two hoots what films her daughter watched. And of course Gillian would be the first in the class to develop a chest, when Nancy and the rest of them were still flat as pancakes. Unless Carmel was padding her daughter out, which Olive wouldn't put past her.

She switched off the engine and turned to regard her pouting passenger. 'I'll see you later, sweetie. Will you give your old mum a birthday hug?'

'You're too *fat* to hug.' Nancy snatched up her schoolbag and opened the door and scrambled out, and raced after Gillian Fennessy, who was disappearing through the school gates. Maybe Olive should have asked Mark to have a word, out on the boat. Nancy adored him; she might listen if he asked her to go a bit easier on her mother. On the other hand, it might make things worse if Nancy thought Olive had been discussing her with Mark. A minefield, and the girl just turned twelve: what on earth lay ahead?

She drove to the shop, parking as always in the laneway at the back, next to Fred's van. She lumbered from the car, wincing at another twinge in her back. She entered the premises through the rear and put the kettle on for the first of many cups of tea.

She went through and unlocked the front door, and turned the sign from *Closed* to *Open*. She gathered up the small bundle of post with the litter-grabber she'd been using since she'd lost the ability to bend down. Mostly rubbish, and a pink envelope with Nancy's name on it, written in what looked very like Beth's neat hand. Funny: Beth had never given her a birthday present before.

She slipped the envelope into her bag and placed a call. 'Beth, it's me. Am I right in thinking you're responsible for the envelope I've just found at the shop for Nancy?'

'Yes. Mark mentioned her birthday was today, and I thought she might appreciate something small this year, with the baby coming and everything.'

Mark mentioned: she filed that away. 'That's sweet of you, thanks so much. She'll be thrilled.' She'd have to persuade Nancy to write a thank-you letter – or she might save a row and commit forgery.

Tom dropped in not long afterwards to collect his earnings from the clock. Mark rang a little later to check in with her, and she found herself telling him of her row with Nancy.

'Want me to have a word?'

'No thanks – I think it might come back to bite me. Let her enjoy her birthday without a lecture.'

'Right, I'll let you get on. See you at dinner time.'

'Safe trip.'

The rest of the morning passed with a satisfying trickle of customers. Early tourists already about, another reason for her to keep the shop open as long as she could. She'd kept to the reduced winter hours, not having gone to a full week like she normally did at the start of May. This year, she simply didn't have the energy.

At lunchtime she hung the *Closed* sign and went next door to the pub. 'I need something salty,' she told Fred, so he got her a bowl of chips and a salt cellar, and a pint of water. Thirty minutes later she was back behind the counter, showing a puppet theatre to a German couple while another customer browsed among the teapots.

At three, she took a call from a man who wanted her to look at his bog-oak sculptures. 'Monday morning,' she told him. 'Bring in your favourite two.' She added that she was going out on maternity leave soon, and he congratulated her and asked how long she thought she'd be closed for. 'That depends,' she told him. 'I'm due on June the eleventh, but it's a first baby, so it might be late. I'm hoping to be back early July.'

She smothered a pang of guilt. A first baby sounded disloyal to Nancy. She remembered when they'd got her, just a few days old. Everything about her had been fascinating: the pink ovals of her fingernails, the minuscule whorls of her ears, the sweet dimples behind her knees. The adorably comical wobble of her chin just before she wailed, the way the back of her head fitted so perfectly into Olive's cupped hand, the clasp of her tiny fingers around the enormity of Fred's thumb.

And soon it would all begin again with another baby – and before she knew it, Nancy would be caught up in the magic of it too. She would. She *would*.

Just before four o'clock, she was startled by a sudden bright flash. While she was trying to figure out what had caused it, the bell above the door tinkled and Fred appeared, his face tense. 'Storm coming,' he announced. 'I can't get hold of Dad.'

Olive's heart skipped. 'Storm? What storm?' She clicked off the radio and hauled herself to standing, and heard a loud rumble of thunder. Rain was spattering onto the window – how had she not noticed it?

'Just starting up,' Fred said. 'Getting windy. They need to come in. I've tried ringing him, but I think something's up with his phone.'

'I'll try.' She found her phone, and scrolled to

Mark's name. She pressed *call*, and listened to dead silence as the rain began to slap in earnest against the window. She felt stirrings of panic, and tamped them down. 'Probably just out of battery.' But he always made sure to have it fully charged before he went out on the water, on her insistence. 'They're probably on the way back, Fred, if they're not back already.' Trying hard to keep her voice calm. 'Can you send someone down to the pier?'

Nancy, in a boat, on a wild sea. Storms came out of nowhere here, no warnings. What had she been thinking, letting her off with Mark?

Stop. Don't panic. *Don't.*

'I've called the café,' Fred said. 'Jack has sent someone down to check. I'm going there now myself. You keep trying Dad.'

Just then the shop lit up with another flash, followed almost immediately by a loud bang of thunder that made her grab his arm in fright – and suddenly it was all too real. Suddenly she felt a folding within her.

'Fred,' she began, and couldn't go on. 'Fred,' she said again. The only word she seemed able to get out. Her legs felt as if they were filled with water. She couldn't draw in breath. 'Fred.'

He helped her back to her chair. 'You want me to stay with you?'

'No, I'm OK. You go.'

But she didn't feel OK. She felt miles from OK. The lunchtime chips were sitting like clods of mud in her stomach. 'Put up the *Closed* sign,' she told him. Customers she definitely couldn't handle now. She concentrated on breathing. In, out.

'I'll ring you,' he said, 'from the pier.'

'Do, the minute you find them.'

They were back on land; they had to be. At the first sign of wind, Mark would have made for the shore. He wasn't a daredevil, and he certainly wouldn't take any chances with Nancy. They were probably on their way right now to the shop. Fred would meet them between here and the pier. She'd lock up as soon as they arrived. They'd go home and have an early dinner.

She tried calling Mark again, kept trying, kept getting the same silence. What if they'd gone further than planned? What if he'd decided to take Nancy out beyond the bay for her birthday?

Breathe, she told herself. She cradled her bump, lowered her head, drew shuddering, terrified breaths as the storm continued to rage. And with every new lightning flash, and every thunder boom, her fear increased.

Beth. She'd phone Beth. Beth would be calm. She'd say all the right things, she'd reassure her.

Beth answered on the first ring. 'Olive? Are you alright?'

'Nancy is out with Mark,' she said, in a frightened, stuttering rush. 'They're in the boat.'

'Where are you?' Beth asked sharply.

'In the shop. Fred is gone to the pier. Beth, I'm so scared.'

'I'm on the way.' She disconnected before Olive had a chance to tell her not to come, to stay safe at home.

Tom. She'd call Tom, get him to stop Beth coming out. But Tom didn't answer his phone either. Twice she tried him; twice it rang out. She got up, sat down again, got up again. She walked to the door like an old woman, holding on to shelves for support. She returned to the desk and called Fred. She could hardly hear him over the roar of the wind at the pier. 'No news,' he shouted.

No news. No sign of them. She tried Mark again, and Beth again as the storm raged on, and got nowhere with either. Beth was on her way here, driving through that weather because Olive was frightened.

Please keep them safe. Please keep them all safe. Nancy, Nancy. She felt a twinge in her abdomen that she ignored – not now. A sharp pain ran down one leg, drawing a gasp from her. She stood and pulled on her coat. Rang Fred again, got no answer this time. Dear Jesus. She sent him a text.

Coming to the pier with Beth.

She slipped her phone into her pocket. She dragged her chair to the window and sat there waiting, the minutes crawling by, until she saw Beth's car pulling up outside.

She went out. The wind snatched at her coat, the rain spat in her face. She pulled the door closed, keys left in her panic by the till. Didn't matter. She wrenched open the passenger door of Beth's car and tumbled in, ignoring the fresh pain in her back. 'The pier,' she said. 'We must go to the pier.'

'Olive, you can't—'

'The pier!' she cried, tears spurting. 'Please! I must go!' and Beth switched on the engine she'd just switched off and drove the short distance to the pier, wipers flipping furiously from side to side, swiping away rain that was instantly replaced with more. Olive felt another pull in her abdomen, a horrible tightness in her chest. Everything felt wrong. 'Sorry, Beth – I'm just terrified.'

'They'll be safe,' Beth replied. 'They'll have taken shelter,' she said with such authority, such certainty, that Olive clung to it. Beth was right. Beth was always right.

There were small knots of people on the pier,

all eyes directed towards the churning, roaring sea. Olive recalled similar scenes in the past, people waiting in fright for boats that had gone out, waiting for fishermen who sometimes didn't come back.

Stop. Don't. Breathe.

Cars were parked willy-nilly. Beth found a space further along, and Olive clambered out and strained for a sight of the red boat on the water, half blinded from rain and tears, the wind whipping angrily again at her clothing, her hair. There was another flash, another peal of thunder. No red boat was to be seen – the only craft she could make out were the usual grey trawlers, heaving and thrashing at their moorings. She told herself that only meant he'd pulled in somewhere else.

She clung to Beth's arm. They clung to one another as they fought their way back towards the pier. Another sharp stab of pain, high in her thigh, made her draw in her breath sharply. As they drew closer to the onlookers, she spotted Fred standing with Mark's friend Dougie O'Farrell. 'Fred!' she called, but it was snatched and swallowed in the gale. 'Fred!' she roared, and this time he heard, and hurried over.

'Go back to the car,' he said to her, to both of them. 'You'll get soaked.' He was soaked himself, his jacket useless against the heavy rain, his uncovered hair plastered to his head as he attempted to steer her around. 'There's no point in all of us getting drenched.'

'I'm staying here!' Olive cried, pulling away from him. 'I must be here!' She flinched as another abdominal spasm hit. 'Where are they, Fred?' she begged. 'Where are they?'

'The lifeboat's gone out—' which made her burst into fresh terrified tears and beat at his chest in helpless anguish. Nancy, Nancy, Nancy.

And just then there were shouts from the crowd, and she swirled around and craned out to sea, praying it was the lifeboat returning with them, but it wasn't. It was a section of the cliff collapsing, tumbling into the churning water some distance out, and something, some structure, rolling and crashing right along with it, breaking up as it fell, the whole mass landing with an almighty splash in the sea.

Watching the destruction, Olive felt a sense of unreality. How could this horror show be happening? How could the cliff face simply shear away like that? Was the world ending, folding in on itself? What hope was there for one little boat in all this chaos? She clung to Fred, fearing her own collapse.

And in the direct aftermath of the cliff fall, while everyone stood in shocked silence as the storm still raged around them, Olive heard another faint cry, this time behind her. She turned – and gave a wail of relief. There they were, there the two of them were, there Mark and Nancy were, coming not from the water but from the road, Mark holding Nancy by the hand, both of them searching the crowd.

'Nancy!' Olive screamed, and held out her arms for her daughter, and at the sound of her voice Nancy broke free from her grandfather and ran towards her mother, and Olive caught her and pressed her close as best she could, and yelled at Mark over Nancy's head that she'd kill him, *kill* him for doing this to her, and how could he not have seen the storm coming, was he so stupid that he hadn't realised the danger he was putting her daughter in, and why had he not answered his phone, was he trying to send her out of her mind with worry? And all through her rant he just stood there, getting wetter and wetter while she shouted herself hoarse and clasped Nancy to her.

And as she ran out of breath, she felt a searing pain along her back that made her arch and cry out, and a gush of warm wetness down her thighs, and she turned back to Fred without releasing her hold on Nancy and told him, and at least half of the gathering, that something was wrong with the baby.

Beth

As she was making her bed, having washed and dried the breakfast things, her phone rang, and it was Mark.

'Good morning,' she said, sitting on the edge of the bed.

'Good morning to you. I wanted you to be the first to hear the good news.'

'What good news is that?'

'I went for a walk just now up the Bog Road, and I heard the cuckoo.'

She smiled. 'Really? That's marvellous.'

He'd been bemoaning the fact at dinner on Wednesday that he hadn't heard the cuckoo yet. The middle of May, he'd said, and not a peep, and Beth had had to admit that she and Lil had heard it every week since the middle of April, on their Sunday afternoon walks.

She liked how little things made him happy. A cuckoo's song, buds on his rose bushes, the bottle of ginger beer she'd brought him on her last visit to his house, because he'd mentioned how he'd always wanted to taste it after reading about it in the Enid Blyton books of his boyhood, and how he never had. Such a small thing – but the glee he'd shown when she'd handed it over, as if she'd given him the crown jewels. She loved how close he lived to happiness, how eager he was to embrace it whenever it came along. She loved the child-like joy he took from life.

'Are you ready for your boat trip?' she asked him, and he told her he was. She'd never before felt the need to acknowledge Nancy's birthday, but for some reason – the imminent new baby, the friction Olive had reported between her and Nancy – she thought a gift might be appropriate this year.

After mulling it over for a while she'd settled on a voucher for a manicure, which she thought might appeal to a young girl. She'd dropped an envelope through the shop letterbox last evening, on her way home from the supermarket, and Olive had rung to thank her, half an hour before Mark's call.

'Flapjacks,' he said now.

'Pardon?'

'I'd like to know how to make them. It's Dougie's seventieth next month and he loves them, so I want to surprise him with a batch. Will you let me have the recipe?'

Dougie was his childhood friend, widowed like himself. The two of them played cards with a few others once or twice a week, and met for a drink in between. 'I'll show you how to make them,' she said. 'Your house or mine?'

'Yours, I'm sick of mine – and maybe Lil would be interested in a few rounds of gin rummy.'

'You'll have to teach her. Wednesday, half past four?' Wednesday was turning into their day.

'Wednesday it is.'

'And you'll stay to dinner.'

'I'd be delighted.'

Nothing had been said, but they'd reached a sort of understanding. Little by little, they were trying each other out for size. Somewhere along the way they'd passed a point, and they both knew it. She'd suggest a walk in the next week or two. He'd propose dinner in a restaurant some night after that. Another night they might go to the cinema, if there was anything on that took her fancy. No need to rush – at their stage in life, what was there to rush to?

And a mystery had been solved.

It's me, he'd admitted, on her last visit to his house. She'd decided after all to tell him about the little deliveries, the trinkets and flowers left for Lil by a door, or on a windowsill. It might seem silly, he'd said, but I was trying to let you both know that someone was thinking of you.

Both of us? They were for both of us?

Yes.

The packet of sweet pea seeds. She remembered then the conversation they'd had. He'd asked about her favourite flowers, and she'd mentioned sweet peas, among others. She thought back to the tea light and the beach pebbles and the paper cone of snowdrops, and all the rest. And there had been a gap in the offerings for the time he'd been on crutches, and unable to travel under his own steam.

And the Valentine cards, she'd asked, with no name on the envelopes?

I don't know anything about them, he'd replied, but he was a poor liar, and she'd let it drop rather than make him uncomfortable. He hadn't sent one the year of the accident, knowing it was too soon, just a month after, but he'd sent one last year and this year, and it was clear now that they hadn't been intended for Lil, as she'd assumed.

She was happy she'd hung on to them. She must find a way to let him know that something more than an *x* would be appreciated next year. A woman liked a tender little message in her Valentine card.

She spent the rest of the morning baking bread

(she should show him how to do that too) and writing to a cousin in Offaly, and taking her summer clothes out of storage. Another summer without Maria and the others, the various annual milestones acting as poignant reminders. Always would, no matter how far she travelled from their last year together.

After an early lunch she made her way to the library. Lil's dental appointment wasn't until half past two, but she was getting the bus to Listowel, and it tended to take the scenic route. Beth could have driven her – the library would have survived being shut for a couple of hours – but she hadn't offered. Lil mightn't speak, but she was capable of taking a bus journey on her own.

'No need to hurry back,' Beth told her. 'I'm happy to stay on till closing, so take your time in town. Do the shops, get yourself something new to wear.'

But even as she said it, she knew there was little chance of it happening. Hollie had been the shopper, not Lil. Lil shopped only when she had to – and over the last two years, with her silence adding to her reluctance, Beth almost had to propel her into a shop when the need arose.

Do you want anything? she wrote, and Beth said no, and just then Carol Slattery arrived with her little boy whose name Beth couldn't get into her head, and while she was trying to decide yet again if he was Shane or Shay, Lil slipped away.

The Slatterys' previous borrowings were produced, each one giving off a faint whiff of cat, as all books returning from that house tended to do. Beth would set them outside for a while later, when mother and child were safely gone. While they hunted for replacements she took her book and a pack of hand wipes from her bag, and hung her jacket on the chair. Even in May the cabin could become chilly after a bit, although today seemed mild enough.

The new books were brought to the desk and stamped. 'Say thank you to Mrs Sullivan, Shay,' his mother said. Shay. Beth vowed that this time she would remember it.

The Slatterys had barely gone when Tom arrived with a couple of books under his arm. On seeing her, she imagined his face fell – or maybe it didn't. Such a fleeting thing; she couldn't be sure. After he'd left she brought a chair outside and placed the cat-scented books on it.

The afternoon passed quickly, thanks to Olive's book club choice, which was engrossing. People came and went, most of them making some remark about the heaviness in the air. As it approached four, hearing taps of rain on the roof, she went out and retrieved the chair and books, and resumed her reading. No callers for the past half an hour: she'd close early if the weather deteriorated further.

It did. The rain quickly grew heavier. The wind started up. A sudden bolt of lightning was followed some seconds later by a distant boom. She didn't remember hearing of a storm warning – but some came unannounced, and could be vicious. Short-lived mainly, but fierce while they lasted.

She thought suddenly of Mark, going out to sea with Nancy. She closed her book and called him, but his phone didn't even ring. Maybe he'd cancelled the trip. Maybe when he'd picked Nancy up from school he'd seen the signs. Hopefully he'd cancelled. She tried him again, and again got silence on the line.

She decided to close the library. Nobody would come out in this weather. She pulled on her jacket and was on the point of leaving when her phone rang. She took it out, thinking it might be Mark, but it wasn't.

'Olive? Are you alright?' Another bright flash lit up the library, which had grown ominously dark.

'Nancy is out with Mark. They're in the boat.' Fright in her voice.

'Where are you?'

'In the shop. Fred is gone to the pier. Beth, I'm so scared.'

'I'm on the way.'

She disconnected and stepped out – and even though she'd heard it, the force of the wind took her by surprise, batting against her, seeming intent on pushing her over. She jammed her bag under her arm and locked the door quickly. She battled her way up the path, head bent against the driving rain.

She'd left the back porch unlocked: she hurried in. 'Lil?' she called, and heard no answering footfall, no sound at all. Still in town, or on the way home. She should leave a note – but even as the thought occurred she dismissed it, recalling the panic in Olive's voice. She'd text Lil from the gift shop, let her know where she was.

On the short drive into town she could feel the wind buffeting at the car. The rain battered against the windscreen. Intermittent lightning flashes caused her to clamp the steering wheel more tightly. She'd always been nervous of lightning.

At one stage a car overtook her, driving too fast for the conditions. She thought it looked like Noel Hurley at the wheel, a volunteer lifeboat man. Noel, driving in a hurry in the direction of the pier on a stormy day. She refused to think about the implications of that. No point in letting her imagination run away with her.

She'd try to phone Mark again when she got to the gift shop. She would text Lil and call Mark – but she didn't get a chance to do either. She'd barely pulled up outside the shop and turned off the engine when Olive appeared. Before Beth could move, she'd wrenched open the passenger door and practically fallen onto the seat with a thump.

'The pier,' she said, struggling to pull the door closed against the wind. 'We must go to the pier.'

She was in no state to go anywhere. Had she forgotten she was eight months pregnant? 'Olive, you can't—'

'The pier!' she insisted, eyes swimming. 'Please! I must go!'

What could Beth do? Arguing would only add to her panic. She started the car again, the storm continuing to whirl about them. Not a soul on the street, everyone with sense remaining indoors, a paper bag swooping towards the car like a ghost before being snatched away again. Beth thought of Lil, and hoped she was sheltering somewhere.

Olive leant forward in her seat, knuckles white on the dashboard ledge. 'Sorry, Beth – I'm just terrified.'

'They'll be safe,' Beth told her, trying to sound

far more certain than she felt. 'They'll have taken shelter.' Let them be safe, she prayed silently. Let both of them be sheltered and safe.

They approached the pier. Beth made out a small crowd, maybe twenty, assembled there. She thought she spotted Fred among them, but couldn't be sure in the driving rain. A line of carelessly parked cars forced her further on until she found a space, and took it.

'We should stay in the car,' she said – but Olive was already getting out, so Beth had little choice but to follow. The wind tore at them as they pushed, huddled together, back to the pier. Beth avoided looking at the sea, kept her focus on the onlookers as Olive shouted for Fred.

He heard, and came to them. He tried without success to persuade them back to the car. By now, to Beth's increasing nervousness, Olive was almost beside herself with fear, in turns clutching at Fred and lashing out at him.

A commotion among the others made them turn – and Beth watched in disbelief as a large portion of the jutting cliff face broke away and went crashing into the sea – and what had it taken with it?

Wasn't that close to her house?

As she was still trying to process it, trying to gauge the distance, a new shout caused her to turn in the other direction and see, with a wash of relief, Mark and Nancy materialising from the roadside, drenched but intact. Olive gave a scream at the sight of them, and Nancy ran towards her, and mother and child came together. Beth tried to catch Mark's eye but he was fixed on Olive, who had begun to berate him, shouting wildly at him, calling him an idiot.

Of course her outburst was understandable, prompted as it was by her shock and fear, but still Beth willed her to stop as he stood there wordlessly, not attempting a defence. And then Olive did stop. Her face changed, she let out a different cry, and turned to Fred with fresh panic.

'Something's wrong!' she cried. 'Something's wrong with the baby!'

Fred reacted quickly, easing Nancy from Olive's grip. 'You stay with Gramps, sweetie, OK? I must go with Mum.' Mark stepped forward and put an arm around Nancy as Fred hustled Olive away, Olive calling to the child that they'd be back soon.

Back soon, with an unborn baby in jeopardy. Maybe not so soon.

The storm was easing off, ebbing away as quickly as it had sprung up. The rain was lightening, the wind abating. She gave Mark a smile she felt he could use. 'I'm glad you're safe.'

For once, he didn't return the smile. 'Safe and

sound,' he said, running a hand across his wet face. 'Been an adventure,' he said, 'hasn't it, Nance?' and the girl looked up at him with big, frightened eyes.

'Will my mum be OK?'

'She will,' he said, and he caught Beth's eye then, and she saw the worry he was attempting to hide.

'Come to my house,' she said. 'It's closer than yours – and I can do dinner, and you can tell us all about it.'

'That'd be good.'

Beth crouched in front of a silent Nancy. 'Let's go, dear. We'll get you warm and dry in my house.'

'But will Mum really be OK?' she asked, chin trembling. Maybe she'd also seen the uncertainty in her grandfather's face.

'Of course she will,' Beth replied stoutly. She'd better be, or the child would never forgive either of them. 'Come on, we'll go in my car.'

Before leaving the pier she glanced back at the quietening sea – and saw something washing up on the beach. Two somethings. She looked further out and saw lots of somethings, floating on the calming water. Lots and lots of somethings, tumbling one after another onto the sand.

Not somethings. Books.

And then it came to her.

The library.

Her library was gone, swept away with the crumbling cliff into the sea. All her lovingly collected books, gone.

And Lil might have been in it, but for the dentist. She herself might have been in it, had she not decided to shut it early.

'Beth?'

Yes. She was needed. She turned back to them. 'Come on,' she said, and led them to her car. As they were getting in, her phone rang – and about to answer the call, she saw *Lil* on the display.

Lil? Lil didn't call. Lil never called, she texted.

Something had happened to Lil. Someone else was using her phone to call Beth.

She pressed the answer key, full of dread. 'Hello?'

A gasp, then – 'Gran, you're alright! You're alright!' The words rushing out in a high-pitched, instantly familiar voice, followed by a burst of loud weeping.

Lil's voice. Lil. Lil was speaking. No, Lil was crying. 'Lil? Hello?'

'Beth? It's Tom. I'm with Lil. She – well, she was worried about you. There's been some – damage, in the storm, and—'

'I know,' she said, her mind racing. 'I saw it, I was at the pier. I'm coming home. Tell Lil I'm fine, and

I'll see her soon.' She dropped her phone into her lap – did she drop it or did it fall? – and sat unmoving in the driver's seat.

'Beth, are you alright?'

She looked at Mark's face, full of concern. 'Lil,' she said. 'Lil was speaking,' and then she had to press her mouth shut and put a hand to it, because she didn't want a twelve-year-old child, who was already frightened enough, witnessing tears or hysterics, both of which were threatening.

'I'll drive,' Mark said, not waiting for a response before getting out, and she slid over to the passenger seat, afraid to risk a glance at Nancy, who was sitting silently in the back. Poor child: what a day she was having. What a birthday she was having.

'Right,' he said, adjusting the driver's seat, tilting the rear view mirror, 'let's get this show on the road,' and she sat back as he drove them away, and she closed her eyes as they travelled home to Lil.

Lil

Mum, Dad, Hollie. The three people she'd loved most in the world. The people she'd grown up with, the ones who'd taught her and formed her and made her who she was. Two and a half years on, their loss was still immeasurable – and what tormented her now was how she'd taken them for granted, how she'd tossed the miracle of them aside every single day.

She'd just turned twenty-one, and was halfway through her third year of college. Life was good, and the four of them had all the time in the world – except they hadn't. Three of them had come to a sudden end on a wet January afternoon, three of them had stopped breathing, stopped living, abruptly and violently, and then it was just Lil, alone in the house that used to be filled with them, alone with the spaces they'd left behind, the gaps where they used to be, the silences their words could no longer banish.

In the days immediately following the accident she'd wandered, dazed and dumbfounded, through the house, entering rooms and leaving them again, opening drawers and cupboards for no reason. She'd found leftovers of them everywhere, waiting to ambush her: her mother's untidy scrawl on the utility room calendar – *dentist 3.45, book NCT, cat worm tabs*; a half-full tub of mint ice-cream in the freezer, her father the only one in the family who liked it; Hollie's running gear still in the tumble drier, navy top, grey pants, sports bra, knickers, headband, the shocking jumble of them when Lil opened the door causing her to slam it shut again. Lives interrupted, cancelled, wiped out by a layer of water on the road that had sent Hollie's car aquaplaning, spinning and whirling and careening into a garden wall.

Six days Lil had lasted in the emptied-out house, just her and Hollie's cat, and Gran every now and again, as bewildered and dazed and speechless as herself. Six days of doorbell rings and careful, tearful voices, and hands reaching for hers, and food offerings that ended up, most of them, in the cat's dish or the bin, and coffins being lowered into holes dug out of frozen ground, and phone calls that she'd had to ignore because she couldn't answer them, because she had lost the ability to form and vocalise words. She'd tried, she'd strained to speak, but the sound had been caught, held, tangled up somewhere within her traumatised self. She had literally been struck dumb by grief.

Six days she'd lasted before packing a bag and rapping on the back door of the house next to hers, her grandmother taking her in without question, the cat following half a day later, tired of waiting for Lil to return and feed it.

And then, a few days after moving to Gran's, lying in bed for much of the time because she was sick with loneliness and desperate to see them again, hear them again, she'd begun to conjure their remembered voices in her head. *Would you ever be a darling and run upstairs for my slippers, Lil?* Mum asked, and *I like your hair pulled back like that*, Hollie said, and *Will you be looking for a spin to town on Saturday?* Dad enquired.

Of course they weren't real, these disembodied utterances. They were figments of her fevered imagination, sounds that she couldn't touch, or draw close to her. But they were the voices of her lost ones, familiar and loved, and in their way they offered a kind of comfort.

She'd hungered for more. She'd roamed around inside her mind and dug among her memories until more came. *That dish needs extra chillies; it hasn't enough of a kick*, Mum said, and *Have you by any chance borrowed my pink top again?* Hollie asked, and *I met Aoife in the bank this afternoon*, Dad said. *She's going to ring you later, Lil.*

And as the days drifted by, the voices in her head had become part of her new silent life – and almost, on occasion, seemed to occur without any help from her. Unlocking one morning the door of the library that Gran had reopened just weeks after the tragedy, Lil had heard Hollie say, *That cat would sleep for Ireland*, so clearly that she'd turned to see where her sister was. *I'm playing golf with Paul tomorrow*, her father said, again unexpectedly, as Lil had brushed her teeth that evening. *Olive has got beautiful vases into the shop*, her mother said the following morning, while Lil had been twisting her hair into a knot.

She would puzzle over these instances. Was it her subconscious, throwing up long-ago remarks that had lodged quietly in her memory? Were the voices still all her doing – or had her parents and sister somehow managed to tune into the workings of her head from whatever place they inhabited now? Had they taken ownership of their voices, wanting as much as she did to keep in contact?

But it hadn't mattered how it was happening. She hadn't cared. She'd clung to them, these precious, fragile connections. She'd tried questioning them

– Where are you? Are you together? What's it like? Do you miss me? – but her questions had remained unanswered, so eventually she'd stopped, and contented herself with listening.

She'd also stopped trying to reclaim her own voice – for who knew whether the sound of it would somehow break the spell, and cause her family to fade away? She'd become convinced that she needed to keep quiet, to allow whatever pathway to remain open for them to be heard.

She'd shared what was happening with nobody. Not the succession of doctors Gran insisted on bringing her to, not her friends, not even Gran. Least of all Gran, who Lil had known would be distressed and worried at the development, and who would attempt to find a means to stop it happening. No, better to keep it to herself, to remain alone with her inner voices. Others managed without words: so would she.

Texts had become her means of communication, and the little notebook that was always on her person, or within easy reach. It wasn't ideal; she knew that. There was only so much you could type into a text, or scribble in a notebook. Her friends, the ones who lived locally, dropped into the library now and again to pass on news. So-and-so had got engaged, so-and-so was moving away, so-and-so's parents had split up. They never stayed long. She couldn't blame them. It was tricky, sustaining a conversation where only one party was speaking, difficult to remember to ask only questions that needed a nod or a shake of the head in response, or a short written comment. Lil had felt bad to be inflicting her silence on them, but powerless to do anything about it.

There was no more college. Her business studies course had lost its appeal. Accounting, economics, risk management, marketing – why had she ever thought any of it important, or interesting? Gran's library, and the books in it, became her main focus, with walks or swims when it was closed, and occasional Saturday afternoon trips to Listowel with Gran – although those particular outings, full of cars and crowds, were ones she quietly dreaded.

A year passed, and another. She and Gran continued to live together, and Lil remained in her silence, the voices of her family drifting in and out of her head, growing fainter as time went by, but still there. Still there.

And then Gran had installed a stranger in Lil's house.

To be fair, she'd given Lil the option of rejecting the idea, and Lil had put up no protest. It was better, she knew, that the house was lived in – and having someone else there, anyone else, took the pressure off her to return to it. But it was so strange, so disorienting, so sad to look across and see smoke curling again from the chimney, or a light on at night, or to hear music coming from it.

At first she'd avoided him. She'd stopped using the lane, which would force her to walk past the house. She'd dreaded coming face to face with him, particularly after she'd heard him yelling at Skimbleshanks – but when it happened, when he finally walked into the library, she was astonished to discover that she didn't feel the resentment she'd thought she would. She found nothing in him that she could object to, nothing she could hold against him.

Oh, he talked too much in her presence, but so did everyone else around her now, except Gran. Embarrassed by her silence, they felt compelled to throw words in its way, and he was no different. She understood this, and didn't think badly of him for it – but behind his talk she sensed something else. The loss, the ache in her recognised something similar in him, and instead of dislike, what she was most conscious of feeling towards him was curiosity.

She'd left the cat book at his gate on a whim that

she could hardly explain. And the more times she encountered him after that, the more she observed him working in the garden that belonged to her, the more times he dropped into the library, the more she looked forward to seeing him.

She didn't question it, didn't try to analyse it. He was likeable, and she liked him, that was all.

And today, with its drama, and the terror she'd felt at the thought of losing Gran along with the others, today the wall of silence she'd hidden behind for so long had come crashing down, as surely as the library had tumbled into the sea.

She'd walked about Listowel for a bit after the dentist, not venturing into the shops as Gran had suggested – she dreaded being approached by shop assistants, having to mime her inability to speak, and endure their pitying looks, or worse, their attempts to communicate – but knowing that Gran would be disappointed if she arrived home too early.

When she boarded the bus to Fairweather the day was still fine, but by the time she got off at the top of the lane the storm had taken hold, making the short walk back to the house a battle against the elements. She'd been surprised to find no sign of Gran in the house. Could she still be in the library? Surely she didn't think anyone would come out in this weather.

She'd hurried upstairs to dry her hair and change her wet clothes before venturing down the garden – but as she'd glanced out her bedroom window she'd seen the unbelievable, impossible sight of the library moving, tilting, shifting. No, it had to be the rain blurring her view of it, making it appear to move – but then it had happened again, the cabin had given another lurch, and she'd known it was real, it was happening, and in the awful knowledge of that, she'd opened her mouth and a loud scream had burst out of her as she'd flown downstairs and out again into the storm in her wet clothing.

She didn't dare approach the moving cabin on her own, but the only place she could find help was next door. Without giving herself time to think about it she was there, and throwing open the back door she'd thrown open so many times, and she was shouting at him, and he was looking at her in amazement, and she was dragging him with her down the garden, in time for both of them to witness, as she'd screamed and cried for Gran, the horror of the library plunging from view.

The nightmare of that, thinking Gran to be inside it, thinking her to be gone, like the rest of Lil's family – and when Tom had managed to persuade her back into Gran's house, when she'd tried with shaking hands and no hope to call Gran, the call had been answered, Gran had answered, Gran was alive, and Lil had passed the phone to Tom, so overcome she was unable to say more, and he'd learnt that Gran was at the pier.

And now they were waiting for her, the two of them. And while Lil had been changing into dry clothes, heart still fluttering, hands still trembling, Tom had found Gran's brandy and insisted on Lil drinking some when she'd returned downstairs. 'Just a little,' he'd said, so she'd taken a little, and felt its warmth pouring through her.

And she was calmer now, and the storm was nearly over, and she wasn't speaking, but not because she couldn't. She was sitting at the table in the kitchen and Tom had put on the kettle without being asked, and he was finding milk and tea and sugar, and not trying to make her talk.

And her family's voices were gone.

She knew they were gone, without quite knowing how she knew it. And it wasn't because she'd spoken again: it was because it was time for her to let them go. She knew this. She knew it. She would miss them desperately, she would miss them deeply for a long time, but she had to learn to live without them.

'How are you feeling, Lil?'

She turned towards his voice. His real, living voice.

'Better,' she said, and he gave her a smile, and she managed to produce a tentative one of her own.

'I like your dimple,' he said.

And then she heard the sound of a car.

'Gran is here,' she said, and hurried out to the hall and opened the door and ran straight into Gran's arms.

The Day After

All the prayers she'd offered up, ever since she'd known for sure that she and Fred had started another baby. All her pleas, all her entreaties, all her imploring. All the bargains she'd struck with an invisible God whom she'd cursed and despised over the years. Let my baby be safe and I'll never get cross with Fred again, I'll never gossip about anyone, I'll never scold Nancy for leaving her room in a mess. Let my child be healthy and I'll be a better wife, a better mother, a better everything. Let it live, and I will do anything, anything you ask.

'How're you feeling this morning, Mrs Purcell?' The nurse, all blonde highlights and perfect pearly nails, looked sixteen, not a day older. She smelt of those violet sweets Olive's grandmother used to suck to keep her breath fresh. Tiny gold dots winked in her ear lobes. 'Are you experiencing any pain?'

'No. No pain.'

That was a bit of a lie. Her stitches hurt if she moved an inch, or breathed deeply. Her pelvis ached. Her neck was stiff from a night on the firm hospital pillow. Her throat was sore from the roaring she'd done during what felt like a week, but which turned out to be just six hours, before she'd finally pushed out a baby who clearly wasn't in any great hurry.

But she hadn't wanted painkillers. No epidural, no anything. She'd wanted to feel it all, to endure it all. She wanted to remember everything about this time, every single detail, from the minute she'd got the first darts of pain yesterday that she was too frightened to pay attention to.

'How is he?' she asked the nurse.

'He's getting on fine, not a bother.' She took Olive's pulse and temperature and blood pressure, humming lightly all the way through, and then she wrote on Olive's chart. 'The doctor will be doing her rounds in a couple of hours – and look, here's your breakfast now!' The excitement in her voice, as if Olive was being presented with the Oscar for Best Patient instead of a bowl of grey mush and a slice of limp toast, already buttered but not all the way to the edges. The clock on the wall that faced Olive's bed told her it wasn't even six thirty. Who ate breakfast, or any meal, before six thirty in the morning?

'Up you sit, love.' The orderly, short and broad, slapped Olive's tray onto the trolley by the bed while Olive struggled, wincing, into the best semblance of sitting she could manage. 'Anything else I can get for you?'

'Marmalade?' Olive asked. Toast without marmalade was like a boiled egg without salt. The woman promised to return with some, but when it hadn't materialised ten minutes later, Olive did the best she could.

In due course the doctor arrived, wearing a white coat over a blue dress, and shoes with thin straps at her ankles. She read silently through Olive's chart, her placid expression unchanging.

'How's he doing?' Olive asked.

'Fine, just fine. Any bowel movement?' she enquired, and Olive admitted to a minor incident after breakfast for which a bedpan had had to be requested. Such indignities hospital afforded.

'Sleep?'

'I did.'

But she hadn't got nearly enough of it. Not half enough blissful hours of unconsciousness, woken as she'd been at six twenty.

'Have you eaten?'

'I have.' As much as I could stomach.

'Keep it up,' the doctor said, and tripped away on her high heels.

Soup arrived at noon, brown in colour and thick

enough for Olive's spoon to stand briefly in it. Mercifully, Fred showed up not long after, looking like he'd got about two minutes' sleep, and bringing a flask of chowder and a pair of crusty buttered rolls, and two new books.

'Did you see him?' she asked.

'I did. He's doing great. You'll have him soon.'

Her heart smiled. 'How's Nancy?'

'Fine. She wanted to come in with me. We had a small battle, which I won. I thought I should check out the lie of the land before I brought her.'

Nancy wanted to visit. Hallelujah. The hug on the beach was all very well, but Olive had feared it was simply the instinct of a scared child who might momentarily have forgotten that her mother was the enemy. 'Were you able to contact all the party people?'

'I was.'

The birthday party, of course, had been cancelled – or rather, postponed. 'Did you call Evelyn's nephew?' Poor lad, his career as a deejay over before it had begun.

'I did. By the way, Dad's staying in the spare room while you're here. He's going to bring Nancy in this afternoon.'

Mark. She couldn't think about him without a

rush of shame. Mark, who'd got the brunt of her anger, in front of everyone.

'He knocked his phone into the sea,' Fred told her. 'He was taking out the picnic and the phone came out too, and fell into the water before he could grab it.'

He told her that Mark had brought the boat in to shore shortly after that, as soon as the weather had begun to change. 'They'd just rounded the headland so he pulled into a cove, and they made their way up to the road, and hitched back to Fairweather.'

He'd lost his phone so he couldn't get in touch. He'd pulled the boat in as soon as he'd seen a change in the weather. He'd kept Nancy safe, and in return he'd been yelled at by a large, demented woman.

'Will you tell him I'm sorry?'

Fred grinned. 'Too late for that. He says he'll use it against you at every opportunity in the future.'

'It's no more than I deserve.'

'Don't be daft – he could see you were upset.'

'Still.' There was making up to do there, big making up. She'd think of something.

'He's cooking dinner for us this evening,' Fred said.

'*Mark* is cooking?'

'Yes indeed – we're getting blue cheese burgers.

He says Beth taught him. They went to Beth's for dinner last night, Dad and Nancy.'

'Did they?' She couldn't keep up.

'And Ollie, there's something else,' Fred said then.

'What?'

'The library. Beth's library.'

'What about it?'

'It's gone. It collapsed with the cliff—' and Olive recalled the terrifying sight, in the midst of the other terror, of the crumbling cliff face, and the structure it had taken with it that she'd failed to recognise.

'Was anyone hurt?'

'Nobody. There was no one out on the path, and Beth was just closing the library when you rang. Lil had just got back from Listowel when it happened. She was at the dentist.'

'Lil saw it happening?'

'She did, and so did Tom – and Ollie, here's the amazing thing. She's talking again.'

'Lil? Lil is talking?'

'She is – she phoned me earlier to tell me all this. She thought Beth was still in the library, and the shock of that brought her voice back.'

'God …'

How horrifying it must have been for Lil to witness that, imagining Beth to be inside – but it had restored her voice to her. Whatever mental shift had occurred, one trauma seemed to have undone the damage of the other.

The library, Beth's library, was gone – but her granddaughter could speak again. Libraries could be replaced; that loss they could cope with. And nobody had been hurt, which was another blessing.

'The shop,' she said, suddenly remembering. 'I left it open when I went to the pier.'

'Not to worry – Connie spotted you leaving in a rush and went to check. She locked up and dropped the keys into the pub.'

Connie in the hardware shop across the road, known as neighbourhood watch because she missed nothing that went on in the street. Olive would bring her flowers when she was back in action.

After Fred left she dozed for a couple of hours, waking briefly when a different nurse appeared to check on her – and waking again to find her brand new son being wheeled in.

'Look who's here!' said the nurse, and Olive pulled herself up, ignoring the aches.

'He's OK?'

'He's perfect, all grand now.'

She feasted her eyes on him. Her and Fred's son, who'd been conceived against all odds and born three and a half weeks early, jaundiced and with breathing difficulties. He'd been whisked off the previous night, taken from them just seconds after she and Fred had had their first glimpse of his tiny outraged face. He'd been placed in an incubator in a special unit so his breathing could be monitored, under lights that shone on his jaundiced skin and helped it to heal.

Their healthy son, weighing six pounds and twelve ounces, with wisps of black hair and cloudy blue eyes and a beautiful snub nose, and a mouth whose full bottom lip caused an obstruction in her throat, and a chin that came straight from Fred, and cheeks that begged to be stroked, and skin smooth as silk, smoother than silk. Nothing in the world was as smooth as his skin.

Their son, their baby, who had yet to be given a name. Her and Fred's miracle, their little fighter, after all their years of trying, all their failures, all their heartbreak. Her prayers answered, someone listening to them after all. Who would have thought it?

'Now,' the nurse said, 'let's see if this little man is hungry' – and she guided Olive through her first attempt at breastfeeding, which went from shaky to shakier, and then got a little better, and then a little better again. 'You're getting the hang of it,' the nurse assured her. 'Another couple of times, you'll be a pro.'

A pro breastfeeder. She'd been called worse. She lay back against the pillows, feeling the small heft of the brand new human she and Fred had made, the wondrous tug of his mouth on her nipple. Worth waiting for, worth all the heartache that had preceded him. When feeding was over he burped obligingly and went to sleep, and she went back to gazing at him, and wondering what colour hat she'd buy when he won his big award.

Not long after, her door opened again.

'Are you decent?' Mark asked, and she checked her neckline before beckoning him in, and he was followed by Nancy, who went straight to the bedside, into her mother's outstretched arms. Olive mouthed, 'Sorry,' at Mark, who flapped it away and went to say hello to his new grandson, leaving mother and daughter to have a whisper.

'I'm sorry,' Nancy said into her chest.

'For what, you goose?'

'For being so mean to you. I was scared when you said there was something wrong with the baby. I thought it was my fault, because I didn't want him to come.'

Oh Lord. 'And why did you not want him to come, darling?'

'Because he's yours, and I'm not.'

And there it was. Olive drew back, just far enough that she could look at her. 'Nancy Purcell, you're just about the biggest goose I know.' She held her daughter's face in her hands. 'Sweetheart, you *are* ours. You're mine, and you're Dad's. You became ours the day we got you, and you belong to us every bit as much as that little fellow does. The fact that I didn't give birth to you just means that it was easier getting you. You should have heard me moaning and groaning last night – your dad was looking for ear plugs.'

Nancy gave a tiny smile. 'That's not true.'

'About the moaning and groaning? It certainly is. Ask Dad.'

'About the ear plugs.'

'Well, he didn't say it out loud, but I bet he wanted them. Ask him that too. Listen,' she said, 'when I was on that pier yesterday, not knowing if you were safe, I was like a mad woman, I was so scared. I was more scared than I ever was in my life, and so happy to see you. You *know* that – you were there. You saw me, and you heard me giving out to Gramps, just because I'd been so scared.'

Nancy nodded.

'So you know how much I love you, and how much I will always love you, no matter how mean you are to me. And guess what else?'

'What?'

'My two children have the same birthday, which means I'll only have to make one cake every year. Am I not a clever mother?'

Nancy considered this. 'But I might want a girl cake, and he might want a boy one.'

'Good point. Two cakes it is then. Sorry about your party, by the way.'

'Doesn't matter.'

'Yes, it does. We'll have an even better one when I'm home.'

'You don't have to.'

'But I want to. Now go and get to know your brother – and start thinking about a name for him.'

Nancy's eyes widened. 'Me?'

'Yes, you. Dad and I can't decide on one, so I think we should give you the job. You can take a few days to think of your favourite.'

She hadn't cleared it with Fred, for the simple reason that it had just this minute occurred to her. She knew he wouldn't mind; he'd understand why it was a good idea. She hoped Nancy would steer away from the likes of River or Apple, and present them with a name they could live with. Then again, did it really matter what they called him? Didn't names always grow on you when they belonged to someone you loved – or had been chosen by someone you loved?

When Nancy went to the baby, Mark took the chair beside the bed. 'He's a beauty,' he said. 'The spit of his gramps.'

'Thank you,' Olive said quietly, reaching for his hand.

'For what?'

'For keeping her safe. And I'm so sorry for the horrible stuff I said. You know I didn't mean a word of it.'

'Of course I know that, you foolish woman. When are they letting you out?'

'Monday, all going well.'

'Excellent. I could do dinner that night, if you liked.'

She smiled. 'Yes, I hear you're quite the chef now.'

He suddenly became interested in his fingernails. 'I wouldn't say that exactly. I can do a couple of dishes, that's it.'

She wouldn't push it. 'Well, that would be delightful, thank you. Oh, and Fred told me the good news about Lil.'

'Yes, it's wonderful, isn't it? And I presume he told you about the not so good news too.'

'About the library? How could it have happened,

Mark? That cliff edge must have been very unstable.'

'Must have been – and the weight of the books wouldn't have helped. There's going to be an investigation – some council fellows were around this morning. I heard the entire cliff path is cordoned off.'

'Well, it would have to be. What about Beth's garden? And Tom's?'

'Yes, they're bound to be impacted. We'll know more soon enough. They all send their love, by the way.'

They left soon afterwards, and Olive dozed some more, and woke to her phone ringing.

'Well,' Tom said, 'talk about drama.'

She laughed. 'I like to cause a bit of a stir.'

'I believe it. How are you?'

'I'm great. I'm deliriously happy. And I'm now officially a mother of two.'

'So I hear – congratulations. I'm so glad it all worked out. You'll have to wait for your present, springing it on us like that.'

'Tell me,' she said, 'about Lil. Tell me what happened,' and he told her.

'Is she alright?'

'She is, I think – or she will be.'

Now he could get to know her properly. 'So how is it there today?' she asked. 'The gardens, I mean. Yours and Beth's.'

'Well, we haven't really got a good look at the damage. We had council people around first thing this morning.'

'Mark mentioned them. What did they do?'

'They taped off most of the two gardens, and said we weren't to go beyond it. They're doing an inspection of the whole area. We'll have to wait and see, I suppose. It's a good job the gardens are so long.'

'Good job is right. Such a thing to happen.'

'You're telling me. If I'd known Fairweather was so dangerous I'd never have come near it.'

'Oh, how can you say that? You'd never have met me!' Or Lil. 'Will you call to see me when I'm home next week? You don't have to bring a present.'

'Sure. Give me a shout when you're up for a visitor.'

After dinner Beth and Lil arrived, bringing a Ziploc bag full of orange segments, and two bars of Olive's favourite chocolate, and a tube of lavender hand cream, and four books.

'We're not staying,' Beth said, 'just wanted to look in, and see you and the baby.'

'Hello, Olive,' Lil said, and the shy happiness

on her face was beautiful to see, and the sound of her voice brought tears to Olive's eyes, because it brought everything else, everyone else, back with it. 'Congratulations.'

'Thank you.' Olive dabbed her eyes with a corner of the sheet. 'How are you, Lil?'

'I'm good, I'm OK. And I'm delighted for you. And ... Mum would be delighted too.' Dashing away tears of her own.

She was fragile, of course she was. She would be fragile for some time, but she'd heal and become stronger. And eventually she'd blossom again.

Fred was Olive's last visitor of the day. He reappeared as the baby began to whimper. 'Just in time,' Olive said, 'for his next feed. Will you take him out?'

As she was feeding him – and feeling more and more like a pro – she told Fred about letting Nancy choose a name. 'I thought it might help them to bond.'

'Did you now? And what if she picks something we hate?'

'We won't hate it. We couldn't hate anything she picked.'

'I'll remind you of that when you're the mother of Frankenstein Purcell.'

She looked at him in alarm. 'Oh, Fred. She wouldn't.'

'If it's really bad, we can say we'd like three to choose from, and take the least dire.'

'Good idea.'

She was so lucky he'd married her. He wasn't perfect, but he was perfect for her.

Mind you, he was lucky too.

The May
Book Club Meeting

'Olive has asked me to be godmother,' Lil said, pushing an armchair further along the wall.

Beth was plumping cushions. 'Has she?'

'Yes.' She slotted a kitchen chair into the space she'd created. 'She's also asked Nancy.'

'Two godmothers? Any godfather?'

'No.'

Beth smiled. It was so Olive.

Lil left the room and reappeared with another kitchen chair. 'And she's decided that she'd like to be a stay-at-home mum for the next few months, and she's wondering if I'd fill in for her.'

'In the gift shop? She wants you to run the shop?'

'Yes, over the summer.'

Wonderful Olive. Doing everything she could to help Lil find her feet again – especially now that there was no library to occupy her. 'And what did you say?'

'I told her I'd love to.'

'I'm glad to hear it. You'll be great. And after the summer?'

Lil hesitated. 'I'm not sure, Gran. I know you'd like me to go back to college, but …'

Beth studied her. 'What would *you* like to do, Lil?'

'I don't know – but working at Olive's will give me time to think.'

'That's true.'

'And there's another thing, Gran.' She'd left her hair loose today; now she gathered up a handful and swept it behind her shoulder. Such wonderful hair she had. 'I've decided to move back home, when Tom's lease is up.'

Better and better. 'Only if you're ready, love.'

'I'm not sure that I'll ever be ready, but I think I should.'

'I think you're right. Have you said anything to Tom?'

'I mentioned it to him yesterday.' Preoccupied all of a sudden with the cushions that Beth had already attended to. 'I offered to let him rent a room from me – I wouldn't like to see him stuck – but he thinks it might be best if he found his own place.'

Beth digested this interesting information. 'I see. So he's going to stay in Fairweather then?'

'For the time being.'

And just then, as if they were summoning him, he rang the bell. 'I wanted to get here before the others,' he said. 'I wanted to give you this. It's for both of you, if you'd like it.'

He handed it a little hesitantly to Beth. She and Lil examined it.

It was the library in miniature. It wasn't skewed like his other little creations, but regular in shape. Every side was accurate; he must have walked all around it, taken photos maybe. Every detail of it was faithfully reproduced. The welcome sign on the door, the little overhangs above the three windows, the knobbly surface of the pitched roof, the skylight. The colours were true, yellow pine walls and door, bottle green roof. It was a small work of art.

'When did you make it?' Beth asked.

'A while ago. I wasn't sure either of you would want it, but maybe now ...'

Maybe now that the library didn't exist any more in reality, this little model could serve as their reminder. Not so much right now, when it was still fresh in their minds, but later. Months and years from now, when the image of it would have faded, long after the last book had washed up on the beach, sodden and useless, they would still have this to help them remember.

And it would remind them of the interior too. It would call to mind the shelves of books, the faded

Turkish rug on the floor, the desk, the cushions, the chairs. The heaters on the walls. It would conjure up the smell of the books, how it felt to run a hand along the spines, the peace of sitting there on an afternoon surrounded by stories, the made-up ones and the true ones.

As libraries went, it had been humble and limited, but it had been hers, it had been her labour of love, and he had captured it with his carving tools.

'Thank you,' she said. 'It's a thoughtful gift.'

'It's lovely,' Lil said, and Beth caught the look that passed briefly between them. Oh, my.

It was a dozen days after the storm, and the book club was meeting in Beth's house – and since the previous day's conversation with a council engineer, the content of which she had yet to share with Lil, Beth wasn't at all sure how long the new venue would last.

Climate change, the man had said. More extreme weather instances, causing more cliff erosion. We're seeing it all the time. You were very lucky you weren't in that shed.

She hated when anyone called it a shed. It was a privately run book borrowing service, she'd told him, thinking to keep the word library out of it in case that raised awkward questions. He'd shaken his head and told her that was the problem. The weight of all those books, he'd said, and located so close to the cliff. An accident waiting to happen, if you don't mind my saying so.

She *had* minded him saying so. She'd minded it very much. Is it not up to the council to keep an eye on the condition of the cliffs? she'd asked. Haven't you been inspecting the path that people use every day? He'd smiled at that in such a condescending way that she'd had an impulse to slam the door in his face.

We can't monitor all the cliff paths, Mrs Sullivan – we'd get nothing else done. We do spot inspections, and keep as good an eye on every place as we can, and we follow up any concerns that people bring to us. We *will* be carrying out a major survey now of this area—

After the horse has bolted, she couldn't help putting in, and of course he'd ignored that.

—and we'll know more then. In the meantime, I'm sorry that most of your back garden must remain out of bounds – and I have to warn you that your house, and the one next door, which the occupier tells me belongs to your granddaughter, might not be viable in the long term.

Not viable? What on earth do you mean?

If the area is found to be generally unstable, I mean.

For goodness' sake – the gardens are surely long enough for the houses to be well out of danger.

For the moment, yes – but if it's felt that the condition of the coastline poses a future risk to the buildings, you may have no choice but to move out at some stage.

Move out? Move out of the house she and Gerry had bought when they'd married, the old Carmody place that had stood here for generations? And the house next door, the one that Maria and Killian had built, not *viable*? What a horrible word. What a cold, clinical, awful word.

How long will this survey take? she'd demanded, and he'd shrugged and said hard to know, possibly a few months.

We'll be in touch, he'd said, and she had shut the door then. Not quite a slam, but not far off. She'd gone through to the back and stood outside the porch and looked at the gaudy yellow and black tape they'd strung across her garden the morning after the storm, just above the coal shed that she'd converted into a toilet, and she'd let her gaze travel beyond it to the space where the library had stood, and beyond that to the sizeable gap that had been created in the cliff path, the rest of which was now out of bounds too. Since the storm, anyone wanting to access the big beach from the town had to go around by the road, which took far longer.

She'd had a lucky escape. She was well aware of it. She could be dead now, or Lil could. And others might have died too, if they'd been on the cliff path, or in the library when the ground under it had given way. Lucky escapes, she'd realised, had a tendency to put things into perspective, to sort out what was important and what wasn't.

She'd walked as far as the tape and turned to look back at the house, at both houses. Really, what were they but bricks and mortar? Full of memories, yes – but memories could be packed up and taken away. Memories, in fact, insisted on accompanying whoever stored them. It wouldn't be the end of the world if she had to move out, if the houses were deemed unsafe in the next few months.

The three of them took seats while they waited for the others to arrive. 'You heard about the petition?' Beth asked Tom.

'I did. I signed it a few days ago in the supermarket.'

An official library for Fairweather, a petition started by a few of Beth's regular borrowers, and by all accounts gaining momentum quickly. This new lobby group might have better luck than Beth had had when she'd looked for the council's help all those years ago. Their case a bit stronger than hers, given the publicity the loss of the old library had got, and the demand that was there for a replacement.

'Will you get involved,' Tom asked, 'if a regular library comes to town?'

Beth shook her head. 'Lack of qualifications, and too old to be considered for a job. But it wouldn't interest me anyway – I've done my bit for the readers of Fairweather. I hope it happens, though. No town should be without a library.'

He turned to Lil. 'What about you? Would you think about training up as a librarian?'

'Maybe,' she said, and Beth thought this a distinct possibility.

The doorbell rang again just then, and Lil went out to let the others in, and the May meeting of the book club got under way. Charlie Purcell, whose middle name was Mark, and whose attendance had been sanctioned in advance, had the good grace to sleep through most of it, and only woke when it was time for his mother to feed him in the next room.

Afterwards, Lil served the usual tea – and Mark, with a flourish, produced a carrot cake that he swore he'd baked all by himself. 'Beth will vouch,' he said, and Beth told them that she had indeed given him the recipe, but that she couldn't swear his claim of having baked this one was true.

'He's been known to cheat at cards,' she said, and Fred and Olive nodded in agreement, and he had the grace to look momentarily abashed.

'The cake is mine though,' he insisted, and Beth thought it probably was, and a very good effort too. She'd make a baker out of him yet.

She thought it likely that he would suggest that she move in with him, in the event that she had to leave her home.

That would not be happening.

She liked her own space too much to give it up, and she suspected he did too. No, she'd find a new house to live in, or maybe a nice apartment, and they'd conduct their relationship, if both of them still wanted it, in a different way. She loved the wonderful freedom of being older, when you could live exactly as you pleased, needing nobody's permission.

And Lil?

Lil would be fine. Ironic that this new uncertainty about the houses had presented itself just when she was preparing to move back into hers – but no matter. She'd find her way. She was already finding her way.

As they chatted among themselves, Beth regarded the people who were gathered in her sitting room. Fred and Olive, who'd finally been granted what had been denied to them for so long. Mark, who'd managed to surprise and disarm her, and who was, she had to acknowledge, becoming a little indispensable. Lil, who had a journey to travel but who'd begun it at last, and Tom, who seemed to have found a way to banish his own demons, and who might just make Fairweather his permanent home.

To think he'd been in jail for assault.

Only last night she'd discovered it, when she'd been scouring the council website for any reference to the cliff collapse. About to log out, her search having proved fruitless, she'd put Tom's name into Google on impulse, just out of curiosity, and found the newspaper article from the previous August. A rising star in the London computer world, she'd read. A pub brawl, a man in a coma, Tom behind bars. Who would have thought it? No wonder he'd looked so haunted when he'd arrived.

She assumed the man had recovered, or Tom would more than likely still be in jail.

He might tell them sometime. He might explain it all. Or she might ask him, if he and Lil looked like they were going somewhere definite. In the meantime, he'd done wrong and he'd been punished for it, and everyone deserved a second chance.

She allowed her gaze to travel about the room again. Things weren't fully sorted, far from it. When were things ever fully sorted? But for now they were all fine, more than fine – and collectively moving, she was sure, in the right direction.

And that, she felt, was quite enough to be getting on with.

Acknowledgements

A big thank you as ever to all who make my writing life easier:

My extended family at Hachette Books Ireland, in particular Ciara Doorley, Joanna Smyth, Breda Purdue and Ruth Shern.

My agent Sallyanne Sweeney, there when I don't even know I need her.

The eagle eyes of copy-editor Hazel and proofreader Aonghus.

My research assistants Máire Logue and Philip Gleeson, ever ready with the answers to my questions.

Book bloggers and fellow authors, faithful broadcasters and journalists for early reviews and spreading of the word.

Anyone who's shared or retweeted my pre-book blather online – it hasn't gone unnoticed. (Extras when I land the film deal.)

And a special thanks to you, for choosing me.

Roisin xx

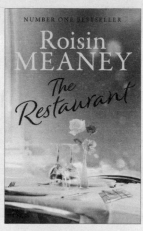

When Emily's heart was broken by the love of her life, she never imagined that she would find herself, just two years later, running a small restaurant in what used to be her grandmother's tiny hat shop. The Food of Love offers diners the possibility of friendship (and maybe more) as well as a delicious meal. And even though Emily has sworn off romance forever, it doesn't stop her hoping for happiness for her regulars, like widower Bill who hides a troubling secret, single mum Heather who ran away from home as a teenager, and gentle Astrid whose past is darker than any of her friends know.

Then, out of the blue, Emily receives a letter from her ex. He's returning home to Ireland and wants to see her. Is Emily brave enough to give love a second chance – or wise enough to figure out where it's truly to be found?

Also available on ebook and audio

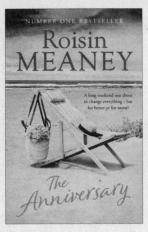

It's the Bank Holiday weekend and the Cunningham family are escaping to their holiday home by the sea, as they've done every summer for many years.

Except that now, parents Lily and Charlie are waiting for their divorce papers to come through – and have their new partners in tow.

Their daughter Poll is there with her boyfriend and is determined to make known her feelings for Chloe, her father's new love. While her brother Thomas also has feelings for Chloe – of a very different nature...

And amid all the drama, everyone has forgotten that this weekend also happens to be Lily and Charlie's wedding anniversary.

Will any of the couples survive the weekend intact?

Also available on ebook and audio

One
Summer
Roisin
Meaney

NUMBER ONE BESTSELLER

Nell Mulcahy grew up on the island of Roone so when the old stone cottage by the edge of the sea went up for sale, the decision to move back from Dublin was easy.

But when Nell decides to rent out her cottage for the summer to help raise money her forthcoming wedding to Tim, she's unprepared for what"s about to happen ...

As she welcomes holiday-makers to her cottage, Nell must face some truths: about her upcoming wedding to Tim, and her friendship with his brother, James.

And, meanwhile, her father delivers some astounding news which leaves Nell, her mother and the island reeling ...

But will Nell make it down the aisle? One thing's for sure, it's a summer on the island that nobody will ever forget.

Also available on ebook and audio

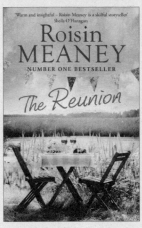

It's their twenty-year school reunion but the Plunkett sisters have their own reasons for not wanting to attend ...

Caroline, now a successful knitwear designer, spends her time flying between her business in England and her lover in Italy. As far as she's concerned, her school days, and what happened to her the year she left, should stay in the past.

Eleanor, meanwhile, is unrecognisable from the fun-loving girl she was in school. With a son who is barely speaking to her, and a husband keeping a secret from her, revisiting the past is the last thing on her mind.

But when an unexpected letter arrives for Caroline in the weeks before the reunion, memories are stirred.

Will the sisters find the courage to return to the town where they grew up and face what they've been running from all these years?

Also available on ebook and audio